Note on the Author

Mary McCarthy teaches English and French in a secondary school in Dublin. Her first novel, the best-selling *Remember Me,* was published in 1996 ~~b~~ ~~~~ ~~~~ in 1997, an~~~~

Also by Mary McCarthy

Remember Me
And No Bird Sang
Crescendo

SHAME
THE
DEVIL

SHAME
THE
DEVIL

Mary McCarthy

POOLBEG

Published 2001
by Poolbeg Press Ltd
123 Grange Hill, Baldoyle
Dublin 13, Ireland
E-mail: poolbeg@poolbeg.com
www.poolbeg.com

1 3 5 7 9 10 8 6 4 2

A catalogue record for this book is available from the British Library.

ISBN 1 84223 033 6

Cover design by Slatter-Anderson
Typeset by Patricia Hope in Garamond
Printed by
Omnia Books Limited, Glasgow

Acknowledgements

I would like to thank my family, friends and colleagues for their ongoing support.

A huge thankyou to my editor, Gaye Shortland, for her understanding, encouragement and insightful observations.

I am indebted to the following for their advice: Pauline Gildea who read and reread the novel – meticulously!, Sioned Parry of The Ritz, London, for her help with the research and Susan Daly, a former student of mine, for her expertise and brilliant notes on veterinary studies.

A special remembrance for my "Millennium Sixth Years", particularly the Prefects for making my job in school a lot easier.

Thanks to my brother, Des, for his kindness and help.

To my son, Dara – thanks for being you!

Thanks to Loretto and Colma with all my love.

Thank you Maeve, for everything!

For the staff in school: "You're the tops!"

For Niall, my late Brother.
I miss him.

"What's gone and what's past help
Should be past grief."

Shakespeare: *The Winter's Tale*

One

The voice is persistent. It is not a pleasant voice and it is not welcome. For days, weeks and months Amy Kennedy has tried to banish it but the house, conspiratorially, has let it in. It seeps from the ceilings and the walls or from under the floorboards. It is everywhere around; a pervasive malignant influence. The voice is her enemy: a thief creeping slyly inside her to steal her spirit.

Her husband, Maurice, loves this house. He grew up here in the stylish seaside suburb of Blackrock, Co Dublin. In its day it was a fine family residence but over the years it has become run-down. Its once-imposing façade, now shamefaced, suffers its neglect with painful embarrassment. The ancient gates are rusty, the paint peeling pitifully and the almost-pebbleless driveway oozes mud and slime through grooved tyre-tracks. Weeds choke the shrubbery under the large bay window, whose greying nylon curtains shut out the light, rendering the interior dark and dismal.

The spacious hall is shabby, its dark brown carpet faded and threadbare near the front door. Standing haughtily in the corner, the old-fashioned hatstand seems ludicrously out of place beside the bookcase with the broken leg. The mahogany banister cries out for a coat of varnish.

At the end of the hall, down two steps, lies the kitchen, its great green range now redundant, sitting superfluously in the centre – another sorry example of the waste. Pots and unwashed pans cover the draining board. Cobwebbed dust and grime, embedded in the crevices between the presses and the sink, add to the impression of decay: a testimony of negligence which constantly berates Amy.

To the right of the entrance hall, a dark brown door leads into the high-ceilinged living-room that has stayed the same since Maurice inherited all those years ago. A faded dusty red settee and two armchairs, never used, wait in vain for visitors.

It is four o'clock in the afternoon. Upstairs in the front bedroom, Amy Kennedy, partially dressed, lies on top of a creased duvet. Her eyes are half-open, vacantly watching the flickering images on the portable television, conveniently set on a table at the bed's end.

She stares, unfocused and unseeing. She has an ache somewhere – a dull, throbbing ache which she can't identify but which threatens to devour her. It started in her head, she thinks, but it has spread throughout her body, pickling her pores, her muscles, her very bones.

Bones, other bones, disintegrate in the cold clay. The wrinkled flesh must be wasted away from the bones by now. In what condition is the body? Have the worms done their worst? Are the maggots still in there, gouging and gorging? In the deep recesses of her mind these ominous thoughts scratch and scrape. Battle as she might, she cannot blot them out.

Amy stretches out her hand and gropes among the empty biscuit packets and discarded sweet papers on the filthy floor. Panic rises in her chest, palpitations pound. She must have a cigarette. Heart thumping, hands shaking, she clutches at the packet. Not the voice again. She can't bear to hear it now.

Not again.

Two

April is the cruellest month, the poet said, and maybe it was true. Five days had passed with no word from Dawn, but she'd done this before, just her way of showing her annoyance, of teaching her mother a lesson. The withdrawal of love – it was a typical female thing, wasn't it? As a child, Dawn would try to hurt her by not eating. Now it was not speaking. Same treatment, different method. Never mind, Amy would phone her at the flat and apologise. Again.

The whirlpool went round and round, at ever-increasing speed, sucking her in.

What have you done now? her mother would ask, in her strident voice. She'd stand, hands on bony hips and shake her head disdainfully. Her mother had always disapproved of her.

April 10th. First anniversary.

This morning Amy had gone to the cemetery, dutifully placed her multicoloured bouquet on the grave, tidied the tiny white pebbles and dug out the weeds. She'd stood there for a long time, staring at the black marble tombstone . . .

Lead, kindly light, to eternal rest the soul of Elaine Shiels,
beloved wife and mother.

Beloved wife?

Not the epitaph Amy would have chosen, but that's what Claire had proposed and Claire always got what she wanted. Amy's father hadn't interfered. He never did. He was happy to let others take over.

A wave of sadness washed over Amy as she thought about her father. Staring at the grave, she spoke silently to her mother. Unheard words in a one-way conversation – had it always been so?

Dad likes it in the Home, Mother. Says he does anyway. They give him a daily paper and he still does the cryptic crossword, chews his toffees in the day room. No smoking or eating in the bedrooms. No visitors after seven p.m.

Why did you do it, Amy? Put your father in a Home? Have you no shame? No sense of decency? Or honour?

Amy winced. She didn't have to respond to that. She no longer had to justify herself. She could just keep talking.

The house fetched a great price – over £400,000. Prime location. Good amenities. Room for extending. The Dublin property boom. Dad insisted that Claire and I each got £100,000 He convinced us that his pension and insurance policy, added to his share of the sale of the house, would cover his costs.

You obviously didn't need much convincing. Things have come to a pretty pass. Now your father is forced to pay for his care.

It's not that simple, Mother.

It is to me. Why are you telling me this, Amy? Why did you come here at all? To do your duty? To salve your conscience?

Just thought you'd like to know the details, Mother. You were always a stickler for details.

Go home, Amy. Go home to your husband.

Amy had stood at the grave in the pelting downpour, a year to the day after her mother's demise, and earnestly tried to pray for the repose of that tormented soul; tried to wipe out the years of misery, the constant criticism, the snide remarks. The bitterness. In her heart she wanted to forgive her mother, but the words wouldn't come.

Outside the bedroom window the storm howled. An eerie wind whipped around the corner of the house, wailing banshee-like, and the rain bashed mercilessly against the windowpanes, jeering at her. Pulling the white cotton sheet snugly around her shoulders, Amy turned on her side and reached over to the mahogany bedside table to get her gold watch, the one her husband had given her for their last anniversary. An unusual extravagance for him.

She squinted at the tiny digits. Nine o'clock. He'd be home any minute. Maurice never stayed out late on a weeknight but, with any luck, she'd be asleep by the time he made his way upstairs. He liked to have a brandy at the kitchen table after his long day, glance through the newspaper and, on the rare occasions when she was not in bed, have a chat. She made sure she was up less and less frequently.

Yes, her mother would gloat, *I always knew it would come to this.*

And what had it come to? She raided her brain for the right word. Misery? Too strong. She hadn't the energy for such a demanding emotion. To be truly sad you had to feel something – moved, excited, motivated – *any*thing.

Since Dawn's departure to go to college the house was lonely. Amy missed her daughter. She missed female company: the laughter, the loud music, the telephone ringing, the school stories, the friends calling. All her life, it seemed to Amy, she'd been vaguely dissatisfied but certainly not miserable. The right word hovered at the corners of her mind but tauntingly eluded her.

Her headache hammered. She'd slip downstairs and make a cup of tea, have one of the scones she'd made earlier – the hallmark of her day – a few lousy scones.

But then he'd come in and she'd have to stay and chat. Chat, chat, chat: he'd go into minute detail about every case, each injection or eye examination or teeth-scaling, gingivitis or worming or any bloody thing, the worst being when he had to put an animal to sleep.

"I did it as humanely as I could," he'd mumble sadly, "but, all the same . . ."

All the same, her husband would feel guilty – losing a patient was a failure, no matter that it was a dumb creature. Sometimes she

5

thought that he felt more for his beloved animals than he did for her. The best vet for miles around – his reputation sacrosanct.

She'd sit and watch him and nod and agree and he wouldn't notice whether she was smiling or frowning or frothing at the mouth. He never listened to her and if she did make a comment he ignored or dismissed it. No, that wasn't quite fair – she didn't contribute much to any conversation – that was hardly his fault.

There was no need to converse when Maurice was around. He could talk the hind legs off an ass, eat and lower his drink all at the same time. Sometimes she marvelled at how many words could come tumbling out of his mouth in the space of a few minutes. Hundreds and hundreds of words: nouns, adjectives, verbs, adverbs – all spewing out, the interjections adding suspense or horror or surprise – whatever the need of the moment. She'd sit and say "yes" or "no" or "maybe you're right" in the appropriate places.

He was a great one for the midnight chats; came to life at the witching hour; went over the day's events one by one and then filed them away in that tidy mind of his. Order, method and regularity in his house, in his practice and in his life. Meticulous in everything he did – her slovenly ways must enrage him but he was too polite to make a comment. Didn't like rows, either, our Maurice: "All I want is a peaceful life, Amy."
Not too much to look for.

He'd absentmindedly ask for her news. Then the real panic would set in. What would he think if he knew she'd spent half the day in bed, her only effort that day having been to make a batch of twelve pathetic-looking scones? She'd mutter something about having no news.

No news is good news.

Shut up, Mother, shut up.

Amy would stare at her husband and rack her brains for something to tell him, some bit of gossip or trivia or neighbourhood news . . . anything. But what, in her paltry life, could possibly interest him? Where did she go to get any news? What did she do or even *think* that would engage his curiosity?

I think, therefore I am.

Depressed. Down. Going out of my tree. Losing it. They're right, I am losing it. Who cares? Isn't it easier to just go on and on and on, not complain, do my duty and accept my lot? And he can't see how I am, how I really am. He couldn't understand because I'm not sure I do myself. And what does it matter, anyhow?

Why should he care, Amy, if you don't?

She sighed and switched off the light. Squeezing her eyes shut, she prayed for the respite of sleep. Not so tight, Amy, don't squeeze so tight. Relax. Relax. The yellow, purple and red dots would flicker magically under her eyelids if she managed to relax. She loved this: the changing shapes dancing, running together, separating and moulding again into different patterns and more elaborate forms.

From downstairs the grandfather clock ticked and ticked, louder and louder till it reached drum level. Too tired to get out of bed and close the bedroom door. Anyway, he didn't like her door closed, she knew that – it made him feel rejected, shut out. He'd feel shut out; she felt shut in.

Sleep. Sleep. Go to sleep.

Tick, tick, tick, tick, tick.

She couldn't let this tiredness beat her. She'd have to start cleaning the house; it wasn't fair to leave it all to Dawn at the weekends. She'd plan tomorrow: shopping in the morning if she had the energy – a visit to Nancy in the bookshop. Yes, the bookshop.

She'd promised the old lady ages ago that she'd call in and help her tidy up and price the books in the stockroom. Some of those books were first editions and very valuable. Nancy wasn't getting any younger and sometimes her memory wasn't the best – Amy wondered how many customers took advantage. The shop was ancient and musty but Amy adored that special smell of old books – there was no smell in the world like it. In her Brontë-bred imagination it was redolent of elegant English drawing-rooms, white-aproned serving-girls carrying in highly polished silver teapots on silver trays, hot buttered muffins and a blazing fire. Nancy, with her cultured accent, genteel manner and pristine-clean old-fashioned lace blouses was quaint. Civilised. The bookshop was an oasis of calm, courtesy and civility, incongruous in the surrounding suburban labyrinth of fast-food joints, honky-tonk computer stores, blaring music shops and antiseptic supermarkets. Every time Amy stepped into the bookshop she stepped into an ancient graceful world.

Tomorrow night she might call to see her sister, Claire.

Claire, she who always had news and insisted on inflicting it on the nearest available pair of ears, would be in high spirits as usual – she'd natter on and on and on about her day in the jewellery shop: who came in, who bought a bracelet for his wife's birthday, who was going out with whom, the butcher next door, the newsagent opposite, the woman in the flower shop . . . on and on and on. Claire should have married Maurice. They could have babbled into oblivion.

Claire had dated Maurice for a few months before she had introduced him to the drama club. When Amy had met him that fateful night of the dress rehearsal, she'd thought he was nice. Nice – such a horribly inane word – but that's what her initial impression had been. After a few weeks, he'd asked her out for a drink. Claire hadn't minded, by then she was seeing someone else. How could she explain to her sister now, after twenty-two years, how she felt?

Count your blessings, Amy, she'd say. You have it all – a beautiful, brilliant daughter at college, a fine home and a decent man for a husband. You're not the only one with problems. I'm on my own. I have to make a living and there's always something to be done – last year rewiring and have you seen the state of the windows? I'll have to take out another loan. So, don't tell me you're feeling down. Stop moping and complaining. With a good cleaning and a coat of paint, your house would be grand. Why not get a part-time job? You were better off emotionally and in every other way when you worked in the surgery. If you don't want to work again with Maurice, there are loads of jobs out there for the asking. Take a ride on the Celtic Tiger, Amy. What about the £100,000 you got? My mortgage ate mine. Invest your money in something you'll enjoy: take a holiday, renovate the house, start a business. Do something constructive. You're an intelligent woman. Get up off your arse, go out there and start living again.

No, a visit to Claire would not be helpful. After her diatribe on the importance of a working life, Claire would try to persuade her to take up a hobby. The drama club. A hobby – the panacea for all problems, according to Claire. The elixir.

The last thing she needed was to hear Claire's pedestrian opinions and trite advice. She couldn't betray her deepest feelings to her sister; she'd never been able to do that.

You've little to complain about, Amy.

I know, Mother, I know. He's not a bad man: a good provider, dedicated to his career – not overly giving in the money department, mind you. Why was he so opposed to her doing up this house? It was in such bad shape. If he loved it so much, why did he neglect it?

She'd given up asking to visit Paris. He kept putting her off, despite her offer to pay – preferred his holidays at home, he said. Didn't like the hassle of air travel. Their last proper holiday had been to Brittany and that was years ago. Maurice hadn't enjoyed it. His excuse nowadays was that he couldn't leave his practice.

Angrily she reached under the pillow and opened another packet of crisps. Comfort eating.

Never marry a mean man, Amy.

Mean? He didn't mind lashing out on Dawn's third-level education; gave the girl a fortune in pocket money; never quibbled about her house-sharing rent in Stillorgan or the price of her books. Dawn had him eating out of her hand – more power to her.

With his wife he was careful. Prudent. It infuriated her but why complain now? Wasn't that one of the reasons she'd married him in the first place – because he was safe? She'd known all along what he was like. You didn't expect a man to change after marriage. If you did you were a fool.

You walked into this with your eyes open, Amy.

Yes, thank you, Mother.

What did you expect, anyway?

Expect? She hadn't expected anything. Maurice had ambled into her life without fuss. They went out together, enjoyed one another's company. She was young and pretty. Clever but not too clever to upset a man's ego. More to the point, Amy was accommodating – a quality a man like Maurice prized. He told her he loved her. Was that the rock she perished on? When a man told a woman he loved her – wasn't there something deliciously irresistible about it? Did we automatically love where we were loved? Amy thought it might be so. Maurice had a lot going for him in those days. She admired him for his intelligence and his ambition. He was kind. He was good to her – then. Her friends were getting married. Middle twenties – that's what you did – you got married. They decided to tie the knot. It was easy. Inevitable.

And you thought a marriage like that would work?

Yes, Mother, because that's what you had and, on the surface, it worked for you. I don't remember much passion between you and Dad. You were more like polite acquaintances than husband and wife, immersed in your own little world, but you didn't complain because you knew and I know that after years and years together, that's all there is – mutual tolerance . . . if you're lucky.

Enough of this! You've made your bed, Amy.

And then it struck her – the word she was looking for. Overwhelmed. Her life had overwhelmed her. She woke up one day and felt, with a dire certainty, that she was lost. Utterly lost in this big barracks of a house that she'd grown to despise.

I warned you, Amy, but you wouldn't listen. You never listen.

Dear God, make the bitch leave me alone.

Three

Maurice Kennedy had a last quick look in on the grey Siamese: still out for the count but breathing more easily. Pulse normal. Hopefully the pin in the hip would do the trick for the poor little bugger. Personally he'd have opted to put the cat out of its misery, but Mrs Mangan wouldn't hear of it. The moggie had been her only company for years past.

He checked the other animals, left on a dimmer light and locked the surgery door. Buttoning up the collar of his crombie overcoat, he made his way to the black Merc parked up the road. It irritated him the way every Tom, Dick and Harry parked outside his premises for easy access to the supermarket next door.

There was a distinct nip in the April air and it had begun to drizzle. He hated this time of the year: setting out for work in the dim half-light of the early morning and coming home again in darkness, the daylight all but lost to him. Fine for those who had time to appreciate that the evenings were stretching, but he hadn't noticed, not with the hours he worked. How did they cope in the Scandinavian countries?

He settled himself behind the steering-wheel, turned the key in the ignition and switched on the lights. Nine-twenty on the car clock. Later than he'd intended but enough time for a quick pint in Delaney's. Amy would be in bed. No sense in rushing home to a dark, unwelcoming house.

His wife's depression was infectious; trying to pretend he didn't

11

notice was impossible. He'd been patient with her, God knows he'd been patient, but for how long more could he endure it? He'd urged her to go back to the doctor but to no avail.

She'd taken her mother's death very badly and her father's admission to the Old Folk's Home had been sudden and upsetting. Since Dawn had gone off to college, his wife had become even more jittery. Her relationship with their daughter had deteriorated during the past year and he'd presumed that the tension in the house would have eased a bit after Dawn had left, but it was palpably worse. When the girl came home at weekends, there was nothing but friction.

His wife needed a pastime, some creative outlet to occupy her mind and her time. Everybody should have an interest outside the home, so he'd always believed, anyhow. If it weren't for his weekly game of squash and the odd night in the Yacht Club, he'd be totally stressed out.

Why had she been determined to give up working with him in the surgery? She'd been a wizard with the accounts and he'd resented having to employ a secretary as well as a receptionist, particularly now that he'd hired another vet. More salaries, more pressure. He didn't take kindly to giving away wages that could have been his wife's. Luckily, in a few more years, Dawn could join the practice.

The pub carpark was practically full – unusual enough for a Wednesday night. He found a place near the exit, a tight fit between a Starlet and a Saab, but he manoeuvred skilfully. He grinned as he remembered the time, when they were first married, that Amy had roped him into giving her driving lessons. She'd hit a brand new Corsa in the car park at Golden Strand – only one car parked there and she'd managed to hit it. He'd thought she'd abandon all attempts at driving thereafter but, by some fluke, she'd passed the test first go. Wanted her own car ever since, but that had been out of the question until now – now she'd got her hands on her inheritance. A hundred thousand quid – no doubt eventually, when it had sunk in, she'd plan to do up the house, have a holiday – God knows what. Disruption, he hated disruption. Of course, if she continued the way she was going . . .

"Hi there, Doc. A Guinness, is it?" Vinnie Parkinson moved up at the bar to give him room.

"You're all right, thanks. I'm just in for the one." Maurice beckoned to the barman. "A pint, please, when you're ready, and a cheroot."

"Listen, Doc," Vinnie whispered, "thanks a million for what ya did for Molly. She hasn't looked back since the delivery and it's all down to you." He took a filthy handkerchief from his pocket and blew his nose noisily. "You've a great pair of hands, God bless them!" He turned to his bearded drinking-buddy who was propping up the bar. "Thirteen stitches Molly got and she moanin' and whimperin' and trying to bite the bejaysus out of the good Doc here."

Maurice found this type of flattery highly embarrassing and unnecessary; being plámásed by a local who'd obviously had one too many.

"Just my job, Vinnie. Just my job."

"Ah, get away outa that, weren't ya up with Molly the whole night and if ya hadn't a been there, I'd never a managed to deliver them four healthy bitches. No, siree. Sold three of them for a tidy sum and the runt, tha' I kept for meself- I know me onions – a fine strapping collie bitch the likes o' which I haven't seen in over twenty year." Lowering the rest of the pint, he gestured to the barman for a refill, and prodded Maurice in the ribs. "How's the missus?"

"Fine." Maurice shuffled on his seat. "She's fine."

"She didn't come in with ya?"

She never came with him these days.

"Working late, were ya, Doc?"

"That's right."

"It's a curse, isn't it? The hours I put in meself are cruel."

Vinnie Parkinson worked on a dairy farm past Bray. The way he boasted about the cattle, you'd swear he himself was the owner of the estate but tonight Maurice didn't care about the little man's idle chatter; in one way he welcomed it. Vinnie's drone had a calming effect and it required very little concentration.

He spotted his sister-in-law coming in by the back door. She was dressed in a dark green trouser suit he hadn't seen before. Smart. Sophisticated. He also noticed the way she'd swept her long dark curls back from her face. She was a very handsome woman, turned all the men's heads as she passed by. He waved to her and she edged her way through the crowd at the bar over to him.

A peck on the cheek. A broad smile. "Maurice, this is a pleasant surprise."

He smiled back, stood up and gave her his stool. "Hardly a surprise, Claire. You know I often drop in on a Wednesday night for a quick one."

She ordered a Scotch and soda which he insisted on paying for. Vinnie was visibly put out by the unexpected arrival of this glamorous intruder. "I'll leave you to it, Doc." He raised his tartan cap slyly to Claire and slithered off.

"The smell!" Claire shuddered. "Do these people never wash?"

Maurice laughed. "He's working with cowshit all day. What do you expect?"

"That he'd have a shower before he comes out in the evening."

Maurice lifted a hand to her nose. "I smell of disinfectant. Is that any better?"

"No," she agreed, pushing his hand away, "but at least it's hygienic. Anything strange or startling?"

"Not really. Had an interesting evening, though. A pet hare – my first."

"A hare? I've never heard of anyone having a pet hare."

"Nor I, until now. Apparently bought from some couple in Meath who rear them. Parents domesticated. Good pedigree."

"So, what was wrong with the well-connected hare?" She took off her jacket and draped it carefully around the high-backed stool.

"He got hit by an up-and-over garage door. Not badly hurt, but he pulled a tendon in his back leg trying to drag himself away."

"How do you treat that?"

"Just painkillers. He'll be brought back tomorrow for an X-ray."

"Never a dull moment, Maurice."

Was she being sarcastic? With Claire you never knew. "No two days are the same, that's for sure. There's a guy in Monkstown who has a huge garden, a protector of wildlife. I think I told you about

14

him before. He's a committed conservationist, does great work. Tonight he arrived with three baby hedgehogs."

"Hedgehogs? Cute, but aren't they full of fleas?"

"Smelly as well when they've got diarrhoea."

"Disgusting!"

"He was feeding them on brown bread soaked in milk. The cows' milk didn't agree with them so they got the runs."

"You're not going to tell me you gave them Immodium?"

"No." He laughed. "I've advised him to change to goats' milk."

Claire quite enjoyed talking about Maurice's veterinary experiences; she knew he liked to and he rarely got the chance with her sister nowadays. You had to let a man talk about his job. "Is that the guy who brought in the woodpecker last week?"

"The same. Mauled by a cat, not seriously hurt but in shock." Maurice lit his cigar; he allowed himself one a day since he'd packed in the cigarettes and he was careful not to inhale. "Recovered his composure, I'm happy to say, so I brought him out to the fields and he flew off. It was a bit of a risk. He could just as easily have dropped dead from fright after an experience like that."

Hard to reply to that. "Let me buy you a drink. Another Guinness?"

"Thanks, Claire."

"How's Amy? I phoned this morning, got the damned answering-machine."

"She went to the cemetery."

"So I gathered. I was going to go with her but . . . just as well. I called over myself at lunchtime and saw the flowers. She'd tidied up the grave. Still trying to please Mam."

"She never managed to when the old girl was alive, so it beats me why she still bothers."

"Amy never broke the umbilical cord – that's her problem. I thought she'd be able to put everything behind her after the funeral but obviously she can't."

"It's been a year, Claire. How much longer is this mood going to go on? Do you know what she told me last week? That she can hear your mother talking to her. That's off the wall."

"Is it? Mam was always and forever on and on at Amy, moaning

15

and giving out about something or other. I'm not surprised that she can still hear her bloody voice. It's hard to erase something like that from your memory. Mam was a pain – you know that. She was desperately strict with Amy, expected a lot of her, being the elder. Not that she was very affectionate to me either, but I didn't care. She had peculiar notions about discipline."

Maurice had heard it all *ad nauseam*.

"I have a very hazy picture of Dad when we were growing up. He kept himself to himself, came home every evening, ate his dinner alone in the kitchen and then buried himself in the newspaper. Mam invested far too much time and energy in Amy and myself and I'd say that Dad felt neglected."

"He was, Claire. That's the reality. She took very little interest in him – or so I gather from Amy."

"Mam left him to his own devices, which seemed to suit Dad, but when it came to us she was a control freak – a sadistic one at that. Amy still has the mark on her leg of the poker Mam threw at her. I learned to stay out of the way."

"We all got the odd smack when we were growing up."

"This was more than the odd smack, Maurice. Mam was vicious."

"It's time Amy got over it. She's too sensitive and she's so wrapped up in herself lately that she doesn't see the problems she's causing at home. You could cut the atmosphere in the house with a knife. Dawn has bent over backwards to please her mother, but nothing she does is any good."

"History repeating itself."

"That's what makes it impossible to understand. You'd think that Amy would have learned the lesson from her own upbringing."

"It doesn't always work that way, Maurice. They say that when you have children you end up making the same mistakes as your parents did. But Amy's not remotely like Mam. Surely you don't think that? She's gentle and kind and she adores Dawn. She must miss her living at home."

"Yes. She can't seem to let go."

Claire looked wistful. "The tyranny of motherhood. I'm glad I didn't have kids."

"Dawn is my saving grace, Claire. If it wasn't for her, I'd be lost."

"I know. I know."

Maurice stared glumly into his pint but Claire had to pursue the conversation. "I dropped in to see Amy on my way here this evening – yet again, there was no answer. The bedroom light was on and it was only nine o'clock."

"She spends most of her time in bed looking at TV5 or reading those damned depressing French novels." He sighed.

"Reading is a refuge, Amy always used to say, and she had a weird taste in books, even when we were teenagers. She must have read *Madame Bovary* five times. I tried the English translation once but I abandoned it after a few chapters. Too dark by far for me. It was on TV a while ago. Amy taped it, she told me."

"Yes, Flaubert has a strong appeal," he said ironically. "Reinforces something she feels is in herself, I suppose. I wish I could get through to her, Claire. She's getting beyond me and it's frightening."

"I'll talk to her again. Sarah Goodman was in the shop today, buying cufflinks for Jack. She's very put out that Amy is avoiding her."

"I can understand why. She and Amy are friends since their first year in primary school. Friendships like that are few and far between. They've always looked out for each other."

"I don't like Sarah." Claire flicked back her fringe from her face. "She's full of her own importance."

"Sarah? No, she's not. She genuinely loves Amy and she's worried about her. Jack knows about the situation too. I couldn't hide it from him. As you know, we play squash once a week – he asks questions, naturally, but he won't gossip."

"He's learnt to keep his mouth shut," Claire said abruptly. "Maybe I could try again to persuade Amy to go back to the doctor?"

"She'll refuse. Won't even discuss it. She can't admit that she has a problem. Clodagh Heffernan came to see her last night but Amy wouldn't even get out of bed. She'll have no friends left."

Claire paid the barman. "People get fed up. You can't blame them."

"No," he agreed, "you can't."

"If she'd only do something to help herself – of course that's the problem with depression: it's totally debilitating. Perhaps I could get her to rejoin the drama group? It would get her out two evenings a week and that way I could keep my eye on her. Surreptitiously, of course. I'd hate her to think I was interfering, Maurice, because I'm only out for her good."

"I know that and Dawn is there for her too but she takes every comment as a criticism. I doubt if she'll listen to you, Claire. No offence. She still sees you as her little sister."

"Dismisses me, is that what you mean?"

"Perhaps, though secretly maybe she envies you your vitality."

"Vitality? That's a laugh. I spend my time running around, trying to catch up with myself. I refused to do more overtime tonight but we have to keep the shop open, what with all these late-night shoppers. It used to be only Thursday nights, now it's Wednesdays and Fridays as well. I told Mrs Punton that she'd just have to do without me. I'm only an assistant manager, after all. You can be walked on."

"That's for sure."

"It's hard to fathom Amy. She doesn't see her own strengths. She was the success in our family: the one who went to college, got a good degree, mastered a foreign language. She has no need to feel envious of me."

Maurice stubbed out the cigar.

"Well, what about the drama idea?" she asked.

"Try again if you like; Claire, maybe, just maybe, it'll work. She used to enjoy it – wasn't a bad actress."

"She was terrific as Pegeen Mike – of course she was much younger then. Young and feisty."

"And a bundle of energy. In those days we used to take treks in the Wicklow mountains; miles and miles and I was always the one who begged for a rest. And Amy was a powerful swimmer. Remember when she used to go to the pool every morning?"

"Religiously. Winter or summer she'd be up with the larks and off."

Maurice remembered other things: his wife's kindness to his mother in the endless weeks of her final illness; the night she announced her pregnancy when they'd celebrated with a bottle of champagne; the decorating of the back bedroom as a nursery; the day they brought Dawn home from the hospital; when their daughter cut her first tooth, took her first step; her excitement when she first understood Santa Claus. All the memories jumbled together . . .

He saw her clearly – standing in the doorway of their new premises, her brightness and enthusiasm on that glorious day when they'd finally opened up their own practice. It had been hers as much as his – then. She'd been his rock, his anchor – he couldn't have done it without her. And she'd been happy in those days, he was certain of that.

"Maurice? You OK?"

"Sorry, Claire. What were you saying?"

"About Amy's swimming. She could take that up again."

"She takes no exercise of any kind these days," he said wistfully, "and she does damn all around the house."

"Signs on; she's put on a lot of weight, that must add to her depression. I could go swimming with her. And then, if she agrees, she could rejoin the drama club." Claire was becoming more optimistic. "It's just a matter of getting the ball rolling, isn't it?"

"The drama group," he pondered, "might be the answer. A start at least. Get her out to meet new people."

"Very few new recruits, I'm afraid. It's the usual gang. This year we're putting on *Death of a Salesman*. Rehearsals start next Monday." Claire bit her lip. "I'm talking pie in the sky here, really. That's what you're thinking, isn't it? Amy hardly goes out the door – how can I get her involved in a play? I was mad to think I could talk her into it."

"Give it a try, Claire. That's all you can do." He finished the remainder of his pint in a single gulp.

Four

Dawn Kennedy gathered up her textbooks and photocopied notes from the college reading-room table. While pleased with the amount of work she'd covered, she was exhausted. Friday evening. The cubicles were all occupied – lots of students crammed their study now in order to have Saturday and Sunday free for more pleasurable pursuits. Exam time was fast approaching. She'd have to call to the library on Monday after her physiology lecture and see if the veterinary statistics textbook she'd asked for had come back yet; the librarian was always helpful.

Should she reconsider and go home for the weekend? Two days of doom and gloom. Could she face it? Her mother had refused to employ a housekeeper because her father didn't want a *stranger* in the house. But why should she have to give up her valuable time to be their domestic help? And yet, her father had been very generous to her; she should do something to repay him. Her mother's apologetic phone call on Wednesday had been pitiable.

She wished her mother and the whole goddamn mess would just disappear, vanish in a puff of smoke, then she immediately chided herself for the thought. Her mother was going through a rough patch; it wasn't fair to condemn her.

She'd go down to The Barge and see if Paul was there yet. She'd arranged to meet him at eight o'clock to go to the cinema but she wasn't in the humour for a film now. Her brain was jam-packed with chemistry, histology and biochemistry. Not to mention anatomy; she'd read and reread and finally managed to memorise the primary vessels of the thoracic limb: subclavian, axillary, brachial, median. *Miller's Guide To The Dissection Of The Dog* had become her bible.

All she wanted was to unwind; to flop down in a comfortable lounge seat, knock back a few beers and have a chat.

Nothing too taxing.

* * *

"A Heineken, Dawn?" He put his arm around her waist in that proprietary way she'd grown to like. It made her feel cherished, appreciated.

He noticed the dark circles under her eyes; they were there this morning as well. She wasn't sleeping properly because she insisted on reading late into the night. Paul didn't miss his student days. Not one bit. Too much pressure, too much study, never enough money. And for Dawn, with all of her father's expectations, it was worse; First Year Veterinary – bloody gruelling. No, he preferred the world of work. He liked his job in the Department of Social Welfare; regular hours, reasonable income, good prospects. "You look done in."

"What a day I've had! One hour of embryology followed by an hour of physiology then histology. I spent three hours today looking down microscopes at slides of tissue – skin, liver, brain, lungs. Then two and a half hours in the anatomy lab followed by three hours of study."

"Rather you than me!"

"At least I'm able to differentiate between the tissues now – they all looked the same at the start! Listen, I want to type up my chemistry notes into some kind of order on the computer. Did you get the toner cartridge for the printer?"

"Hadn't the time." He'd completely forgotten. "Sorry."

"Paul Tennyson, you promised."

"I know." He kissed her cheek. "Monday, I swear. I can drop in after lunch."

He paid the barman for the two pints and led her to a seat near the window, overlooking the Grand Canal. "OK. What film?" he asked, opening the entertainment page of *The Irish Times*.

Dawn chewed the inside of her lip. "I'm famished, Paul. I skipped lunch."

"Fine, we'll eat before the film."

"A meal as well? You've got to be kidding. I'm skint."

"No worries, my treat."

He turned to the sports page and she slowly sipped her drink. The sharp taste was welcoming, reviving. The truth was she didn't fancy the long walk the whole way to Parnell Square. She just felt like sitting here all evening and getting smashed but that wasn't a good idea.

"I was thinking of going home tomorrow, Paul."

"What?" He folded the paper and shoved it into the inside pocket of his suit jacket. "Have you forgotten last weekend? For Heaven's sake, that was a disaster. You came back all in a tizzy because you'd got practically no study done. You don't have to be trotting up and down to Blackrock every Saturday. My parents haven't seen me since February."

"That's different; they don't expect you to travel to Cork. I'm only down the road. Dad likes to see me."

"Dawn, you'll have to stop this. I know that there are problems there but they're not *your* problems. You're not the one to solve them. Your mother is responsible for her life, *you* certainly aren't."

"It's easy for you to say that, Paul. You don't realise how good Mum was to me. She worked her hours in the surgery around my needs; she'd be there every afternoon when I came in from school, hot chocolate and kind words waiting. She used to drive me to hockey matches, the cinema with my friends, the discos when we were older. We'd go into town together to buy clothes and she always treated me to lunch out even though she hadn't that much money. Dad didn't pay her a fortune. You see, Paul? She invested so much time in me. She'd listen to my problems without dismissing them. She always treated me as an intelligent human being even when I was a kid."

Paul took her hand.

"She's a truly kind person."

"I know you and your mother are close." He stroked her hand.

"We used to be and that's what makes this so sad. I have to do something."

"Maybe so but –"

"It's only in the last year since Gran died . . . I don't know, she's changed – lost her spark. I feel so sorry for her and I wish I could do something to help. She was always there for me. I can't desert her."

Paul nodded but he didn't agree.

"And it's not just Mum I'm concerned about – it's Dad too. He has to cope with her all week on his own. If I'm there for the weekend, it gives him some sort of a break."

Paul scratched his moustache thoughtfully. Where was the point in arguing with her? He'd been through this so many times. Her innate sense of duty was dogged. Resolute. He'd never met anybody like her in that respect. Most of his friends didn't give a toss about their parents; leaving school meant leaving home and that was that. Of course if the Mammy felt like doing your ironing or your washing when you turned up, that was grand.

"I'll go down tomorrow," she said, knowing he was peeved. "Tonight's for us. OK?" She snuggled up beside him. "Are Ben and Isobel going out?"

"Yeah, to a twenty-first. They'll be home late."

"Good, why don't we get a takeaway and a bottle of wine and stay in?" She kissed him lightly on the lips. "It'll be nice to have the place to ourselves for once. We can go to a film any time."

"All right," he conceded. "We'll light the fire and put on some music. You need to relax."

"I need you," she murmured in his ear and her cool breath tickled.

* * *

Dawn lay innocently in the crook of his arm, like a little girl. The dying embers of the fire glowed blue and pink and purple. He watched her as she slept. Her breathing was deep and even, her face calm, no flicker of worry now on her brow. Her skin glistened. He loved the scent of her, the feel of her. He wanted to protect her. These were the special moments. He softly kissed her hair, making sure not to wake her. In a while he'd carry her into their bed and they'd make love.

The phone rang. Loudly. Shrilly. She groaned.

"Shh, shh, Dawn. Go back to sleep. It's OK." He eased himself out from under her arm and crept out to the hall to answer the phone.

"Paul? Hello. It's Maurice Kennedy. Is Dawn there?"

"No," he lied. "She's out."

"Oh, I see. I was hoping to catch her."

"She'll be late. She stayed on in college to study. She's up to her neck in it," he said pointedly.

"Could you give her a message?"

"Sure."

"Ask her to ring me early in the morning. I have to play a squash match in the afternoon and I'm not sure of her plans. I was hoping she might come home. Em, her mother's not . . . not well."

"I'll tell her, Mr Kennedy."

"Thanks, Paul. Everything all right with you?"

"Super."

"That's good."

"Bye."

Paul hung up abruptly. Dawn's father took the biscuit. Could he not let his daughter have one weekend free? He went back to the sitting-room. Dawn was awake now, reaching for a glass of wine.

"Who was that on the phone?" she asked sleepily.

"Wrong number."

"Ooh." She stretched. "My back hurts. This damned rug."

He rolled her onto her stomach. "I'll give you a massage."

She relaxed as his hands kneaded her back and shoulders, rubbing and squeezing, ironing out the tension.

"You're turning me on." She turned her head and smiled up at him. "I love you, Paul."

He leaned down and whispered, "Let's continue this in bed."

Five

Dawn squeezed the sodden mop into the sink and ran it under the tap. Even though she hadn't managed to remove all the dirt and grease, the floor looked slightly more presentable. Now to attack the sink. She rummaged through the miscellaneous packets, tins and bottles in the press and found a scouring powder. She wished she'd remembered to bring her rubber gloves; this kind of cleaning would play havoc with her hands. She was sprinkling the white strong-smelling powder over the enamel draining board when the doorbell rang.

A visitor? Maybe Claire, she sometimes visited on Saturdays, if she wasn't in the shop. Dawn dried her hands in a newly washed tea towel and went to answer. A familiar figure stood on the doorstep. Blonde streaks. Mid-forties. Well-dressed. Impeccably groomed.

"Yes?"

An outstretched hand. "Dawn, how are you?"

Sarah Goodman. Her mother's best friend.

"Is she in?" The woman stepped, uninvited, into the hall. "It's been a while since we met. Your eighteenth birthday, I think? Yes, your mum and dad brought you out for a meal in Killiney. My husband and I joined you."

The trying-to-be trendy guy who played squash with her father. "I remember."

"Is your mother in?" Sarah repeated.

"Yes, but she's asleep."

"Not to worry."

Dawn assumed that the woman was about to leave but, instead, she headed for the stairs, as brazen as anything, and was halfway up before Dawn could stop her.

"Front bedroom if I'm not mistaken?"

"No, oh no, please, wait! You can't go up there."

Sarah waved her fears away. "Your mother will be glad to see me. We haven't had a chat in ages."

Glad to see her? A barrage of phone calls, notes through the letterbox, knocks at the door at all hours of the day and no response. Could this woman not get the message?

"I know the way to her room. Your mother and I have a lot to catch up on. I'm sure she'll be glad of the company."

"I really don't think so. I'm sorry but I think you'd better go. She doesn't want to be disturbed."

"Nonsense, Dawn. I'm her friend."

"Please, Mrs Goodman –"

"Sarah, call me Sarah, love. Don't be worried." The woman lowered her voice and leaned over the banister. "I know all about it."

Dawn flushed.

"You'd prefer if I didn't see her?"

"Not today. You'd be wasting your time. My mother is very low. She wants to be left alone – doesn't even want me in there. She's drifting in and out of sleep all day. She had another row with Dad this morning. Nobody can reason with her." Dawn couldn't believe what she'd just blurted out. Why had she given vent to her frustration now when she'd always manage to camouflage it so well?

Sarah came back downstairs, crossed the hall and took the girl by the arm. "Why don't we have a cup of tea and a little chat? I can help, you know."

Help? Who could *help* in this situation? After everything she and her father had tried? Months and months of begging her mother to see a doctor, to try counselling. Anything. Even to get out of bed. Coming down here every weekend, pleading with her mother to get medical help for herself. Now this . . . this stylish vision arrives and bullies her way in. Did this woman honestly think she could

28

land in here, out of the blue, wave a magic wand and solve their problems with a 'little chat'?

"Mrs Goodman, thanks for your concern but, if you don't mind, I'm not up to it."

"All right." Sarah noted the agitated expression. "Maybe another day? Tell your mother I called. And, Dawn, I *am* more than willing to help, if you need me." Sarah took a small white card from her handbag; her husband's business card. She got a pen and scribbled her phone number on the back.

"Thanks." Dawn politely glanced at the card.

"There is help available. You're not on your own."

Dawn smiled weakly.

"Will you do one thing for me? Will you phone me and let me know how things are? And tell your mother I called?"

To get rid of the woman, Dawn would have agreed to anything.

"Who was that?" the sleepy voice lisped.

"Mrs Goodman," Dawn sighed. "Wanted to come up. Imagine!"

Amy blinked. She couldn't make out her daughter's features but she knew by her tone that Dawn was still cross. Amy yawned and stretched in the bed. "Who did you say?"

"Sarah Goodman. I practically had to physically restrain her from coming up here to the bedroom. Are you getting up today? It's almost five o'clock."

Her mother made no reply.

"Am I to cook dinner?" A harsher tone.

"If you like," Amy mumbled. What did she care about dinner?

Sarah popped a Polo mint in her mouth and started the car, then abruptly switched off the engine. She stared up at the front bedroom window. Did the curtain move? Yes, by God, it did. She was being watched. Right, that settled it. She was going back in there this minute. She had to see Amy. Whatever resistance the girl put up, Sarah would handle it.

The bedroom was in a state of total disarray; newspapers littered the carpet, a teeming ash-tray spilled its contents over the locker and the curtains had been drawn again. A feeble light over the bed illuminated the pallid features of Amy Kennedy, who, propped up by pillows, gaped at her helplessly.

"I'd like to talk to your mother alone, if I may."

Dawn stood by the door, her bewilderment preventing her from making a reply.

"If you'd be so good as to bring up some tea," Sarah said firmly, "that would be a great help."

"Mum, I'm sorry. I tried to stop –"

"It's all right, Dawn. Do as she asks." The voice was hoarse and very faint.

The girl nodded dumbly and left the room.

Sarah stood, hands on hips, a stance which immediately reminded Amy of her mother. "Right, what the hell is going on here?"

Amy groped for a cigarette.

"Look at the state of you," Sarah admonished. "This is appalling, Amy. What's happening to you at all?"

"Sarah, it's good of you to call – very thoughtful –"

"Don't start babbling. We've no time or use for idle pleasantries. Something is horribly wrong and I can't stand by and do nothing. Amy, what are you doing to yourself?"

The sickly face in the bed contorted and glared. "What am I doing? What am *I* doing? What are you doing, that's the question. Who do you think you are? Mind your own business. How dare you come blustering in here bossing me around!"

Sarah Goodman wasn't in the least perturbed by this outburst – she'd expected it. "I'll tell you who I am. I'm a friend of yours for forty years and that gives me rights, Amy. I know you've been avoiding me but I have to step in whether you like it or not. I'd never forgive myself if –"

"If what?" Amy challenged.

Sarah wouldn't be drawn on that one. "Now, first I want you to get up out of that bed and get dressed. It's late afternoon. You can't loll about in bed all day."

"Why not?" The voice was irritated but slightly stronger.

"Come on, Amy, up out of the bed and into the shower. Dawn will bring us tea in a moment and then you'll feel better."

"Sarah, Sarah, I . . . can't." Her eyes filled up and she started to shake. "I don't want to."

"No, no tears, Amy. Here, I'll help you." Sarah, her own eyes filling up, went to the bed, put her arms around the heavy shoulders and tried to hoist the sagging body. "That's it. Lean on me."

Amy made a huge effort to rise, then shivering, she flopped back on the pillows. "I can't."

"You can, Amy. I'll help you. Please, for my sake."

Sarah, alarmed, watched her friend struggle with the teacup, her hands shaking. "When did you last see the doctor?"

Amy sipped and said nothing.

"This can't go on. We have to get you back to health, Amy. When did you see your doctor?"

"A few months ago."

"A few *months* ago? That's ridiculous. What does Maurice say? Has he not insisted that you get some help?"

"I think he's given up on me."

"Given up on you?"

"Maurice and I are not communicating very well at present. My fault."

"Why is it your fault? It usually takes two."

"No, no, it is my fault. I'm dragging him down – that's what he says." Her voice was tiny, feeble. "Dragging him down."

Sarah bristled. "Typical bloody man. Only sees his side."

"He's tired, he works very hard, as you know, and then back home to me, his ailing wife who moans and groans and hasn't the energy to do diddly-squat." Amy smiled sadly. "That was one of my mother's favourite expressions: diddly-squat."

"Listen, Amy –"

"I'm worn out listening. There are no words you can say to me, Sarah, that will make any difference. I've heard every word on the subject."

31

"Maybe you're not hearing the right words. Maurice obviously is not tuning in to what you're saying?"

"I don't say much these days. Why keep at it when you end up going round and round in circles? We're at cross-purposes most of the time."

"Sure, Jack's the same. But I force him to listen. I make sure he takes me out at least once a week for a meal. Once I get him over the dinner table, I have his undivided attention."

Poor Sarah, did she honestly think that a weekly dinner out would solve her marital problems? "Maurice is doing his best but I'm a hopeless case."

"Rubbish."

"Is it?"

"You have to work at these things."

"I'm so tired, Sarah." She looked at her friend pleadingly. "I just want to be left alone."

"Don't be so bloody melodramatic." Sarah pulled a face. "You're not Greta Garbo! I'm going to ask you again. What has Maurice to *say* about all this?"

"And I'm going to tell you again. He's fed up and lost patience and interest and I can't say I blame him. He's making a life for himself that doesn't include me."

"I'm sure you're wrong." Sarah wasn't one bit sure. She'd seen Maurice Kennedy dining out with his sister-in-law only a few weeks ago, laughing and chatting and looking anything but troubled. Then she'd spotted them together at the yacht club. Very palsy-walsy.

"Amy, you've got to pull yourself out of this . . . this apathy."

"You don't understand, Sarah."

"No, I don't. How can I know what's going on in your head? But I can see one thing – you're depressed and have been for a long time. You've stopped going out, answering calls. You haven't contacted me since before Christmas when you refused the invitation to our dinner party. Clodagh is worried about you too. To all intents and purposes you've dropped out of sight."

"I don't feel like going out."

"It's not healthy, Amy, to hide yourself away like this. You've got to get help. It's not fair to yourself and it's certainly not fair to your husband or daughter. You don't even see the strain that poor girl is under. You're not a cruel person, Amy. Take a good look at yourself. You have to acknowledge what you're doing." A small stifled moan made Sarah regret her harshness. She softened her approach. "I'll help you, Amy. I'm here to help you."

"I'm not going back to that doctor. Never again. No more of those sedatives. They made me feel worse."

"I've no time for sedatives myself," Sarah agreed, "but there are other ways. Homeopathy for one thing, I swear by homeopathic cures – tried them for headaches and I got great relief – but that's probably no use for you at the moment, the state you're in. You need counselling."

Her friend's forthrightness was disconcerting. "I'm tired all the time. I don't have a scrap of energy. I know you're right, I should be up. I should be doing something with this place but . . . Sarah, I hate it. I loathe the house. It's really getting to me."

"And he still refuses to think about moving?"

"He keeps stalling. He's been fobbing me off for years. He's no intention of selling. I wish to God I could get out of here. Every day it gets worse."

Sarah walked to the window and drew back the long linen curtains. "Let's have some light. Daylight has a way of clearing the mind." She looked around her in dismay. "Your room is awful, Amy. This house is in a desperate state. It would depress anyone."

"I'd like to put a match to it."

Sarah opened a window. "No need for such a drastic measure: you can employ the Mini Maids. You're not short of a few bob now."

"No, no," Amy protested. "Maurice would hate the disturbance."

"Then let Maurice clean up the mess. I'll give them a call. Book them in for – when would suit you? I know you do hate the place, Amy, but at least if it was cleaned up it would be a bit more cheerful."

"I'm telling you, Maurice wouldn't like it. He can't tolerate strangers in the house."

"Tough."

"But —"

"No buts, Amy. This has nothing to do with Maurice, OK? You'll be paying. It's your home too. You have rights."

"We'll see."

"Grand. After that, we can start planning the decorating. New colours can transform the place."

"Maurice will have a fit."

"Let him. I ignore Jack's fits all the time. Never let a man put you off doing anything, Amy; they like to take control, and the more they get, the more they want, that's the nature of the beast. Decorating, yes. I can help to organise it. Maurice needn't be discommoded at all. The colour schemes and the drab furniture in this house would get to anyone. That red monstrosity downstairs that poses as a suite will be the first thing to go."

If Maurice was a fly on the wall — if he only could hear Sarah's grand plans for his mother's furniture. Amy had to smile.

"Good, that's more like it. Now, don't lose the rag before you hear me out; you definitely should go for therapy."

"I don't think so, Sarah."

"Hold on. Normally I wouldn't recommend this type of thing either but I have to say that it has helped many people, turned their lives around."

"People like me?" Amy asked sceptically.

"Yes," Sarah said, "and people who were worse than you. Much worse. I can't give you the particulars, but I know of one case where therapy literally saved a life. I have that from the horse's mouth — you know what I mean."

"Therapy? But I'd have to talk, bare my soul, spill out my guts."

"You can go at your own pace, Amy."

"I couldn't sit there and yap about my life to a total stranger. Give all my intimate thoughts, feelings, for scrutiny. No, I don't want anyone probing and pumping me for information. I'd hate it."

"Therapists aren't like that at all; they're trained listeners. You get out of it what you put into it. Nobody is going to force you to say anything you don't want to. Of course, there's no point in going if you don't co-operate."

"Co-operate? Just what I mean, I'd have to talk."

"Is that such a bad thing?"

"It would be for me."

"Give it a try. Make one appointment and if you don't like the session you need never go back." Sarah patted her hand affectionately. "Just once, Amy, please."

"But wouldn't I need a referral from a doctor?"

"Not necessarily. I know someone here in Blackrock. I could have a word."

"I'm still not sure. I wouldn't feel comfortable –"

"That's just where you're wrong. This woman would *make* you comfortable, believe me, that's her trademark. She has such an easy manner, you'll find yourself very relaxed, I promise."

"I'd feel like a fool."

"For being depressed? Don't be mad . . . I mean don't be daft. These people are used to hearing all sorts of stories. There's nothing you could tell her that she hasn't heard before. Nothing."

"I'll think about it."

"Amy Kennedy, the time for thinking is past. I'll phone this minute. Don't look so forlorn. Everything's going to be all right. If you really want to know, I used to go to her myself – she was terrific."

"*You* went for therapy?"

"I was very depressed after my brother died. This woman got me through it. She's particularly good on bereavement counselling." Sarah took an address book from her handbag. "Right, here's the number." She picked up the telephone receiver.

"Wait, Sarah . . . I can't."

"You can, Amy. If you want to, you can."

"I'd be afraid." Amy paused. "I'm feeling too insecure."

Reluctantly Sarah hung up. She picked up a hardback novel from the floor. "What are you reading?" She examined the cover. *À la recherche du temps perdu*. Proust. What's it about?"

"The decay of society among other things."

Sarah tutted. "Nancy, I presume?"

"Yes, and do you know what else she managed to get for me? A first edition of *Les Plaisirs et les Jours*. She met someone last summer from a publishing house in Paris who has great contacts."

Sarah was unimpressed. "On my way home I'm going to pick up a book for you in Eason's: *The Power of Negative Thinking*."

"You mean *positive*?"

"No, I mean negative – that's the point. You'll understand when you've read it. It's well-written, full of common sense and sound thinking and much better for you than this –" she looked disdainfully again at the French novel, "this type of morbidity. It'll help you. It helped me when I was feeling particularly inadequate."

Amy wasn't about to make a defence of Proust, not to Sarah. "When did you ever feel inadequate?"

"Lots of times. When I went into Mount Carmel to have Gerald I was a bundle of nerves. I know everyone having a baby is nervous but I was terrified. I wasn't much better on the other two, despite the epidural. At the last job interview I did for the bank I was a gibbering idiot. And when Anna fell that time from the tree and had to get ten stitches on her face, I wasn't worth tuppence, I swear to God. That's when a nurse in Casualty told me about Rescue Remedy. It calmed me down."

"Rescue Remedy?"

"Mmh, a homeopathic cure. I'll get you some. And exercise is good too. There's no point in going to see a therapist if you don't make an effort yourself."

"I know,' Amy said dejectedly. "If I could only summon up the energy. The more tired I get the more depressed I become."

"I think that's part of it, Amy. We'll get you through that as well. There *is* an answer to every problem. You just have to find it."

"You've such a positive attitude, Sarah." Positive but naïve in the extreme.

"Amy, you will get better, I promise you that, but you've got to make an effort."

"I'll try," she said wearily.

"And you'll make that appointment?"

"Maybe."

Sarah knew she'd have to work harder on her. It wasn't going to be easy.

Six

Sarah drove over to Clodagh Heffernan's house. This sprawling housing estate wouldn't be her cup of tea but, fair play to Clodagh, she'd certainly got her act together after Gareth dumped her. Five years together and he chickened out of their arrangement, told her it wasn't working out and hightailed it off to England, leaving her to carry on with the mortgage repayments on her own. It was a good job she hadn't married him; at least there were no legal entanglements.

"Hi, Sarah. Come in. I wasn't expecting to see you today." Clodagh, dressed in pale blue dungarees and a white T-shirt, ushered her into the tiny hall and opened the door on her right. "Sorry about the mess." There was material strewn all over the sitting-room floor. "I'm nearly finished the costumes. I'll need a lot more stuff for the men's jackets, though. Not sure what to try for Biff. Should I have more or less the same costume as for Happy? What do you think?"

"You'll have to ask Niall about it; he's in charge of costume design. Listen, I didn't call around about the play." Sarah shifted from one foot to the other.

"Oh?"

"No, I've just been to visit Amy. She's in a terrible state."

"I called a few times but she obviously doesn't want to see me. I left messages on her answering machine as well. She's definitely avoiding me."

"She's avoiding everyone. When I saw her today, quite honestly, I got a fright. She looked awful. She was still in bed at five o'clock. I hadn't realised how bad things were until I called there. She told me she's not sleeping properly at night. She wakes up at five in the morning and then she can't get back to sleep. That leaves her washed out for the day and the vicious cycle continues."

"Why doesn't she try sleeping pills?"

"Clodagh, she doesn't need sleeping pills. They won't solve her problem. She needs therapy."

"What makes you the expert?"

Sarah bit her tongue. "Look, it's not simply a matter of lack of sleep with Amy – you know that. She's depressed."

"Not her mother again? Why can't she forget it; put it out of her head and get on with her life? She's obsessed."

"That's the bloody point." Sarah saw red. Did Clodagh have no understanding at all? "You want her to snap out of it – if only she could. It's not as if she chose to be ill, is it? You make it sound like she's looking for attention."

"Maybe she is. All I know is that some of us have to work for a living. I couldn't afford the luxury of lying in bed all day. That's selfishness."

Sarah sighed. Clodagh was so judgemental. "I think you should have a little more compassion. Amy is having a terrible time. I've never seen her so unhappy and it's tearing me up."

Clodagh softened a little. "Was she on her own when you called?"

"No, the daughter was with her. The girl is under a lot of pressure and there's dissension between them – I couldn't get over it. When I think of how Amy idolised that girl!"

"You're great, Sarah. I wouldn't have the nerve to interfere."

"I'm not interfering," Sarah said stiffly, waiting for Clodagh to clear a place for her to sit. "Somebody had to step in. Amy's low, very low. Frighteningly so."

"What can *you* do? You said yourself she needs professional help."

"Yes, precisely. I'm hoping to persuade her to go. But there are other things we can do too." Sarah hated the way Clodagh always managed to avoid trouble. She was a good friend so long as everything was all right but, if trouble brewed, she wouldn't get involved. "Amy needs all the support she can get. I've called to rope you in. If we could get her to come out with us, it would be a start. We used to have some great nights out, remember?"

Clodagh shook her auburn curls. "Not the last few times – Amy drank too much. I found it a terrible ordeal, Sarah. I don't like scenes and when Amy drinks she gets maudlin."

"That's very harsh." Sarah, tired of waiting for Clodagh to clear the clutter, moved a box of needles and thread and sat down on the couch. "I blame Maurice for a lot of her troubles. He's hopeless. Mind you, most men are when it comes to women's emotions. He was always a bit of a stick-in-the-mud but lately I think he's worse."

"In what way?"

"More remote. Do you know what Amy told me today? That they've had separate bedrooms for the last six months. That's a recipe for disaster for any couple."

"I suppose so but sometimes there are good reasons: Amy's insomnia, for instance. Maybe they visit each other's room for passionate interludes."

"Cop yourself on. If Maurice Kennedy is indulging in romantic interludes they're not with his wife."

Clodagh frowned and sat beside her. "Why do you say that?"

"I think he might be seeing someone else – having an affair."

"Another woman? Maurice Kennedy?" Clodagh scoffed.

"Stranger things have happened. Some women might even find him attractive. I personally don't go for that clean-shaven little-boy look but some women love it."

"But he's not the type, is he?"

"He might think he has an excuse now with Amy being the way she is and every man is the type, given the chance, Clodagh. You, above all people, must know that."

"I'm obviously not as cynical as you."

"It's not cynicism, it's realism. Jack wouldn't be beyond a little fling if I didn't keep a good rein on him."

Jack-the-lad's lead had stretched far enough to allow him more than one fully fledged affair, Clodagh knew, but she kept the observation to herself.

"And another thing I can't stand about Maurice Kennedy is that he's so bloody tight-fisted." Sarah's nose twitched. "That must be awful to live with. Remember when we all went away for that weekend in Carlingford? He counted his change meticulously any time he bought a round – which wasn't very often. Even Gareth commented on it to me."

"I don't give a damn what that louse thought."

Sarah was on the wrong track here. Better to avoid the subject of Gareth. "Are you free tonight? Jack's going to some business do and the kids are staying in a neighbour's house for a sleepover, so I hoped we might go out for a meal. I asked Amy of course but she won't come. I'm going to keep asking her out no matter how often she refuses."

"There's no point pestering her, Sarah."

"I don't see it as pestering. Even if she doesn't accept invitations, it's important for her to know that people still care."

"Mmh."

"So, are you free for dinner?"

"OK. I've no other plans. My social life isn't exactly hectic at the moment."

"That must be the worst thing about being on your own – Saturday nights. I always feel as if I'm short-changed if I have to stay in on a Saturday night."

Did Sarah ever listen to herself? Being married hadn't stopped *her* from being on her own tonight. "Where do you fancy eating?"

"What about the Boulevard Café? Wasn't it Amy who discovered it? Remember that lovely meal we had on her birthday two years ago? God, she was in great form that night. Different times."

"I wasn't there."

"Weren't you? Oh no, it was Maurice and Jack. We had a foursome. Maurice was all praise for the place and he's not easy to please. I'll give Sharon a ring and see if she has a table free for seven-thirty."

"I'll drive; I'm off the jar for Lent."

* * *

Amy stared and stared at the name in her address book. Sylvia Gibson. A local number. Sarah said the practice was five minutes away – she wouldn't even have to borrow the car. Maurice needn't know. But why shouldn't he know? Wasn't that what he wanted? Wouldn't that make him happy? And Dawn? And Sarah? She lit a cigarette and inhaled deeply. All she had to do was dial the digits. Then things would take off. Is that what *she* wanted? She heard Maurice coming up the stairs and she shoved the address book under the pillow.

* * *

The Boulevard was buzzing as usual. This was one of the reasons Sarah had chosen this restaurant : it was popular, the chat was animated, the music lively without being too intrusive and the waiters were good-humoured and friendly – plus the food was excellent.

Sharon, who owned the restaurant, wasn't there. Her mother, Elizabeth, a very glamorous woman, greeted them both warmly and showed them to a candle-lit table set for two by the window, looking out on Exchequer Street. Saturday-night revellers rushed by in the pouring rain, umbrellas doing battle with the gusts of strong wind.

Good to be in here, cosy and warm.

Darragh, the flamboyant waiter, who called his female patrons "petal", discussed the merits of the Californian Pinot Noir versus the Spanish Rioja with Sarah as Clodagh had a quick glance around. Suddenly she spotted him.

Maurice. With his sister-in-law. They were sitting at a small table by the stairs. Deep in conversation. How could she keep Sarah from seeing them? She dragged her chair a little to the left, sat up as tall as she could and hid her head behind the menu.

"I ordered the Pinot Noir in the end. I think it's the one Jack chose the last time we were here. I didn't forget your mineral water."

"Thanks."

"Have you decided on your starter? The Seafood Chowder is delicious. I'm going to have that."

"I think I'll have the Garlic Mushrooms." Clodagh lowered the menu but sat up straighter.

"You all right? You look a bit uncomfortable."

"No, no, I'm grand."

"Right, now for the main course. I'm going to opt for the Chicken Sunrise. I love Brie cheese."

"And tomato and spinach filling," Clodagh read aloud.

"It's scrumptious."

"I'm in the mood for pasta. What's good?" She decided to defer to her friend's culinary wisdom.

"The Linguine Prawn Arrabiata is terrific. But that would be more garlic for you."

"No problem. Don't forget I've no man to worry about."

Sarah looked at her suspiciously. "Have you decided?"

"I'll have the Tagliatelle Carbonara." She winked. "Better cut down on the garlic – just in case."

"Are you winding me up, Clodagh Heffernan?"

"Who? Me?"

"Sometimes, I don't understand you."

Ditto, Clodagh thought.

"Do you want dessert, Clodagh? Jesus H Christ. I don't believe it!"

"What, what?"

"He's here. Maurice-fecking-Kennedy is sitting over there, as large as life and twice as ugly. I don't bloody believe it."

"You sound exactly like Victor Meldrew!"

"He's with her. I knew it all along. He's definitely with her."

"Who? Who is he with?" Clodagh pretended ignorance.

"Amy's sister. Yer woman, Claire. Claire Shiels. Oh my God, what am I going to do?"

"Nothing, Sarah, you're going to do absolutely nothing. Leave it. We've enjoyed our meal. Don't go stirring things. It's none of our business."

"It damn well is. I'm not going to let him get away with it."

"Get away with *what?*"

"With thinking he's home free. No way. I'm going to make Mister-Squeaky-Clean squirm."

"Shh, shh, Sarah. Everyone will hear."

"I don't care."

"Please, Sarah, will you just drop it –"

"Have to pay my respects." Sarah jumped up from her chair, waved and called: "Maurice, Maurice! Over here!"

He whispered something to his companion, rose quickly from his table and strode over, all smiles.

Clodagh was dying a thousand deaths.

"'Evening, girls. Nice to see you."

"And you, Maurice, and you," Sarah gushed.

"Is Jack at the club tonight?"

"He's at some business dinner, then he's going to the club." She paused for effect. "He said you'd be there."

"No, couldn't make it. Something came up."

Something came up? Sarah could well believe it. And it most likely would come up later again tonight. "You know Clodagh, don't you?"

Maurice nodded politely. "How are you?"

"Fine, thank you."

"Isn't that Amy's sister with you?" Sarah said innocently. "Would you care to join us?"

"No, thanks all the same. We're on our way in a few moments. I must thank you for calling to see Amy."

"It's the least I could do. I'm very worried about her." Sarah stared at him. "Was it wise to have left her on her own tonight, Maurice?"

"Unfortunately, she prefers to be on her own. I'd have thought you'd have gathered that from her today." He surprised them both by pulling up a chair and sitting between them. He gestured over to Claire that he'd only be a minute. "I'm delighted you're taking an interest, Sarah. Amy needs her friends. I was afraid she'd lose you all."

"There's no chance of that, Maurice." Sarah took a little sip of wine. How could he have the gall to sit there and pretend concern for his wife when he was dining out with her sister? The man's audacity knew no bounds. "She's seriously depressed in my view."

"Yes, she is. But your visit worked wonders, Sarah, I'm glad to report."

"I don't think so, Maurice. We had a long talk but I didn't make much headway."

"That's where you're wrong." He beamed. "She told me tonight she was going to ring the therapist you recommended."

"Did she?" Clodagh, amazed, turned to Sarah. "Well done!"

Sarah shook her head. "I wouldn't go congratulating myself yet. It's very early days."

Maurice nodded. "But it's a step in the right direction."

"She could change her mind," Sarah warned. "She might have just told you that, Maurice, to placate you or something. Amy needs careful handling. I intend to keep a good eye on her."

Maurice didn't doubt it. Sarah liked adopting causes and now she had one which would demand her fullest concentration. He was relieved. It might take some of the pressure off him. Amy had given up listening to him. She might pay some attention to her friend.

Seven

Joe Shiels sat reading the latest John Grisham which Claire had brought to him on her last visit. Was it his imagination or had he read this story before? At his age, maybe there were no new plots?

He'd pulled the armchair away from his bedside to the window where there was better light. He shared the room with a retired British army captain, who regularly regaled him with stories of his exploits during the war. The latter was now happily snoring away in the other bed. He was a nice old codger, if a bit of a bore. Joe had opted to share the room; it made him feel less isolated.

A polite knock on the door and a pretty red-haired nurse entered.

"Mr Shiels, a visitor for you in the day room. Your daughter."

"Claire?"

"Your other daughter, I think."

"Amy?" Surprised, he rose from the chair more quickly than he'd intended and tottered slightly. He gripped the armrest and gritted his teeth. Blast these legs.

"Steady on." The nurse linked him. "Why don't I escort you down?"

Brusquely he disengaged his arm. Oh hell, why take it out on her? She was only trying to help. "No, I'm fine, Nurse, thank you."

"Good."

"I'm not totally dependent yet." He couldn't resist the barb.

The nurse smiled comfortingly and pretended to straighten the curtains. He was a proud old gentleman. Still, since that stroke, his balance wasn't the best and his arthritis didn't make walking any easier. She'd stay a few steps behind to watch him on the stairs.

Amy looked out on the meticulously kept flower-beds and wondered if her father missed his own little patch. He'd always had a keen interest in gardening but in the past few years he'd had to employ a local boy to mow the lawn and do the weeding; the effort had become too much for him.

She wasn't looking forward to this visit, hadn't been here in weeks: it was painful to watch her father deteriorate before her eyes, reliant on the kindness of strangers. She'd have to learn to accept it – it had been his decision to come here. But what choice had he? Claire was out at work all day and an apartment wouldn't have suited; they can be lonely places. In any case he'd never have settled with Claire. Not that she'd offered to have him.

Dawn had made a tentative suggestion that, since they had room, her grandfather should live with them but Maurice had pooh-poohed the notion. The old man needed round-the-clock minding. Even Amy had to admit that was beyond her. She couldn't have invited her father to stay with them – not the way things were.

And yet . . .

"Amy, Amy." His eyes moistened as he hugged his elder daughter to him. "How lovely to see you!"

"Come and sit down, Dad. How are you?"

He followed her to the four-seater settee and slowly eased himself into it. "Oh, pulling the divil."

"Here, for you." She handed him a small brown-paper bag.

With childlike glee he opened the present. "Butterscotch – my favourite." He seemed genuinely pleased.

"How are they treating you, Dad?" She was afraid to hear the answer.

"They're kind, Amy, very kind. A bit fussy sometimes, but you can't have it every way. The food's good and nourishing; plenty of meat and veg – lovely big floury spuds like you used to get in the old days. One of the Sisters keeps a little vegetable garden out the back. Nothing like fresh vegetables; they've a much nicer taste and texture than those supermarket ones."

Her father had always enjoyed his grub.

"We get lots of rhubarb too, when it's in season, and they make their own brown bread, just like your mother used to. "

Amy squeezed his hand.

"Hard to believe she's gone a year now, isn't it?" he said. "Where does the time go? I had a Mass said for her here in the chapel on her anniversary."

"I went to the cemetery . . ." She should have brought him. It was the least she could have done.

"That wasn't easy for you, pet."

"I'm sorry I didn't call for you, Dad. I wasn't thinking straight. It never occurred to me."

"It's all right, Amy. I never liked graveyards," he said simply. "Intimations of mortality and all that. I'd rather remember your mother in her little kitchen, shoving batches of brown bread into the oven or washing out the front porch. God knows, that woman never rested easy; always busy – knitting, darning, sweeping, cleaning out presses. She ironed everything in sight – even my underpants. What's the point in ironing underpants? But she *had* to be doing something. Didn't know the meaning of relaxation."

"No," Amy agreed.

"I miss her much more than I'd ever have thought."

"Do you, Dad?"

"Indeed I do. You remember the way she used to chatter on about all and sundry and I, God forgive me, wouldn't be paying a blind bit of attention to her – that used to rattle her cage, all right." He smiled at the thought of it. "Oh, she'd words at will, your mother, words at will. I miss all her little sayings."

Amy didn't.

His daughter's glum expression was a worry. "Your mother's gone to a better place." He tittered. "That's what they want us to believe, anyway."

"And do you?"

"Naw, as far as I'm concerned, there's only one life in it. The chaplain here would give out yards if he heard me saying that. I've had some right old barneys with him."

"With the priest?"

"Oh aye. I set him up and he falls for it every time; give him all sorts of ecclesiastical questions which addle the poor unfortunate – he leaps in with his theories, definitions and philosophies, then, in the next breath he contradicts himself – I'm telling you, it's mighty."

"Dad, you're a terrible tease."

"Sure there's no harm in a bit of fun."

"No."

"How long is it since you've had any, Amy?"

"Too long, Dad."

"Well," he said emphatically, "isn't it time you went out there and got some?"

"What exactly did you have in mind?"

"Listen, love, enjoy yourself while you can – don't let matters go too far."

"Matters?"

"You know right well what I mean, Amy. Go out and see a bit of life before it's too late. You're not getting any younger."

"I'm well aware of that."

"But you're not too old to enjoy yourself. That's why I gave you the money. Use it. Spend it, girl. Money is meant to be enjoyed not hoarded away, gathering dust in a bank."

"That's what Sarah says."

"She's right."

"Mmh, I was thinking of doing up the house."

"The house? Ah, not at all. What good is that? The house will be there long after you."

"I thought it might cheer me up."

"It never cheered your mother up, did it? If she wasn't painting she was stripping wallpaper, varnishing the woodwork, always at the damned house, week in, week out. Far too finicky."

Who dropped the glass of milk on the kitchen table? Was it you,

*Amy? The truth now. Clean it up. Quickly. Another glass broken –
do you think I'm made of money? You're the clumsiest little pest that
ever wore shoe-leather. Hurry up. Now look – you've cut your hand.
No, I do not have bandages. Run it under the tap. No tears, no tears
or I'll give you something to cry about. When you're finished
mopping the floor, go up to your room and tidy it properly. That
room is a disgrace. A disgrace.*

"At the end of the day – what does it matter, eh? There are more
important things in life, Amy. You'd be better occupied going off
on a nice holiday for yourself."

"You're probably right but Maurice is busy and he's difficult to
budge."

Her father took off his glasses and wiped them in the end of his
cardigan. "Who said anything about Maurice?"

She was taken aback. "On my own? Go off on my own?"

"Just what you need."

"I couldn't, Dad. Dawn has exams coming up and –"

"And what?"

"I couldn't just up and leave Maurice on his own. He wouldn't
take to the idea at all. He expects me to be there."

"Maybe he expects too much, then. You were always there for
him, Amy, and for Dawn too. You've done your bit and signs on;
she's a grand girl and she's made a life for herself. You've no cause
for anxiety on that score."

"But I do, Dad." Amy's eyes filled up. "I've become a burden to
her."

"That's the very thing none of us wants to become." He took the
packet of butterscotch from the bag and unwrapped it. Watching
him breaking off a piece, putting it in his mouth and starting to
chew made Amy sad. It brought her back to the steaming kitchen
where her father would sit after dinner, sharing his sweets with her
and helping her with her homework.

"I've watched you over the last few months, Amy. Don't think I
haven't noticed. I didn't think it was my place to tell you how to
live your life but since I've come in here I've had a lot of time to
think. You're very unhappy, aren't you?"

49

Amy turned away. Her father was old, tired; he deserved some peace. She was here today to comfort him, to give him attention, not to foist her problems on him.

"Amy, love, life's very short."

"There's no use complaining –"

"I don't hear you complaining, Amy. I've never heard you complain. Maybe it's time you did. Why don't you do something for yourself, child?"

She had. She'd made an appointment with the counsellor. Fifty quid a session. Fifty pounds to sit with a stranger and tell all. Sad and self-indulgent. It was complete self-indulgence, wasn't it? She turned back to him slowly and the vacant look on her face dismayed him.

He patted her hand gently. "You can see no way out?"

"I don't know, Dad. I can't think straight. Any time I make up my mind to do something I change it just as quickly. I can't concentrate on anything. What to make for dinner has become a momentous decision."

"That's not like you, Amy. You were always so competent."

"Past tense."

"Focus on what you want for yourself. Forget Maurice and Dawn and the bloody old house. It will be there long after you. Ask yourself what it is *you* really want."

"That's just it; I don't know what I want. I try, every day I try to make a fresh start, to make plans, to be happy, optimistic . . . but nothing works. Maurice can't understand where I'm coming from and Dawn has her studies. She's been great but she can't solve my problems, can she? It's hard to explain. I feel as if I've woken up in the middle of a play but I've been cast in the wrong part."

"You've got to get that idea out of your head, Amy. You can change your life if you want to. But you must want to."

"Dad." She hesitated. "Were you happy with Mam?"

"We muddled through, I suppose. I didn't hope for too much, you see. That's the secret of contentment. In our case, Amy, it was your mother who was unhappy. Not that she ever said anything. She was a great believer in duty, your mother was, but I knew she

50

was just going through the motions most of the time. She was one of those people who do the right thing at the expense of themselves. Self-sacrifice has repercussions."

"I never felt close to her, Dad."

"She was a hard woman in lots of ways; hardest of all on herself. But then she carried around a huge weight of guilt."

"Guilt?"

He sighed gently and his eyes took on that faraway look she'd seen before. "There's a lot you don't know about her."

"I'd like to know, Dad."

"Let's go out for a stroll in the garden? It's allowed when we have visitors. A bit of exercise would do me good. We can escape through the French window there, otherwise Sister Martha will see us and make me take the Zimmer frame and I hate the cursed thing."

Amy helped her father to his feet. He was very shaky, much more feeble than she'd realised. "What about a coat, Dad? It's chilly today."

"Would you run up to my room? The grey overcoat is hanging in the wardrobe nearest the door."

"Of course. Sit on the piano stool and I'll be back in a second."

"We had a session here at this very piano last night. Sister Alphonsus plays a mean Scott Joplin." He smiled. "A sing song at night, just like when I was a lad. We didn't have telly in those days and we were better off for it. Made our own entertainment."

Amy visualised them sitting around in their wheelchairs or propped up on the sofa and the armchairs singing half-forgotten tunes from a bygone era. Together but ultimately alone.

She wanted to ask him to explain about her mother. She needed to know, but the old man seemed to have forgotten all about what he'd been saying and she didn't want to fluster him.

* * *

Joe was awake late into the night. Amy's visit today had disturbed him greatly. He should have taken more care of his children. He'd opted out of their upbringing, taken a back seat. Too bloody scared to step in and do his part. What could he do for his daughter now? What had he done for her when she was a child? If he couldn't help her then, what could he possibly do now? He closed his eyes but the images wouldn't go away . . .

The kitchen door was locked. He heard her weeping softly on the back step. It was raining heavily and she was soaked.

"Amy, child, Amy! What on earth are you doing out there in the dark? Come in out of the rain. You'll get your death."

She flung herself into his arms, her scorching tears wetting his face. "I'm sorry, Dad. I'm sorry. I won't do it again." She gulped between sobs. "I won't be bold any more. Tell her I'm sorry. I won't do it again."

He hugged her tighter. "Do what, darling?"

"I made a mess, left my toys around the bedroom and the baby tripped and cut her head on my tin drum. Mam shouted that I shouldn't have left it on the floor, that she'd told me to tidy up but I forgot, Dad. I didn't meant to hurt Claire." Another loud gulp. "Mam slapped me hard and put me out in the garden. She said it was to teach me a lesson."

How long had the child been out there?

"I'm sorry, Dad. I'm sorry."

He carried his daughter over to the fire. "It's all right, chicken. It's all right."

He lifted her wet dress up over her head. She stood shivering in her vest and knickers, her little body blue with the cold, her teeth chattering.

He thought his heart would break. "Come upstairs, pet, and I'll run you a hot bath. We have to get you warm again."

"Dad, I'm afraid to go upstairs. Mam's up there with Claire. She's really cross."

"Don't worry, love. It'll be OK." He patted her wet curls. "I'll talk to Mam about it."

But he hadn't, had he? Not then or at any other time.

Eight

Yesterday's conversation with her father played on Amy's mind. What had he meant about her mother feeling guilty all her life? Guilty about what? Her failure as a wife? Her children's upbringing? The oppression in the house? All of these seemed plausible, and yet, it was as if her father had been talking about something different. Amy had wanted to ask him to talk in more detail, fill in the gaps, but she'd no wish to push him into saying anything he might later regret – she'd sensed that he'd already confided more than he'd intended.

Just as Amy stepped out of her morning bath, the phone rang. She wrapped a towel around her and, still dripping wet, went into the bedroom to answer.

"Mrs Kennedy?"

"Speaking."

"This is Helen Broe."

Helen Broe. The woman who'd bought the family home; married to an auctioneer; three grown-up kids. She hadn't heard from the Broes since her father had signed the deal on his house and she hadn't expected to.

"Yes, Mrs Broe. How can I help you?" she asked cautiously.

"Well, it's rather difficult. I don't quite know how to begin."

Please, nothing unpleasant, Amy prayed.

"A most peculiar thing happened this morning – a letter arrived here, addressed to your mother. I was going to post it on to you but then my husband and I talked it over and we thought – we thought it would be better to phone first."

Amy sat down on the bed. "A letter for my mother?"

"It must be distressing for you," the woman faltered. "I wasn't sure what to do."

"You did the right thing." Amy's thoughts raced. "I . . . I'm sorry, this is a bolt from the blue."

"Yes. Look, my husband can drop it in to you on his way into work, if that's a help. It would save delay."

"I don't want to put you out."

"Not at all. Fancy – a letter after this length of time. It's strange, you know, coming like this, as you say, out of the blue – obviously from someone who doesn't know that your mother has passed away. That's why I was reluctant to phone you but I suppose –"

"Mrs Broe," Amy interrupted, "could you check the postmark?"

"I already did. It's from London."

"London?"

Vague childhood memories stirred: birthday cards, Christmas greetings, a parcel now and again.

"So, Hugh will be there in an hour or so."

"I'm actually on my way out. I have an appointment which I can't cancel, unfortunately. Of course he could post it in my door."

"Fine. I'm awfully sorry about this. It's bound to be unpleasant. To tell you the truth, I was about to throw it out but Hugh thought it might be something important."

"You're very good." Amy felt she had to say something to ease the awkwardness. "Everything all right with you?"

"Oh yes," the woman's voice lightened. "We're thrilled to be here in Glenageary – settled in within a matter of weeks. The neighbours are wonderful, very helpful. You wouldn't know the house. We built a conservatory off the dining-room and Hugh converted the attic. My youngest, Danny, sleeps up there, delighted with the privacy. It's more like a Virgin Megastore than a bedroom, you know what teenagers are like."

"Indeed."

"Right, I better let you go, Mrs Kennedy. Nice to talk to you again. Take care."

"And you. I'm very grateful, Mrs Broe. Goodbye."

Amy replaced the receiver. Her hands were shaking, she was ashamed to admit to herself. It's only a letter, it's only a letter, she repeated mantra-like. What was the name of that friend of her mother's? She lived in the south of England. Corr? What was it they used to call her? Aunt Cathy? Aunt Catherine? Yes, that was it. Amy had a picture in her mind of a walk on the pier in Howth, the breeze blowing her dress skywards and her mother turning to her and laughing. That was what stuck in her mind – her mother's laughter.

* * *

The room was painted pale yellow. It was a cheerful colour and Amy guessed this was deliberate. "Sit down, please." Sylvia Gibson smiled encouragingly as she showed the client to a chair. "Now, how can I help?"

"I eh . . . you were recommended to me by a friend." Amy faltered. "She said if I spoke to you . . . she thinks you can help me."

"I hope so, Amy." Sylvia Gibson leaned a little closer. "Can you start by telling me how you're feeling now."

"Stupid for being here," Amy admitted. "Is it OK if I smoke?"

"If it makes you more comfortable, by all means." Sylvia took an ash-tray from the drawer of her desk. Then she pulled her own chair out from behind the desk and moved it closer to Amy's. "That's better." She pulled a large writing pad off the desk. "Do you mind if I take notes? It's just that it helps me to focus and it's a record if you decide to come back because we can trace what's happening. Also, I've a head like a sieve – I need to write everything down," she confessed.

"Me too." Amy lit a cigarette and balanced the ashtray on her knee.

"Right, now you said you felt stupid being here. Why so?"

"More than stupid, Selfish. I think it's quite self-indulgent."

Sylvia Gibson smiled. "I don't agree, naturally. You owe it to yourself to look after yourself. If you were physically sick you'd go to a doctor, surely?"

"I'm mentally ill. Is that what you're saying?"

Sylvia Gibson kept her face very straight. She mustn't register any emotion that would alienate this woman. Wisely and slowly.

"The real reason I'm here is that I can't sleep. I didn't want to go back on pills." Amy furiously flicked the ash. "Maybe I should try massage? The thing is . . . well, I can't say, really."

"It's all right, Amy. You can say absolutely anything you like."

"I don't honestly think I should be here."

Sylvia nodded. "Go on."

"I shouldn't need to be here. It's utter failure. I think there's something awful about having to come to a stranger – sorry, no insult intended – coming to a stranger to tell your problems. I should be able to solve them myself. I'm a grown woman but I feel – out of control. That's the best way to describe it. And I think I should be able to talk to my family and friends about it and I can't. I did, I tried to, but it . . . they didn't understand. Don't get me wrong – they're very good but . . ."

"Amy," Sylvia said gently, "do you feel loved?"

* * *

The writing *was* familiar. Putting on her reading glasses, Amy sat by the kitchen window and, trembling, tore open the envelope. One page folded over. Amy flicked to the bottom, her first thought to discover the sender.

Catherine Cole.

Yes, yes, Cole. How could she have forgotten? The small freckled face swamped in the collar of the fur coat with its sickly-brown colour. Cole the Mole – as a child that's what Amy had nicknamed her.

Other memories came flooding back. A red pleated dress with a white belt. She couldn't have been older than six or seven. She'd torn it climbing on a fence. Amy didn't remember receiving the dress but she remembered, in vivid detail, the stinging slap across the face . . .

"You've ruined it, absolutely ruined it. Have you no shame? You're the most ungrateful little witch that ever walked. Wait until I tell your Aunt Catherine! She's not made of money, you know. Do you realise how much that dress cost, my girl?"

Amy shivered in the corner of her room. The evening light was fading and her mother's face, contorted with rage, took on a yellow, evil hue.

"Throwing away her hard-earned money on the likes of you." Her mother tossed the dress on the bed. "You'll stay up here and mend it," she screamed. "Do you hear me?"

Amy wasn't good at sewing. Sister Agnes had smacked her in class the day before for unravelling a grubby sample. Sister cut pieces of seersucker material into square patches for practice. You were only allowed one sample per week and you had to be careful. "They don't grow on trees, girls," the nun would scold.

Amy started to whimper as her mother lunged at her. "Come here, you pest!"

Amy shrank against the wall.

"Don't dare back away from me." Another sharp slap, this time on the leg. "You'll sit up here and you'll mend this dress." Her mother stormed out and within seconds was back with the sewing-basket. She cut a small piece of thread. "Don't double it and don't, I repeat *don't* let the stitches be seen on the outside. Make them small, neat. I'll be back in twenty minutes to check. Is that clear?"

Amy stared down at the carpet. If she didn't look up, her mother mightn't hit her again.

"Is that clear?"

"Yes." Her little voice shook.

"Yes what?"

"Yes, Mam."

Amy sighed aloud in the cold kitchen. Butterflies somersaulted in her stomach and her forehead felt clammy. Heart beating fast, she started to read.

My dear Elaine,

I'm sorry for the long delay in getting in touch with you. Hope this letter finds you and yours well.

Amy lit a cigarette and took a long pull.

I deeply regret the row we had and always meant to write and make it up with you but time passed and I never got around to it. We were both foolish; nothing is worth losing a friendship. I hope you find it in your heart to forgive me.

A row. That explained why the visits and the post had stopped.

I'm writing to let you know that I'll be in Dublin for a few days at the end of this month. I'll be staying in the Shelbourne from the 27th. I'd love to meet up with you. Please phone the hotel and we can arrange a get-together. There's something extremely urgent I have to tell you but I'd need to see you in person. It relates to JE and, needless to say, I don't want to be more specific until I see you. Just one thing – <u>nothing</u> was as you thought.

Sorry for the scribble, I'm hurrying to the post. Please contact me, Elaine. I'd really like to see you again.

Love,

Catherine [Cole].

Amy sat for a long time, her hands gripping the letter, her thoughts flurried.

* * *

Claire stood on the doorstep, her cheeks glowing from the cold wind. "Well," she brushed past Amy into the dark sitting-room. "Where's the letter? What's all the fuss about?"

"I burned it."

"You *what?*"

"I burned it – nothing important after all."

Claire flopped into the old red armchair. "Nothing important? Let me be the judge of that. Do you know after you phoned I drove over here like a mad woman – even skipped lunch?" She folded her arms. "Who was it from?"

"Just somebody who worked with Mam years ago in London. It was an invitation for a holiday."

"That's a bit macabre. Why did you burn the letter? You'll have to let this woman know about Mam, won't you? It's only common politeness."

"It's OK. I phoned her." Amy was surprised at how easy it was to fib once she got into her stride. "She was sad to hear about the death and sent us all her condolences."

"That's that, so."

"Yes."

"Make me a coffee, will you?" She sniffed. "Any chance of a sandwich?"

Amy went to the kitchen to fill the kettle. Today was the 25th. In two days' time she was going to phone the Shelbourne and arrange to meet Catherine Cole. No need for Maurice or Dawn or Claire to know anything about it. She needed the luxury of privacy for the moment.

The visit to the counsellor had been her first step – a big step. She felt relieved it was over but she knew she'd go back.

Did she feel loved? A painful question.

Sylvia Gibson had been good. Amy had left the session no longer feeling stupid or embarrassed. The woman had assured her she wasn't going mad; that she needed time and they'd take it as slowly as she liked. Amy had told her about her mother's death and her father being in the Home. She'd talked her about her feelings of loneliness, guilt and despondency – nothing about her anger, but the counsellor had probably surmised. Weren't they trained to hear what was unspoken? They'd covered recent events although Amy had skimmed over her marriage problems – she knew there'd need to be more than one session on them. Sylvia had scribbled copious notes but Amy hadn't felt uncomfortable. They hadn't dealt with her childhood yet, although from what Sylvia Gibson had said, that was where all her behavioural patterns had been formed. So, Amy would go back next week and continue. She didn't know what would come out of it but at least she was no longer frightened.

Then this letter out of the blue. Strange and not so strange. It was fate stepping in, she thought and Amy had a strong belief in destiny. She had to find out who this JE was. Clearly Catherine Cole hadn't wanted to risk committing too much to paper. *Nothing,* underlined, *was as you thought*. What on earth did that mean?

"Amy!" Claire stood in the kitchen doorway. "Do you need a hand?"

"No, no, everything's all right. I'm just buttering some bread. Ham and cheese OK ?"

"Fine," Claire said, surprised that Amy was bothering to go to the trouble. Her sister looked and sounded different today. More with it. Claire was puzzled but she wasn't complaining. Any change was a change for the better.

Nine

A silver layer of early-morning frost blanketed the garden. Maurice stared gloomily at the drooping red and pink geraniums in their terracotta pots. He'd warned Amy that they should have been kept inside for a few more weeks – you could never trust the Irish weather. Last year they'd had snow in April.

He'd brought her up a cup of tea earlier but she hadn't opened her eyes. He got into his car and drove off to his other life, his infinitely better life, at the surgery.

Amy heard the car door slam. 7.30. He was leaving for work earlier every morning, coming home later at night; spending more and more time out of the house. She stretched lazily for the remote control. *Sky News*. She sipped the cool tea and lit her first cigarette of the day. She opened the locker drawer and took out her address book where, yesterday, she'd jotted down the telephone number of the Shelbourne. She'd phone in an hour, probably the best time to make contact before Catherine Cole went off for the day.

* * *

"Sam, Sam," Catherine Cole called her husband in from the adjoining bathroom.

"Was that the phone? Not the dining-room surely? They haven't stopped serving breakfasts, have they? It's only eight-thirty.

61

"No, no. You'll never guess. That was Elaine's daughter. Amy."

"Why would *she* phone you? Is anything wrong?"

Catherine swallowed. "Elaine died a year ago."

"Died?" Sam Cole dabbed at his face with a towel, removing the last bits of shaving-foam. "How awful! And you never knew a thing about it. I'm sorry." He came over and hugged her. "That's rough, Cathy. What was it? A heart attack?"

"I never even thought to ask – my mind went blank."

"Naturally." He sat on the bed to pull on his socks.

"I feel numb," Catherine said. "I've thought about Elaine often, more so in the past year – and all this time she was dead. It's dreadful; I should have kept in contact."

"That cuts two ways. She didn't bother to keep in touch with you, either." He searched under the bed for his shoes. "It's not your fault. She was difficult."

"Dead for over a year, I can't credit it." Catherine sighed. "I couldn't wait to give her the news. Now she'll never know."

"It wasn't meant to be," he said stoically.

Catherine hated the way he did that – put everything down to fate.

"It might be all for the best," he continued. "You don't know how she might have taken it, Cathy. I wasn't convinced you were doing the right thing anyway; it could have opened up a can of worms. This way the whole thing is over and done with."

"No, it's not." She bit her lip thoughtfully. "Amy, the daughter, is coming here at twelve-thirty to meet me for lunch."

He looked at his wife, waiting for an explanation.

"She read the letter and she's very curious." Catherine went to the window and looked out over the trees of Stephen's Green. The curling fibres of the cirrus clouds merged with the patchwork of grey and blue. Catherine watched, feeling an increasing sense of foreboding. "She seemed anxious to meet me. I couldn't refuse."

"You're treading on dangerous ground, Cathy. I'd say nothing if I were you. Why should the daughter be dragged in? What can *she* possibly do?"

"It concerns her mother. She has a right to know, Sam."

"Does she? What good can come out of it? Why stir up trouble? You've no way of foreseeing the consequences. Stay out of it, Cathy. You've done all you can – Elaine is dead and I think the story should die with her."

Catherine pulled her suitcase from the wardrobe and took out a photograph album. She flicked through it and stopped at the old black-and-white snapshot. "Look at this." She handed it to him. "I wanted Elaine to have it; a record of happier times: Amy playing in the garden with the hula-hoop I bought for her. She was so excited, not used to getting presents."

"You were kind to her."

"I should have done more."

"No, Cathy, it wasn't your responsibility. You couldn't have influenced the way she treated her children. No mother takes kindly to criticism."

"I was mad about Amy. And now on the phone her voice was – I can't describe it – kind of faint, delicate. She was such a gentle creature."

"Timid, as I recall," her husband interjected.

"Yes, that was part of the problem."

* * *

Depression was not necessarily a bad thing, Sylvia Gibson had explained. Often it was a wake-up call to get us to look hard at our lives and at ourselves. It often signalled the necessity for change. Sylvia had advised Amy to start the change by being nice to herself. It was now 9a.m. Plenty of time to get her hair trimmed and treat herself to a manicure. She'd get up in a moment or two, have a shower, put on the new navy suit she'd bought yesterday in a local boutique and take the bus into the city. It was so long since she'd bothered about her appearance that it had been a real effort to force herself to go into the shop. It was when she was trying on the suit and looking at herself in the dressingroom mirror that she'd had a good look at herself for the first time in months. She was shocked by the ashen face that looked back at her. Pallid and drawn, eyes lustreless. No wonder Sarah was so worried. Amy truly didn't recognise herself or what she'd become.

She'd have to do something drastic and a haircut was the best option. She'd ask the girl in the chemist's for help in choosing some make-up to give her back a bit of colour in her cheeks. But these were only stopgaps. Amy knew she'd have to take herself in hand and it wouldn't be easy. What had Sylvia Gibson told her to do? Focus on one thing at a time. It was when all the thoughts crowded together that she became panicky.

She'd focus on this morning. Catherine Cole sounded like a sensible woman. She'd been very upset when Amy had told her about the death but agreed immediately to the lunch meeting.

Amy heard the letter box click and went downstairs to take in the mail. There were two envelopes – one from Eircom, the other addressed to her. She opened it: her new Visa card. Brilliant. Imagine, her first credit card at her age. It gave her a strong sense of independence. She could do what she liked with this without any unasked-for *advice* from her husband. It had been Sarah's idea. Amy didn't know why it hadn't occurred to her before.

* * *

The black-and-grey cocker spaniel stood shaking on the table. His distraught owner, a tall middle-aged woman, hovered. "What is it, Doctor Kennedy? His legs are weak; he can't get up on the chairs and this morning he couldn't make it onto the bed. He usually jumps up to wake me but this morning he just sat on the floor and whimpered. I'm very worried."

Dogs shouldn't be allowed up on furniture, Maurice thought. This little guy was a typical example of the dominant dog that ruled the household, but both animal and owner were too long in the tooth now to change their ways.

"Pity they can't talk and tell you what's wrong with them, isn't it?" the woman brooded. "They're more trouble than kids."

He felt around the dog's abdomen. "The gastro-entiritis has cleared up?"

"Yes, completely. He was back on his food by the weekend. I only gave him little bits of boiled chicken and rice, like you told me."

64

Maurice stuck a thermometer up the dog's backside. The little chap squirmed but made no other objections. His owner cooed and patted his head. "Temperature normal, Mrs McCluskey. I don't think there's anything seriously wrong with him." He put twenty-four antibiotic tablets in a plastic container. "One morning and evening."

"But what about the weakness in his legs, Doctor?"

"He's had a bit of trouble with his bowels lately and that often causes a sore stomach or abdomen. He won't jump because it hurts him. He'll be right as rain in a few days."

She looked doubtful. "It's not arthritis, is it?"

"No, it wouldn't come on that quickly; you'd notice a gradual deterioration."

"Of course."

"If it continues, we'll have to X-ray him to eliminate other possible causes – anything neurological, but he's showing no signs of that and, at his age, anaesthetics are to be avoided if possible."

Mrs McCluskey nodded. "I don't want him to suffer, that's all."

"He'll be fine but if you don't see an improvement after a few days ring the surgery, and one way or the other, bring him back next week for a check-up."

"The crustiness has gone from his eyes. Should I continue with the drops?"

"By all means; cockers tend to suffer from their eyes. I'll just check his ears as he's here." He lifted the long curly flaps and peered in. "Grand."

"He's as deaf as a post, Doctor. I have to roar to make him hear me. He's startled if anyone walks up behind him."

"Deafness in dogs is not as bad as it would be for you or me, Mrs McCluskey. Their sense of smell is what they go by."

"Thank goodness for that, Doctor Kennedy." She lifted the dog off the table. "Say thankyou to the doctor, Jacko."

On cue, Jacko wagged his tail, glad to be safely back on the ground, sensing that his ordeal was over. Dog and owner left the examination-room, both equally relieved.

Marie, the pretty blonde receptionist, stuck her head around the door. "Just two more cases before lunch: a kitten for inoculation and the Brewster's bulldog for his booster and kennel cough vaccines."

"Thanks, Marie. Could you phone my wife, please? Tell her I'll be late tonight."

"Certainly."

He went to the press to get Intravac. "Marie, on second thoughts, leave it."

"Right." She went to call in the next client.

He was going to see Luke Yarker's new veterinary clinic in Sallynoggin after evening surgery. Luke had bought the place lately, had renovated and expanded to include boarding facilities for cats and a grooming parlour. He'd invited Maurice to the official opening, no doubt hoping to impress. Nonetheless, it would be good to meet some of the lads from his college days.

Why bother phoning Amy? She wouldn't notice whether he was late home or not. There was a time when such things mattered, but it had long passed, he thought ruefully.

* * *

Amy gazed critically at herself in the salon mirror. Her dark hair was cut shorter, in layers, wispy bangs framing her face. It gave her a gamine look.

"It's taken years off you," the stylist said, standing back to admire her handiwork. "You should keep it like that; a trim every six weeks."

"Yes," Amy agreed.

As she paid the bill, Amy invested in some of the Redken products recommended by the stylist. They were expensive and she had to quell the niggling guilt. She smiled to herself as she realised she then had to dampen the guilty feeling about feeling guilty. Whoever said change was painful wasn't kidding! A lifetime of conditioning wasn't going to be shed that easily.

She walked up Grafton Street. The pedestrianised street was crowded: busy shoppers filed in and out of the chic department stores; buskers sang in twos and threes and further up, towards St

Stephen's Green, a street entertainer amused a crowd of spectators. He was painted all over in silver – face, hands, clothes, everything, from his top hat to his big boots. The music, the sunshine and laughter lifted Amy's spirits.

The receptionist looked up absent-mindedly from the register. "May I help you?"

"I'm Amy Kennedy. I have an appointment with Mrs Catherine Cole."

"Yes." He consulted his notepad. "She left a message to meet her in the lounge." He pointed towards the open door on the right.

"I'm not sure what she looks like." Amy felt foolish.

The receptionist stood up and peered. "That's Mrs Cole, at the table in the centre, reading the newspaper."

Nervously, Amy walked into the lounge. She took advantage of the few available seconds to observe the elderly lady, who was immersed in her reading: small, thin, neatly dressed in a beige two-piece, grey hair and gold-framed spectacles.

"Mrs Cole?"

Catherine Cole looked up and a big smile spread over her face. "Amy!" She rose from her seat and threw her arms around her visitor. "Sit down, my dear. Sit down. How lovely to meet you after all these years."

As Amy settled herself in the armchair beside her, Catherine studied her: nice hairstyle, expensive suit, slightly overweight, no resemblance whatever to her mother. Edgy.

Catherine wondered how to begin. "Would you like a drink before lunch?"

"Maybe a sherry?" Amy suggested. It would be an icebreaker.

As Catherine Cole spoke to the waiter, Amy's thoughts were in a whirl. What would they say to each other? How would she broach the subject of her mother's past? Could she ask her about the row? This meeting was difficult for both of them but something in Catherine's manner, some softness in her tone, convinced Amy that everything that needed to be said would be.

Ten

Catherine stepped tentatively off the kerb onto the busy road outside the hotel. "I feel I'm taking my life in my hands here."

Amy hopped out of the way of a speeding taxi. Her mind was miles away. When was Catherine going to get around to the subject? Every time Amy tried to steer the conversation Catherine would get diverted. Over lunch they'd talked about Maurice and Dawn and Joe in the Home. When was Catherine going to discuss the real reason for this meeting? Amy was finding it excruciating but how could she be rude?

They walked in the direction of Grafton Street and went into the park by the entrance directly opposite the Stephen's Green Shopping Centre. They crossed the humpback bridge and found a free bench near the pond.

"I haven't been in here for years." Catherine looked around at the colourful flower-beds. "Isn't it beautifully maintained? It's just as I remember it – not like the rest of the city. Gosh! Dublin has certainly changed – I wouldn't recognise it; so many new buildings and restoration work. I'll have to pay a visit to Temple Bar; someone told me it was like the Left Bank with all its restaurants." Catherine moved closer on the bench. "Right, you've told me a lot about yourself and I'd like to thank you for being so open with me."

"You're easy to confide in."

"I know things haven't been easy for you," Catherine hesitated, "and it's definitely not my place to counsel you –"

Not when she was paying fifty quid an hour!

"People care about you, Amy. From what you've told me, your daughter certainly does."

"It's been difficult for her since I . . . since I became ill. She gets frustrated with me. Until recently we used to get on really well; I did everything I could to give her a happy childhood."

"I'm sure you did."

"It's important, what you see and hear as a child, isn't it? Dawn was a great kid; full of life – good at sports and music and brilliant academically. She has such confidence."

"That's down to you, Amy."

"And to her father. He doted on her – still does. They're very alike: go-getters, optimistic, ambitious."

"Not like you?" Catherine suggested.

"No, not like me. It's a funny thing; you can make other people secure without necessarily being so yourself." Sylvia's words.

"Self-esteem," Catherine agreed, "there's so much talked about it nowadays – I've always thought it varies with different stages of your life."

"But surely the foundation is built when you're young?"

"Yes."

"On the surface my mother seemed in control. She had such definite ideas, but the older I get the more I realise that she had her own inadequacies to deal with. She drove Claire and me very hard, was very critical. She was so negative. It was horrible growing up in that house. I feel bad saying that about her now that she's dead."

Catherine drew closer to Amy. "I know what you went through with your mother," she said. "That's what caused the argument between us."

Finally, she was going to explain the letter.

"One day, when she was too harsh with you, I spoke up. Told her to go easy, to control her temper."

"She had a vicious temper," Amy said, kicking herself for interrupting at this crucial moment but she couldn't control the rising anger. "I never knew when she was going to flare up. That's what made it frightening. At any moment, she'd lose it, fly off the handle for nothing at all. I was terrified of her but Claire was different. She did her own thing – stood up to my mother, even answered her back." Hands shaking, Amy took out the white packet and lit a Silk Cut Ultra. "I never had the nerve to do that. Catherine, I've so few happy memories of growing up. I'm not looking for sympathy or anything like that but maybe I'm still suffering the effects?" Wasn't that what Sylvia had intimated? "Maurice tells me to let it go, to forget it – I wish I could but it eats at me all the time. I can still hear her voice scolding, criticising, castigating me for something or other."

"Your mother had her problems, Amy, no doubt about it, and she obviously took them out on you, but you're an adult now. What she did is done, can't be altered, but how you *deal* with it can. Hark at me! A few years working in the psychiatric wards and I'm still dishing out the advice. Sam's always telling me to stop analysing everything but old habits die hard, I'm afraid."

"If I could only understand, if I could just explain it to myself. After she got cancer, I tried my best to help her. I gave up the job in the surgery – it wasn't much of a sacrifice – and I went to Glenageary every day to look after her." Amy paused. "I think she resented it. She couldn't bear to have me help her, to be dependent on me, to thank me – not that I was looking for thanks. I thought that her illness would have made us closer but it didn't. I spent hours every day with her, trying to get her to talk to me but she wouldn't."

"Elaine couldn't abide pity."

"The night she died – and she knew she was dying – I'm convinced of that – she sent me away. Didn't want me with her at the end." Amy dragged heavily on the cigarette. "That really hurt."

"None of us knows what was going through her mind. She wanted to spare you, I'd say." Catherine knew her words sounded hollow. "It's now time we got down to why we met – the letter. Maybe what I have to unfold will help. How much has your father told you?"

"Since she died, he seems to remember only the good times.

71

He's sanitised her behaviour, canonised her memory. When he talks about her it's not the woman I remember."

"Joe was a good man, gentle and soft, although he may have contributed, unwittingly, to Elaine's behaviour. He should have made a stand."

That's what Amy the child had always hoped for – that her father would make everything right.

"OK, now down to brass tacks. You know that your mother and I worked together in London after the war?"

"Yes, in a hospital. She was a nurse's aide, she told me. She was the youngest of a very large family – I never even met half of them; they'd all emigrated. Leaving school at fourteen meant she'd no qualifications. Dad said she'd worked in a biscuit factory in Drumcondra but hated it so much that she'd taken off to England. They were doing a line, as he called it. He was very disappointed when she left."

"I can fill in more of the story now." Catherine pulled on her gloves; it was getting chilly. "Let me get my thoughts together – I want to get my facts right. It was the summer of 1951 I remember because by then I'd met Sam. I was a junior nurse in the hospital and your mother was, as you know, a nurse's aide. She didn't like that job either, by the way – called herself a glorified skivvy. I think that not being well educated gave her an inferiority complex which is most likely why she pushed you and your sister. Education meant everything to her. She must have been thrilled when you married a vet."

"She was never excited about anything I did," Amy said fixedly. "Except I think she was secretly pleased when I got my degree. The day of my conferring," Amy reminisced, "it was a lovely summer's day. We posed for photographs in the campus grounds. I can still see her face, the self-satisfied expression. But she never said a word. No congratulations; nothing. Dad hugged me and told me it was the best day of his life. It wouldn't have killed her to have said something encouraging, would it?"

"It wasn't in her nature – Elaine found it difficult to give praise."

"I learned to accept that, finally. Sorry, I'm interrupting your story."

"Where was I?"

"She hated her job in the hospital," Amy prompted.

"Yes. At the time, there was a young doctor there, an obstetrician, a brilliant man, who took a shine to her."

"Took a shine to my mother?" Amy echoed incredulously.

"Not in the way you mean," Catherine added hastily. "He liked her, thought her hard-working, efficient and well-mannered. She had a soft Irish brogue which amused him. Anyhow, to cut a long story short, he asked her to come and work for his wife as a live-in housekeeper. The wife was very delicate, had a series of miscarriages. She was about five months gone on her third or fourth pregnancy when Elaine agreed to go and work for them."

"It sounds like one of those saga novels – impoverished working-class girl meets rich benefactor. I never knew any of this."

"No, you wouldn't. Elaine never spoke about it after she came back to Ireland."

"What happened. Why did she come back? Because of my father?"

"That's what she pretended at the time to everyone but me. Back to the story: Elaine went to Surrey at the end of that summer to take up the job. She got on very well with the doctor and his wife at first. He'd bought a huge house in Esher – the wife came from moneyed people." Catherine smiled. "The rich people of your typical saga novel, as you say. Anyhow, Elaine had every second weekend off and she'd come to stay with me in my flat near the Tottenham Court Road. We made the most of our weekends; two young women exploring London together – you can imagine. After a while the visits stopped abruptly.

"Elaine wrote and told me that Mrs Edwards was very ill and couldn't be left on her own; that she wouldn't be coming up to London until the situation had improved. Oh, the baby had arrived by then, a boy. Elaine took full charge of him, by all accounts."

"So she'd become a nanny?"

"Yes, and she continued to look after Mrs Edwards as well. She was kept very busy and claimed she was happy but, reading between the lines of her letters, I felt something wasn't right.

Meanwhile, at the hospital, Doctor Edwards was a changed man – softened unbelievably. He was delighted with his son; as proud as Punch. He kept a picture of the little fellow with him and showed it to all and sundry." Catherine looked wistful. "Having waited for so long to have a child – you'd understand that."

"Yes," Amy said, feeling Catherine's sadness. She hadn't been able to have children of her own, as she'd confided over lunch.

"I didn't see your mother for ages and, according to her letters, everything was going fine but I still had my doubts. Then, she telephoned me one night at the hospital. I'll never forget that phone call – she was in tears, extremely emotional. The Edwards agreed to let her have a week off – she was exhausted."

"Looking after a small child and an invalid couldn't have been easy," Amy said.

"No, indeed. I persuaded her to spend the week with me." Catherine shook her head sadly. "Amy, when I saw her, I was horrified at the state she was in – as thin as a whippet, dark circles under eyes, no energy – she was utterly worn out. I kept her in bed for two days and wouldn't let her lift a finger. She was at the end of her tether."

"Overworked?"

"Completely. I gave out all sorts about exploitation, how the Edwards were taking her for granted and I begged her to give up the job."

"So that's why she left."

"No, about five days into her visit with me tragedy struck. The child died."

"Oh my God," Amy gasped.

"A cot death. He was about eight months old then. The doctor and his wife were distraught. Elaine was blamed."

"Blamed for the death?"

"Yes," Catherine continued, "I suppose they had to blame someone. Isn't that what happens in tragedies when people can't accept what's happened? They have to direct their anger somewhere."

"But she wasn't even there. How could they blame her? And a cot death . . . ?"

"Mrs Edward accused Elaine of neglect and . . . other things."

"What things?" Amy's voice rose.

"Being rough with the child, shaking him." Catherine looked away.

Amy was filled with dread.

"At the time, I refused to believe it," Catherine spoke very softly.

Shaking the baby. Being rough with him. Amy fought the rising nausea, the repulsion.

"Doctor Edwards came to my apartment with Elaine's suitcases. He was a broken man. He said that Elaine wasn't fit to look after children and that his wife had feared the worst for some time past."

"Then why had they kept her on? If they were unhappy with the way she'd been treating the baby, why hadn't they dismissed her?"

"I suppose that's why they felt guilty: that they hadn't acted sooner. They paid her fare back to Ireland – shipped her off without any references, refused to let her attend the funeral. I tried to intervene and, for my trouble, he had me removed from paediatrics to a general ward. I rarely had any contact with him after that."

"But he continued in the job?"

"Yes, put all his energy into his work. He was a brilliant doctor, as I've said. Men can compartmentalise their feelings better than women can. I assume that he got comfort and strength from his work."

"And my mother was destroyed. It's horrible."

"Elaine left England and never spoke about it again – certainly not to me. Your father married her a few months later. We kept in contact for some years after you were born. Then Sam and I married and we bought our home in Suffolk – a converted schoolhouse, you'll have to come for a visit."

"I'd love to."

"I was convinced that the Edwardses had used Elaine as a scapegoat; that they'd treated her abominably . . . but . . ."

"But?"

Catherine coughed gently. "When Sam and I came to Ireland on our regular visits over the years, we became more and more concerned about Elaine. I couldn't condone the way she treated *you,* Amy. She was far too strict, sometimes violent. After we had that row I told you about, I didn't hear from your mother ever again."

Amy couldn't speak.

"That was the end of the story, as far as I was concerned, until a month ago. A new children's wing was opened in the hospital – they dedicated it to the memory of Doctor Valentine Edwards. Big plaque on the wall. He'd passed on about ten years ago but it had been his idea: his brainchild. The widow, Jane Edwards, was there to officiate at the opening ceremony – unveil the plaque, say a few words."

"Jane Edwards . . . JE?"

"Exactly. And do you know who attended the ceremony with her?"

"Who?"

"The son, Henry." Catherine folded her arms. "The son who supposedly had died."

"But . . . but how?"

"I was astounded when he appeared on the platform. I couldn't catch my breath. I was baffled."

"He was *alive*?" Amy blurted.

"Very much so. A tall tanned handsome man. Also a doctor."

"How do you know it was him? Maybe she had another child after?"

"Not with the same name. Nobody would call a second son after a dead child."

A tiny pulse throbbed in Amy's right temple.

"I was going to confront Jane Edwards there and then but I didn't get the opportunity. There were so many people milling around – old friends and colleagues of her husband's and other hospital staff."

"You didn't speak to her at all?"

"Oh, I did. I introduced myself. Told her I'd worked for her husband in my early career and that I'd respected him greatly – even went as far as to mention that I was a friend of your mother's."

"And?"

"She got very uptight, clammed up completely, stiffly shook my hand and walked away."

"But why? Why would they have *pretended* that their son had died? Why would anyone do anything so awful?"

"That's precisely what I'd like to find out, Amy. Your mother had been made to feel responsible for the death of that baby. Imagine trying to live with that."

That's what her father had meant. It was heart-rending.

"I have to meet this Jane Edwards." Amy gritted her teeth. "I have to find out why this happened. It's . . . it's a horrible story. It's criminal. Jane Edwards has to answer for it. I'll have to see her."

"That won't be easy to organise. They don't live in England any more, my dear. Moved to France – I'm not sure where. The son, Henry, runs some sort of a clinic there. I managed to wheedle that out of one of the doctors at the opening ceremony. I wanted so badly to be able to tell your mother all this."

"She went through torture," Amy said bitterly. "All those years she must have been going through torture – and for what?" Another thought occurred. "Did my father know about it?"

"Yes, she'd never have married him without telling him. He supported her completely. I'd say he was relieved that the Edwards hadn't pressed charges."

"Sweet Jesus!"

Catherine's eyes grew wider. "If a crime had been committed, why didn't they? Of course we now know that they had no reason to. They couldn't because there was nothing to press charges about. The whole story was a fabrication – a lie."

"Why didn't she fight back? Why did she let them get away with it?"

"She was completely traumatised, Amy. She was scared witless. She wasn't going to take on the Edwards. All she talked or cared about was to get home." Catherine brushed a crumb from her skirt.

"If the child had really died," Amy mused aloud, "there would have been police inquiries. A postmortem. But colleagues and hospital staff? Didn't they think it odd?"

"Remember his position. He was above suspicion. I don't know who exactly was misled with this wrong information. Possibly nobody but myself and he had me moved. Your mother was devastated. I couldn't console her. Then, when she got a little stronger, she left my flat and came back to Dublin, met up again with your father and started a new life. She tried to put the past behind her."

Amy watched a small boy fly a kite with his father. "But she wasn't able to, was she?"

"Apparently not." Catherine shook her head sadly.

Eleven

Paul Tennyson gently stirred the bolognese sauce and watched the penne come to the boil; then he turned down the gas. He'd waited and waited for Dawn to arrive home, to present her with a nice meal and a bottle of Merlot, but his hunger had finally got the better of him.

Almost nine o'clock – she was buried in the books, he presumed. The last few weeks before exams were tough – really tough and, fair dues to her, she didn't take out her anxiety on him. When he was sitting for his Uni exams, five years before, he'd got on everyone's nerves – attacked anyone who looked crookedly at him.

He grimaced as he spotted the greasy saucepan, abandoned on the draining board by Ben. He'd have to have another word; the lazy git never did his share of the tidying-up – such a slob. Isobel wasn't bad, at least she mucked in once in a while but she refused to clear up Ben's mess – and why should she?

Wouldn't it be brilliant if he could afford to buy a place – but a mortgage these days was out of the question. Not on one salary. He'd squirrelled away almost nine thousand pounds but that wasn't nearly enough with Dublin's prices; he'd need a hell of a lot more for a deposit.

This sharing lark was beginning to pall. It had been fun at the start when they'd all moved in, and the house here in Ballsbridge was spacious and ideally located, especially for Dawn for vet college, but he'd been far happier when he'd had privacy in his little bedsit in Ranelagh. Paul liked his own space.

He switched off the gas, poured the pasta into a colander and opened the kitchen window to clear the steam. A key turned in the hall door.

"Ben? Is that you? Get your fat arse in here and wash this manky pot, you slovenly pig!"

"Charming!" Dawn sauntered in, slung her leather briefcase on a kitchen chair and grinned. He'd teased her about the yuppie image of carrying the case, but her father had given it to her and Dawn put a lot of store on any present she got from him.

Paul hurried over and kissed her lightly on the mouth. "Perfect timing. Dinner will be ready in a jiffy."

She breathed in the spicy aroma. "Smells delicious and I'm absolutely ravenous – only had a ham sambo at lunchtime."

"Take off your jacket and sit down." He took the wine and handed it to her with a corkscrew. "You can do the honours."

"What did I do to deserve all this?"

"I'm damned if I know." He turned from the cooker, his eyebrow raised in his well-practised Connery impression.

She poured a glass for each of them. "Dish up the grub, Tennyson, and cut out the crap!"

"It's your eloquent turn of phrase that makes all this worthwhile." He served the meal, threw her a napkin and sat down to eat.

"What? No side salad or garlic bread, Paul?"

"Don't push it, sunshine!"

"It's the bio-chemistry that has me flummoxed. I spent three hours today going over notes and I haven't a clue. Everything gets mixed up in my mind."

They were still sitting at the kitchen table an hour later, the dirty dishes soaking in the sink.

"Make key words," Paul suggested. "That helps."

"Yeah, done that, been there. I'll just have to keep at it." She rotated her shoulders slowly.

"Stiff?"

"As a plank. I sat too long at the computer, obviously."

"You tend to hunch," he said. "You'll end up with round shoulders."

"Very consoling! Enough about me, how was your day?"

"Fine, fine." He finished the dregs of his glass. "Want coffee?"

"No, ruin the effects of the wine. I'm nice and sleepy now and I'm stuffed – or satiated as my father would say. Thanks for dinner, Paul – you did yourself proud. You'll make someone a lovely wife!"

"Cheeky brat!"

"How did your meeting go this morning?"

He paused. "I was offered a job in Longford. I told the boss I'd think about it."

"Longford!" Dawn gasped. "Are you insane?"

"Only kidding." He stroked her hair. "It'll be a few months before anything's on offer. I wouldn't mind a change, though. Oh, I almost forgot. Guess who I saw in the Green today?"

Dawn picked up the evening paper and glanced at the headlines. "Who?" she asked idly.

"Your mother."

She lowered the paper. "My mother? In Stephen's Green?"

"Yep."

"No way."

"She was there, I'm telling you."

"You made a mistake, Paul. Sure she hasn't been in town for over a year. She hardly goes anywhere now."

"It was definitely her. I went back for a second look. She was sitting near the duck pond with another woman, deeply engrossed in conversation – she didn't notice me."

"Are you sure it was Mum?"

"I'm positive. And," he added, stressing every word, "I've never seen her looking better."

She waited expectantly for him to continue.

"Nothing much to tell. She's had her hair cut and she was wearing a navy get-up. Looked very smart."

"My mother doesn't have a navy suit. It wasn't her."

Paul got exasperated. "It *was* and she *was* wearing a navy outfit. How could you possibly be familiar with all your mother's clothes? You don't live there any more."

Dawn pouted.

"Phone her if you don't believe me. Go on. Do it now."

"I do believe you – it's just that it's so long since she's been out of the house, never mind to the city. I wonder who the other woman was. Probably Sarah."

"I wouldn't know," he said, slightly irritated by her scepticism.

"What did she look like? Blonde hair?"

"Grey. A little lady with grey hair and glasses, your average granny type. Satisfied?"

"Not all grannies are small and grey-haired. Mine was tall and gaunt. Tell me more about this woman."

"I didn't go marching up to scrutinise her – didn't realise I'd get the third degree from you. The next time I see your mother, I'll take out my notebook and jot down all the particulars: what she was wearing, what her facial expressions were, who she was with. I'll even interview her if you like."

Dawn chortled.

"Glad you find this funny."

"I do," she said, "here we were, having a very pleasant evening, good conversation, nice food, both of us in grand form and, the minute the subject of my mother comes up, we're arguing."

"*I*'m not arguing."

Dawn didn't retaliate. She was shattered; a hot bath would ease her aching muscles and some lavender in the burner would soothe her overworked brain.

* * *

Amy stood on the weighing-scales. Eleven and a half stone. She'd never been this weight in her life – except when she was expecting Dawn. She'd have to shed a stone – no need to overdo it. Ten and a half stone would be ideal for her age and height. She hung the new suit in the wardrobe. Her feet were killing her; the shoes had pinched her toes while she'd traipsed around town; it would take a while to wear them in.

All in all today had been remarkable. Her meeting with Catherine Cole had surpassed anything she had expected. She'd learnt so much about her mother's past that she'd have to mull it over, piece by piece, detail by tiny detail.

Once Catherine had got over the pleasantries, Amy found herself able to talk, not mere chit-chat but genuine, heart-to-heart communication. Maybe it was because Catherine was older, more like a mother figure, that Amy found herself able to be honest with her? Or maybe it was because Catherine herself was so open? And age brings its own wisdom. The best thing about today's *tête-à-tête* was that Amy didn't feel she was being judged.

No sign of Maurice although it was almost midnight. Not that it mattered whether he was home or not – the spare room was his domain now.

She needed time to herself for serious reflection. She'd get into bed, smoke a cigarette – no TV tonight – and then she'd turn out the light.

It was easier to think in the dark.

Maurice got into second gear and eased the car slowly up the driveway. The rain pelted down the windscreen, making visibility dire. It was past two o'clock and he didn't want to disturb his wife. He hadn't spoken to her in almost three days.

The house was in total darkness – she could have left the porch light on for him. He switched off the engine, flicked off the car lights, and was plunged into blackness. The roof light, as he opened the car door, allowed him a few seconds to find his footing on the slippery wet ground. Cursing, he locked the car door and fingered his key ring until he found the hall door Yale. Then, his mouth set as the raindrops soaked his head and shoulders, he cautiously picked his way up the two steps to the house.

Once inside, he managed to locate the hall light-switch. A strange smell assailed his nostrils – lemon, was it? He glanced up the stairs. Something was very different. Then it hit him – the place was clean, spick and span. The carpet had been vacuumed and, to his astonishment, the banisters shone. Polish. That's what the unfamiliar smell had been – furniture polish.

* * *

Sam Cole, a bit the worse for wear after trotting around the pubs, poured himself a glass of water and added two Alka Seltzer. "Don't want a head in the morning," he told his wife, who was already in bed, browsing through a brochure of coach excursions.

"Amy is a very troubled woman," Catherine said, watching him lower the fizzy concoction in one go.

He belched. "But you got on well with her?"

"Once I broke the ice. I've invited her for a visit."

"Will she come?"

"I'd say so. Her marriage is a bit rocky at the moment, so she'll play it by ear."

"I wonder what the hubby's like."

"A very successful vet; ambitious and work-driven, by Amy's account. The daughter's studying veterinary – a chip off the old block. Amy feels quite isolated. A few weeks with us would do her the power of good."

"A few weeks?" he gasped. "Catherine, we'd want to think this through. You said she'd been suffering from depression."

"So?"

"At our time of life, we should be relaxing. You can't take on this woman. You hardly know her."

"Come on, Sam. She's Elaine's daughter and I feel I owe her."

"You don't. You don't owe her a thing," he grumbled.

"You'll like her. She's good-hearted."

"I don't relish the idea of having strangers in my home." He got into the double bed beside her and pulled the duvet over to his side.

"She's not a stranger." Catherine tugged the duvet back – he wasn't going to hog it. "Nothing's arranged as yet, anyhow, so there's no need to get excited. I have her number and I'll call her when we get home."

"All right." He resigned himself like he always did. His wife usually had the last word. "Where are we off to tomorrow?"

She handed him the brochure. "You decide."

Catherine snuggled back on the pillows as her husband took his reading glasses from the bedside table. A few weeks in their home, enjoying a new scene, would work wonders for Amy – give her a new outlook. And a temporary separation from the husband wouldn't be any harm, to boot.

"What about a trip to The Japanese Gardens and The National Stud?" Sam suggested.

"Perfect."

Twelve

"And that's the story – or as much as I know of it." Amy was sitting with Sarah in the latter's immaculate kitchen in Newtown Avenue. It was the morning after her meeting with Catherine Cole.

"Your poor mother – and she was so young at the time. Alone in England, no family or friends around, apart from this Catherine Cole. And it wasn't something she could tell people even after she came home. A baby dying under her care – the scandal of it; the disgrace. You know the way people talk – no smoke and all that. She'd have been shunned. Or worse." Sarah shuddered. "Imagine her isolation, Amy. At that age and in those times she'd have been gullible, vulnerable and then, of course, this Doctor Edwards was an eminent man; she'd have accepted verbatim anything he'd told her. Doctors were gods then. The lie would have been Gospel."

"That's what Catherine said. My mother was almost seventy years old when she died last year, Sarah, and for fifty of those years she grieved over a tragedy that had never occurred."

"It makes you wonder how well we ever know anyone and what they might be going through. But to be blamed in the wrong is appalling."

"And yet, you know, in one way I can understand the Edwards. The doctor maintained that my mother wasn't fit to look after a child." Amy pursed her lips. "I know, from my own experience, that there was truth in that. She was cruel . . . sometimes violent. My father was aware of it. So was Catherine Cole."

"Amy, are you saying your mother abused you?"

"Abuse is such a general term, isn't it?" Amy stirred her tea. "One person's notion of abuse is another's idea of discipline. My mother didn't believe in sparing the rod."

Ireland of the fifties wasn't an idyllic place for any child. Corporal punishment was rife. Mother Church had a very firm grip and many parents followed its lead.

"She certainly wasn't the perfect mother," Amy muttered.

"But killing a baby? You don't believe she was capable of that?"

"No."

But secretly Amy wondered. When her mother's temper got the better of her, anything was possible. Accidents happen and angry people often don't know their own strength.

"They said that the baby was *dead*. Why? What normal parents would say something like that, for God's sake? There's no justification, none whatever."

"I don't know." Amy, her elbows leaning on the table, rubbed her forehead slowly. "I'm getting a headache; have you any aspirin?"

"Panadol OK?" Sarah got the tablets from a press and poured Amy a glass of Ballygowan.

"Thanks." Amy washed down two with the spring water. "When you examine the facts it doesn't fit together – something about the whole saga bothers me. If they wanted to get rid of my mother, why didn't they simply fire her? They were the employers, they had the power, so why resort to such an extreme?"

"They had their reasons, and they must have been damned good reasons to be so malicious as to lie like that. There *is* more to it, definitely."

Amy lit her fifth cigarette since she'd sat down but Sarah wasn't going to nag her about smoking, not with the efforts her friend was making. "Your hair's fabulous. Henna, is it?"

"No, a mixture of some kind, the stylist said. Burgundy, I think."

"Looks terrific." Sarah studied Amy's face. "There's something else different about you."

"I got my eyebrows tinted. Thought I might as well go the whole hog. And it does make you feel good to pamper yourself now and again."

"Absolutely." Sarah helped herself to another custard cream.

"My therapist – I sound like an American, don't I? My therapist," Amy drawled, "convinced me to be nice to myself. Well, are you not going to ask me how I got on?"

"I wasn't sure you wanted me to. How did it go, Amy?"

"Much better than I thought. The hour flew by. Once I got started there was no stopping me. She put me at my ease and she's a good listener – you were right. She has a knack of asking the right questions but she made the whole thing seem natural; like any conversation. It's only afterwards you realise that you did all the talking. "

"You're going to go back, then?"

"I'd say I need quite a few visits. We've a lot more to get through. I need to shed the – what's that you call it – psychological baggage? Yeah, it's a weird experience when you do start talking about yourself. Some of the things that came out – I wasn't even aware of them myself and then . . . when you hear your own voice saying the words it's like a sudden gush, a release – a kind of cleansing. One minute I felt like bursting into tears and the next I was laughing. But some of the mist in my mind began to clear. I like her, Sarah. I trust her."

"I'm thrilled, Amy. I really am. Take it one day at a time. The first step is the hardest. The next time you go it won't be half as bad. You're over the initial awkwardness."

"When I told her about the constant tiredness, she advised me to get a blood test done as well."

"Oh?"

"I may have started the change."

Sarah's face fell. "What? The menopause?"

"Yes, don't look so horrified. It's not contagious!"

"You're going through the change? No way – you're far too young."

"Forty-six isn't too young, Sarah. Some people start in their thirties. It depends on when your mother . . . it's different for every woman."

"Huh," Sarah snorted. "I've no intention of succumbing to it for years yet – if ever."

Amy laughed. "I don't think we get to choose. Smokers usually start earlier, if that's any consolation to you."

"The menopause?" Sarah was still in shock. "I don't believe it – sure you're not getting hot flushes or anything like that, are you?"

"Not everyone gets flushes. My periods have become very erratic, closer together and heavier, and the insomnia thing is par for the course, apparently, not to mention the depression –"

"You go and get tested if you want to, Amy," Sarah said, "if it makes you feel better to have some doctor pronounce you over the hill."

"It doesn't mean being over the hill." Amy smiled. "To tell you the truth, I'd be happy to be diagnosed as menopausal. The stopping of periods will be cause to throw a party, not to mourn. It's only the end of one phase but it's the start of something new. I like the whole idea of change – it's stagnation that's terrifying. It actually might make me feel better about myself. At least I'd know I wasn't going mad."

"You're not going mad – such a thing to say."

"Sometimes I feel as if I am."

"Like I said, Amy, go ahead. Enjoy your menopause if you must but I think it's absolutely . . . I don't want to discuss it."

Taboo. An unpleasant subject. Why? Why did it have to be taboo? It was just a natural occurrence that every woman had to accept sooner or later. If any of Amy's symptoms had been caused by this natural change in her body she'd be only too happy to know about it. To know and accept and get help if necessary. Why was Sarah so frightened by the notion? Once again, Amy felt cut off.

Lately this feeling of estrangement was irrepressible. Maybe she expected too much from others? It was just that she and Sarah used to share so much. They still did but something had changed. It was something subtle and intangible and Amy knew it was in herself. She loved Sarah. They'd always be friends, hopefully, but something definitely had changed. Was it possible to have complete intimacy, full understanding with another human being? Did soul mates truly exist? Or were we destined to be always separate entities?

"So," Sarah asked as she cleared away the teacups, "about Catherine Cole's story, what are you going to do, Amy? What *can* you do?"

"I have to get to the bottom of it. I'll never rest easy until I know the full truth. The trouble is that I haven't a clue how to get in contact with Jane Edwards. She's living in France. Catherine is my only lead at the moment."

"And will you go to visit her?"

"I think so. Maurice knows nothing at the moment; I'll just tell him I'm going away. I won't divulge anything else. He'd only tell me to forget the whole thing – he's sick of what he calls my *fixation* with my mother and I don't want to involve Dawn when she's so near her exams."

"What about Claire?"

"I've already lied to Claire – my first time ever. I feel bad about it." *The truth, Amy. Tell the truth and shame the devil.*

Sarah had her opening now. Time to voice her suspicions. "How close *are* you to Claire?"

"We used to be much closer," Amy admitted, "but lately she finds me difficult, I'd say." Another example of alienation. Her own sister found it hard to understand her.

You're too sensitive, Amy. You always were. And odd. No wonder your sister can't understand you. You're secretive.

Amy clasped her hands to her ears and shook her head.

"Are you all right?" Sarah stood up and went to her. "You've gone very pale."

"Just this blasted headache," Amy said. "The Panadol will kick in soon. What were we talking about? Oh, Claire. Yes, we've grown apart but she's still friendly with Maurice."

"And that doesn't worry you?"

"Why should it?"

"Forget it." Sarah munched on a chocolate biscuit. She'd finished the custard creams. Amy wondered how she kept her svelte figure. Metabolism just wasn't fair.

"Sarah, what's on your mind?"

"Look, Amy, I wasn't going to say a word about it, but since you brought it up – I've seen Claire out with Maurice on more than one occasion." She leaned over in a conspiratorial way. "They were *real* chummy."

Amy laughed. "There's nothing going on with Claire and Maurice, Sarah. Take my word for it. They've always been good friends – that's all. Sure he knew her before he knew me."

"More fuel for the fire," Sarah exclaimed.

"I've never had any reason to mistrust either of them. Claire's my sister and Maurice isn't . . . he isn't like that. He'd hate subterfuge. You know that Maurice isn't cut out for intrigue of any kind – wouldn't have the interest or the energy. He likes things to be clear-cut and simple."

"Well, I think you're too trusting, Amy. And even if it *is* only a friendship between them – does that not bother you?"

"Quite frankly, no, because it's my own fault. Maurice needed Claire to talk to during my . . . my fall from grace, shall we call it?" Her fall from grace – more self-recrimination. Hadn't the therapist warned her against putting herself down all the time?

"*I* wouldn't like it. Your partner, not your sister-in-law, is supposed to be your best friend. That kind of relationship can be more destructive than an affair."

Amy puffed thoughtfully. She'd never seen her husband's friendship with her sister as any kind of threat.

"And I'm convinced there's more to it," said Sarah. "Claire, may I remind you, hasn't the same moral compunctions as you or I have. Remember, a few years back she went out with that married guy, the stockbroker?"

"Sarah, you'll never forgive her for that."

"I don't like cheats."

"You're barking up the wrong tree. If there was anything going on, I'd know."

"The wife's always the last to know." A ring at the door prevented Sarah from further debate.

Maurice and Claire? For a second Amy considered the

possibility. They did spend a lot of time together recently. Claire was outgoing and attractive and Maurice *had* dated her first – but an illicit liaison? No, it wasn't Maurice's style. Whatever he was, he wasn't a fraud. Deception was totally alien to his nature. And Claire wouldn't be capable of such betrayal – not of her sister. They had their moments, like all siblings do, but they did love each other.

"At last!" Sarah hurried back to the kitchen. "The rubbish removal van. I have to open the garage for him – my old double bed and a washing-machine to get rid of. I waited in three days last week for this cowboy to arrive." She unlocked the kitchen door. "Can you rely on *any*body any more? He's a crabby little man – I'm paying him way over the rate but you'd swear he was doing me a favour!"

* * *

Almost lunchtime, Claire thought, as she wrapped the silver earrings in tissue paper. She'd skip her usual sandwich and dash down to the lingerie shop. She had her eye on a black negligee. She didn't want him getting bored. Once a man took you for granted, things started to slither down the slippery slope. Claire was all too aware of the importance of keeping a man's interest and she knew just how to add spice to a relationship.

"So, is there?" the customer repeated.

"I'm sorry, I was miles away," Claire apologised.

The girl frowned. "I was enquiring about a silver bracelet to match."

"I'll get the tray for you." Claire took it from the window display and placed it on the glass counter. "Some of these might suit."

As the customer examined the bracelets, Claire made a mental shopping list: new toothbrush, moisturiser, cleansing lotion, cotton-wool pads, deodorant. And what would she wear this evening? Her red dress – he liked her in red, or her silver top and black trousers? How formal was the restaurant?

"No, I'll leave it." The girl handed back the tray. "Just the earrings, thanks."

Claire dealt with the purchase. She was about to shut the shop when she decided to make a quick phone call to her sister.

"Claire, hi! I'm just back from Sarah's. Good to hear you."

The voice was high-spirited. So, Amy's mood was still up. "Just phoning to see how things are."

"Grand, thanks. I'm feeling a lot better. Treated myself to some new clothes and I got my hair cut when I was in town yesterday – I'm pleased with the result."

"You were in town?"

"Mmh. Next you'll be seeing pigs fly!"

"You sound different, Amy."

"I *am* different."

"What brought all this on?"

"I took your advice. I'm seeing a counsellor. Sarah persuaded me."

"Amy, I won't pretend to understand what you're going through but I'm relieved you're finally doing something to help yourself."

"Sarah had a lot to do with it. She's a good friend. She cares."

"I care too. I wanted to help. I did my best."

"I know, Claire. Don't think I'm ungrateful. You've been very good. Maybe I needed an outsider- not a family member – to point me in the right direction. Sarah's a rock of sense."

"Is she?"

Claire's miffed tone was not lost on Amy. "She's very balanced."

"I never thought so." Claire was sorry she'd phoned now. "I always found her brusque to the point of rudeness. And she's a bloody know-all."

"That's just her way; she doesn't mean to offend. She's been very helpful." Amy hesitated, not wishing to exacerbate her sister's hostility. "You *all* have. Are you doing anything tonight? Would you like to come for dinner? Maurice will be working late – surprise, surprise!"

"You're going to cook?"

"I can still manage a casserole."

"I'd love to, Amy, but I have other plans. I'm going out for a meal with a friend."

"Of the male variety?"

"Yes. I've known him for ages. No big deal."

"I'd like to meet him. Maybe you'd bring him for a visit?"

"Maybe."

"What's his name?" Amy asked eagerly.

Shite. Now what? Claire racked her brains for a credible name.

"Paddy." Not very original, she reprimanded herself.

"Paddy what?"

"Paddy Whelan," Claire said quickly. "I haven't time to talk now. I'll come over tomorrow night."

"Bring him with you."

"He's going away on business." The inspiration flashed – she had to think on her feet here. "Talk to you later. Bye."

* * *

Dawn couldn't get over how well her mother looked and the fact that she'd dropped by. Amy had never visited the house in Stillorgan before, despite many invitations. Dawn had brought her mother on the grand tour and Amy praised everything she saw; the green curtains, the cosy armchairs, the bright fitted kitchen, the tiled bathroom. From the evidence of double beds you didn't have to be Inspector Morse to work out what the sleeping arrangements were, but her mother wisely ignored the evidence.

"Off to England on your own?" Dawn was more than surprised. They'd settled in the sitting-room and, as Amy made herself comfortable in an armchair by the fire, Dawn poured them each a glass of white wine from the bottle her mother had brought.

"She's a friend from way back. I've known her since I was a child." That was no lie. "If you'd prefer me to stay home during your exams, I can always change the dates," Amy offered.

"No, don't do that. I don't need you here when I'm doing the exams, Mum." She groaned. "If I could only get rid of Dad! He'll be analysing the questions, suggesting answers – driving me nuts! Maybe," she added, brightening up a bit, "he'll have a conference to go to – anything that would take him away from Dublin would be a godsend."

"Don't let your father put you under extra stress, Dawn. These are *your* exams, your life. You don't have to discuss the papers with anyone. When I did my finals, a girl from my class convinced me that I'd totally misinterpreted one of the questions. I worried all summer but it turned out *she* was the one who had to repeat."

"But Dad will want to see the papers – you know that full well. It's as if he's living the experience again through me."

She wondered if her daughter had made a mistake – going on for the same profession as Maurice. Competition would be inevitable. "Don't get too uptight if you can help it." Amy opened her handbag and took out a small dark brown bottle. "Take four drops of this before your first exam."

Dawn glanced at the name. "Rescue Remedy?"

"Sarah got me on to it – it keeps me relaxed. It's not a drug – all natural ingredients. Homeopathy." She noted Dawn's sceptical expression. "Try it anyway. It won't do you any harm."

"I'm fairly calm most of the time," Dawn said. "Paul understands what it's like and he doesn't bug me."

"You two have it sorted, haven't you? Paul's a nice lad. What time does he get home?"

"Around six usually, depending on traffic. Why don't you stay and eat with us?"

"No, no, I only called to see you and the house. I'm not going to disrupt your evening."

"Mum, please stay. I'd like you to – and Paul would be glad to see you – especially in that lovely suit."

Amy glanced down at her attire. "My *suit?* What would Paul care about that?"

"It would give him the greatest satisfaction."

"I haven't the foggiest what you're talking about!" Amy checked her watch. "I can't stay for dinner today, I have an appointment in the Well Woman in an hour."

"A routine check-up?"

"Would be if I went when I should – I'm long overdue a visit. At my age the body needs constant monitoring!"

Dawn laughed. "You look better than ever. Your hair, it's really great. And eyeshadow, no less. What colour is it? Dark green. It accentuates your eyes. I might try it."

"You don't need it, love. You're blessed with gorgeous hazel eyes – just like your grandmother." Dawn had Elaine's beautiful eyes but she didn't share the dark dour countenance. She had a soft mild expression – like Maurice's.

"So, when will you go to Suffolk?

"Next week. I have to tell your father yet." Amy rummaged in her open handbag. "Is it OK if I smoke?"

Dawn got an ash-tray. What a conversation: make-up, hairstyles, clothes, holidays. Trivia. Glorious trivia. She marvelled at how her mother had transformed in a few days. This was not the woman who'd lain in bed for weeks, silent and sullen. Dawn hoped she wasn't dreaming.

Amy sat back in the taxi. Another ordeal over – her first visit to her daughter's house. Crazy, wasn't it? To be nervous about a visit to her own daughter. But Amy had caused Dawn a lot of hassle.

Ah ha! Not so easy being a good mother, is it?

Amy took out a tissue and wiped the sweat from her brow. The driver, glancing in his rear-view mirror, noticed her unease: "Don't worry, love. I'll get you there on time. This bloody traffic's chaotic but I'll get you to your appointment."

Another examination. Internal. The dreaded smear test. More poking and prodding and questions. Testing. Analysis. Diagnosis. She was beginning to feel like a specimen.

There you go again, Amy. Getting yourself in a tizzy. Grow up. Have you no courage? Always a worry wart. You'll never change.

Amy opened the passenger window. She needed air.

Thirteen

"So, Amy. How do you feel about the results from the clinic?" Sylvia offered her a mint, which she refused.

"I guessed as much. They've started me on HRT. I know a lot of women don't like the idea but I'm willing to give it a try. As I told you last week, I feel out of control – as if my body no longer belongs to me and it's soaring and dipping on a never-ending rollercoaster, so if hormone replacement helps – great. Any relief would be welcome." Amy lit a cigarette.

"Very positive," Sylvia approved. "Now, any other developments? How are things with your husband?"

"The same. Worse, if anything. I've decided to go to visit a friend in England. Just for ten days or so."

"Good for you." Sylvia jotted it down.

"I'm going tomorrow morning. I think we need a break from each other."

"It never hurts," Sylvia agreed. "OK, this evening maybe we should deal with your childhood. At our first meeting you were asking me what caused your constant need to please others and you'd started to tell me about your parents. From what you said, I gather that you didn't have an easy relationship with your mother. Would you like to discuss that?"

"Not particularly." A shaky laugh. "What was that poem about your parents fucking you up? It's easy to lay the blame on others – I want to let it go, Sylvia."

"And you will be able to – eventually. First you have to get it out there and look at it. Deal with it – then move on."

"I've tried to deal with it – believe me I have – I've spent my life trying to understand and forgive and . . . it's her voice in my head," Amy blustered. "I still have her bloody voice in my head and it . . . I hate her." Amy blushed crimson. "I'm sorry. I didn't mean to say that – it just slipped out. You must think I'm some sort of a monster. I'm sorry."

Sylvia leaned forward and stroked Amy's arm. "Please never apologise to me, Amy. You're free and safe to say anything you want to. Anything. That's why we're here."

"But to say I hate my mother! It's not even true. I don't hate her, of course. I . . . I love her. Loved her." Tears welled. Sylvia passed her a tissue.

"Tell me about the voice," Sylvia said gently.

* * *

Nancy Mulhearn looked tired. She'd had her steel-grey hair cut into a bob which made her seem younger than her eighty years but, nevertheless, she did look tired. She was dressed simply in her usual attire of black skirt and white blouse. She brought her guest into the back of the shop where she had the kettle on the boil and a plate of cream cakes waiting. "It was nice of you to agree to come, Amy. I've missed your little visits. I heard you weren't well."

Amy took in at a glance the untidy piles of books, the dust, the disorder. "I'm a lot better now, Nancy. Women's troubles."

Nancy nodded sagely. "Do they ever end?" She smiled sympathetically. "How's Doctor Kennedy? Still working as hard as ever?"

"Indeed." Amy accepted a cup of tea and a cake. Overweight or not, she wasn't going to refuse when Nancy had gone to the trouble. "I'm going on a short holiday tomorrow to England."
The old lady paused. "Will you be gone long?"

"No, a matter of days."

"Amy, do you intend to go back to work at the veterinary surgery? I'm not asking out of idle curiosity. The reason I wanted you to come and see me was that I have a proposition to make to you."

"Sounds interesting," Amy said, half-afraid of what might be coming.

"As you can see the shop needs reorganising. It's getting beyond me, to be honest about it. Since my sister died last year I'm a bit lost. I need help. As you know I don't do a roaring trade here but I'd be loath to sell up. The shop keeps me going."

Amy couldn't imagine the bookshop not being run by Nancy. She was an institution in the area.

"So," the old lady went on, "I was wondering if you'd be interested in working for me? I have a few bob put away and I'd be willing to invest it in the business but I don't want to take on the hassle of refurbishment at my age. I know what you did for your husband in setting up his practice. I need someone of your business expertise and experience and someone I can totally rely on. The fact that you're so interested in books is the icing on the cake. I'd trust my little kingdom in your hands."

Amy was stunned.

* * *

Maurice gazed in awe at his wife. She was packing a small suitcase, humming to herself. Standing there beside the bed, bare-footed and dressed in a black lace slip, she was alluring. How long was it since he'd looked at her properly?

He handed her the walking-shoes she'd pointed at. "Amy, I wish you'd consulted me before you made these plans."

"Consulted you?" She continued with her task. "Maurice, when are you ever *here* for me to consult you? I haven't seen you for a week."

"I've been busy," he retorted sharply. "Some of us have to work."

"I've been busy too." She closed the clasp on her toilet bag.

"So I see." He took a deep breath. "Nice hairdo."

A compliment. "Thanks."

101

"You're definitely going then?"

"Early morning flight to London." She folded her mauve cupro dress in the plastic cover from the cleaners. "Then a train from Liverpool Street. The journey takes just over an hour. I've to get off at Stowmarket and Catherine will meet me there."

"An old friend?"

"Yes."

"From school?"

"Pass me that hanger, will you? The wooden one."

He did as she bade. "Well?"

"Well, what?"

"This person you're visiting – an old school-friend, is she?"

"I knew her when I was in primary school." Amy put the lid down on the suitcase and zipped it. "Are you going back to evening surgery?"

"No, it's Rodney's turn. Amy, could we go out to dinner?"

She hadn't expected that.

"If you must go on the trip," he went on, "and I feel you're being very impulsive about it – you hardly know this person – I don't want you going with bad feelings between us."

"Maurice, there needn't be bad feelings. I want to get away, that's all."

"Get away from what?"

"From this house." Her voice remained calm.

"From the house or from *me*?"

"Both," she replied frankly. "You won't miss me, Maurice. You'll barely notice that I've gone – you're not home often enough for it to make any difference whatsoever to your life."

"Is this another attack?"

"I don't want an argument, Maurice. The facts speak for themselves: we don't see each other, we hardly talk – and when we do we row, we don't go out together any more, we don't make love. It's been a long time since we had a proper relationship."

"And that's *my* fault, I suppose?"

"I didn't say that – don't put words in my mouth. We're both at fault."

"No, we're not, Amy. *You're* the one who's changed. You've shut yourself off."

"I'm trying to sort myself out. Your criticism is a bit hard to take at the moment. I've gone for help, as you wanted me to, and you should be supporting me. Already I think I've made some progress." She sat on the bed and took a perfume bottle from the bedside table. A dab behind the ears had a refreshing effect. "I wish you'd stop putting me down."

His cheeks flushed and his eyes burned. "Another accusation."

"A justified one – I'm tired of the constant fault-finding. Give me credit for something, will you? I know things have been hard for you, Maurice, and I am truly sorry about that but you've got to give me time. I will get better; I'm determined to make a new start. You've no faith in me and that hurts."

"No faith? Amy, you haven't been yourself for months and your judgement has been warped. You were getting quite paranoid. Now that you've temporarily cheered up, you're running away."

"I'm not, Maurice. I'm doing the exact opposite." She put the atomiser into her handbag. "And about my thinking being warped, you're wrong. I've never seen things so clearly. I'm only going for ten days. There's no need to overreact. I've made up my mind."

"And where do I fit in?"

"That's up to you. Maybe you could use the time to have a long think."

"A long think about what?"

"About us. About where we are and where we're going."

"Give me strength! Where we're *going*? What the bloody hell does that mean? We're not going anywhere."

"Precisely. We've stagnated."

"Crap!"

"It's not. We've nothing in common any more."

"We've been married for over twenty years – that's what we have in common and that's where we are. I don't know what you want."

"Excitement, companionship, consideration – a bit of romance. Do you want me to go on? Fun might be nice."

"Fun, she says! What bloody fun were *you* for the past year, eh? Amy, you're full of it! Romance! At our age? Get a grip. We have what every married couple has."

"No, we haven't." She softened her tone. "Maurice, we used to be nice to each other, remember? We used to laugh."

"Grow up, Amy."

Told you, Amy. What did I tell you? Did you listen?

"There you go again," she said, trying her damnedest to ignore the other voice as Sylvia had recommended. "When I try to explain how I feel, you dismiss me – you're oblivious to anyone's opinion but your own. You're wrapped up in your own life, your job, your friends –"

"Yes, I am. What else could I have done?" he shouted. "I tried to include you. You're the one who cooled off – not me."

"You're right, you're right. But didn't you ever wonder why? Didn't it occur to you that I wasn't happy?"

"What *occurred* to me was that you were being utterly self-absorbed – wallowing in your misery, not giving two hoots about your family. And after what you claim you went through as a child, you, above all people, should know better."

"That was below the belt, Maurice. I don't claim anything that wasn't true." She could feel tears of frustration forming but she wouldn't give in to them. Not this time. "I *do* care about my family. It's very unfair of you to suggest otherwise. I've always put you and Dawn before myself. I'm not demanding any gratitude; that was my duty but maybe, just maybe, I neglected my own needs."

"Amateur psychological shite. Jesus, is this what therapy is teaching you? Lovely! We all have problems and we have to deal with them – usually on our own. What makes you think your situation is unique? Not everyone is in the privileged position of going for counselling."

"I'm paying for myself," she reminded him. "And it was your idea. You can't have it every way, Maurice."

He knew he'd gone too far. "I apologise – I shouldn't have said that."

"No, you shouldn't have."

He sighed. "We're a lot luckier than most, Amy. You should be grateful. Maybe if we went back to the way things were, you could come back to work with me?" he asked hopefully.

"No," she said, aghast at the notion. "That would be a backward step, Maurice. I've other plans in mind. Nothing definite but I'm considering a recent offer."

"What offer?" His suspicion was mounting.

"We'll talk about it when I come home. Going back to the surgery is out – I need to move forward."

"*You* need? When I hear you talking about duty and lack of gratitude and your needs it makes my blood boil – what about *my* needs?"

She ignored his sulky expression. He was behaving like a spoilt child.

"Go then, go off on your holiday," he said at last. "Be as selfish as you want. And what about your daughter? Her exams next week. You don't give a fiddler's."

"That isn't true," Amy said quietly. "I've discussed it with Dawn. She needs space now – not interference."

"Interference? What's *that* supposed to mean?"

"You're not to pressurise her during the exams."

"Pressurise her?"

"Maurice, it's hard for her trying to live up to your standards. Just go easy on her."

"Do you think I'm a fool? I wouldn't do anything to make life difficult for Dawn. You've done enough for both of us." His blood pressure rose. "*Me* upset her? Christ! You've one hell of a selective memory. I'm not going to waste my breath trying to talk sense to you, woman! You're impossible."

He stormed out of the bedroom, raced down the stairs and banged the hall door after him.

The knot in Amy's stomach tightened.

"I'll come and see you as soon as I get back, Dad."

"Please do, Amy. Tell Catherine I sent my best and the next time she's in Dublin I'd love to see her."

"Will do. Apart from anything else, I'm glad to have renewed the friendship. She's lovely."

"She always was."

"Goodnight, Dad. See you soon. God bless."

Amy put down the receiver. She was glad she'd come clean with her father. As she'd guessed, he'd kept what he'd known of the story from her in order to save her from undue worry. On the phone he still sounded wary. She'd told him everything that Catherine had revealed except the crucial news that Henry Edwards was still alive. That would have been too much of a shock.

* * *

"Let me get you another, Jack." Maurice signalled to the barman who was run off his feet. The local was packed; they were lucky to have got standing room at the bar. "So, she's going in the morning to God-knows-where. Wouldn't it be marvellous if we could all just flit off whenever we liked?"

Jack said nothing. This diatribe was boring beyond belief. Maurice was a pain in the proverbials tonight.

"I never knew she could be so hotheaded and stubborn." He drummed the beer-mat on the wooden counter. "*Give me time to think* – bullshit. And do you know what else she said?"

Jack accepted the drink and pointedly looked at his watch.

"That I wasn't to pressurise Dawn. The barefaced nerve of her. *I'm* the one who encourages Dawn, takes an interest. Amy's truly lost it."

"Take it easy, Maurice. You're far too uptight. Go with the flow, that's what I do."

"You wouldn't know anything about it, Jack. Sarah's a different type altogether. At least she listens."

Jack smiled to himself. His wife listened all right, but only to what he chose to tell her.

"What's it all about, eh? I break my balls every day in the practice just to keep her in the comfort she thinks she deserves. She hasn't worked in almost two years. Two years! Nice one, if you can get it."

106

"Come on, Maurice. She gave up her job to look after her mother and for no other reason. Amy put years of her life into building up your business. No wife could have done more. You're not pretending you dislike work? You live for it, man. You're the one person I know who's consumed by his career – so don't hang that on Amy."

Maurice glowered into his pint.

"Let her get on with it; that's my advice. Women always do what they want to do in the end – accept the inevitable." Jack wondered when he could make a bolt for it.

"I'm not going to pander to her any more. Let her go. She can bloody well stay away for all I care. Then," he fumed, "when I asked her to come back to work she pretended she'd another offer. What the hell does that mean? Did she go behind my back and apply for jobs without even telling me? God, I never knew she was so sneaky."

"Maurice, drop it, will you? Look, there's that bird who works in Madigan's. Did you ever see anything like the tits?"

Whatever part of his anatomy Jack thought with, it wasn't his brain.

"Finish your pint, Maurice, and we'll head into Leeson Street."

"A club? Tonight?"

"Why not? Start enjoying yourself. Two weeks of freedom on the cards, you lucky bastard! You know what you need?"

"No, thanks. We're not all sex-mad like you. You'd want to be careful, Jack. Sarah's bound to find out sooner or later. It's not worth risking your marriage. You're too fond of playing with fire."

Jack elbowed him jocularly. "Maurice, if you weren't so sanctimonious, you'd be a riot. You take things too seriously, mate. A bit on the side adds an extra dimension to any marital arrangement. What they don't know doesn't hurt them."

His friend's cavalier attitude was infantile. "One of these days you'll get your come-uppance."

Jack took his car keys from his pocket. "No chance if I'm careful, Maurice, and careful is my middle name."

* * *

Joe Shiels tossed and turned in the bed. His roommate snored blithely on. Amy's phone call this evening had unsettled Joe. Catherine Cole – a blast from the past. He remembered her with fondness; she was a generous, affectionate woman. He'd begged his wife to make up that horrible row but Elaine had stuck to her guns. Wouldn't give an inch. She'd cut off her nose to spite her face – Catherine was a good friend. Elaine had chosen to forget all the kindness, the comforting words, the support.

Joe sat up and thumped the pillow.

Now Amy was going on a visit. Was it time for his daughter to know all? Not that Catherine knew the full story but she might set her on the trail. How would Amy cope with the real truth?

So, the great Valentine Edwards had passed on to his reward, with honour, success and his sainted name preserved. No suggestion of dishonour, no hint of impropriety had scarred his meteoric career whereas . . . Elaine. Poor Elaine. She'd never recovered from the gruesome business. It had dogged her for the rest of her days. It had scarred their marriage and Amy's and Claire's childhood like some painful cancerous growth, eating away at the soft core. Now his elder daughter was determined to find out the reasons. He hadn't tried to dissuade her; didn't think he had the right.

Maybe Amy's search would come to nothing? France was a big country and it would be very hard to trace Jane Edwards. But with Catherine's contacts it wouldn't be impossible and if Amy *did* manage to find her . . .

What then?

Fourteen

"What's this?" Paul picked up a sealed envelope from the hall table. "It's addressed to you, Dawn. No stamp."

She came downstairs, her wet hair wrapped turban-style in a towel, and took the envelope. "Mum's handwriting. She must have left it here the other night. I never noticed."

"How could you? It was hidden under the phone book." He kissed the top of her head. "See you tonight. Have a good day."

"Very smart!"

"I mean it. Don't study too hard." He grabbed his jacket, kissed her again and left.

Dawn went into the kitchen and poured herself a coffee from the percolator – Paul made a fresh pot every morning. She loved the smell permeating the house – brought back memories of afternoons in Bewley's on the hop from school with her friends. Great, he'd left her two croissants.

Carefully she tore open the envelope. A short letter and a cheque book. A lodgement docket fell out of it onto the floor. She picked it up.

£10,000.

She sat there, stupefied.

A new current account with the princely sum of 10,000 quid. Hastily she grabbed the letter.

Dear Dawn,

I knew you'd refuse to accept the enclosed if I gave it to you in

person. I'm not trying to make up for all the distress I've caused you
– money wouldn't compensate for that – but I want you to have this.
I've never been in a position before to do much financially for you.
It's just my way of saying "thanks".

> *I love you,*
> *Best of luck with the exams,*
> *Mum.*

Dawn started to shake with excitement. A windfall! She jumped
up and danced around the kitchen. She'd phone her mother this
minute and . . . wait! She checked the clock on the windowsill.
Too late: her mother would be landing in Heathrow at about this
very hour.

She grabbed the letter and kissed it. "Mum, Mum, you're a life-
saver! With Paul's stash we'll have enough now for a mortgage. A
bloody mortgage. No more renting; no more sharing. Oh, Mum!"
Dawn burst out laughing.

The kitchen door opened. "What are you guffawing about?"
Isobel sidled up to the cooker, avoiding Dawn's gaze.

"Nothing." She slipped the cheque book into her dressinggown pocket. "I got some great news, that's all."

"Good for you." Isobel, her blonde hair dishevelled, her
dressinggown half-open, hunched over the sink as she filled the
kettle.

"Izzy, what time are you supposed to be in work? It's after
ten."

Isobel worked as a buyer in Roches Stores in Henry Street. "Not
going in today."

"I thought Thursday was your day off."

"I called in sick." Isobel turned around. A big purple bruise
stained her right cheek and the eye above it was half-closed.

"My God!" Dawn jumped up and ran to her. "What happened?"
Isobel shrugged. "I walked into the wardrobe."

"Izzy!"

Isobel went to the fridge and took out a pint of milk. Her
movements were slow, stiff.

"Who did this to you, Izzy?"

"Don't want to talk about it, Dawn. Forget it."

"Forget it? Have you looked in the mirror?"

"I don't have to," Isobel said bitterly. "I can feel it."

"Izzy, it was Ben, wasn't it?"

No reply.

Dawn took her by the arm and led her to a chair at the table. "I'll make your breakfast. Then we're going to the doctor."

"No, no doctor. I'll be all right in a few days."

"You're going to the doctor – no arguments."

"I can't, Dawn; he'll ask awkward questions."

"And you'll answer them. This isn't the first time, is it?"

"He swore he'd never . . . it's when he has a few jars. He doesn't mean it."

"Stop it! Stop making excuses for him."

"He's sorry. Genuinely, he is. He won't do it again; he promised."

Dawn made her a cup of strong sweet tea. "I'll go to the doctor with you," she said firmly.

"It's only a bruise. It's nothing."

"I want you thoroughly checked out. That eye looks nasty."

"No, Dawn. Maybe you could get me some ointment from the chemist? I don't want to go out like this. Make-up won't cover it."

"Why should you cover it?" Dawn raged. "Where is he?"

"Still asleep."

"God! He lays into you last night, beats you up and leaves you looking like that and now he's merrily sleeping it off. Bet you didn't get much sleep."

Isobel sat and stared.

"What about his job?"

"He was fired yesterday – that's what got him mad." Isobel sipped the tea and winced.

"Your mouth is sore too." Dawn was torn between fury and distress.

"He lost the rag. Ben wasn't himself last night. The manager threw him out without a reference. He went on a binge, got madder and madder and then came home and took it out on me."

"Why was he fired?"

"He was drinking on the job."

"Izzy, he's a disaster."

"He attacked one of the customers – verbally, I think. The guy messed up his betting slip and there was a commotion at the counter. Everyone was shouting at him and this guy was pissing him off. Anyway, Ben snapped."

"At a customer? That's not on."

"I know. The manager came to have a word and Ben turned on him." Dawn looked despondent. "He punched him."

"He hit his *boss*?"

"Yeah. The manager restored order, calmed down the punters, then, as coolly as you like, went and got Ben's coat and told him not to come back. Just like that."

"Who could blame him? Ben's a liability. I'm going upstairs now to tell him in no uncertain terms what I think."

"No, don't!" Isobel was horrified. "Let him sleep it off, please."

"He's out of here. Paul will insist on that and I agree with him."

"Out of here? Oh, Dawn, you can't do that. Where will he go? He has nowhere else. He hasn't seen his family in years." She looked beseechingly at her flatmate. "And what about me?"

"You're welcome to stay, Izzy, until you find somewhere else. Anyway, our lease is up in two months. We'll all be on the look-out then."

"Stay? Without Ben? I couldn't do that."

"You'll be far better off without him."

Isobel sat and nursed her jaw.

Dawn piled the dirty dishes into the sink and started to scrub them vigorously. Why did Isobel put up with it? Couldn't she see what he was?

"I love him," Isobel murmured.

"No, you think you do." Dawn turned to her. "Will I make toast for you?"

"I'm not hungry."

Even if she was, she couldn't chew with her cut lip. And her jaw – what if it was broken? She should go to the hospital.

"Please, Dawn, do you have to tell Paul?"

"I won't have to – one look at you and he'll know everything. Listen to me, Izzy. Someone has to make you cop on."

"This will blow over and everything will get back to normal. I have to give him another chance. I know you find this hard to believe, Dawn, but Ben does love me."

"So he knocks you about?"

"He needs me, Dawn."

"But you don't need him. You don't. He's a lazy drunken scumbag. You deserve better."

Isobel started to weep softly. Dawn put her arms around her. "Shh, shh," she crooned, "it'll be OK."

"Sure." Isobel sniffled into the sleeve of her dressinggown. "Sure."

"You could go home to your parents for a while," Dawn suggested.

Isobel's face twisted into a wry grin. "Out of the frying-pan."

"What?"

"Into the bloody fire. Why do you think I left home in the first place? My father's an asshole – knocked the shit out of my mother and the rest of us. My brother ended up in the hospital once. We all left home at the first available opportunity. I only visit her when I know he's not there. I haven't spoken to my father in years – hate the sight of him."

Dawn was flummoxed. "You never said a word."

"No, not the kind of round-the-table conversation people would appreciate."

True enough, Dawn thought. Why should Isobel have confided in her, anyhow? They shared a house, that was all.

"I can't go back to my mother now. She has her own problems. Funny, isn't it? You'd think I'd have seen the warning signs but I didn't. Ben was good to me at first. He made me laugh." She rubbed her swollen mouth.

Dawn knew enough to know that this was typical: children of abusive parents often end up with violent partners. "It doesn't have to continue," she asserted. "We'll get him out."

"I don't want to leave him, Dawn. Ben's had a raw deal most of his life. If I finished with him, I dread to think what might happen. He relies on me."

"You're not a social worker, Izzy. If he loved you, he'd respect you, not treat you like a punch-bag."

"There are all sorts of love," Isobel murmured.

Dawn was out of her depth.

* * *

Maurice came home at lunchtime. Maybe Amy hadn't gone? He turned his key in the lock. The house was empty. His footsteps echoed down the lonely silence of the hall. The place was desolate, like a football ground after a match. There was a note on the kitchen table.

Maurice, I've stocked up the fridge. The meat is in the freezer. You've enough to last you for about a week. I'll phone in a few days.

Amy.

He went into the sitting-room. His books had been rearranged tidily in the bookcase. The discarded newspapers which usually littered the coffee-table had been removed. He checked the mantelpiece. Not a speck of dust. The room was as neat as a new pin. But cold.

He went upstairs to her bedroom. This used to be *their* room. It was also tidied; the bedside table was gleaming; he could smell the residue of polish. The radio-alarm clock had been unplugged.

Unplugged.

He sprawled out on the double bed and closed his eyes, letting his mind travel back . . .

Nights of passion, sweet words, gentle touching. He could hear her voice softly urging him on. Her laughter. Tender kisses, caresses, stroking, fondling.

Aeons ago.

Gurgles and chuckling as their baby daughter got into the bed at ungodly hours of the morning. Tickling, pinching, high-pitched screams of delight.

Another life. Other people.

Her old cotton nightdress lay abandoned on the pillow beside him. Maurice picked it up and buried his head in it. The nightdress, the pillow, the sheet – all were redolent of Amy. He lay there for a long time staring at the ceiling.

Fifteen

Stowmarket Station was quaint; an old red-brick Gothic building, ornate with high-pointed arches and clustered columns, but smaller and more intimate than the typical stations found in big cities, where the noise, the scrambling crowds, the large flashing notice-boards and the loudspeaker announcements every few seconds added to a sense of confusion and agitation. Here it was easy, manageable.

A fellow traveller helped her alight, handing down her luggage. This chivalrous gesture calmed her slightly but, as she followed the other passengers to the exit, Amy's spirits began to droop. She was apprehensive about this visit; all the way down from London in the train she'd asked herself if she was doing the right thing. Ten days with a woman she hardly knew, and a man of whom she had the dimmest memory, didn't bode well.

An elderly gentleman with a bulging suitcase bumped into her and apologised. He was accompanied by a stout buxom woman who, Amy presumed, was his wife. The latter was talking loudly, pointing frantically and issuing instructions to the harassed husband. For a moment Amy worried that the woman wouldn't make it through the narrow gates but before she had time to further ponder the problem, two arms were thrown around her.

"Amy, lovely to see you." Catherine hugged her. "Had a pleasant journey?"

"Very nice, thanks."

117

"Here, let me help with your luggage."

"It's all right. It's not heavy; I can manage." Amy felt awkward.

Catherine didn't seem to notice. "You look well, Amy."

"And you."

Excruciating. Amy was useless at small talk.

"At least let me carry the small bag."

"That's for you." Amy smiled and handed it to her.

"Dear, oh dear, what did you go and do that for?"

"It's nothing; just some chocs and a bottle of cognac for Sam. You mentioned he was partial."

"You're a terrible woman – there was no need to go to that expense." She took Amy by the arm and led her out of the station. "I'm parked here. The green Opal. We'll be home in about ten minutes. Sam will have the kettle on, I hope."

The countryside was gorgeous on this sunny May morning: rolling fields, tall trees bordering the narrow winding roads and, dotted here and there, houses with latticed windows and colourful window-boxes. English villages were immaculately maintained, Amy thought. There was a reassuring sense of order and tradition. You'd almost expect to see bowls on the green.

"All the houses are so individual," Amy remarked as Catherine negotiated a curved bend, "and the gardens are lovely."

Polite stilted conversation.

Catherine indicated left and took the turn. "That's the main occupation around here – gardening. One neighbour planted bright orange marigolds, then he painted his garage door purple - there's no accounting for taste. Most of the folk here are retired and elderly – like Sam and me. You won't be moving in hectic social circles, I'm afraid."

Amy was about to protest but Catherine talked on.

"You see those cottages with the slated roof-tiles? They're mediaeval – were all once thatched."

Giving her the tourist spiel? Maybe Catherine was as nervous as she was? Maybe she was having second thoughts about this visit as well?

118

"The old roofs were very pretty but an accursed nuisance; attracted bugs and had to be redone every couple of years," Catherine prattled on. "The tiles are more practical, if less aesthetic."

Amy decided to show more interest. "Is that the library?" She pointed to her right.

"That's the village hall. They have all sorts of functions there: flower-shows, bring-and-buy sales, even slide shows."

"Slide shows?"

"Nothing too exciting, my dear. Old Tom Weston, the curate, regularly organises little evenings to show off his slides from the 1940s. They're quite interesting – the first or second time. Still, he's a good sort and does wonders for the village. He's a regular visitor with us. Has a keen interest in animals, also.

"Tom has a liking for all God's creatures. He organises an open-air blessing ceremony for the animals every July in the church grounds. People come from miles around with their pets." Catherine slowed the car to a halt, which was easy to do as there was no traffic. "This is our little village; twenty houses, a telephone kiosk and the village hall which you've seen; that's it *in toto*."

"No pubs?" Amy grinned. "Not like Irish villages."

"There was one but it closed down. So did the corner shop but we're only three miles from Ipswich, which is very convenient. I go up to London once a month – never lost my love for the city but I prefer to live in the country now. The pace of life here suits us better."

"You have the best of both worlds."

Catherine drove on to another bend in the road and pulled in to a carpark space opposite a splendid old greyflint stone building, erected on higher ground.

"That's the school?" Amy was agog. "It's magnificent."

"Used to be," Catherine said proudly, "now it's our humble abode."

It was far from humble. "I tried to imagine it, when you told me about it, but my imagination didn't do it justice, Catherine."

"It's been converted nicely but Sam will tell you all about it. That's one of his hobby-horses: talking about the house. Finding this place was his triumph."

Amy got out of the car. To the right of the schoolhouse were a Gothic church and a small graveyard. Would it be strange to live so close to the dead? It reminded her of Haworth Parsonage where the Brontës had lived. She'd visited Yorkshire once, on a school trip years before, and the barrenness and bleakness of the moors was what struck her most, but Catherine's home, nestling at the edge of this exquisite village, was far from lonely or desolate.

It exuded restfulness, stillness.

Catherine helped take her case from the boot. They crossed the road and entered the house via an archway.

After a substantial brunch, which Sam had prepared, of rashers, eggs, hash browns and mushrooms, Amy felt more at ease. Catherine decided to drive over to Ipswich on the pretext of getting more supplies but Amy guessed this was a ruse to allow Sam and herself time to get acquainted.

"You have a beautiful home," Amy told her host.

"It's what we wanted, Amy; no noise, no pollution. You'd only see a car every hour. The postman comes in the morning and, apart from the infrequent visit from a neighbour or a trip to the pub in the next village, we live quietly."

"Peace, perfect peace, as my father says."

"We spent most of our married years in London but the hustle and bustle and constant rushing became too much for me once I'd retired from the insurance company. It took Catherine a while to get used to it here but now she wouldn't live anywhere else."

Sam was a tall, thin man with longish grey hair and a bushy moustache and beard. He had the same ruddy complexion and kind eyes as the captain from the Birds Eye commercials.

"Tell me about the house," Amy said.

He stood up from the table. "Why don't I show you around?" He led her out to the hall with its latticed windows which had once served as a large classroom. "The school was built in 1868." He pointed to an old wood-burning stove. "We left that – adds to the atmosphere, we thought."

"Do you still use it?"

"We do, yes. Gives off great heat." Sam was in his element. "Now, if you look closely at the wall behind you, you'll see hook marks where the children used to hang up their coats."

It brought Amy back to her own primary school: rows of tiny desks, hooks for their gabardines, the unforgettable smell of chalk and Plasticine and the angelic face of a young, enthusiastic novice who'd taught them *The Owl and the Pussycat*.

"When did the school close?" she asked.

"Not until 1960."

"As recently as that?"

"The schoolmasters used to live in the adjoining cottage and then, years later, the last schoolmistress bought the whole place and converted the school part into living quarters for herself."

"I love the old cragstone floor."

"Me too, although Catherine says it's hard to clean. She'd prefer wooden floorboards."

"There's something solid and earthy about stone."
Sam was pleased by Amy's discernment. "It was quarried locally for all the houses in the village. Stonemasonry is a craft. Withstands the test of time."

"And old houses have their own personality." Amy thought of her home. What personality did it have? "But they need a lot of maintenance."

"You can say that again. There's always something to be done – not that I mind; I like DIY. I took off those oak doors and dipped them myself. They came up very well."

Amy duly admired them.

"Cathy made all the curtains herself. She's got a good eye for colour. We added on the upstairs storey when we took over in the eighties."

Amy followed him up the wooden stairs to a narrow landing off which were two small bedrooms and a bathroom.

"We put you in here," he said, as he opened a door to a third room, located at the back of the house.

The bedroom was bright. A large French window opened onto a small balcony.

"Thought you'd like the view," he added, waiting for her reaction.

Amy gazed down. The window overlooked the back garden with its willow and oak trees and then the view swept further: field after green-and-yellow field stretched to the horizon; trees and pretty hedgerows vied beautifully for attention; on and on, down and down to a meadow sloping majestically to a road in the valley below.

"It's breathtaking," she gasped, truly delighted.

"You should see it in winter when the snow comes. Picture-postcard stuff." He was chuffed.

"Thank you, Sam." She turned to him, her eyes glistening. "Thank you for giving me this room."

"I hope you'll be comfortable," he said gauchely.

"I will, oh, I will."

"I left you some books on the shelf. Catherine said you were a great reader. There's one or two on the history of the area you might be interested in."

She was touched by his kindness.

Amy started to unpack. The coming days would be pure pleasure. These were good people. She'd read, go for walks, engage in pleasant conversation. No stress, no pressure.

She sat by the open window, looking out at the landscape. A cool breeze drifted in, lulling her. She relaxed her shoulders, breathed in deeply and felt the tension ease.

Sixteen

Sam unpacked the groceries as his wife put a match to the living-room fire.

"Is Amy having a lie-down?" She blew into the grate to get the flame started. "I suppose she's tired after her journey."

"Not a bit of it. She's gone for a walk. Wanted to explore."

"Sam, you didn't let her go out?" Catherine scolded. "It's going to rain."

"How do you know? Your hip acting up again?" He shoved two batch loaves into the bread bin. "That hip of yours is more reliable than the BBC weather forecast!"

"No, my hip's fine, thank you very much. It was beginning to drizzle when I came in."

"Not to worry; I lent her your raincoat."

A thin wisp of blue smoke curled up the chimney, then the spark spat and died. "This damned fire won't light," Catherine complained. "I don't think you dried the wood properly. That big log is damp."

"Here, woman, out of the way." He tore a sheet from an old newspaper and spread it out over the chimney breast.

"That's dangerous, Sam. Someday we'll be found here burned to a crisp."

"Stop worrying, will you?"

"One spark and the whole thing could ignite. Or you could start a chimney fire."

"There, look! The flame's caught. It never fails." He screwed the paper into a ball and threw it on the fire. "We'll have a great blaze in a moment."

"That's what I'm afraid of."

"Why do we have to light the fire in here, anyhow?"

"It's chilly in this room in the evenings."

"We usually sit in the kitchen."

"Not when we have visitors."

Hadn't they spent their evenings in the kitchen when his brother, Charlie, came to stay at Easter? The kitchen was more homely.

"I hope Amy didn't go far," Catherine fretted. "She doesn't know her way around."

Sam rose stiffly from his knees. "She won't come to any harm. Don't you know full well that she'll bump into one or other of our illustrious neighbours who'll be only too pleased to stop and chat and show her the way if she does get lost." His wife's fussing irritated him. "Not that she's going to get lost."

"I still don't think it was wise letting her wander off like that."

"Wander off? She's not a child, Cathy."

His wife took up her knitting and sat in her favourite armchair by the window. "What do you think of her, Sam?"

"Very affable."

"And?"

"She seems agreeable."

She clacked her knitting needles impatiently.

"What do you want me to say?"

"Nothing."

The silence eventually got to her. "Did you notice anything else?"

"Like what?"

"Did you think she was very quiet? Subdued?"

"Not subdued, no. She went into ecstasies about her room and was very interested in the house but she's probably a bit uneasy being here since she hardly knows us. It will take her time to thaw out."

"She'll settle in. I want you to do your best, Sam."

"Meaning?"

"Be nice."

"I *am* nice."

"Make a special effort. Amy needs all the support she can get."

"You told me."

"Did she mention her husband?"

"No, we didn't get around to that. She said her daughter had started her exams."

"That's on her mind, too."

"Too?"

"I think Amy is at a crossroads in her marriage. She needs her own space; time for reflection."

"Cathy, be careful. You're not to dish out any marital advice. Outsiders should stay like that – on the outside."

"If she asks me . . ."

"She won't. She doesn't know you a wet week."

"She trusts me, Sam. People in trouble need to be able to talk."

"She has her family and friends, I'm sure."

"I'm her friend."

"Well, be a good one. Don't interfere."

"She's already confided in me," Catherine persisted.

"Let her work things out for herself, Cathy. She seemed – I'm not sure how to describe it – fragile, I think. I mean she's a fine figure of a woman, looks hardy enough, but she's a bit insecure."

This kind of observation was unusual for Sam.

"Some country fresh air will bring the colour back to her cheeks," he continued, "although she may get bored here quickly. When are you going to take her up to London?"

"Wendy Barrett said she'd booked afternoon tea in the Ritz."

"Book for afternoon tea?"

"You have to – weeks in advance. I must ring Wendy for the details. I haven't seen her in a long time. It will be nice to have a chat."

"Pump her for information, you mean." Sam picked up the sports section of the morning's paper.

"Well, what's wrong with that?"

Mary McCarthy

"Nothing." He sniffed behind the page. "So long as you don't go involving Wendy Barrett in your little scheme."

"Sam Cole, I don't know what you're wittering on about."

* * *

Amy pulled up the hood of the wax raincoat. Walking along the narrow road in the soft shower, she felt exhilarated. No cars, no motorbikes – nothing but the patter and plop of raindrops falling on leaves. She spied a robin pecking for worms under a hedge. A young man cycled by and waved hello.

A little girl with curling wet hair ran to post a letter in the red mailbox. She smiled coyly and stepped out of Amy's way into a big puddle. The child was totally unperturbed – getting wet was an unexpected bonus. She jumped up and down, splashing her yellow Wellington boots and her navy jeans. How would her mother react when she got home?

Amy would have received a thrashing. Elaine had never approved of childish frolics.

The smell of freshly cut grass from a nearby garden added to Amy's growing sense of wellbeing. Rain is romantic, she decided, as she wended her way back towards the village.

* * *

"Wendy? It's Catherine Cole. How are you? That's great. Did you manage to get the booking? Well done!"

Sam wasn't eavesdropping. But Catherine's voice on the hall phone boomed through the door. Maybe Wendy Barrett was deaf?

"We're both fine. No, he's inside reading the paper. Sends his love."

Sam grunted. Why should he send his love to a woman he hardly knew?

"I've been meaning to ask you something."

Ah ha! Now the real reason for the phone call.

"About Jane Edwards."

126

He had to hand it to her – his wife didn't beat about the bush.

"Yes, I met her the day of the opening of the new wing. It was extraordinary meeting her again after so many years. Were you talking to her? So was I. She's aged very well, hasn't she? Of course, money is no object."

Sam grinned.

"I believe she's emigrated. Where? Is that right? I would have imagined somewhere more up-market. I was sure it would have been Paris or St Tropez or one of those fashionable places. And the son lives there too? You don't say."

Why did people utter those immortal words *you don't say* straight after the other person has just said whatever they had to say? Mind-boggling, it was.

"Yes, Amy's here. Arrived this morning. No, no, I haven't said anything to her yet, not until I knew for sure you'd got the booking. She'll be delighted."

Sam wondered about that.

"So, what did you think of the opening? Very formal, wasn't it? No, I didn't eat anything – I hate finger food. The champagne was good, though. I'm sorry I missed you but there was such a big crowd. Were you talking to Henry, the son? Is that right?"

Cathy's skill at interrogation would be the envy of Scotland Yard: she asked seemingly innocent questions, made innocuous comments, added her own observations and, before you knew it, the other party was spilling the beans.

"Anything else strange or startling? How are the boys? Is Ralph still in Warwick? And Poppy? Pregnant? Another grandchild? Wonderful."

It was hard for his wife to have to hear that news.

"Are you enjoying your retirement? That's good. Me too."

Not strictly true. Sam knew his wife really missed work: missed meeting people, being busy, dealing with daily crises and most of all she missed the patients who'd adored her.

"What time are we meeting? Two-thirty? Amy will be tickled pink. Wednesday it is, then. Terrific. See you then. Super."

Now she'd come back to the room and repeat word for word

the whole telephone conversation and he'd have to fake ignorance. These little games appealed to Sam.

"You met Mrs Rogers, did you?" They were relaxing in front of the fire after dinner. "She's a nice soul. Husband died a few years ago but her son is very devoted; visits every week."

"She pointed out some nice walks to me and she asked me to remind you about the Friday night game of whist."

"I think I'll give it a skip this week." Catherine stood up. "Must open those chocolates you brought, Amy."

"Don't, on my account," Amy begged. "I'm trying to lose weight."

"You're fine the way you are," Sam interjected. "I hate scrawny women."

"Do you?" Catherine looked askance. "You never mentioned it before. You think I'm too thin?"

Sam had walked himself into this one. "No, you're just right, Cathy. Perfect."

"Liar!" She flung a cushion at him, then turning to Amy she went on: "He always lamented my lack of a bosom, dear. What's that you used to say, Sam? Better to have something to shake than something to rattle."

"I never said any such thing," he refuted, laughing.

Catherine opened the parcel. She took out the bottle of brandy and a huge box of Black Magic. "My favourites." She was about to discard the bag when she felt a small package at the bottom. "What's this?"

"Open it," Amy said eagerly.

Catherine did so and found a ring: white gold embellished with tiny vine leaves and grapes, a ruby in the centre. She was astonished.

"It's Georgian," Amy explained.

"I can't possibly accept this."

"I want you to have it; it was Mam's."

"But you should give it to Dawn. It rightfully belongs to her."

"I know Mam would have liked you to have it, Catherine."

Sam sipped his glass of brandy and smacked his lips appreciatively. This stuff was damned good.

Catherine leaned over and kissed Amy's cheek. "Thank you, dear, I'll cherish it."

"Catherine," Amy said at breakfast the following morning, "don't put your game of whist off for me, please. I want you to carry on with your usual routine while I'm here. Otherwise I'll feel as if I'm in the way."

"In the way?" Sam scoffed. "Stuff and nonsense! You're like a breath of fresh air, Amy. It's nice to have some younger company."

A breath of fresh air? Catherine had wanted her husband to be friendly – there was no need to overdo it. "You're sure about Friday?" she asked Amy.

"Positive."

"It's settled, so," Sam said. "I'll bring Amy to the Bull and Bear. Introduce her to a few local characters."

"The Bull and Bear?" Catherine echoed derisively. "That flea-pit?"

"I'd love a visit to an English pub," Amy said.

"And this Wednesday you're off to the Ritz, young lady." Sam passed her the marmalade. "Have to get out your glad rags."

"The Ritz?"

"Just afternoon tea to meet a friend of mine," Catherine told her. "A visit to the Ritz is always a treat and you'll find my friend, Wendy, interesting."

"I'm sure," Amy replied cordially.

"Oh, you will." Sam wiped jam from his moustache. "Cathy's up to her old espionage tricks."

"Pardon?"

"Don't pay any attention, my dear," said Catherine. "I worked with Wendy Barrett years ago in the hospital."

"The hospital where . . ."

"The same, the very same," Catherine said, eyes full of mischief. "Wendy retired as matron three years ago. She's kept up with many of the staff." She paused for dramatic effect. "Wendy's the very one who can fill us in on all there is to know about the Edwards."

Seventeen

Dawn glanced up at the clock in the exam hall: just twenty minutes to go before she handed up her anatomy paper. The Latin inscription under the clock did nothing to relax her.

Tempus fugit.

Time flies and she had to get her last answer finished. She'd written enough about the two cerebral hemispheres; now she had to develop her paragraph on the cerebellum. Shit! She'd hoped for about ten minutes at the end to reread her other answers.

Luckily, her practical exam had gone well; four minutes to identify the nerve in the tagged disembodied leg of a dog, then the bell rang and she had to hurry to the next: *what muscle is this? Where is its origin? Where is its insertion?* Next bell, next question. Thirty tasks in all. She'd run about like a blue-arsed fly.

She smiled as she remembered her first days in the lab: the shock of seeing fifteen dead dogs in the Anatomy Hall. Four students were assigned to each of these formaldehyde-preserved greyhounds, who 'hadn't made the speed'. Greyhounds were chosen because they had minimal fat cover and their muscles were more easily defined and identifiable. Dawn had avoided touching anything for weeks and she'd got away with it because "Mac-the-knife" in her group relished the experience, bludgeoning through nerves and vessels with unconcealed glee.

Pelvic limbs, sciatic nerves, proximal end of tibia, tuber coxae – it must have been easier in the old days when the students had learnt Latin. How she'd managed to score such high marks in her anatomy assessments was a mystery.

Still, there was no room for complacency: a few students were always weeded out of First Year and she didn't want to be one of them. The thought of repeating in August fuelled her resolve to get on with the written answers.

Exam technique was vital, Dawn knew, and timing was the key. It didn't matter how much you'd studied and crammed if you weren't able to demonstrate on the day what you knew.

She met Paul upstairs in Crowe's. He was standing by the fireplace, nursing a pint.

"How did it go?" He pulled up a chair for her.

"Not sure. I got the paper finished at least."

"That's good. A pint?"

"No, a rock shandy, please. I'm parched."

"Coming up."

Dawn sat down wearily and closed her eyes. Maybe she should have written more on the muscles of the abdominal wall? She'd kind of skipped over the inguinal ligament. There was nothing she could do about it now. She'd have to clock it up to experience and focus on her next exams. She'd tell her father everything had gone brilliantly.

"Here you go. I got you peanuts as well."

"Thanks, Paul. Listen, I don't want to stay long. I have to study my chemistry notes. I met Angela Redmond this afternoon; she's up the walls about it; she didn't do chemistry in school and that makes it all the harder for her."

"You did, though."

"Yes, but I still need to swot."

He'd just bought himself another pint.

"Do you mind if we go home after this one?"

"No," he said resignedly. "I think you're overdoing it, though. You'd be better off relaxing tonight. Have a proper drink."

"I can't; I need my wits about me."

"You're the boss."

* * *

"Come here, bitch!" Ben Cosgrove snarled. He'd ransacked the bedroom in an effort to find his money. His eyes glinted malevolently and spittle had dried on his lower lip. Where had the little cow hidden it?

"Isobel!" He came lunging into the bathroom after her. "Get me the fucking wallet."

Isobel cowered against the sink. "Please, Ben, please! We need that money for our rent."

"Bollocks to the rent! I need a drink." He wagged his finger threateningly. "If you know what's good for you, give it to me now."

"I promised Paul we'd settle tonight."

"You settle tonight, then. When were you paid? Yesterday? You give him the shagging money."

"I paid for the electricity and the phone. I need the rest for groceries, Ben. Be reasonable," Isobel said, in a half-sob.

"Stop whining!"

Her shoulders shook and she breathed deeply in a supreme but vain effort to control herself. She knew from experience that crying drove him mental.

"No waterworks, for Christ's sake. Stop blubbering and give me the wallet. It's mine. Right? Is that all-fucking-right with you?"

She couldn't move, couldn't even nod – she was paralysed with fear.

"So, tell me!" he roared. "Where the hell is it?"

"Ben, if you'd just –"

He leaped forward and grabbed her by the arm, twisting it painfully behind her back. "I'm going to count to three and then you're going to tell me where it is." His foul breath washed over her. Pain shot into her upper arm, pain so intense that she thought she'd pass out.

"It's in the pillowcase," she panted, squirming away from him.

"The pillowcase?" He smacked the back of her head. "Very fucking clever, aren't you?" Another smack.

How had he missed it? He hurled her away from him, sticking out his foot and tripping her up. She crashed to the floor.

"Now, you're for it, you little shit!" He lifted his leg and repeatedly kicked her in the back while she writhed and moaned.

"Ben! Please, Ben! Stop!"

"Stop? I'm only starting." A vicious kick to her side.

Isobel screamed out in pain as she felt his boot for the third time. He's going to kill me. This time he's going to kill me. She thought she heard something crack.

"You no-good tramp!" Another kick. "Did you think I'd let you away with this? You should know me better."

Her mind went numb.

He cursed and swore and kicked her harder. The veins stood out on his neck as he puffed and wheezed and lifted his boot again. "I'll teach you not to mess with my stuff."

Isobel stopped screaming.

Her vision blurred. Adopting the foetal position, she tried desperately to shield her face from the blows that rained down unmercifully. His boot smashed into her chin. Choking, she swallowed her own blood.

* * *

Paul opened the hall door. "I'll do a stir-fry for the dinner; it's quick. You go up and have a long soak in the bath."

"Thanks." Dawn put her arms around his waist and kissed him. "I'm dying to get out of these clothes. I'm sticky from the heat of the exam hall. Why is it always sunny and warm when I do exams? It was the same last year during the Leaving."

"These are the trials sent to test us, Dawn."

"When I come down, we'll have to discuss the cheque Mum gave me."

"I know. I've been thinking about it." He drew away from her. "I'd prefer if you kept it in your own account."

She was taken aback. "Why?"

"Safer for the moment." He went into the kitchen and took out the frying-pan.

Dawn followed him, determined to pursue this. "Why would it

be safer? I thought we'd agreed on a joint account. Much easier to get a mortgage."

Paul took some red peppers and onions from the vegetable rack. "I don't want to rush into anything, that's all."

"What do you mean?"

He turned to her, his face flushed. "I don't feel it's the right time for either of us to make that kind of commitment. Where's the sharp knife? I think it would be better if . . ." he said hesitantly. "I know we've been going out for a year now and we get on really well and all that, but –"

"But?" Dawn frowned.

"It's a very serious business: buying a house together."

"I thought that's what you wanted. A house. Paying rent is just throwing money down the drain – that's what you said."

"And I still go by that. I do want a house eventually."

"Well then?"

"I'm not ready." His voice was muffled.

Dawn couldn't believe what she was hearing.

"If we buy a house together, Dawn, it could lead to all sorts of complications. You're very young; you've years of college ahead of you."

"So?"

"What if something happens?"

"Like what?"

He faltered. "What if we break up?" He finally found the knife at the back of the cutlery drawer. Dawn stood stock-still, his every word wounding her.

"You might need that money later," Paul went on. "You can never foresee the future. An investment like that is a safeguard."

"I thought we were an item," Dawn replied coldly.

"We are. Of course we are but it's early days yet. I just don't think we should walk ourselves into anything we might later regret."

She kept her face straight.

"So, you keep that money in the account your mother opened for you and I'll continue saving. Then whatever happens happens." He laughed, glad to have got that out of the way.

Whatever happens happens.

She felt like a fool. She'd presumed that he'd jump at the chance of owning their own property; of having something solid, something real, something that would bind them. Now, she realised, he didn't want to be bound to her. Living together was a casual arrangement that suited him. It was *playing* house.

"Are we going to share next year, Paul?" She adopted his business-like approach.

"Why not? We'll renegotiate our lease here. I'd prefer Isobel and Ben out of the picture, but we'll find someone else to take their room. It won't be a problem."

"No," she said slowly. "I suppose not."

He finally managed to look her in the face. "Right, everything's game-ball?"

"Yeah." The operative word was *game*. She left the kitchen.

He loved Dawn, he wanted to be with her but neither of them was ready to make such a momentous decision. She'd obviously misunderstood. When he thought about buying a house, and some day he would, he'd always thought it would be *his*. Joint ownership had never occurred to him. Marriage was a long long way off. Sharing rent was one thing but owning a house together could become very complex, legally and every other way. He'd planned to own his own home and, hopefully, Dawn would want to live with him. But the house would be his. He hoped she understood this now.

He started to whistle. Now what other vegetables had they got to go with this chicken stir-fry? He opened the fridge. Mushrooms, great!

Dawn was furious with herself. Why had she opened her big mouth? She tore off her jeans and blouse angrily and threw them on the bed.

I love you, Dawn.
Did he?
You're the best thing that's ever happened to me.
So much for words.

She'd have to reconsider her options. He'd worried about such a big *commitment*. What were they now if not committed? They lived together, looked out for one another, shared everything. What was *that* if not commitment?

What was it for him? An idyllic little fun-loving set-up with no serious attachment? She wanted more. She wanted him to put his money where his mouth was: to be in this for the long haul. Why should she settle for anything less? She grabbed her shampoo from the dressing table and stomped out of the bedroom.

The bathroom door was closed. Dawn knocked. "Izzy, you in there?"

No response.

"Izzy, are you in there?"

Maybe it wasn't locked. She tried the handle and the door opened to her touch. She walked in. Isobel was lying on the floor, in a heap.

Dawn gasped. "Izzy, Izzy," she mouthed but no sound came from her lips.

Blood, dark-red blood smeared the side of the bath. Dawn, trembling, approached the inert body. Isobel's legs were twisted underneath her and one arm was outstretched, lying limply, like a broken doll's. A pool of blood from her mouth spread out on the tiles.

"Oh, sweet Jesus," Dawn moaned. She opened her mouth to yell. Again nothing happened. Dawn's breath stopped for a moment, then came back in rasping, jerky gasps. Her head began to swim.

Get help, get help. Quickly.

Zombie-like, she backed away from the gruesome scene. She leaned over the banisters and screamed with all her might: "Paul! Paul! Phone an ambulance."

Frantically she peered down as he ran into the hall below.

"What is it? What is it, Dawn?"

"Phone an ambulance. It's Isobel . . . she's . . . she's . . ."

"What? What?" he shouted.

Dawn sank onto the floor, grasping the wooden bars of the

baluster. She started to shriek, a wild piercing shriek that stopped his heart.

"What's happened?" He was up the stairs in a flash. "Where is she?"

"In the bathroom – she's lying on the floor. There's blood, so much blood. Go in there and look. No, no, first call 999." She clung to him. "Do something," she bawled. "There's blood everywhere."

Eighteen

Maurice had rushed over to the house in Stillorgan, after his daughter's frantic phone call. He gave her a stiff brandy and got her into bed.

"Try to get some sleep, Dawn. Isobel's in good hands now. There's nothing more you can do tonight."

"Oh, Dad, I'll never forget it; seeing her lying there . . . I thought she was dead."

He tucked in the sheet like he used to when she was a child. Then he sat on the bed and took her hand. "She's going to be all right. When I phoned the hospital, they assured me of that."

"Two broken ribs." Dawn shuddered. "And they might have to wire her jaw. Dad, what makes people *do* things like that? How could he?"

Maurice didn't know the answer. When Dawn had asked him questions over the years, he'd always tried to deal with them openly and truthfully. Parents were supposed to know all the answers. Brutality – what caused it? Nature, nurture – was a propensity to violence genetic?

"I'll never understand it. He's wicked – an animal. No, an animal wouldn't behave like that but he's not human. Isobel was so good to him, put up with all his moods and his meanness and selfishness. I suppose that's why he walked all over her but – tonight, tonight he was savage. Has he no feelings?" She shook and shivered. "I despise him, Dad."

"The police will get him, Dawn. Leave it to the police."

"Is Paul back yet?"

"No, he rang from the station. They're making out a full report."

"That bastard could be anywhere by now – off on one of his pub crawls, getting pissed."

"Where does he drink? If they could narrow down the likely pubs, it would make finding him easier."

"Everywhere he's not barred from. His cronies drink in the some of the pubs in Camden Street, I think." Dawn was suddenly struck with a new fear. "What if he comes back here tonight? Oh God, Dad."

"He's not going to do that. He wouldn't take such a risk. He must know he's in serious trouble."

"But his things? He's not going to leave his clothes and his stereo equipment. He's such an arrogant pig; he's so perverted he won't even know the damage he's done."

"He must know."

"Not if he'd already started drinking when he hit her. He's not rational when he's drinking. And there's more to it. There's a fierce misogynistic streak in Ben Cosgrove. He was always having a go at me."

"A go?" Her father looked even more concerned.

"Nothing physical – I don't mean that. He was always slagging me about my studies; saying that a woman's place was on her back, that sort of thing."

"Delectable."

"Yeah – a real bastard. He thinks life owes him a favour; sees anyone else's success as a slap in the face for him."

"And Isobel told you he lost his job?"

"Ben Cosgrove could never hold on to a job – interfered with his drinking. He expects Izzy to fork out her salary to supplement his social fund. I bet that was what caused this beating: money. They were always arguing about money. The way that creep's mind works – as far as he's concerned Isobel got the hiding she deserved. The more I think about it the more I feel he *will* come back here."

"We'll make sure the door is bolted, Dawn. He won't be able to get in. I'll stay tonight."

"Would you?" Relief spread over her face. "Paul's great but I'd feel safer knowing you were here, Dad."

"Not a problem."

"Thanks."

"He won't be back; I guarantee it. They'll pick him up, Dawn."

She bit her lip. "I hope they lock him up forever and throw away the key."

Maurice wondered, if and when they got him, how long he would actually be locked up. Free legal aid, an experienced barrister and he could be out on the street again in days. "Has he any previous record?"

"Not that I know of. Izzy once told me that his brothers had got done for stealing cars."

How did a nice girl like Isobel get hooked up to such a slimeball? Maurice thanked his lucky stars that Dawn had found Paul. "It's up to Isobel to press charges – when she's ready."

Dawn was dismayed. "I don't know if she'll do that. I tried to talk reason with her last week. Dad, this wasn't the first time he attacked her. She makes light of it, tries to justify his actions, understand his feelings – *his* not hers – then persuades herself he'll never do it again."

Maurice held the glass to her lips and she sipped, grimacing at the strong taste. "Try to drink it, Dawn. It will do you good."

"What time is it?"

"Twenty-to-eleven."

"I can't stay in bed. I have to study. How am I going to concentrate when Isobel is lying in bits in a hospital bed?"

"There'll be no study tonight. Get some sleep – you need it."

"But the Chemistry exam is the day after tomorrow and –"

"Dawn," he said carefully, "don't worry about the exams. There are more important things. Would you like me to phone your mother? She'd come home if you wanted her to."

"No, Dad, don't do that." Dawn lay back on the pillows. "I don't want Mum to be involved. She'd only worry and she's already had a lot on her plate. Anyhow, what could she do? Let her enjoy her holiday."

"Hmm." Maurice's resentment rose. His daughter was in shock. Finding her flatmate like that was an horrific experience. And where was her mother?

Off enjoying a *holiday*.

* * *

Donnybrook Police Station. The drunk in the corner started to cry. A teenage girl, high on drugs, was brought in by a passing motorist; the girl had flung herself in front of his car. A man stood at the far end of the room filling out a report on his stolen Honda. The phone hadn't stopped ringing: four house burglaries, one disturbance of the peace, an attempted rape, a domestic assault complaint. A typical night's work and it was only eleven o'clock. By pub-closing time there'd be a lot more action, the garda at the desk knew. First he had to calm down this irate young man and get him to give a coherent account of his story.

Paul, irritated, scratched his nose. "I'm not sure what age she is — early twenties, I guess. What difference does it make?"

"As I've told you, I need to get the initial details, sir," the policeman answered evenly. "Let's go over it one more time. Name: Isobel Dillon. Next of kin? Mother, you think? Address, yes, I've noted that. And you say you live in the house with her?"

Was there an implication that *he* had something to do with it? "I live with my girlfriend; we share the house with Isobel and Ben."

"This would be Ben Cosgrove, the victim's boyfriend?"

"Yes, yes," Paul snapped. "I told you. He's the one responsible."

The policeman nodded and noted it on his pad. He wrote slowly and meticulously. "You haven't seen him this evening?"

"No, he'd scarpered."

"Any idea where?"

"On the gargle as usual. Listen, can you not get a squad car out there to look for him? As we're here talking, he's making a break for it."

"All in good time." He kept writing.

Paul saw red.

The policeman lifted the phone. "Just take a seat over there, sir, and I'll have someone out to talk to you."

"What? Someone else? To talk to me? What have *you* been doing for the last ten minutes? Haven't I given enough information? I've told you everything I know. What's going to be *done*?"

The garda kept his cool; he was used to this. "If you just let me make this call, sir, someone from the DDU will be with you shortly."

"The DDU?"

"The District Detective Unit," he explained. "You'll have to give further details."

"I don't believe this!"

"Given the gravity of the situation . . ."

Paul groaned. More bloody red tape, more time passing and that piece of shit was out there on the loose.

The detective was huge, a big bull of a man. He had a craggy, lived-in face and steel-blue eyes, which, if it weren't for the circumstances, might have intimidated Paul.

"Where is she now?"

"Tallaght Hospital. She'll be in there for at least a couple of weeks."

"I'll have to call and see her. Get a statement."

"Why do you need to do that?"

Paul's exasperation had absolutely no effect. "This is your story, Mr Tennyson. I need to get the victim's account."

"You don't believe me?"

"It's not a question of that. You weren't present at the time. You didn't witness the attack."

"No, but I bloody well witnessed the aftermath. The girl was in a desperate state. She'd been brutally beaten. Battered. I dread to think what might have happened if we hadn't come home early. She could have bled to death. My girlfriend, Dawn, got such a fright I couldn't leave her alone this evening. Her father is in the house with her now."

"Very wise."

Paul felt like punching him.

"How long have you known this Isobel Dillon?"

Jesus, what was the point of all this malarkey? "About ten months. I advertised in the *Evening Herald* for two people to share. They applied and I took them. Dawn liked her on sight. Neither of us particularly liked him."

"And why was that?"

"I don't know; he looked sort of shifty."

"Shifty? I see."

"Look, with all due respect, Detective Dunne, this isn't getting us anywhere. I know this bollocks did it because it wasn't the first time he hit Isobel. He's vicious."

"Was there a prior report of his conduct made to us?"

Paul sighed. "No."

"I see."

If he said *I see* one more time, Paul *would* thump him.

"Right, let's get on with it, shall we? You got home at about six-thirty?"

"Yes, but we didn't go upstairs straight away. We were talking in the kitchen."

"You and . . . ?" He consulted his notes. "Dawn Kennedy?"

"Yes. Then Dawn said she'd go upstairs for a bath."

"And you were still in the kitchen?"

"Making the dinner." Next he'd be asked what he was cooking!

"What happened?"

"I heard Dawn screaming. I rushed upstairs and she told me."

"What exactly did she tell you?"

Jaysus! This was the pits. "She was crying hysterically, screaming and shouting about Isobel in the bathroom. I went in and found Isobel unconscious on the floor. There was blood spattered all over the tiles – a big pool of it on the floor. Her face was bleeding badly and I thought she might have head injuries too. I covered Isobel with a bath towel, then I ran to phone the ambulance."

"Did she regain consciousness?"

"Yeah, the ambulance guys brought her around. She was

whimpering and moaning. Her eyes looked funny; she wasn't focusing properly and when she tried to speak she couldn't."

"Anything else?"

Christ, wasn't that enough?

"Think very carefully, sir. Go over the scene in your mind."

"I don't have to – I can't get it out of my mind. When the ambulance men were putting Isobel on the stretcher I noticed more blood. A big dark red stain. I had to shield Dawn from seeing it. It was a horrible mess."

"Blood where, sir?" He ignored Paul's revulsion. "I have to know."

"On her stomach, her legs, between her thighs." Paul sucked in his breath. He thought he was going to vomit. "What the fuck could that bastard have done to cause so much blood?"

The detective kept writing. Was he taking this down word for word? Paul decided he'd better tone down his language.

"Thank you, Mr Tennyson. I'll need to question your girlfriend, as well."

"Why? She can't tell you any more than I've already told you."

"She'll have to corroborate your story, sir."

"Not tonight? She wouldn't be fit."

"Tomorrow or the next day will be fine."

"But what about Ben Cosgrove? Aren't you going to pick him up?"

"Not yet. Look, I'll be straight with you," the detective said. "I'll go to the hospital, get Miss Dillon's story and we'll take it from there. She has to make a formal complaint before I can do anything."

Paul, seething with rage and frustration, stormed out of the station.

Nineteen

Afternoon tea in the Ritz would be a treat for Amy and a nice memory of her trip to England – civilised and refined, a reminder of a more genteel world that Catherine missed.

Amy was amused at the whole idea and wondered what to expect: cucumber sandwiches, delicate pastries, muffins? Something vaguely Wildean and very, very British!

The Palm Court, the last vestige of elegant Edwardian London, is plush. Very sophisticated. But calm – an oasis of tranquillity within walking distance of the designer boutiques and auction houses of Bond Street and Jermyn Street. There are no clocks here; the tempo of life slows down. A quick glimpse of Piccadilly's taxis and buses flashing by is possible, if you look in the direction of the swing doors.

But it's much nicer to forget the world outside.

While Catherine went out to the central gallery to greet her friend, Amy sank into a rose-coloured Louis XIV chair at their reserved marble table with its delicate pink tablecloth. Time to study the scene. Amy wanted to relish every detail, store it up for future memories. She glanced up at the frosted glass ceiling and pink-capped chandeliers. The lighting was soft, delicate, flattering.

There was the famous nymph of the Palm Court fountain. Tritons, blowing conches above her, and goldfish at her feet, flicking their tails. Opulent gold-leafed walls and mirrors added to the elegance.

147

Two ladies sitting nearby debated whether they'd make Wimbledon this year. A waiter, immaculately turned-out in his three-piece suit, served tea and coffee from Heritage silver tea and coffeepots. The blue-and-white floral china particularly appealed to Amy who, despite her original misgivings, was thoroughly enjoying the whole experience. It wasn't every day you visited the Ritz!

Wendy Barrett was a cheerful, sensible woman whom Amy liked on first impression. She was tall, well-built and had a round face with dark curly hair and amazing brown eyes that danced as she spoke. Her intonation was like Betty Turpin's from *The Rover's Return*.

After indulging in a selection of cucumber, smoked salmon, cream cheese and mustard-grain sandwiches, melt-in-the-mouth scones served with home-made strawberry jam and clotted cream, and the pastries and cream cakes on offer, Catherine led the up-to-now idle conversation around to more important matters. "When did you actually work with Valentine Edwards? Was it before he got married?"

"Before and after. I joined the paediatric unit as soon as I went to St. Gabriel's. The fifties – another world. Although, just like today, we were overworked and underpaid. But I loved the job – we all did, didn't we, Catherine?"

"Yes, felt we were making a difference."

"And Valentine Edwards certainly made changes. He reorganised the whole wing; had really innovative ideas. The staff was in awe of him. As well as his organisational abilities, he was a brilliant doctor – gifted."

Catherine didn't want to hear all this. Today's meeting was not for the purpose of eulogising Valentine Edwards. She wanted Amy to find out something useful. "I remember him as being self-important; arrogant to the nurses – whom he regarded as underlings – and dismissive of the women in the labour ward."

Catherine's vehemence surprised Amy.

Wendy rushed to his defence. "He didn't care about being popular – although he was."

148

Amy, felt compelled to say something. "Anyway, he was a good doctor and that's what women want – to feel they're in good hands."

"He was the best. Safe deliveries and healthy babies were his first concern. People put absolute trust in him, Catherine." Wendy turned to Amy. "You had to wait months to get an appointment to see him; I actually believe some women planned their pregnancies to suit Dr Edwards's schedule."

"That was what was said at the time," Catherine muttered, "but it was all exaggerated; a tall tale, no doubt reinforced by the great man himself. Nobody could accuse him of modesty."

"Catherine, the facts speak for themselves: the older mothers who'd attended his clinic from the outset of their first pregnancies, wanted him present at the birth of *all* their children. The younger ones were half in love with him."

"He was handsome?" Amy asked.

Catherine sniggered. "A walking Adonis!"

Wendy grimaced. "You never liked him, Catherine."

"No, I didn't. I freely admit that. He was pompous, conceited and he used his position – a power-monger, that's what he was."

"Do you mean the way he treated staff?" Amy wondered why Catherine hadn't told her this before. She was getting two conflicting views here.

"Yes, that's exactly what I mean." Catherine poured more tea for the three of them. "Wendy, you have to admit that he was very dictatorial and even manipulative when it came to the younger nurses."

"He was a bit of a flirt," she admitted, "but it was all light-hearted, Catherine. Nobody took it seriously."

"That's where you're wrong. I knew one nurse who was propositioned by him after a long night in the delivery room. The girl was very upset. I advised her to report him but, of course, she didn't. Next thing she was moved to Accident and Emergency. It ruined her chances of ever becoming a midwife. She left the profession afterwards."

"I never heard that," Wendy said.

"No, it was all hushed up. I was *there*, Wendy. I know what happened."

"And you didn't speak up for her?"

"No, to my shame, I didn't. As you've already said, he was the senior physician. I was a junior nurse. Who was going to pay any attention to me? And, when I asked awkward questions some years later about another incident, I too was shifted. You can't have forgotten that?"

"You mean when you went to the general ward?"

"Yes."

"Catherine, I thought you asked for that move."

"No, I did not. But as it turned out, I enjoyed my time there. Later, I qualified as a psychiatric nurse, so, I suppose, unwittingly, he did me a favour."

"It's all so long ago." Wendy sighed. "What did you do that annoyed him?"

"It wasn't anything I said; it was what I knew."

"Something about his son," Amy interrupted suddenly, "and a nanny who minded their baby."

Catherine threw Amy a warning look. "A woman Amy knows used to work for them," Catherine explained.

"Oh?"

"Yes," Amy replied, sorry now she'd been so blunt, "when the baby was small."

"Right, right, the Irish girl. She left suddenly, didn't she? Wanted to return home?" Wendy had heard stories of neglect but she knew better than to state this in present company.

"I heard the child died," Catherine said.

"Died?" Wendy was astonished.

"One of those silly rumours." Catherine sniffed – something she did when she was ill at ease, Amy noticed.

"I never heard that at all." Wendy was extremely puzzled. "Who would start a rumour like that? Very curious. And this friend of yours told you about the Edwardses, did she, Amy?"

"She just mentioned them once in passing," Amy replied quickly. "I didn't pay much attention."

Amy was very uncomforable. Surely this woman wouldn't believe it was a coincidence that she had heard about the Edwards family? She must have guessed that Catherine had deliberately set up this meeting. But if she was suspicious, she was masking it well.

Wendy had supposed that the Irish nanny was too young, too inexperienced and that she'd been fired. The doctor had very strong ideas on child-rearing. She'd have to be careful not to embarrass this woman. "I do know they never employed a nanny after that. The wife devoted her life to the little boy. They were very loving parents, both besotted by him."

"What is Mrs Edwards like?" Amy asked casually.

"A lovely woman; sophisticated, well-spoken, very gracious. She was the model wife," Wendy went on. "Gave all her time and energy to her son and her husband."

"She wasn't healthy," Catherine butted in. "If she was sick all the time it must have put a strain on the marriage."

"You mean the miscarriages? Yes, they'd been very unlucky. Years of disappointment. But once she had her son, things changed." Wendy daintily stirred her tea. "She grew stronger, hardier. My guess is that the constant pregnancies had worn her down. Once he had his son and heir, I suppose they stopped trying for more children. No, Jane Edwards is far from feeble; she's a very strong woman who knows her own mind – very determined."

Amy looked at Catherine.

"I heard a story once that the little boy, Henry, was being bullied in his public school." Wendy paused. "Bullying used to be a dreadful problem in schools. Still is, I imagine."

"Probably." Catherine was anxious for her to go on.

"Jane Edwards apparently went to see the headmaster and gave him what for; threatened to take the parents of the bully to court despite the fact that the father was a High Court judge. She'd have done anything to protect that child – a lioness fighting for her cub." Wendy smiled. "Most mothers are, when it comes down to it."

It was beginning to make more sense to Amy. *A very strong woman who knows her own mind*. And Amy's mother was a young woman, insecure and alone in England. Jane Edwards felt her baby was under threat. *Fighting for her cub.* She'd had to get rid of the troublesome nanny. Why not simply dismiss her? Why had this *lioness* felt the need to lie to an employee? Her mother had been a powerless servant – an underling. It was bizarre but what was clear was that she wasn't going to get the answers she needed from Wendy Barrett – if anything she was more confused.

"You told me Henry has settled in La Rochelle," Catherine said, in an effort to move the story along.

"Yes, some time after Valentine's death. He wanted a new life. Henry runs a clinic there in partnership with two others, he told me. I had a long conversation with him the day of the function. You didn't speak to him, Catherine?"

"I don't know him at all."

"He's charming and very handsome."

"A chip off the old block?"

"No, Catherine, he's not a bit like his father, except in looks; same dark complexion. In manner he takes after his mother – extremely courteous and polite. He remembered me from the hospital; said some very nice things. And," she added, "invited me for a holiday any time I liked. I thought that was very generous of him."

"It was." Amy was doing her damnedest to be pleasant. She looked around to see if anyone was smoking. She was dying for a puff. "Is he married?"

"Divorced. The wife stayed on in the family home in Esher. It was an amicable separation, apparently. No children."

Catherine glanced at her watch. They had to leave for their train in a few more minutes. "His mother moved to France too?"

"Only for the summer months; she comes home to Surrey every winter."

"Amy happens to be going to La Rochelle for a trip," Catherine declared, her face straight. "That's why the story interests her. In fact, that's how the whole thing came up. She mentioned her holidays and I remembered about Henry Edwards."

Startled, Amy twitched in her chair.

"You're going to La Rochelle, Amy? Well, that's terrific. If you like I'll drop Henry a line to let him know. He'd be only too glad to show you around, I'm sure, when he hears of the connection."

"The connection?" Amy's heart thumped.

"With me." She smiled. "I'll tell him you're a friend of mine. When are you going?"

Amy looked helplessly at her friend.

"July," Catherine said, without batting an eyelid. "Her husband has to work so she'll be travelling alone."

"I love holidays on my own," Wendy said. "It's much better; you can come and go as you please and you've nobody to suit but yourself. Last year I took off by myself on a coach tour of Scotland. I thoroughly enjoyed it."

"That's bit different. On those organised tours you're guaranteed to meet people." Catherine took a tissue from her handbag. "But it can be daunting in a strange place and it takes time to find your feet. She'd be grateful to meet up with someone who knew the place well. Wouldn't you, Amy?"

Twenty

"Catherine, I can't believe you did that." They were settled in their train seats beside the buffet car.

"Needs must, Amy. Time is of the essence."

Amy took a long look at her companion. There she sat, in her pale pink suit, immaculately groomed, her lipstick perfectly applied, her glasses perched on the tip of her nose – as if butter wouldn't melt in her mouth and she'd told her friend, Wendy Barrett, a whopper of a lie.

"We needed that information, Amy. I'll be able to get his address now; Wendy has it at home. And his telephone number."

"You don't think I'm going to contact him?"

"Why not?"

"How could I? The man doesn't know me from Adam. Am I supposed to phone him out of the blue?"

"You won't have to. Wendy will set up a meeting. All you've got to do is let me know where you'll be staying and I'll pass it on to Wendy. Nothing simpler."

"Where I'll be staying?" Amy gasped. "You think I'm actually going to go to La Rochelle?"

"Of course you'll go."

Amy folded her arms stiffly.

"We'll book you a flight as soon as we get home. I told her July so that gives us plenty of time. You can get a flight to Bordeaux, as far as I know, and then it couldn't be far on the train. French trains are fantastic. Or else, if you'd prefer you could fly to Paris. I think the train from there is a TGV – high-speed."

"*Train à grande vitesse.* I know what it means."

"Now, about your hotel, I'll pick up a few brochures. I'll drop into the travel agents in Ipswich tomorrow morning and . . ."

Catherine's voice droned on and on and Amy began to drift off into her own little world. She looked out of the window at the fields rushing by. Catherine was talking hell for leather, competing with the *ra-ta-ta-ta, ra-ta-ta-ta* of the speeding wheels.

It was happening again. Everything was being planned for her, she was being told what she must do, advised, organised, talked down to as if she were a child.

Her mother, Maurice, Dawn, Claire, Sarah . . .

What you should do, Amy . . .

What you must read, Amy . . .

If I were you, Mum . . .

Listen, Amy . . .

Why don't you cop on, Amy?

Get your act together, Amy . . .

You could never manage to do it properly. Take a leaf out of your sister's book.

Why can't you listen?

"La Rochelle – isn't it where the French holiday? You'll love it there. I can see them all in their navy-and-white striped tops, eating *en famille.* There are islands off the coast and you could take boat trips. I mean the main aim, of course, is to get to know Henry and find out all you can but you may as well see the sights too. Maybe you'd get to meet Jane? Oh, Amy, think about it! You could solve the mystery."

Like everyone else in her life, Catherine was starting to take over. Why was it that they all felt entitled to do this? What was it about her that encouraged people to take control?

"Catherine, please stop it." Amy was mortified to realise that she'd almost shouted.

"Pardon?" Catherine was dismayed.

"Stop planning my life. Please."

"Amy, what's got into you?"

"I can't stand it any more. I'm sick of people bossing me around and telling me what to do –"

"But –"

"But nothing, Catherine. I have to make my own decisions."

Catherine sat upright, shoulders rigid.

"I need to work out things for myself," Amy said, gently but firmly.

"I was only trying to help." Catherine took up the newspaper.

"I know that but –"

"We'll say no more about it, shall we? I apologise for interfering."

Oh, God, she was hurt. Amy shouldn't have snapped like that – if only she could be assertive without being aggressive. "You weren't interfering, Catherine, but everything's moving too quickly for me. You can see that?"

"Forget it, Amy. We've had a nice afternoon and we don't want to spoil it."

A nice afternoon? Amy had been self-conscious during the whole conversation. She'd felt like a spy, a fraud, worming information out of an unsuspecting innocent. And Catherine had annoyed her although the Ritz had been wonderful: other-worldy, relaxed, serene.

"I'm sorry." Catherine's voice shook.

How could Amy manage to atone? There she went again – trying to please, trying to be nice, to be grateful, to be caring, to be everything people wanted her to be. Blast! "I'm sorry, too." Amy's upper lip quivered.

"Close your eyes and have a nice little nap," Catherine suggested.

"I appreciate everything you've done for me. I don't want us to fall out – I've had such a lovely time with you and Sam. But when and *if* I go to France, it must be by my own volition."

"You were very anxious to find out about the Edwards," Catherine reminded her.

"I know."

"You've changed your mind?"

"I'm not sure. I have to think. I can't make spur-of-the-moment decisions, Catherine. I have to consider my husband and my daughter. Whatever plans I make affect other people's lives."

The older woman nodded and pretended to read. Amy was more unstable than she'd realised – her reaction was over the top. What did she want? Catherine had gone out of her way to set up the meeting and get this information and now she had it thrown back in her face. Amy was her own worst enemy. Either she wanted to pursue the story or she didn't.

Twenty-one

Another exam over. Dawn hadn't done too badly – not that she cared as much any more. She wasn't as nervous as she had been for the first one because now she had a different outlook. What really mattered? What was important? How could she *worry* about diagrams, statistics, facts and figures when Isobel was in hospital, battered and violated?

Paul brought her dinner into the sitting-room on a tray. "Your mother's on the phone. Will I tell her you're out?"

"No, no, I'll speak to her."

"I'll pop this back in the oven. Are you sure you're OK? I can put her off."

"No, I'll take the call. I want to speak to her."

"You won't . . . ?"

"I won't say anything about Isobel."

"Better not, I think."

Paul took the tray back to the kitchen as Dawn went out to the hall. Gearing herself up for a good performance, she picked up the receiver. "Hello."

"Dawn, how are you? Lovely to hear your voice."

"And yours, Mum."

"How did it go today?"

"OK. Not half as difficult as I'd imagined."

"Good, good. You got what you expected?"

"For the most part, yeah."

"Well, that's the worst one over."

159

"Mmh."

"You all right, Dawn? You seem a bit down."

"I'm just tired." Dawn felt the tears welling.

"Have an early night, love. Is Paul treating you well?"

Why did she have to say that? How Paul was treating her was a moot point. He was doing everything in his power to help out in this dire situation but he had hurt her. Burst her bubble.

"Paul's all right, Mum. How is your holiday going?"

"Fine. The house here is amazing, Dawn. You'd love it. I'll tell you all about it when I get home."

Dawn thought she detected something in her mother's voice but she wasn't sure what. "How are you getting on with your friend?"

"She's very kind."

It sounded false.

"We went up to London yesterday to the Ritz."

"Very impressive!"

"It was an experience."

"So, you're enjoying yourself, Mum?"

"I am – it's a nice change."

"What's the hubby like?"

"He's a darling. He's a bit of a tease and he has a real sardonic sense of humour which I love. He's bringing me to the local tomorrow night so that should be a bit of fun."

"Mum, just enjoy yourself. Life's too short."

"Dawn, are you sure everything's all right? Your dad's not at you, is he?"

"No, on the contrary, Dad's been great."

"Is there something you're not telling me? I feel you're not in the best of form."

"You're imagining it, Mum."

"Am I?"

"Yes, everything's fine, honestly. I'm just knackered after the exams. You know the way you build yourself up to them and then afterwards there's a horrible anti-climax."

"I can perfectly understand that. Try to unwind over the next few days."

"Mum, thanks a million for the money. You're so good and –" Dawn's voice quivered.

"Dawn, I'm not convinced that you're OK. You sound . . . emotional. If there's anything going on, I'd like to know."

Maybe she should say something? But not about Isobel. "I need to talk to you about Paul. It's nothing urgent but I need your advice."

Romantic problems. Amy had thought that Dawn was in some kind of serious trouble – not that romance wasn't deadly serious at Dawn's age. "Anything you'd like to tell me now?"

"No, Mum, not over the phone. It can wait. When are you coming home?"

Amy distinctly heard a catch in her daughter's voice. "Next Friday week. I'll come earlier, if you like."

"No, no, stay the time you'd planned, Mum. We're all surviving without you!"

"Very reassuring." Amy laughed. "I miss you."

"Me too."

"How's your dad coping on his own?" Amy hadn't rung him.

"Seems fine. He's calling over here later."

"Good. Mind yourself, pet."

"I will." Dawn would have given anything to have her mother's comforting arms around her at this very minute.

"Goodbye, pet. See you very soon. Good luck with the rest of the exams and don't worry."

"Thanks." It came out like a sob.

Amy instinctively knew there was something drastically wrong. She made up her mind there and then to come home early. She'd try to get a Saturday flight. "Chin up, Dawn. I love you."

"'Bye, Mum."

Dawn replaced the receiver and burst into tears.

Maurice accepted a beer. "Thanks, Paul. How is she?"

"Not great. Her mother phoned an hour ago and she went up to bed for a lie-down straight after."

"Maybe she shouldn't go to the hospital tonight?"

"I hear her coming downstairs. You try to persuade her not to go."

Dawn came in and kissed her father. "Thanks for coming, Dad. I'll be ready in a minute."

"Dawn, we don't have to visit the hospital tonight. Leave it for a day or two until Isobel is stronger. I can just as easily drop you there tomorrow night."

"No, it's a long drive out to Tallaght."

"Not on the motorway, it isn't."

"I don't expect the car at my beck and call, Dad. You're busy."

"It's no big deal. Rodney doesn't mind in the least doing evening surgery."

"I'd prefer to go now. Last night Isobel was asleep – doped from all the drugs. She didn't even know I was there."

"All right, so." Maurice looked at Paul. "You coming?"

"No, I think Isobel would want to see Dawn on her own. I'll call in a few days." He went to kiss Dawn on the cheek but she pulled away.

Maurice wondered why.

* * *

Dawn sat by the hospital bed, trying not to show her horror and disgust at Isobel's appearance. While she talked, she avoided staring at the dark ugly bruises. There were tubes everywhere and a drip going into Isobel's arm. The screens had been pulled around the bed to afford some privacy.

"Paul shouldn't have done that, Dawn." Isobel swallowed. It was painful to speak. "He shouldn't have involved the police."

"But he had to – he had to, Izzy. Ben's a criminal. No, he is. Assault is a criminal offence. He can't be allowed to get away with it."

"He won't be," Isobel mumbled.

"No, because the police will deal with him. I have to make a statement yet."

There were tears in Isobel's eyes. "A Detective Dunne called here this morning."

"Did he? That was quick. Paul told me he'd have to talk to you, but I didn't think he'd move that fast. Fair dues, they're on the ball. What did he say?"

"Asked me a load of questions."

"I hope you gave him the right answers."

"I did; said I'd fallen down the stairs."

Dawn's mouth fell open. "You *what?*"

"You heard me."

"Izzy, You can't be serious."

"I am. Deadly serious."

"But why? After what that piss-artist did to you? Two broken ribs – and your mouth. I can see the difficulty you have breathing. The pain must be excruciating."

"It is but the jaw isn't broken like they thought at first. I was lucky."

"Lucky?"

"That's what the doctor said."

"Ben Cosgrove is a sadist. He deserves to be strung up. Why won't you press charges, Izzy? Why?"

Isobel shifted uncomfortably in the bed.

"Here, let me fix that pillow. Do you want a drink?"

Isobel shook her head.

"Come on, Izzy, speak to me. Tell me why."

"Why? Because if the police got him, he'd be out on bail in a few days and then he'd come after me."

"You can't be sure he'd be out in a few days."

"He would," she said bitterly. "Read the papers, Dawn. Ask any cop."

Dawn didn't feel competent to argue. "He needs to be taught a lesson." She moved her chair nearer to the bed. "You're not going to tell me you still love him?"

"No, I certainly don't."

"You agree he must be punished?"

"He will be. My brothers were in here today. They'll handle it."

"Izzy!"

"They know people."

"People? You mean *heavies?*"

Isobel nodded. "I'm glad – I hope they tear him limb from limb. I hate him. I hope they kill him. Slowly. He's a killer." Isobel looked away. Her body started to tremble and a loud choking sob filled the cubicle.

Dawn leaned over her and kissed her wet cheek. "Ssh, ssh."

Turning in the bed, the tears now running freely, Isobel grabbed Dawn's hand. "You don't know the half of it, Dawn."

"Izzy, I'm so sorry we didn't get home earlier. If only we hadn't gone for that drink – we could have stopped him. We could have done something."

"He killed my baby."

"What?"

"He murdered my baby."

"Oh God, Izzy."

"I didn't even know I was pregnant – not for sure. I'd often missed periods before." She gulped and fought back more tears. "I should have known, I should have guessed. I'd been feeling rotten but . . . a little baby growing inside me, Dawn. A seven-week foetus. He kicked it out of me. Kicked my baby to death."

Dawn felt the flesh on the back of her neck begin to crawl.

"His baby too. I'll never forgive him for that. Never. I don't mind what he did to me; I'll recover – but a baby. My baby. He butchered the baby – I'll never get over that."

Dawn shook from head to toe. All that warm dark red blood on the floor . . . smeared on the cold tiles.

A baby.

Dawn couldn't condone what Isobel's family planned to do – she didn't believe that anyone had the right to take the law into his own hands. Vigilantism was ruthless and dangerous. But what about innocent victims like Isobel and her baby? What justice did they get?

Dawn squeezed her flatmate's hand and cried inwardly.

She cried for the misery in the world, for all the hurt and sorrow and pain. And she cried for lost possibilities – for a little mite, a precious gift, a new and wondrous tiny human being who, up to the moment of its sadistic slaughter, had been cushioned in the protective layers of its mother's womb.

Twenty-two

Catherine scrutinised her face in the bedroom mirror. "Have I too much powder on?"

Sam didn't glance up from polishing his shoes. "You're fine. You look well."

"I think I'll change into my blue dress."

She was fidgety tonight – had been for the past two days since the Ritz business. She hadn't told him much but he'd gathered that things had not gone as planned. Amy had been very quiet. There was a coolness between the two women – a polite coolness.

Catherine took the blue dress from the wardrobe and held it up to herself. "Is this better, Sam?"

"It's perfect."

"You said that about the black. Which do you prefer?"

No matter what opinion he offered now, he'd be sure to say the wrong thing. "Wear whatever you're comfortable in, Cathy. Why create a major issue out of it? It's a game of cards – not a fashion show."

She pouted.

"I prefer the blue," he added, to please her.

"Why?"

"It's a softer colour for you." Was this the right answer?

"You think the black is too severe?"

"Cathy, the black suits you too. Either of them is fine, fine. Wear whatever you want."

She was irked by his impatience. After all, he'd spent ages in the bathroom tonight, had ironed his purple shirt and even pressed his trousers. Now he was busily buffing his brown shoes – and he was only going to The Bull and Bear.

"Keep the conversation light this evening," she advised him. "Amy is tetchy at the moment."

She wasn't the only one. "I'll be very circumspect, I promise."

"Did she ring home tonight?"

"No, she was on to her daughter, I think." Sam came over to the dressingtable, peered over her shoulder into the mirror and fixed his tie.

She sniffed. "New aftershave?"

"Mmh. *Obsession.*" He winked. "Do you like it?"

"It beats me how a man who hasn't put a razor to his face in years could possibly need aftershave?"

"You like me to smell nice, don't you?"

"I hear her going downstairs. You'd better be off." She patted his arm. "Thanks, Sam."

"For what?"

"For bringing Amy out tonight. I appreciate it."

He picked up his jacket from the bed. There was no need for thanks; Sam was quite looking forward to a few hours in his local.

Amy liked the pub. It was small and cosy. There were high stools around the circular bar and dark wooden tables and chairs in the centre of the carpeted floor. Wooden partitions with stained-glass panels separated other sections from the main part.

"Well, Amy, where would you like to sit?"

"Up to you, Sam."

He waved to a red-haired man sitting at the bar. "We could have a chat with Norman, if you like."

He knew by her expression that she didn't want to. "Or, we could go into the snug."

"Yes, I'd prefer that."

The snug was on the left, beside the front door. A hardwood floor, two small tables and a leather-covered bench against the wall made it intimate. To Amy's relief, it was empty. She sat down and took out her cigarettes while Sam went to the tiny counter. "What's your poison?"

"A vodka and tonic, please."

"My plans have changed slightly," Amy told him after the second drink. "I tried to get a flight for tomorrow but they could only offer me stand-by. I'll leave on Monday morning."

"We thought you were staying all next week."

"That was the original plan. I'm a bit concerned about my daughter – she wasn't in good form when I rang. Something's up. I feel I'm needed at home."

"Her exams? It's a trying time for youngsters."

"I think there's more to it," Amy said slowly. She lit a cigarette.

"Catherine will be disappointed."

"I don't think so, Sam."

"I swore I wouldn't ask, but I have to – what on earth happened between you two?" In one way he didn't want to know, but yet, Amy was his house guest and he didn't like the idea of her leaving on a sour note.

"My fault." Amy took a long pull from her cigarette. "I hurt Catherine's feelings. She was excited about all the information we got and she started to make plans and –"

"Plans for you?"

"Mmh, a trip to France."

He stroked his beard. "Sounds like Cathy, all right."

"I know she meant well."

"She always means well. Part of her problem. Amy, don't worry. I know what Cathy can be like. Once she gets an idea into her head, it takes her over. She gets carried away."

"Yes. Things got out of hand. Before I knew it she was discussing planes and hotels and dates."

"Organising – she loves organising."

"Nothing wrong with that," Amy said, "but I need time to come around to new ideas – that's my problem. As a result, I often feel bamboozled by other people. In a way, all my life, I've reacted to others rather than taking the lead myself."

"I'm a bit like that."

"Are you?" Amy found that hard to believe.

"Well, I used to be. Cathy did all our planning: the wedding, the honeymoon, the apartment in London, the furnishing, the annual holidays. It suited me, I suppose. I left her to get on with it – until I retired. It was definitely my decision to move down here permanently and, believe me, she took some persuasion. She was used to being the boss."

"You never struck me as the henpecked type."

"I wasn't; I was just easy-going. But once I make up my mind, that's it. I'm as stubborn as a mule, when I choose to be. Cathy had to get used to it."

"Maurice makes all the decisions in our house."

"And that bothers you?"

"I never minded until now. At least I think I didn't mind. Maybe I did all along? Maybe, deep down, I resented it? That's been pointed out to me and I'm beginning to believe it's true. You know I'm going for counselling?"

"Catherine mentioned it." He took a long drink of his ale.

"I was very depressed. For the past year I wasn't really living at all. Some days I couldn't get out of bed. Anyhow, I'm in therapy now and it is helping. What I'm discovering about myself is a bit scary. I've been bottling up anger for years, according to the psychologist. The minute she said it, I knew it was true. On the surface I was quiet – didn't lose my temper or anything like that, but inside . . . inside I was seething. A quiet rage burning away."

"It doesn't seem like you," he said, patting her hand. "You're very mild-mannered."

"Now that the anger's been released it's sometimes hard to control." Amy stubbed out her cigarette. "Sam, I hope I don't end up like my mother. She was a very angry woman."

"Don't think like that. You're not your mother."

"But this temper thing . . . I'll apologise to Catherine. She's been very good to me and I wouldn't want to hurt her for the world. I did insult her and that's unforgivable."

"It wasn't your fault, Amy. Cathy knows that. I can read her like a book; she realises she went too far."

"So did I."

"Cathy's very maternal and she has to direct those feelings somewhere. When you were a child, she idolised you: couldn't wait to get to Dublin and see you to shower you with presents and hugs and kisses."

"Yes, I remember how affectionate she was "

"And, like most people who've never had children of their own, she thought she was an expert on child-rearing."

"Mmh, I was the very same before I had Dawn. I used to give out about people spoiling their children or letting them into pubs, giving them too many sweets – things like that."

"Cathy wasn't worried about you being spoiled. It was exactly the opposite."

"I know."

"She tried to step in, offer advice and help, but one word borrowed another and –"

"Sam, I don't want to repeat my mother's mistakes. Isn't that how they fell out?"

"Yes, she said things your mother didn't want to hear. Tact was never Cathy's strong point. Maybe she came on too strong with your mother too. We've never heard Elaine's side of the story but she obviously felt Cathy was interfering."

"But that wasn't interfering – it was helping." Amy stubbed out the cigarette in the ash-tray. "It's impossible, isn't it? She tried to help and all she got for her trouble was to be cast off by my mother. Now I'm doing the very same – attacking her for no good reason."

"I'm quite sure you didn't attack her."

"I was rude."

"There's a very thin line between help and interference," Sam deliberated. "But my wife's a good woman. She wouldn't knowingly cause anyone any harm, especially not *you*. You're the child she never had, Amy. She's felt guilty about you for years."

"Why should *she* feel guilty?"

169

"She was sorry she couldn't do more to help you. Now, she feels guilty about Elaine as well. Hearing the news that the Edwards baby hadn't died brought it all back to her. I do honestly believe she's acting out of pure kindness. She wants Elaine to be vindicated and she wants you to be happy."

"I know that. I'll make it up with her in the morning. Sam, could I take the two of you out for a meal tomorrow night?"

"I never say no to food. About France, Amy . . ."

"Yes?"

"I wouldn't rush into it."

"You think I shouldn't go?"

"I wouldn't."

"At all?"

"Not without a lot of consideration. You have to weigh up the pros and cons and think about what good it will do – if any."

"That's what I tried to say to Catherine."

"She hates loose ends. Always wants a proper end to a story."

"Is there ever a proper end?"

"A very metaphysical question." He laughed. "And whose rendition of any story are we to believe?"

"'Beauty is truth, truth beauty'," Amy quoted.

"Keats?"

"Yes. Do you believe that, Sam?"

"I do – but the truth is often down to the interpretation of the individual and that's the problem."

Amy liked Sam better and better. "Maurice says the past is past and cannot be changed but I don't want to change it – just be able to understand it."

"I'm lucky if I understand the present!" He smacked her thigh playfully. "I wish you luck whatever you decide."

"I'll need it."

"You have to do what you have to do." He chuckled. "I'm running out of banalities here, Amy."

"Banalities. People always condemn them. At school we'd be warned off clichés in our essays, but the thing about clichés is – you can't argue with them. They're always true."

The barman called last orders. "One for the road. Will you join me?"

"I'll have a soda water this time. Another vodka and I'd pay for it in the morning. I hate hangovers and lately I can't drink as much as I used to."

"I know," he agreed. "It's bloody cruel. Let me end this conversation with a well-worn cliché – and it's one I totally agree with."

"Which is?"

"Let sleeping dogs lie."

"Is that your advice, Sam?"

"Oh no, definitely not." He grinned impishly. "Nobody can ever accuse *me* of giving advice!"

Twenty-three

There was a line of taxis waiting outside Dublin Airport. Amy got the third one in the queue and gave the driver her address. She hated going home; detested the thought of opening the hall door, going upstairs and unpacking – seeing Maurice again. Her stomach was queasy.

* * *

She sat at the kitchen table, sipping a cup of tea. The blinds were down and Amy didn't bother to open them. The nausea got worse, bile churned up from her stomach and burned her throat. Her hands started to shake. Tension at being back. She put off going up to her bedroom. There was a horrible finality in putting her clothes back in the wardrobe. She couldn't take that step – not yet.

The upstairs loo flushed. Maurice! She'd been sure he'd be at work; that she'd have a few quiet hours to get herself together.

"Dad, is that you?" her daughter's voice floated down, causing Amy to jump up and rush into the hall.

"Dawn!"

The girl dashed down the stairs.

"Mum, Oh, Mum! Thank God you're back!"

They sat on the cast-iron bench in the side garden – Maurice's orchard. There were pear and plum trees in the centre and the large apple trees around the wall provided shelter and privacy. His father had planted the apple trees. Most of the fruit went unused nowadays, which was a shame.

"So, I decided not to go back. I couldn't face it, Mum. I'll never live there now. I could never take a bath in that house again." Dawn shuddered. "I'd see her lying there, covered in blood."

Amy stroked her daughter's hair.

"Izzy won't go back either. When she comes out of hospital, she's going to stay with her sister, Janet, in Clondalkin, to recuperate. Then she's off to her other sister in Jersey. She intends to settle there. She thinks that with her experience in Roches Stores, she'll have no problem finding a job in one of the department stores."

"She deserves some luck," Amy said.

"Imagine losing a baby like that?"

"It'll take her a long time to recover. If she ever does. And there's no news on that louse?"

"No. He could be anywhere. I didn't stick around waiting for him to come back. Dad didn't mind when I moved home. He's been wonderful. I'm not sure about working for him this summer, though. Angela Rigney and two of the lads from college are going to the States. They've got jobs in Atlantic City. They've invited me to go along."

"Dawn, I think you should go. You need to get away for a while."

"Paul will stay in Stillorgan until the lease is up."

"And where does that leave things between you?"

"I don't know, Mum."

"He must be finding it hard."

"I don't care."

"I think you do, love." Amy smiled knowingly.

"Why should I? He let me down. We could have had our own place. That's what he led me to believe he wanted, but then when the opportunity arose – and that was all thanks to you, Mum – when we got the chance, he refused it. We had enough for a deposit on a town house. I spotted an ideal one in Ringsend and the mortgage between us wouldn't have been any worse than the rent we were paying, but he wouldn't listen to me. Is it his male pride or something? I never had him down for that, I must admit. He's so obstinate. Why didn't I realise that about him? I'm beginning to wonder if I know him at all."

"Are you sure it's obstinacy? Maybe he's right, Dawn?"

"Right? How can you say that?"

"I know you're feeling angry about it, but Paul's no fool. He's obviously thought this through."

"So have I."

"Have you, Dawn? Have you seriously considered all the implications? Paul's very sensible."

"Sensible!" Dawn made a face.

"You're very young."

"If anybody else says that, I'll scream. I'm nearly twenty, Mum. I know what I want."

"I'm over twice your age and I'm still not sure what I want. Paul has a lot of foresight."

"I don't see how you can take his side, Mum."

Amy hugged her closer. "I'm taking your side, sweetheart."

"I think I will go to America for the summer," Dawn said petulantly. "Yes, I'll go. I've decided. I'll phone Angela tomorrow."

"You should."

"It'll teach him a lesson!"

Amy took her hand. "Go for the right reasons, Dawn. Go because you want to; because you'll experience new and exciting things; because you'll be with your friends. You'll never get this time back, love. Enjoy it while you can."

"Yeah," Dawn muttered, "the best days of my life!"

"They can be; student life shouldn't be all about exams. You're young and free now, Dawn. Hang onto that freedom. You and Paul needn't be tied. He loves you, he does, but he doesn't want to own you. You're very lucky to have such an understanding chap."

"Huh."

"Someday you'll see it like that, too."

"Should I break it off with him?"

175

"Is that what you want?"

"No."

"Then take it easy, that's all. You don't have to live in one another's pockets. You've missed out on some of your college experiences – you admitted that to me once, remember? The Vets' Ball? You said yourself you'd have enjoyed it better without Paul."

"Because he didn't know people there."

"Yes, precisely. And you stopped going to the Friday night talks, too. They were great social occasions."

"That was a mistake," Dawn admitted.

"Paul realises these things; he doesn't want you to give up your life for him." Amy paused. "You don't have to drop him altogether, love. But you could mix more with other people."

"I know you're right, Mum. I've become too needy."

"Going to live with Paul was your escape from home, wasn't it?"

"No . . . no, of course not." Dawn reddened. "I just wanted to be . . . independent. It was nothing to do with you or Dad. I felt I had to strike out for myself."

"And you did the right thing."

"But I guess I'm not as independent as I thought I was. I came to rely on Paul. I substituted one safety blanket for another. That's not the answer at all, is it?"

"No," Amy said, "it isn't. It's great you've found that out, Dawn. At your age I wasn't half as mature as you are. You've grown up a lot."

Amy hadn't been half as wise either. She'd jumped at marriage to get away from the claustrophobic, oppressive atmosphere of her own family home.

And where had it got her?

Twenty-four

Maurice took off his dark green tunic, threw it in the laundry basket and mopped the sweat from his brow. The operating-room, with the late afternoon sun streaming in the window, was sweltering.

He'd completed his seventh and final procedure of the day. Fluff, a timid Persian cat, had been hit by a car. The X-ray had shown a clean break, so he'd put a pin in the cat's femur but it was risky; cats' bones can splinter easily. Luckily, everything had worked well. The little fellow was now safely ensconced in a cage in the recovery room where he'd stay overnight until his owner came to collect him early in the morning.

It had been a long, busy day: two molar extractions, one teeth-scaling, a cataract removal, a vasectomy, a hernia operation on a boisterous bulldog. Vets were, in effect, GPs, midwives, ophthalmic surgeons and dentists all rolled into one.

Maurice was worn out. He felt the years were beginning to take their toll – at forty-eight, he was no longer a young man and couldn't expect to have the energy he once had.

After a quick word with his receptionist about ordering supplies, and leaving a message for Rodney to keep an eye on Fluff tonight, he went upstairs to the small disused flat over the surgery, where he always showered after work. Rodney had hinted that he'd be willing to rent this place but Maurice didn't like the idea of having a tenant, particularly an unmarried male who had a string of girlfriends in tow. More hassle than it was worth. Besides, this place was a refuge for him: he could read in peace, speak his notes on the day's procedures into his Dictaphone, unwind. Think.

Lately he'd done a lot of thinking.

Since his wife had come back from England, relations between them had altered. Instead of arguments, harsh words, raised tempers, there was a disturbing politeness. They seldom met – a brief nod at the breakfast table or passing one another on the stairs. Their talk consisted of trivialities: who'd leave a note for the milkman, who'd put out the bins.

Domesticity wasn't always cosy.

Amy was deliberately avoiding him but, in a way, he welcomed her silence – afraid that if she said anything, she'd say too much. At one time, he'd blamed her depression for all their problems. But the depression had been a result of something much more serious, much more covert.

Amy was discontented.

When he reflected on everything that had passed between them over the last few years, he had to admit that the trouble had insidiously crept in and had been left to fester like an unlanced boil, oozing. He couldn't pinpoint an exact time or occasion which had marked the beginning of Amy's withdrawal; definitely her mother's death had brought matters to a head. But before that the signs were there and he'd missed them. He sighed aloud and the sound reverberated in the empty room, echoing his loneliness.

And now?

Amy was going for therapy. He wasn't comfortable about it. Yes, of course, he'd advised her to go – pressurised her even. But he had very mixed feelings. What did they discuss during these sessions? Him? Undoubtedly. What did Amy say about him? What secrets did she divulge about their marriage? Wasn't it awful that she had to pay this stranger to listen and she couldn't talk to him? And what miracle was this Wonder Woman working to have created such a change in his wife?

Amy had lost weight. She'd embarked on a refresher course in computers to upgrade her skills. Her nights were busy with the

gym or with her new friends from the class or with those bloody 'talking' sessions. Isn't that what he'd wanted? Hadn't he encouraged her to get out of the house and take up an interest? So, why did he feel threatened?

He went out to the kitchenette to get a brandy. Better watch it, old man, he warned himself; drinking alone was becoming a habit.

He swallowed a mouthful of brandy. He couldn't stop the compulsive thoughts. What did she say in those *sessions with Sylvia?* Did she describe how she hated the house? How they had drifted apart? Did she blame him for her depression? What more could he have done? He'd worked hard all his life; tried to be a good father, a good provider. He cared about his family, his practice. He'd been dutiful, responsible. Did she see that at all?

What did Amy want? He did know, deep down – everything she'd done lately had pointed to it – she wanted a new life, a fresh start. Couldn't she have that with him? Now she had this little job lined up, couldn't they begin again?

Every marriage had its difficult patches, he consoled himself. Now that Amy had started to sort herself out, they could try a new tack: she'd be self-reliant, have her own money, friends, hobbies. They'd both be better off for that.

And what about togetherness, a tiny voice niggled. They could go out again as a couple, as they had in the early days. A dinner out once a week – isn't that how Jack kept Sarah happy?

He sat down on the sofa-bed, carefully holding the glass so as not to spill his drink. What the Goodmans had – he certainly didn't want that. How did Jack get away with it? The lies, the craftiness, the game-playing. Why bother? What pleasure did he get by deceiving his wife? What need did it fulfil?

And it was a need. Jack's selfish little ego thrived on perpetual indulgence. What he didn't get from his wife, he got from his mistress – Jack's cynical motto.

And what did the mistress get?

How could that tawdry arrangement suit an intelligent, attractive woman? Did she enjoy sneaking around arranging clandestine meetings, stolen nights in out-of-the-way hotels? At least neither of them claimed it was love.

"Love, boys, love is commitment and fidelity and trust." Words of wisdom in the Religion class. The Jesuits. A big, burly bully in a soutane, strap in hand, teaching mortified teenage boys about the joys of marital love.

Maurice, the obedient diligent pupil, had got top marks in the Archbishop's Exam – the end-of-year assessment for all Catholic students.

What did that frustrated pedant know about love?

"Marital love is not based on the pleasures of the flesh, boys. We all have to guard against the sinful lure of sex." The ruler would crash down on the desk then for added emphasis.

"Lust, boys, lust."

Bang, bang, bang.

"Pray for temperance. Pray for redemption. Pray for deliverance."

Bang, bang, bang.

"Beware of the evil enticements of fallen women who cast their spell and suck you in." Spittle at the corners of his mouth as he huffed and puffed and grew red in the face.

A titter from the back row. The priest glowered around the class while the students cast their eyes to the floor.

"Sexual intercourse is a gift from God, reserved for the sanctity of marriage. Our bodies are vessels for the Holy Spirit." His voice boomed around the draughty classroom.

"Marriage is a sacrament, boys. A sacred union of a man and woman who are committed to each other and to the laws of God. Is that clear?"

"Yes, Father."

"Never forget that."

"No, Father."

Damn Jack! Damn his *fallen woman* with her dark laughing eyes! And damn the fact that he liked her, too. She'd been a good friend to him all down the years. He couldn't ignore that. Sometimes he thought she was laughing at him – at his simplicity, his *naïveté*.

He was tired of warning them, advising them. It wasn't his job to be moral watchdog to two consenting adults who'd chosen to be utterly selfish and contemptuous of the feelings of others.

And Sarah knew what her husband was like. She'd openly said to him, that time they were in Galway, that she was well aware of what she called Jack's *flings*. She'd smiled as she told him, but behind the smile Maurice had seen the pain, the confusion. He couldn't understand why she stood for it. Her complicity. But what if she knew the identity of Jack's current mistress?

Good God, why was he fretting about Jack and Sarah? He had his own marital mess to mend.

"Fidelity and trust are based on honesty, boys."

"Yes, Father."

"Honesty with oneself and with others. *'This above all; to thine own self be true.' Hamlet*. Repeat."

"To thine own self be true," they chorused.

"Uprightness, integrity, morality. These are the virtues we seek. Repeat."

"These are the virtues we seek."

"We must shun occasions of sin. We must abide by the rules."

"Yes, Father."

"Examine your consciences. Look into your hearts and confess to God Almighty your sins. You, Master Kennedy, are you taking this in?"

"Yes, Father."

"Stand up when I speak to you. I think you were daydreaming there in your desk, idling away the time. Were you, my boy?" He brandished the strap.

"No, Father. I was listening."

"Good, good, sit down. Purity of mind and heart, boys. That's what we must strive for. What did I say, Mr Kennedy?"

"Purity of mind and heart, Father."

"Now, the lot of you, take out your copies and I'll write the salient points on the blackboard. First heading underlined: Honesty.

Right, he'd try to be honest with himself. A cigar might help. He rummaged through his pockets but didn't find one. Maurice decided to think it out in the only way he knew – methodically, on paper.

He took his writing pad from the makeshift bureau he'd made when he'd first bought this place fifteen years before. Maybe it was time to think of investing in some good furniture? No, Amy would go mad; she'd resent him putting money into his premises and not his home. But there were some jobs he'd have to have done or he'd pay later with structural damage.

Start his page with a question: what was Amy's main complaint?

Money. According to his wife, he was too thrifty. Was that a fault? Money had to be spent wisely – he'd done that. He was almost finished paying the mortgage on this place. He'd refused to rent a practice as Amy had advised – he'd recognised the folly of throwing money down the drain.

He owned this three-storey house now – waiting-room, consulting-room, X-ray room on the ground floor; operating-room and boarding for the animals who had to stay for observation and recovery, on the second floor; and this little pad up here which, one day, he *could* rent out if he so wished. Or, a better idea: Dawn could have it.

He hadn't been mean – he'd been frugal. Frugality wasn't meanness; it was prudence. He wasn't like Jack, spending every last penny, throwing it away like there was no tomorrow. If anything happened to him, Amy and Dawn would be well set up. His insurance policy and his pension fund would see to that.

Maurice divided the page in two and ticked off *money*.

Not guilty.

Neglect, hadn't she berated him for that? He worked long hours – but that wasn't a crime. He admitted that he'd been a bit negligent, but that was only during the last year when Amy's moodiness had forced him to stay out of the house.

Stop it, stop it, Maurice. No going over old ground. Amy was making an effort; he could, too. He'd work fewer hours – Rodney would be only too glad of more overtime. Soon he'd be in a position to employ a new vet. That would ease the burden.

Her constant criticism was the *gloominess of the house*. He could agree to her doing it up – slowly. No need to go overboard. A few minor changes were all that was necessary. The decor and the furniture – no extensions or renovation or anything like that.

He carefully wrote down and ticked off each of his resolutions.

Their social life was *abysmal* – her word. Easy to solve that one. They could sit down and discuss what they wanted to do. Amy didn't like squash, so that was out. She'd no interest in golf, either. But Blackrock had lots of possibilities: they could go swimming together once or twice a week; they could drive out and walk in the mountains – maybe join a hiking club. Tennis? Would she like that? They could invite friends around; card parties, maybe. Restaurants. Cinema. Bowling in Stillorgan?

He pencilled in all of these suggestions. Ah, why didn't he think of it before? The theatre. Should have been his first proposition. Amy adored the theatre. He hadn't brought her to a play in years.

He took *The Irish Times* from his jacket pocket and went to the Entertainment section. He scanned the list of theatres and decided on The Gate. He got out his Mastercard and his mobile phone and dialled the number.

* * *

"And we'll be able to have more time together." Jack stroked her back. "Which is what you wanted, honey."

"Really, Jack? You think she'll go for it?"

"Why wouldn't she? It'll be perfect for her and the kids."

She hated when he talked of his wife and children. When they were here in her big double bed, she wanted no reminders. No intruders. This time was theirs and theirs alone. His other life played no part here.

He kissed her shoulder blades and she turned and snuggled up to him.

"Mmh, that was good, Jack."

"You're good." He kissed her deeply, his tongue probing, and eased himself on top, his legs straddling her.

"Let's do it again." He smiled down at her. God, he was horny.

"Jack, Jack, tell me," she murmured, her face taking on a sudden innocence.

"Tell you what, honey?" he teased, circling her nipples with the tips of his fingers.

"Tell me you love me." She ran her hands down his back, then scraped him gently with her long nails.

"Careful, careful."

She pouted.

He laughed into her neck. "No marks, please."

"Tell me, Jack," she begged. "Tell me, just once."

Jack would never say those words to her; they were reserved for Sarah. "You're incredible. I can't get enough of you."

"Tell me, Jack."

"You know how I feel."

She ran her tongue over her upper lip and smiled. "I sure do, lover, but I need you to say the magic words."

He held her hands down on the pillow above her head and she wriggled and squirmed.

"Tell me, tell me."

Her kittenish voice excited him. He threw the sheet off his shoulders. "I'd much rather show you," he whispered.

The phone beside the bed rang, startling them both out of a deep sleep. She reached over him and grabbed it. "Hello? Oh, it's you, Maurice. Yes, he's here. Hang on."

Jack took the phone. "Hi, buddy. No, no, it's fine. I hope you didn't ring Sarah? Good, good. I'm working late here."

His chuckle needled Maurice.

"How are tricks? Just finished work? You'll kill yourself, old man. Any news? Did you? Yeah, I suppose Amy will be pleased. It can't do any harm."

Harm was Jack's department – not his. "I need to see you."

"Oh?"

"I'm thinking of doing up the flat and I wanted you to price new windows for me."

"Come on, man. I never mix business with pleasure." He ran his hand down his lover's stomach. "Phone me tomorrow."

Maurice sighed.

"Look, I'll drop in there early in the morning and give you a rough estimate, how's that? But I have to warn you that it will cost you and we're booked up solid for the next three months."

She moved her leg up and down his in a most provocative way. Jack wriggled. "This woman is killing me. She's a tigress." Another laugh. "She needs to be tamed, Maurice."

"I'm sorry I disturbed you," Maurice said sharply. He rang off abruptly, revolted by what he'd heard, feeling, in some perverse way, soiled by their sordidness.

Jack let the receiver fall as her hand travelled downwards over his belly. "Mmh, nice."

"Why does Maurice always ring at such inopportune times?"

"An uncanny sixth sense. Or begrudgery."

"What was he saying about Amy?"

"He's booked the theatre for them for Friday night." He sniggered.

"What's so funny?"

"You'll never guess what play?"

She nibbled his ear. "What?"

He entered her quickly and she gasped. "What, Jack? What?" She panted in pleasure as he thrust deeper.

He groped her buttocks. *"An Ideal Husband."*

She raised her mouth to his and muffled his laughter.

Twenty-five

Sarah Goodman was flabbergasted. "A mobile home, Jack? Where?"

"Rosslare. It'll be great for you and the kids and I could go down at the weekends."

"But what possessed you?"

"Robbie O'Dea, one of our sales reps, told me he was selling at a reasonable price and I jumped at the chance. It solves all our holiday problems. You know I can't get away for the foreseeable future with the expansion and all. The summer months are when people get in new windows – it's our busiest time. I'm needed in the office for the next three months."

"But you could have told me about it before you went ahead and bought. I thought we'd agreed that we'd postpone our holiday until September. You even said we'd get a good deal on Cyprus or Turkey at that time of the year when the high season is over. "

"We can do that as well."

"It was an unnecessary expense, Jack."

He cracked open his soft-boiled egg. "We're doing very well at the moment; apart from our fast-growing business with private residences, we got a contract for a new estate in Lucan – two hundred houses."

"You kept that to yourself."

"I was waiting for a definite offer. That young advertising manager I hired is a whizz kid. We're giving the biggies a run for their money. Next month we're opening up new offices on the northside and I'll have to oversee the whole of that. I'm going to be up to my tonsils."

"Is that what your meeting last night was about?"

"Yes," he lied easily.

"What time did you get in?"

"Not sure, after one o'clock I think. We took the directors of the building company for a meal and you know how these things drag on."

Sarah packed Gerald's sandwiches into his lunch-box. Her son would be late for school if he didn't come down soon for breakfast. The girls had already left with Betty from next door. The car pool had eased Sarah's daily routine.

Sarah went out to the hall and shouted upstairs for the second time. Usually, on the third yell, his bedroom door opened, he'd bellow back and sleepwalk his way to the bathroom.

"Ger, are you up?"

No response.

"Ger, it's eight-twenty."

The door creaked.

"Hurry up, love. Don't shower this morning. You've no time."

Her twelve-year-old son had recently discovered the bathroom. Up to a few months ago it had been murder trying to get him to wash. Then, out of the blue, his friend, Andy, mentioned Boots. Now it was impossible to drag him away from his toiletries: hair wax, mousse, gel, Lynx deodorant. One day she'd found him borrowing his father's aftershave.

She heard him running the taps upstairs, whistling away, not a care in the world, as time marched on.

"Hurry up, Ger!"

"I'm coming."

Sarah came back to the kitchen. "You're pleased with yourself, Jack. I can see that."

She saw a lot more besides.

"A very lucrative business deal, which I'm not too modest to admit is largely due to me and my persuasive charms."

"Did you talk to Fergus?"

"I did."

"And?"

"He agreed."

"You've a hike in salary?"

"Yes, a considerable one. My brother recognises my worth. And I recognise yours which is why I wanted to surprise you."

"You've surprised me all right, but a mobile home? That's the last thing we needed."

"Robbie says it's a good size. There's a main bedroom, and then a smaller room with bunk beds, a toilet and shower cabinet, a fitted galley kitchen and a small dining area."

"Marvellous!"

"Why the sarcasm?"

"I can't see myself cooped up on my own all week on a windswept beach, cooking in a tiny space, being hemmed in on rainy days with the kids fighting and squabbling and getting bored."

"Sarah, that's precisely why I bought it. It's the end of June and the kids will be off school next week. They always drive you mad during the summer holidays but down there they'll be occupied; there are loads of things to do."

"Such as?"

"Wexford is the sunniest place in Ireland. They love swimming and being out of doors – it'll be exciting for them."

"Until the novelty wears off."

"You can have your friends down, too."

Sarah handed him the shirt she'd been ironing. "My friends are busy people. They already have their holiday plans worked out. Clodagh is off to Amsterdam with her workmates."

"What about Amy? She'd go."

"Amy is doing a computer course, I told you."

"Full-time?"

"For a month. She has a job lined up."

"Maurice must be pleased about that."

"Who knows? They're hardly speaking."

He got up from the table, danced over and ruffled her hair. "You see how lucky we are, honey?"

"Are we, Jack?"

Her stare unnerved him. "OK. I'm off. I'll talk to you this evening. Sarah, I'm sorry you're not more enthusiastic about the mobile home. I thought you'd be over the moon."

"Did you?"

"Yes, I did. And, in any case, apart from using it ourselves, it's an investment."

"I'll see you tonight," she said frostily.

"I'll be late."

"Do you want me to keep dinner?"

"No, you eat with the kids. I'll grab something from the deli."

* * *

Sarah sat back on her hunkers on Amy's sitting-room floor. She was taking up the hem on Amy's new dress. "Boyers, is that where you bought it?"

"Do you like it?"

"It's gorgeous. Red is your colour. The theatre on Friday night – Maurice has got the message."

"A very small part of it."

"Things are better?"

"Not particularly."

"He *is* making an effort, Amy."

"One night out together – a cup of water on an inferno."

Sarah couldn't reply; her mouth was full of pins.

"He's so uptight; creates tension. I used to think it was me, but it isn't. I didn't realise how bad it was until I went to England. Within a day or two there, I found myself calmer."

"It's lousy when someone has that effect on you, but he is trying to make things better. Look at the way he relented about doing up the house."

"He'll put that on the long finger – which is why I went straight into Arnott's and bought those curtains. They had the right size and the exact shade I was looking for. I was sure I'd have to have them made."

Sarah finished the job, stuck the remaining pins back in their box and stood up. "They'll brighten up the room no end. Have you decided on a colour for the walls?"

"Tuscany. It's a rich shade. Even Maurice didn't object. Not that I care any more – I'm sick of humouring him."

"Take a look at yourself in the hall mirror. I think the hem's straight but I want you to judge for yourself."

She followed Amy out to the hall. "And what about the mammy's three-piece suite?"

"He refuses to get rid of it, but he's toying with the idea of having it covered."

"One step at a time." Sarah bent down and adjusted one of the pins.

"It's a small step."

"Hang in there, Amy."

"I'm not sure I want to. I feel like a fraud; like I'm playing a part."

She wasn't the only one. "How's your course?"

"A week and a half to go. I'm an expert now on Database, Microsoft Word and Office, System Folders, Spreadsheets – you name it. I'm enjoying myself although it's very intensive. I knew most of it before but it's amazing how out of practice you get."

"Have you given Nancy Mulhearn an answer?"

"I told her I'd help her to get everything sorted. That should take a few weeks, but I haven't made up my mind about working full-time in the shop. She wants me as manager. Do I want the hassle?"

"You'd thrive on it. Have you heard from Dawn?"

"She phoned last night. They're having a great time. She's selling freshly squeezed orange juice on the boardwalk." Amy took one last critical look in the mirror. "You've done a great job, Sarah, thanks."

"I'll run it up on my machine tonight."

"I owe you one. Yeah, Dawn sounded very happy when I talked to her. And she's working as a waitress at night in a small café. The others are double-jobbing too, but they're young; they've got plenty of energy. A good social life as well from what I gather. She needed this space for herself. Come into the kitchen and I'll make us a brew."

Sarah followed her out and picked up brochures from the table. "La Rochelle?"

"Mmh, I wrote to tourist information."

Sarah flicked through the pages. "The place looks fabulous; old buildings, boats in the harbour, restaurants along the quay. Sunshine."

"It won't be a holiday, Sarah. I'm going for a specific purpose."

"I know that but all the same the place looks gorgeous. You always loved the sea, Amy."

"Everyone who lives in Blackrock loves the sea."

"I don't – not in winter – too bleak."

"Not for me. I love walking by the sea in the wind and rain."

"You're an incurable romantic!"

"Only when it comes to nature." Amy laughed.

"Will it be hot in La Rochelle?"

"Nicely hot – not unbearable."

"Looks like you've made up your mind to go."

"There's no harm in doing some investigation. I might go when my course is finished. For a week. I've discussed it with Nancy and she'd be happy for me to start in the shop in August."

"He bought what?" Amy exclaimed. She took an apple tart from the microwave. "Are you serious?"

"Bloody insane!" Sarah got plates from the cupboard.

"Well, I suppose he's thinking about you and the kids, Sarah. Maurice never considered holidays as important."

"There's something deceitful about it."

Amy handed her a slice of the tart and a jug of cream. "Help yourself."

"Aren't you having any?"

"No, I'm still dieting."

"You're great. Have you kept up the walking?"

"Three miles a day."

"It shows, Amy; you look marvellous."

"I feel much better, fitter. Although I've a long way to go yet. It's hard to shift weight."

"You've unbelievable willpower! How's the counselling going?"

"It's difficult. But Sylvia's such a compassionate woman. She tries to make me feel good about myself. Now I've got to work on doing it without her help. I can't rely on her forever."

"I have to take my hat off to you."

This was easier for both of them – to pretend. Amy couldn't admit to Sarah that she still suffered serious lows – usually at night. Her mind was full of dark thoughts then and the *voice* was a constant. Some days she began to feel like herself again but the mood swings were far from over. Sylvia had advised her to go with them rather than fight. Sometimes you had to go down before you could come up again. "Another helpful thing," Amy continued, "is the gym. When I'm there I feel as if I'm working things out of my system."

"I should go back myself but I don't know if I'd have the energy."

"The more you exercise the more energy you have. I love it and it gets me out of the house at night. When I'm down to ten and a half stone, I'll try to cut out the fags but not at the moment. There's only so much self-improvement a body can take!" She lit one. "Sarah, what did you mean by *deceitful?*"

"Jack's been acting the maggot."

"Oh?"

"He's become very attentive."

"Jack was always attentive."

"Not like this: he's buying me little presents, continually asking me how I am, paying more attention to the kids, doing more around the house – when he's there, that is. And now – a bloody mobile home."

"Some women would be delighted."

"He's plotting. It's obvious."

"What is?"

"He has another woman."

"Sarah, here you go again! First you tried to persuade me that Maurice was having an affair with Claire. Remember? When I went to England you actually spied on him."

"Spying is putting it a bit too strongly."

"It is not. You drove by here every other day. Then, when he spent a few nights away, you were certain he was with her."

"How was I supposed to know Maurice was with Dawn in Stillorgan?"

"You have a very inventive mind, Sarah."

"Speaking of Stillorgan, is there any news on that bastard?"

"Ben Cosgrove? Not since Paul told me that the brother arrived to pick up his stuff. Paul thinks Ben might have gone to England – he has an uncle in Birmingham who's a builder. Good riddance. Paul's looking for a new place but he says some of the rents they're charging are exorbitant."

"Will Dawn move back with him?"

"That remains to be seen. They're phoning each other a lot. I like Paul but Dawn's far too young to be in such a serious relationship."

"I agree. She should sow her wild oats. Time enough to settle down. I didn't get married until I was thirty – not that my marriage is anything to go by. Jack *is* up to his old tricks."

Amy puffed away. She couldn't protest Jack's innocence; couldn't be hypocritical.

"Amy, say something."

"I don't like to meddle, Sarah. For me to pry into your marriage would be ludicrous."

"I need to discuss it. It helps to clarify things in my mind."

"How bad is it?"

"On the surface, everything's smooth. But it's difficult to pretend I know nothing."

"Would you not confront him?"

"No, he'd deny it. Tell me I was imagining things. No matter how good my arguments are, I end up feeling in the wrong."

"Until it's out in the open, Sarah, I can't see how you're going to cope with it."

"I live from day to day. I keep myself occupied. The nights when he stays out late are the hardest."

"He's still taking you out?"

"Oh, yes. He's booked some fancy restaurant for Saturday. Told me to buy a new outfit."

"He *is* generous, Sarah."

"Always was. But now it's as if he's trying to buy my affection. He's so obvious."

"And how is he when you're together?"

"Same as ever. He's funny and affectionate. Hugs and kisses galore – as if nothing has happened."

"Maybe it hasn't?"

"I rang his brother last night on the pretext of inviting him and his wife over for a meal. Fergus answered the phone. It was after ten. This morning Jack looked into my eyes and told me he was with Fergus at a meeting for the whole evening."

"How did you not explode?"

"I've trained myself."

"Have you . . . have you stopped . . . ?"

"Making love? No, on the contrary; our sex life has never been better."

Amy didn't know how to respond.

"I'm going to find out who she is. I'll make it my business to find out." She daintily forked a piece of the apple tart and bit into it. "Delicious."

"And what then, Sarah? What will you do?"

"Then I'll have to challenge him, I guess."

"Hopefully you're wrong."

"I'm not. We both know what Jack is like. He's had women before but it was different. It didn't last beyond a month or two and, while I didn't like it, I learned to live with it. This time it's different; I can *feel* it."

How could Sarah turn a blind eye to her husband's infidelity? How could she sleep at night aware that he was having sex with another woman? Knowing he was with someone else, kissing, fondling, copulating . . . and then to take him into her bed and allow him to make love to her?

"By getting me and the kids off to Rosslare for the whole summer, he'd be free. He said he'd come down on weekends but that wouldn't last. After a while, he'd make excuses – valid excuses for not being able to come."

"He is very busy, Sarah."

"Not as busy as he lets on. Jack's an accomplished liar. I'm under no illusions." Sarah helped herself to more cream. "Crazy as it sounds, I do love him. Faults and all, I can't help liking him."

Liking, Amy noted. That was the core of it all. If you liked someone, you could forgive anything.

"Jack's easy to live with – very even-tempered. I've never known him to raise his voice – not even when the kids are acting up. He's patient and good-humoured, Amy. And I still fancy him like hell. I'm not going to lose him. I refuse to give up everything I've worked for. Why should I? I married Jack for a lifestyle and it suits me."

"A lifestyle?"

"The way we live, Amy, the house, the gardens, having two cars."

"Material possessions don't bring happiness, Sarah."

"They do to me. And it's not just possessions – he gives me free rein with my friends. Jack doesn't demand much. He didn't object when I threw in the job. He's bringing home a lot of money and he doesn't stint." She half-coughed. "No offence meant."

"None taken."

"Jack and I both want the same things: a nice home, holidays abroad, a good education for the kids, dining out – all of that."

"If it's that good, what makes him go after other women? Have you asked yourself that?"

"It's quite simple: Jack needs more than I can offer him. He needs excitement."

Excitement. Amy wanted that too but not at anyone else's expense.

"I can't provide the romance he craves. We're too used to each other for that."

Romance? Jack wasn't having an affair for romantic reasons – he was a lecher.

"I give him other things: companionship, love, support." She smiled ruefully. "And steadiness. That's the thing; Jack needs to be steadied and he knows it. He does love me, Amy. I know he loves me and he's mad about the kids. In every other way we have a good deal going. That's why I have to fight for him."

"If," Amy hesitated, "if he's serious about this other woman?"

"Jack used to compartmentalise his feelings. Home, work, hobbies. The other woman was always a hobby – up to now. But if it is serious this time I'll . . . I'll . . ."

"What will you do, Sarah?"

"I have to get my evidence first." She wiped her hands in a paper serviette. "After that . . . who knows?"

Twenty-six

Amy would have loved to live here in Greenview. The three-storey redbrick apartment complex, built in a landscaped area, was half a mile from the sea and, as its name suggested, bordered a large green. The more expensive two-bedroomed apartments, one of which Claire had bought, were located on the ground floor.

Amy rang the bell for number five and waited for her sister's voice on the intercom.

Nothing.

She rang again.

No response.

A light came on and a curtain moved. Claire was in.

Amy pressed again.

Still no answer.

Whoever was peeping through the curtains could see Amy and there was a security monitor in each apartment which identified callers.

Amy kept her finger on the bell.

Finally, Claire's sleepy voice: "Hi!"

"I've rung four times, Claire."

"Sorry, I didn't hear you."

"May I come in?"

"Hang on a sec."

Another minute passed and then the buzzer sounded which allowed Amy entry to the building. She heard scurried movements as she walked down the corridor to her sister's door.

Claire, completely dishevelled, her hair damp, tugged at the belt of her black silk bathrobe as she showed Amy into the small sitting-room.

"I was in the shower."

A sound of something falling came from the main bedroom. Amy took in Claire's flushed cheeks, her sleepy eyes, her agitation. "You're not alone?"

"Em . . ."

Amy hovered by the couch. "I'm sorry, Claire. This is obviously a bad time."

"No, no, it's all right. Sit down."

It was a half-hearted invitation. Amy stayed standing. "I'll go. You're busy. Paddy Whelan?"

Claire grinned idiotically.

"Not a good time to meet him?"

"You could say that."

"Right, I'll be off. Sorry about the intrusion. Phone me later, will you? I want to talk to you about Dad."

"Were you with him today?"

"Yes, I thought he was looking a bit peaky."

"I'll go and see him tomorrow after work," Claire said breathily. She was desperate to get Amy out.

Amy's curiosity soared. She'd almost met the mystery man. For weeks now she'd been begging Claire to bring him for a visit but her sister had adamantly refused. That was nothing new. Claire's relationships often didn't last long and she couldn't see why it was necessary to introduce every boyfriend to her family. But that didn't stop Amy's curiosity.

She walked by the green and was about to exit by the laneway towards the bus stop, when she saw it. The black van. Parked neatly in front of the opposite block.

Goodman Windows.

Amy's heart sank. Jack bloody Goodman – alias Paddy Whelan.

Amy hurried around the corner to the late-night coffee-shop. She ordered a cappuccino and sat down to think. What was she going to do? Anger swelled. Her own sister. How could Claire be so devious?

What should Amy do? Go back there now and confront them? Stomp in, yelling, shouting and calling the odds? Tell them how despicable they were?

She tried to smile politely as the waitress brought her coffee but her face contorted.

Maurice? Did he know? He must. His best friend. How could Maurice have *covered* for them? How had he kept silent? Any time he mentioned Claire he'd given no hint of anything amiss. Was he their accomplice? Their co-conspirator?

She stirred her coffee furiously, drawing peculiar looks from a man at the next table.

Claire. Her very own sister – doing the dirty on Sarah. What madness made her do it? There were enough men in Dublin to choose from besides seducing her sister's best friend's husband. Why would she be so callous?

What now? Amy despaired. Should *she* tell Sarah? Go over there now and inform her? If Amy kept this from her, was she also a traitor?

Tell the truth, Amy. Shame the devil.

Amy cursed the moment she'd decided to visit Claire. If only she'd left it to another night! If only she'd arrived an hour later then . . .? Why hadn't she phoned in advance?

It was useless. Sooner or later the truth always comes out. Her own sister! No, Sarah couldn't be told – certainly not by her.

What could be *done* about the situation? Something had to be done. Immediately. What time was it? Eleven-fifteen. Who should she talk to – Claire or Maurice? It was imperative that she talk to one of them tonight.

* * *

Amy, choking with annoyance, followed her sister into the kitchen. "Start at the beginning, Claire. I want to know every detail and when you've finished telling me that, you can explain why you did it."

Claire feigned ignorance. "Did what?"

"Don't come the innocent with me. I saw the van."

"What van?" Claire eyed her cheekily.

"Jack Goodman's. On the other side of the green."

"So? He was on a job."

"That's one way of putting it."

"I recommended his company to a woman over the road – that explains it."

"Jack was *here* when I called, Claire."

"Says who? You didn't see him, did you?"

Amy bit her lip. She called on every reserve of patience she had. "Was Jack Goodman here tonight? Yes or no?"

"As he was in the neighbourhood, yes, he called here to measure my windows. I told you I had to get new windows. You never listen, Amy."

Never listen.

"Claire, don't make me lose my temper. I know what's going on."

"You know nothing." Claire flopped onto a chair and her dressinggown opened, revealing a love-bite high on her thigh. "I'm not denying he was here. For the last time – he came to measure the windows."

"Fine. So you decided to have sex with him?"

Claire guffawed. "How did you come to that conclusion?"

"I saw you. I recognised the signs."

"I was in the shower when you called, Amy. My hair was wet, remember?"

"Wet from sweat."

"I was in the shower – not that it's any of your damn business."

"Is that the way it is? You screw him in the shower?"

"Don't be vulgar, Amy. It doesn't suit you."

"It *is* my business, Claire. Sarah has been a good friend to me and I won't have her betrayed by my family."

"Won't you? Tough. Go home, Amy. Go home and play happy families with Maurice."

Amy angrily grabbed a chair and sat down. "I'm not going

anywhere. I've all the time in the world – all night if necessary. Now, start again, Claire, and this time the truth."

It was after one in the morning. Amy was drained. Two hours of arguing with her sister.

"I'm sick to death of this, Amy. Do you want a drink before the taxi arrives?"

"No."

"Very commendable. I'll have one." She helped herself to another gin and tonic. "Jack loves gin, by the way. He keeps me in constant supply. Not usually a man's drink, is it? But then Jack isn't typical."

"Yes, he is. He's the typical, dyed-in-the-wool philanderer."

"Amy, you're a riot."

"And what are you, Claire?"

"Get a life."

"Why would you do it? Why?"

"Why not?"

"Claire, please. I want to understand. I want to help. You probably didn't intend for this to happen. It's all a mistake." Amy balked at the emptiness of her words.

"Relax, sister dear. It's no big deal. This type of thing goes on all the time."

"And that justifies it?"

"I'm not looking for justification. That's your bag – always trying to rationalise, explain, excuse."

"There is no excuse for hurting others. And I'm not here to discuss my shortcomings."

"Why *are* you here? To talk sense to me?"

"To try."

"I'm not going to let you lecture me, Amy. You're in no position to do that. Jack and I are having a good time, that's all. We have a great set-up, which is more than you can say about you and Maurice."

"A great set-up?" Amy chided. "Look at what you're risking."

Claire flicked her fringe back from her forehead. "*I'm* not risking anything – I've nothing to lose."

"A sad comment on your life, Claire."

"That's rich coming from you."

"Jack Goodman has something to lose – his marriage."

"His gamble, Amy. I never thought much of marriage. The ones I know are hardly idyllic. And I wouldn't think you'd be such an advocate, either."

"You're impossible! Can you honestly not see anything wrong with what you're doing?"

"I'm having fun. So is he."

"Claire, he has a wife and children. I can't believe you're this selfish."

"And I can't believe you're this innocent. Why should I care about Sarah Goodman? I never even liked the woman. If Jack is willing to forsake his marriage vows – that isn't my fault. I made no promises to anyone."

"Will you make one to me now? Will you stop seeing him?"

"Eventually, I suppose. I'll grow bored with him."

It was all a game to her. A wretched game. Amy stood up. "If you don't care about Sarah, think about the damage you're doing to yourself."

"I won't get hurt. Don't worry."

"Claire, you already have been."

"Bullshit."

"You've been so badly damaged you can't even think straight. Look at the way your life is going – all the broken relationships, the married men, the waste."

The buzzer rang.

"Your taxi."

"Give it up, Claire. Please."

"Amy, just go home. You've nothing to be smug about."

"I know that." Amy went into the hall. "I'm sorry for you, Claire. I truly am."

"Don't be. I'm a grown woman. I'm quite happy. I know what I'm doing."

Amy let herself out.

Twenty-seven

Maurice adjusted the reading lamp. He took an extra pillow from the empty place beside him and propped himself up. The empty space. The spare room. Another indictment of his marriage. This room was now his – he hadn't shared Amy's for months.

He was about a third of the way through *Hannibal* and was thoroughly enjoying it, but it was difficult to lie down with a large hardback – hence the extra pillow. Harris was a writer Maurice admired: spot-on characterisation, mounting suspense, graphic gory descriptions. Maurice felt he was walking the streets of Florence, tailing Dr Fell.

He heard the hall door open. Amy. Unusually late. Her footsteps on the stairs saddened him. She'd head straight for her bedroom. No communication tonight, or any other night.

As he turned a page, his door swung open.

"Maurice!"

Her face was thunder. So, the shit had hit the fan. She rattled her keys. "I was with Claire."

"I guessed."

"How did you guess?"

He folded the jacket cover on his book to mark the page.

Amy stood there, stock-still, in the doorway. "Well?"

"Jack was here. In a panic. He's not long gone."

"He's had a busy night. Maurice, how could you have kept it from me?"

205

He shrugged dispiritedly.

"How long have you known?"

Maurice rubbed his eyes. "From the beginning – almost."

She stood transfixed, refusing to move an inch into the room. "And you never said anything."

"How could I?"

"You're as bad as they are."

"That's not fair, Amy."

"Not fair? How can you talk about *fair?*"

"Please come in, I can't talk to you while you stand there breathing fire. Come in."

"I'm fine where I am," she asserted. "I'm waiting for you to explain this away."

"I can't."

"Try."

"What they do is their own business."

"I mean explain why you didn't tell me. How could you be so underhanded? I always thought you had integrity."

"I thought it wise to keep it from you."

"Did you, did you indeed, Maurice? How very thoughtful." She clenched her hands and the knuckles protruded, bony and white. "Your best friend – my best friend's husband, Maurice, her *husband* – and my sister are having it off," she shouted, "and you thought it *wise* to keep it from me?"

Maurice was infuriated by her attack. "Yes, I did and it was for the best. What possible motive would I have in telling you, Amy? What good would it have done you?"

"That's a cop-out, Maurice."

"I didn't want you involved."

"Did you not? Well, I'm involved now."

He searched his pyjama pocket for matches. She opened her handbag and hurled her lighter.

He caught it, deliberately ignoring her rudeness. "I'm not going to take the blame for this one. Amy, if you'll just listen –"

Listen, listen, listen.

"Shut up, Maurice!"

He sucked madly at the cigar to get it lit.

"Why didn't you *do* something? Why didn't you talk to Jack?"

"I did. Many times."

"Without much success, evidently."

"Without any success. He's a jerk."

"On that we agree." Amy drew herself up to her full height. "I presume you and Claire had your own cosy little confabs about it."

"I tried to reason with her, yes. It was useless. We don't hold the same views on everything."

Amy conceded that.

"What had Claire to say for herself tonight?" he asked quietly.

"She believes she has a right to have *fun.*"

He raised his hands in a gesture of hopelessness. "There you go. You didn't do any better than I did. I'm sorry you were landed in this, Amy. I genuinely am sorry. I acted in your best interests – or thought I did."

"By keeping secrets?"

"Yes, sometimes it's the kindest way. You should know that."

"What's that supposed to mean?"

"Are you saying that you tell me everything? What about your trip to England?"

"That was different; I wasn't cheating on you, Maurice. It was something I had to do."

"Why? What was so important, Amy?"

"You wouldn't understand."

"Try me."

"Not now, Maurice. This isn't the time."

She launched accusations at him, unjust accusations, then she refused to discuss them. "What do you propose we do, Amy?"

"What can we do? It's not of our making. We should just keep out of it. Hope it goes away."

"That's what you want?"

"No, of course it's not what I want. I want none of this to have happened in the first place. It's unbearable. Claire's my sister." Amy's voice cracked.

He looked away. "It's very hurtful for you."

"For me?" Amy squealed. "What about Sarah? You know how fond I am of Sarah. She's a loyal friend. How will I ever look her in the eye again? It's an impossible situation for me."

"Will you tell her?" He fidgeted with the lighter.

"How can I? Tell me. How can I?"

"Now do you understand why I kept it from you? Sometimes it's necessary to hide the truth from those we love."

Amy, conscious of the validity of his words, turned to go.

"Amy, leave it to me. I'll do something."

"What?"

"I'll fix it, some way."

"Maurice, it's not a broken bone. You can't fix everything. You're not God."

"Jack knows that you now know – that puts a different complexion on the whole business."

"I don't see why. What does Jack Goodman care about me or my opinions when my own sister doesn't give a damn?"

"Jack cares all right. He's frantic – petrified you'll tell Sarah."

"He must know I wouldn't do that – couldn't do it. I wouldn't hurt her for the world."

"Jack doesn't think like you or I do, Amy. Tonight I reminded him how close you and Sarah are. How you confide in each other; tell each other everything."

Did she detect a tone of jealousy?

"He'll finish with Claire. No question of it."

"Claire won't be got rid of that easily."

"Claire will have no choice. Jack is an expert at dumping women."

"Maybe this time it's different."

"No, it's not, Amy. She was just the next in line. Hard as it is to fathom that idiot's behaviour, I know one thing about Jack: he loves his family."

"That's what Sarah said."

"She's right."

"But why take such stupid risks?"

"Forbidden fruit – the age-old reason."

"Sick."

"Go to bed, Amy. I'll take care of it first thing in the morning; Jack's calling into the clinic." Better not to mention anything yet about his plans for new windows for the surgery. That would make her madder. "I'll get to talk to him again before Claire has the chance."

"And this time he'll listen?" she asked derisively.

"This time he has no choice. He knows he's done for – playing too close to home."

"That's what it is, Maurice: playing. For both of them."

"Claire will be out of the picture by this time tomorrow, I guarantee it."

"I warned her she'd get hurt." Amy rubbed her forehead. Her head was throbbing.

Maurice picked up his book. "She'll get over it."

Amy tossed and turned until the small hours. She visualised Sarah's face – the desolation, the crushed look in her eyes if she discovered who the *woman* was. Sarah had believed that Claire was having an affair with Maurice – the irony of it.

Images and words flashed though her mind: Claire's smirk; her coolness; her cynical tone; her refusal to look candidly at herself and the situation: her indifference to the misery she was capable of causing.

Fun. A great set-up. I'm entitled to enjoy myself.

What had made her so cold? No, no, she wasn't a cold person. She'd been good to Amy, very good. She'd been kind to Dawn all her life. It was just when it came to men that she . . . what made her so bitter? Their father's inattention? Their mother's domination? Her cruelty? Her manipulation? Pitting her daughters one against the other . . .

"Who loves Mammy the best? Do you, Claire? Amy did the dishes this morning. Is she a better little girl than you are? Who is Mammy's favourite little poppet today? Which of you is telling fibs? The best girl will get ice cream for dessert. Only the one who has

209

broken Mammy's vase will be punished. Which one of you was it? Own up and take your punishment. Was it Amy, Claire? Did your sister break it? Tell Mammy. Tell the truth and shame the devil. Remember, you won't be smacked if you tell the truth. Nice girls don't tell lies."

Claire hadn't come out of it unscathed, either.

Get some sleep, Amy. I'll handle it.

Maurice, the fixer, the mender of broken bones, would solve everything – the blind would see, the lame would walk. There were things he'd never rectify, though.

Maurice's eyes began to blur but he didn't want to close the book. He had to keep reading. If he put out the light he'd be alone in the darkness with his thoughts. He wouldn't let himself dwell on the scene that had passed with his wife. He'd wanted her to stay and have a proper talk. He wanted to tell her that he loved her, that he was doing his best to redeem himself. That things between them would be different from now on. Maybe this trouble with Claire would bring them closer?

You're not God.

What a thing to say! Did she want him to give up like she had? No, he couldn't fix everything. He knew his limitations. He hadn't the power to solve every problem but he had the will to try. Wasn't that the crux of the matter?

He hadn't wanted to talk about Jack and Claire and Sarah; they needed to discuss their own relationship. Not the right time, she'd have said. When would it be the right time? Tomorrow night, she'd dress up and go to the theatre with him. Could they get through a night out together without a dispute? Be pleasant and easy in each other's company? For how long was it possible to keep up the sham?

Twenty-eight

Jack left the veterinary clinic after a long and embarrassing conversation with Maurice, finally accepting what he had to do. He got into his Merc, took out his mobile and rang the office.

"Fergus? Something's cropped up. An emergency. I have to go home for an hour or two. Yes, I know you're tied up. Can you not send Robbie? All right, phone the Lally woman and reschedule the appointment. Why not? I'm telling you I can't. This is an emergency. OK, OK, cool it! I'll call to her first. Just the front windows? Leaded glass in the top panes? Have you discussed price with her? Fine, I'll do it. Yes, I have the brochures here with me. Talk to you later."

Two hours – he could make it home in two hours.

* * *

Sarah was cleaning the bath. She had the radio on in the bedroom and the door open so she could listen to Pat Kenny. He was interviewing a junior doctor: staff shortages, seventeen-hour shifts, incredible fatigue, unbearable pressures, salaries a pittance. The harassed interviewee was proposing that the Minister of Health should spend one day in a hospital, shadowing a doctor, so that he could experience, at first-hand, the hardships. Sarah agreed. The interview ended and The Beatles' familiar voices sang out, telling her all she needed was love.

A movement behind her. She swung around. Jack, his face ashen, stood there, gaping at her.

She got up from her knees. "What's up? Are you home for lunch? I wasn't expecting you – don't know what's in the fridge. I was going to go to the supermarket this afternoon."

He shifted uneasily. "Don't worry about lunch. I have to talk to you."

She turned away and squeezed the sponge into the sink.

"Sarah, can you stop what you're doing and come downstairs?"

She turned on the hot-water tap and rinsed the sponge.

"Sarah?"

"Go on down. I'll be there in a minute."

A heaviness in her chest forced deep breaths. Jack's appearance home at this hour of the day spelled trouble. Big trouble. She opened the medicine cabinet over the bath and took out the Rescue Remedy.

It was crucial she remained calm.

"All I can say is I'm sorry. Dreadfully sorry. I never meant to hurt you, Sarah."

She bit her lower lip. No need to say anything yet. Let him flounder on.

"I don't know why it happened – I didn't plan it."

She kept her eyes averted.

"I know how stupid I've been. Incredibly stupid."

She thought of other words: vain, conceited, selfish.

"Can you forgive me?"

Sarah stared at the calendar on the kitchen wall.

"Please, Sarah. You know that I love you – you and the kids mean everything to me."

"Where did I hear that before?"

"You're the most important thing in my life, Sarah."

"Am I? Am I really?" Deadpan.

He pulled his chair closer. "You know you are."

"Words, words, words. All I know is that you say one thing and do another. It can't go on like this."

"It won't. I swear it. It's over." He went to take her hand but she pulled away.

"Over?"

"Yes, finished completely. I'm so sorry, Sarah. I'll never do it again."

"Who is she?"

"It doesn't matter. She's not important."

"Is she not? And who *is* important, Jack? You?"

"No, no, I didn't mean that like it sounded. Sarah, please don't make this harder."

"Harder for whom, Jack?"

She had learned how to play the game but it wasn't, as John Lennon maintained, easy.

"I'm sorry, I'm genuinely sorry and I promise –"

"What, Jack? You promise to be faithful for the future? You promise never to stray again?"

"Yes, yes."

"A perfect confession, Jack. Now you want absolution?" She banged the table.

He drew back, startled.

"You expect me to *forgive* you?"

"Not expect – hope."

"What would you like me to say, Jack? That everything's fine again? Forget that it ever happened?"

"If you can, Sarah. Please, please, try."

"Tell me who she is."

"Why? What difference does it make? It's over. She's a thing of the past."

A thing. An object. An expendable commodity. "Tell me, Jack. I need to know."

"It won't help matters."

"I'll be the judge of that. Now, tell me."

"I can't."

Sarah got up from the table. "Discussion's over."

"Wait, wait, Sarah. I can't tell you who it is because I don't want to add to your hurt."

"You're such a gobshite," she said so softly he could barely make out her words. "I don't know if I'll forgive you, Jack. I don't think I can. What I've known for too long is that I can't trust you."

"But —"

"Don't interrupt. I'm not going to stand here and listen to your abject apologies because they mean nothing. Nothing. Sorry is easy to say, Jack. You said it the last time and the time before that. I don't believe a word out of your mouth any more, so don't insult my intelligence by making promises you won't keep."

"Sarah, what do you want me to do?' he pleaded. "I'll do anything."

"Your only hope now is to come clean with me. Tell me who the woman is."

Her placid tone frightened him. He cleared his throat nervously. "Claire."

"Claire?" Sarah squealed. "Claire Shiels?"

"Don't look at me like that, please."

"Amy's sister. You were with that *bitch*?" She flew around the table and smacked him hard in the face.

He rubbed his cheek.

Sarah's hand stung from the slap. "How could you? How could you, Jack? Claire Shiels! Dear God, why her? Why that scheming bitch? Why?"

His shoulders sagged.

"Does Amy know?" She shook him. "Does Amy know?"

"Yes," he mumbled.

"Since when? Answer me, Jack. Amy knows since when?"

"Last night."

Her fingers itched to slap him again.

"She called over to see Claire —"

"Poor Amy. My God, how she must be suffering. You cowardly shite!"

"Sarah —"

"That's the *only* reason you're here now, telling me all this. You wouldn't have said a word. You'd have kept on screwing that slut but you were found out. You slime!"

She ran to the sink and poured herself a large glass of water. She shook all over as she swilled down mouthfuls.

"Sarah, it's not like you think. I'd decided long ago to give her up."

She dropped the glass into the enamel sink and it smashed into smithereens. "Long ago? How long ago? A week? A month? You've been with that woman for exactly how long, Jack?"

"Only a few weeks, Sarah. No time at all."

"Since when?" she spat.

"Since the last night of the play."

A wave of nausea churned in the pit of her stomach. "The night you helped at the door?" She wanted to scream, to throw something at him but she couldn't muster the strength to turn from the sink and face him. Couldn't bear to see his cowed expression. "Jesus, you betrayed me on my own doorstep – my drama club – how low are you willing to stoop? There I was oblivious, backstage cueing the cast, while you were out at the front of the hall making up to that cheap whore! Who else knows? Clodagh Heffernan, she *must* know. She must have seen. Oh, God! "

"There was nothing to see. Nothing happened that night, Sarah. I bumped into her by accident a few days later. You've got to believe me. It's the truth, I swear it."

"The truth is something that's in short supply in this house." She marched to the kitchen door.

"Sarah, where are you going?" Alarm.

"Upstairs to pack." Steely voice.

"You're not leaving? You can't leave."

"I've no intention. *You*'re the one who's leaving. I'm going to pack your stuff. Then you're out of here."

"But where will I go? Sarah, please, please. Don't do this. I love you, Sarah. You can't put me out. Where will I go?"

"To hell, Jack. Go to hell." She smiled sourly. "Or there's always your mobile home."

Twenty-nine

"We both knew when we got into this that it wouldn't last." Jack felt inept, inadequate for the task. Couldn't wait to say his piece and get away.

Claire, sitting on the couch a few feet away from him, quietly seethed.

"It's not as if I made you any promises." No argument. This wasn't as bad as he'd feared. He became more confident. "We both knew the score, Claire." He took out his wallet and handed her an envelope.

"What's this, Jack? Pay-off time?"

"The plane and theatre tickets for next weekend – you might as well use them."

She tore the envelope down the middle and then into tiny pieces while he watched. "We were supposed to go to London together."

"Yes, but under the circumstances, it's not a good idea." He regretted the waste – could have used those as a peace offering to Sarah.

"What circumstances are they, Jack?" She wasn't letting him off the hook that easily.

"Amy finding out for one thing. Maurice is on my case too. It's not worth the hassle. What more can I say?"

"You say it best," she lilted, "when you say . . . ah, forget it."

"Look, honey, it was great while it lasted. We both enjoyed ourselves but it's over now."

"Too right."

He was puzzled.

"You don't call all the shots, Jack." She stretched to get her colourless nail polish from the sideboard. Applying the strokes evenly, she blew on her nails to hasten the drying process. "I'm ready to end it; that's why I sent for you."

"Sent for me? I'm not an errand boy."

"That's precisely what you are, Jack. To tell you the truth, I was pleased when Amy found out. My sister can talk a lot of bull, but sometimes, on a rare occasion, she hits the mark. Our affair was a shoddy business, when you boil it down."

"Shoddy?" He was touchy now.

"Mmh." She yawned. "And it was getting repetitive. I was a bit bored."

"You were not, Claire. That's a lie. We both enjoyed it. We were great in bed together. You've said that often enough. OK, it wasn't the love affair of the century but we had a good time."

The pompous pig. "It amused me for a while."

"Amused you?"

"Mmh, a good time-filler. That's what you were for me, Jack – a stopgap."

"Of all the –"

"If you don't mind, Jack. I'd like to go to bed now – alone." She yawned again. "I'm exhausted. Shut the door on your way out, please."

"Stop acting like this, Claire. I know you're angry but –"

"What's the matter? Oh, I get it. I'm supposed to be broken-hearted. Forget it, sunshine. I've known too many like you. And, no doubt, I'll meet a few more before I'm finished. Go to any of the clubs in town – men on the make like you are two a penny."

"But we were fond of each other," he protested.

"We used each other, Jack. Don't embellish it."

"You're not that hard, Claire."

"I'm not that easy, either."

"Don't be flippant. I'd like us to deal with this in as civilised a fashion as possible. I can't see you any more. Now, it would be nice if we could end it as civilly as –"

She laughed.

"Claire, you're a reasonable woman."

"Very."

"I have my family to think about."

"Yes, darling, you do."

Why was she being so facetious? "In all honesty, this would have played itself out in time."

"Quite frankly, darling, it already had."

"Claire, I'm leaving now. It would be better if we avoided one another for the moment. I don't know when I'll talk to you again."

"Tomorrow, Jack. I'm going to visit Sarah to see how she feels."

He grabbed her by the wrist. "No, you are not. I won't have you next, nigh or near my family. Don't threaten me like this."

Now he was showing his true colours. "Jack, relax. *In all honesty* it's only fair to your wife to let her know where she stands. I'll tell her that I'm finished with you, naturally, but she should be made aware of what kind of a man she married. Sarah will deal with it perfectly – the woman who has all the answers."

He tightened his grip. "You're too late, Claire. Sarah knows about us."

Her eyes narrowed. "You told her?"

"Yes, everything."

"My, my, a perfect act of contrition." Claire removed his hand from her arm.

"Sarah understands," he bluffed. "She's a very strong woman."

She's a moron, Claire decided.

"I'm not saying it will be plain sailing but Sarah and I will work it out."

"I'm delighted for you, Jack. You've had your cake and eaten it, haven't you? Now, like a good little boy, back to wifey."

"Don't act the role of the woman scorned!"

"I wouldn't dream of it, Jack. I'm the one who's had a lucky escape." She patted his shoulder in a condescending way.

He stood up and slowly put on his jacket. "I won't leave on a bitter note. We're mature adults."

Mature? He was hilarious.

"Thanks for everything, Claire. I mean that."

"Don't mention it, darling. The pleasure was half mine!"

Her laughter echoed down the corridor as he made his way out into the night. Back to the Bed and Breakfast.

* * *

It was Saturday morning before the two women met. Sarah put the flowers on the kitchen table and gave Amy a hug. "It's all right. I appreciate how you felt. It was awful for you."

"I didn't know what to do, Sarah. I couldn't have told you."

"It's dreadful that you and Maurice were entangled in the whole mess. You were nothing but innocent bystanders. Whatever Maurice said to him, by the way, seems to have had some effect. He was more remorseful than usual. I think he got a right land when you found out. You precipitated their break-up."

Wasn't it sad that it had to come to that? "Thanks for coming over, Sarah. I was worried. And thanks for the flowers."

"I would have called earlier but I had loads to do these past few days. I sent him off with a flea in his ear and two suitcases of clothes."

"Where has he gone?"

"Haven't a clue. Not to *her* place, anyway."

"Claire has a lot to answer for. I'm not going to attempt to defend her conduct." Amy knew that her sister, behind a façade of indifference, had been hurt, very hurt – but that would hardly be much consolation to Sarah. "I'm trying desperately to hate her but I can't."

"She's your family."

"Yes, and I'm ashamed of her."

"We don't choose our relatives. You're not responsible for her behaviour any more than I am for Jack's. But, Amy, I *do* hate her."

Amy nodded.

"After the bugger left, I called a locksmith."

"You changed the locks?"

"Damned right. He has no access to the house now. He can

come knocking but he won't get in. I won't even answer the phone to him – mind you, he's only rung once. I slammed down the receiver."

"But the kids, Sarah?"

"I've sent them off to my sister's for the weekend. Avril adores the girls – she's Anna's godmother. Helen loves going there too – they've a well-stocked playroom and Ger will have his cousin Tommy to play with."

"What did you tell them?"

"That Jack was away on business; they're used to that. I didn't say anything to Avril. My sister has the perfect marriage. No kidding – they still hold hands and look into one another's eyes. Dominic adores the ground she walks on. Anyhow, there's no reason to tell Avril until I decide what I'm doing."

"And what's that?"

"Nothing for the moment. I'm going to let him stew."

"But sooner or later, Sarah, you'll have to do something."

"Ah, I'll take him back when I'm good and ready. He needs his knuckles rapped. He has to stop taking me for granted. Will I fill the kettle?"

"Yeah, do." Amy lit a cigarette and watched her friend make the coffee. If anyone else did that in her kitchen she'd be annoyed but Sarah and herself were more like family. That was the awful thing: she felt much closer to Sarah than she did to her sister. "He has to stop fooling around. I know you say you've got used to his philandering but –"

"You do. You actually do get used to it. The first time – at least it was the first time I found out – was five years ago. I was completely gutted. That was the real reason I went for therapy."

"I had no idea."

"Why dump on you?"

"It wouldn't have been dumping, Sarah. Friends share problems. I'd have been more than happy to try to help – to listen at least."

"You know misery is a dangerous pastime. You can end up enjoying it, wallowing in it."

"Therapy." Amy joined her at the sink to put water in a vase. "I thought it was bereavement counselling after your brother's death."

"It was that too. Bereavement covers a lot of areas. Losing trust is one of them. Anyhow, she helped me to focus on what it was I wanted. I needed to get away to clear my head. I took the kids to Courtown for two weeks, hoping that a holiday would take my mind off my troubles."

"And did it?"

"No, but the kids had a whale of a time. I had to protect them, Amy. They adore Jack. It's not their fault that their father can't behave himself. Whatever goes on between us has nothing – absolutely nothing – to do with them. They have to be kept out of it."

Amy wholeheartedly agreed. Children should never be used as pawns. She arranged the flowers in the vase and placed it on the windowsill.

"Jack behaved himself for about two years after that, as far as I know, then there was the secretary. Classic, isn't it? That lasted about three months."

"He's an awful fool."

"He can't help himself. Monogamy doesn't suit him. But this time he's gone too far. Now part of me wants revenge. But having considered and dismissed the Lorena Bobbit method, I'll opt for Maurice."

"Pardon?"

"Maurice could neuter him. Isn't that how they make tomcats stay at home, stop chasing all the females in the neighbourhood?"

"He'll get fat and lazy," Amy warned her, smiling.

"Better and better!"

"You're great the way you can make light of it." Amy took the milk from the fridge.

"What else is there to do? I've been through the anger and resentment routine and it's a waste of time and energy, Amy. I have two alternatives: I can separate from him for good or I can try to make it work."

"How can you make it work? You can't change people, Sarah. Jack is Jack."

"That's just it, but like I told you, I don't want to lose him. I still love him." She set the cups of coffee on the table and they both sat down. "Enough about me. How did last night go?"

"*An Ideal Husband?* Brilliant production."

"Sparkling wit?"

Amy lit a cigarette. "Yes, but much meatier than *The Importance,* in my opinion. I don't think you'd have been in the mood for it – a bit too close to the bone. The heroine ended up learning to accept her husband's flaws."

"Depressing!"

"Maurice enjoyed it, but he wanted a full discussion afterwards. We had a drink in the bar and he was all for a complete analysis of the plot; tried to insinuate our situation – I wasn't up to it. "

"Yeah," Sarah agreed, "there's only so much talk you can take. What about France, Amy?"

"I've been dawdling up to now. I tried to put my mother's story to the back of my mind; dwell on other things, but it keeps needling me. So, yesterday I phoned Catherine. She got the address of the medical centre from Wendy Barrett. When I've made my travel arrangements, Wendy's going to contact Henry Edwards by way of an introduction for me. I'm phoning the Novotel in La Rochelle this evening."

"Why there?"

"It looks nice – big, modern, air-conditioned. It's beside a park, not far from the harbour. Catherine thinks quite a few business people stay there so it won't look too odd if I'm on my own. I just hope they have a vacancy."

* * *

Sylvia continued writing as her client talked on. She noted the fidgety movements and the fast talking.

"Claire needs a good kick up the bum," Amy said angrily. "She doesn't think like I do – I can see that now. She simply couldn't understand why I was so annoyed with her. Despite the fact that we were brought up together she inhabits a different planet. Is that normal? Sisters being so different? I mean why is she the way she is? OK, OK, I know it's me we're supposed to be analysing here but my sister is my sister and I suppose she's part of the picture . . . she's been a big part of my life. She has been a good sister – I couldn't say anything else but this isn't the first time she has landed me in shit . . ." Amy broke off as the truth of what she had just said hit her. Claire had let her down before.

"When you were children?" Sylvia prompted.

"Yes," Amy said slowly, the scene materialising before her eyes.

"She broke the kitchen window and my mother was furious – I told you how she used to overreact. She charged down the garden after the two of us with a broom, screaming at us to tell the truth about the accident. Claire denied it. She stood and stared into my mother's eyes and lied. She didn't even blush. She was able to face my mother down. She walked away and let me take the blame."

"No, Amy," Sylvia said softly. "You let yourself take the blame."

Amy felt the tears sting.

"What happened then? Did your mother punish you?"

"She broke the broom handle over my back." Her eyes glazed. "My father took me to the doctor that night; said I'd got a whack in school playing camogie. The doctor believed him." She rummaged in her handbag for a tissue and then, very quietly, blew her nose.

"Still, that's all water under the bridge now."

"Is it?"

"Yes, we were just kids."

Sylvia nodded but she recognised the pain.

"But Claire's an adult now and this time her lies were much more dangerous. This time she almost wrecked a marriage – but she won't face up to what she's done and she's put me in one of the most difficult situations of my life. Luckily Sarah doesn't blame me for . . ."

"Why should Sarah blame you, Amy? You've done nothing wrong. There you go again, taking responsibility for other people's behaviour."

Amy smiled. "Are you giving out to me?"

The counsellor smiled back. "Yes, but sometimes that's my job too. Let's get back to our earlier discussion. You've decided to go to France?"

"You think I'm mad, don't you? Pursuing a story that's over fifty years old. I do understand that I should be able to let it go but there's this . . . urge, a compulsion forcing me on. Every time I think I'm beginning to put the whole thing out of my mind, back it comes – the anger, the frustration and the bitterness at my mother. If going to France means that I might get to the bottom of the story and that goes some way to explain everything, then I think I should go." She looked to Sylvia for support. The counsellor made no comment, just scribbled away in her notebook. "It can't make matters any worse, can it?"

"Follow your instincts, Amy."

"I'm worried about Dad too. He hasn't been well lately and I don't want to worry him with this as he might get worse and . . ."

"Amy, let your sister look out for your father for the few days when you're away. He has *two* daughters."

"Oh, Claire hasn't shirked her duty to Dad," Amy interrupted, anxious to be fair. "She's always been good to him and she helped with Mam's funeral and all that. She won't mind keeping an eye on him. There's no problem there."

"Good," Sylvia replied. "It shouldn't be too much bother for her, anyway. After all, she's going to have a lot more time on her hands now, isn't she?"

Thirty

"He had a little turn during the night, Mrs Kennedy, but there's no need for alarm," the nurse assured Amy as she showed her up to her father's bedroom on the first floor.

"Was it another stroke?"

"A very slight one, the doctor came this morning and changed his tablets. He'll be all right but we're keeping him in bed for a few days' rest."

"I've booked for a trip abroad," Amy explained, "maybe I should cancel it."

"There's no need; he's not in any immediate danger. His speech is a bit slurred, that's all."

Wasn't that enough? "And what about paralysis? After the last stroke he couldn't move his right arm."

"No, his limbs are fine. Believe me, it was a very mild attack."

Amy went into the room and found her father propped up on the pillows. He smiled lopsidedly and she tried not to show her dismay.

"Hello, Dad." She leaned over the bed and kissed his forehead, her eyes averted from his crooked mouth.

"Amy, my girl, how are you? I'm glad you're here."

His voice was thick-tongued.

"How are you feeling, Dad?" An idiotic question, she knew.

"A little bit shaky, that's all." It was a huge effort for him to speak. "Nurse Cooper here is minding me like a mother hen."

The nurse smiled in acknowledgement and took away an empty medicine bottle. "I'll leave you to it," she whispered to Amy and quietly left the room.

"Dad, I came to say goodbye. I'm off to France tomorrow morning."

"France, eh?"

"Yes. For a week."

"That's good."

He didn't sound as if he meant it. "You know why I'm going, Dad?"

"You've found out something?" he asked cautiously. Months ago when his daughter had first brought up the subject, Joe had consoled himself with the thought that France was a big country and that Amy would never be able to locate the Edwardses. His presumption had been ill-founded.

"Catherine Cole got me an address for –"

She'd nearly blurted *Henry Edwards*, momentarily forgetting that her father was totally unaware that the infant had survived. He couldn't be given a shock like that. She'd have to be very careful what she said from now on. Amy regretted that she'd told her father *any*thing, but what was done was done.

"An address for Jane Edwards." She kept her voice as light as she could manage. "She's living in La Rochelle."

"How did Catherine discover her whereabouts?"

"A friend of hers. I met her while I was in England."

Only a weak intake of breath indicated that he'd heard.

"I may pay her a visit."

Her father closed his eyes.

"Would you prefer if I didn't, Dad?" She took his wrinkled hand and stroked it tenderly. "I won't go if you don't want me to."

Joe opened his eyes, at first finding it hard to focus, then he stared hard at his daughter, scrutinising her face. "Amy, love, you must do what you must do."

"Not if it's going to affect you in a bad way, Dad."

"It's not me I'm worrying about." Joe sighed softly. "You may find out things you won't like."

228

She pressed his hand again. "I'm prepared for that."

"Are you?"

"Yes, I believe I am. It wasn't a pretty story – I know that much but there's so much more I don't know. I feel that I have to do something, Dad. There are too many loose ends."

"Wrongs to be righted?"

"The truth about what happened to Mam is important for me."

"The truth," he repeated slowly.

"I need to know, Dad."

"Go to France then, if it will help you."

"I'll come and see you as soon as I get back." She paused. "Dad, aren't *you* curious about the whole business?"

"No. Your mother told me as much as I needed or wanted to know. As far as I'm concerned, her story died with her."

"Oh, Dad, you *would* prefer if I didn't go on with this, wouldn't you?"

"Amy, I understand that you'll never rest easy until you put the pieces together."

"It's more than idle curiosity – I can't move on."

"Then go with my blessing."

"Thanks, Dad."

"And whatever you find out, try not to be too hard your mother."

His eyes closed again. Amy sat there for a few moments longer, listening to his breathing become deeper, heavier. She crept out of the room and let him sleep.

* * *

Maurice came into her bedroom early the next morning. "All packed?"

"Yes, the taxi will be here soon."

"Will you join me for a cup of coffee downstairs?"

"What about morning surgery? Won't you be late?"

"Rodney's swapped shifts with me."

"Oh?"

"I presumed I'd be driving you to the airport."

"No need, Maurice."

"Obviously not – you're all organised."

She ignored his wounded expression, his annoyance that she'd sprung yet another surprise on him. She hadn't told him about this trip until two days ago. She'd wanted it to be a *fait accompli* before he'd have the chance to voice his objections. As it happened, he'd said very little but there was no mistaking the undercurrent of hostility.

"I'll follow you down, Maurice, I just want to check my handbag – I always get hassled when I'm travelling – afraid that I'll forget something."

"We're all like that." He left the room and she heard him humming as he went downstairs. He was trying to make the best of it.

Maurice made the coffee. "How long did you say you'll be away?"

"A week. I've left the phone number of the Novotel on the hall table beside the phone. Maurice, would you do me a favour?"

"Sure."

"Would you find time to visit Dad when I'm gone? I'm worried about him."

"Of course."

"Thank you."

"No need to thank me, Amy. I'm fond of your father. I'd intended to go and see him."

His affability threw her. "I rang the Home earlier this morning and the matron said he was much better." She took a J-cloth from the sink-tidy and wiped the table where she'd spilt some coffee. "I wouldn't go if he was still bad," she added quickly, as she sat down again.

"Of course not. I'll call out there in a day or two and Claire will visit him too, rest assured."

"Yes."

Maurice stood up and went to the window. "Clear skies, no sign of rain. It's a nice day for travelling."

"Yes."

"And your train from Paris is at what time?"

"Around six."

"That means you'll be hanging around for a few hours."

"I couldn't get tickets for the earlier train."

He came back to the table and sat down opposite her. "Well, I suppose if you have to kill time, Paris is the place to be."

She couldn't make out his expression. He was staring through her; his eyes round, his jaw set. Amy pushed the coffee cup away from her. The bitter taste was making her feel sick. The ticking of the kitchen clock got louder and louder.

"Maurice, you must be wondering why I'm going to La Rochelle?"

He stared at her.

"It's not just a holiday . . . something has come up."

He continued staring.

"There's somebody I have to visit."

"I see."

He didn't see at all.

"I wasn't going to say anything but maybe I should. I've found out something about my mother and –"

"Amy, I don't want to know," he cut in abruptly.

"But you're always telling me that I keep you in the dark," she retorted, defensively.

"And so you do."

The petulance was back in his voice. His effort at civility hadn't lasted long. "I'm willing to explain everything to you, Maurice."

"Amy, your mother is dead and buried – gone from your life."

"Our parents don't go from our lives."

"They do if we let them," he argued. "We're never going to agree on this."

She tried to light a cigarette but her hands shook. Every time she attempted to talk to her husband it ended up like this.

"Maurice, I *have* to tell you: years ago, while she was living in England, my mother was accused in the wrong of doing something unspeakable and I feel –"

"Unspeakable?" He jumped up from the table. "Then *don't* speak

231

about it," he shouted. "I don't want to listen. Leave me out of this, Amy. Go off on one of your wild-goose chases if you must but I'm not getting involved. It's *here* you should be, at home, looking after your own affairs – not flitting around the continent on some pie-in-the-sky whim. You'd want to get your priorities in order. You're obsessed with your mother and all the imaginary things she did to you."

"Maurice, I wasn't *imagining* anything."

"You've always blamed your mother for what she put you through. You've used it as an excuse all through our marriage."

"An excuse?"

"Face it, Amy. You can't always lay the blame for your misery on other people."

"That's not fair. How can you say that, Maurice? This is not about blame. I only want to understand –"

"Understand? What? Let me tell you a few home truths. None of us had a perfect childhood. We all have to grow up sometime and accept responsibility for our behaviour. Your mother wasn't any worse than most. You're too wrapped up in yourself to see that. There's nothing worse than self-pity. I can't stand it."

"Maurice –"

"Stop acting the martyr, Amy. It's very hard to live with a saint."

"Maurice, please –"

The doorbell rang.

"That's your cab. You'd better go."

Amy grabbed her hand luggage as her husband carried the suitcase out to the driveway. She got into the back of the cab and closed the door. When she turned to wave goodbye to her husband, the front door was shut.

Thirty-one

Amy was inwardly fuming and, although the eighty-minute flight to Charles de Gaulle airport was relaxing, it didn't lessen her fury. She nibbled at the airline food, attempted the *Crosaire* in *The Irish Times* but couldn't sufficiently concentrate.

The more she thought about what happened this morning, the more incensed she became. Her conversation with Maurice had begun no differently from any other time – stiff, strained, but courteous, at least. Then, the moment she'd mentioned her mother, he'd erupted.

Not easy living with a saint.

Of all the preposterous things to say. If it wasn't so outlandish, it would be laughable. *She* was acting the martyr! He was the one who always went on about how hard he worked, how he never had a minute to himself, how he had to pay for everything. Maybe he was resentful that she was taking this break?

Had he always been like that? Laying traps of guilt to catch her? It wasn't Amy who was the martyr. Maurice saw himself as the sacrificial lamb – the one who moiled and toiled, the breadwinner, the one who couldn't be done without. But we can all be done without. He hadn't learned that yet.

She'd oust him out of her head. She'd leave her domestic troubles behind for the next week and concentrate on the job in hand. She passed the tray back to the stewardess. They'd be touching down in ten minutes. Amy would make her way to the train station, find a nice little bistro and have lunch. She'd be able to see the sights as she taxied through Paris. And she could people-gaze. Amy loved watching the French – they were so classy.

* * *

She was jostled and elbowed, pushed and shoved by the teeming throng in the Gare Montparnasse. This was exactly the type of situation Amy detested: crowds, noise, heat, bedlam.

Platform 4 for La Rochelle, she discovered after she had managed to worm her way through the throng staring up at the large electronic timetable. 8369 TGV. 18.50 departure.

Amy followed the crowd, dragging the suitcase and trying not to drop her hand luggage as she battled along. She looked up at the numbers on the first carriage and re-examined the tickets. Typical! She was in one of the last carriages.

The train was spotless, spacious and very comfortable. She had managed to reserve a seat in a *compartiment fumeurs* so she was finally able to light up, having been sorely deprived on the plane and in the taxi. At 18.50 on the dot, the train pulled out of the station – SNCF efficiency. On the continent, time was of the essence – a minute late and you'd miss your transport.

The evening sun shone in a blue-and-white dappled sky as the train sped by. Amy admired the landscape which was neat, groomed, symmetrical: luscious green copses, farms, tiny villages, lakes, multicoloured crops of gold, yellow and green. All was order and harmony.

At eight o'clock the train made its first stop: St Pierre des Corps. Office buildings and towering apartment blocks were all that were visible from the station.

Further south, as the train glided smoothly and speedily on, Amy was charmed by field after field of sunflowers – masses and masses of them with their cheery brown and yellow faces, dancing and frolicking in the sunshine. She was sure that the sensational sight of the sunflowers would remain in her memory long after this trip. She had calmed down considerably and was beginning to enjoy herself.

She started to read some of the brochures and the activities they offered: the aquarium, boat trips to the islands, a night at the casino.

Would she actually do any of these? On her own? Maybe not. It didn't matter – her objective was to meet Henry. But she would be able to spend a few days doing nothing. Just to sit in the open-air cafés sipping coffees, watching the world go by, relishing the sights, the smells and the ambience – that's what she was looking forward to.

Three more stops at Chatellerault, Poitiers and Niort and finally the train arrived in La Rochelle.

* * *

The Novotel was a new, modern, glass-fronted building situated in pretty gardens in the Avenue de la Porte Neuve. The street bordered the magnificent Parc Charruyer but it would be morning before Amy could investigate. She was tired after her day's travel and anxious to get to her room.

"Trois cent vingt-six, Madame." The receptionist turned to the pigeon-holes, took a key and an envelope and handed them to Amy. *"Un message pour vous. Il est arrivé cet après-midi."*

"Merci."

"L'ascenseur se trouve là-bas, derrière vous." The girl pointed to the lift.

"Le petit déjeuner est à quelle heure?"

"Sept heures à neuf heures trente mais vous pouvez le commander dans votre chambre, si vous voulez."

"Bon, merci encore."

Yes, she would have breakfast in her room, she decided as she stepped into the lift. She pressed 3 and the doors shut. She stared at the envelope in her hand. Henry Edwards? She hadn't expected to hear from him so soon. Perhaps this would be easier than she'd thought.

235

Dear Mrs Kennedy,

Wendy Barrett has asked me to welcome you to La Rochelle. Hope you had a pleasant journey. I'll be in touch tomorrow and we'll make an arrangement. Perhaps, if you have no other plans, you could join me for dinner tomorrow evening? It would be a great pleasure for me.

Looking forward to meeting you,

Henry Edwards.

Amy, having read the note, went to the mini bar and took out a miniature bottle of cognac. What did she make of it? The writing was a bit formal but, as he didn't know her, that was understandable.

Brandy in hand, she stretched out full length on the couch. The suite was very comfortable: bathroom, separate toilet, double bed *and* a couch. Modern and bright and clean – the way she'd love her home to be.

She reread the message. He seemed to be sincere about wanting to meet her. Now that it was all happening she couldn't quite believe it. It was exciting – an adventure – but it was also extremely scary. It was one thing plotting and planning in Dublin but now that she was here on his doorstep, she was frightened.

The only comforting thought was that Henry Edwards hadn't a clue who she was. He was just doing the Good Samaritan. He wasn't to know what she was really up to. That's what made it so horrible – Amy hated duplicity.

Thirty-two

Amy opened the bedroom curtains. Blue sky and sunshine. At least the weather was welcoming! Her room overlooked the flower-filled garden and the carpark. She had decided to spend the first day exploring the town on foot. She'd avail of public transport and taxis if she travelled farther afield – the notion of continental driving held no appeal for her. After her shower and a liberal application of suntan lotion, Amy sprayed mosquito repellent all over her body. A knock at her door and breakfast arrived.

She'd finished her second coffee and had just lit her first cigarette of the day when the phone rang. She grabbed an ash-tray and picked up the receiver.

"Madame Kennedy? Vous avez un visiteur."

"Oui?"

"Monsieur Edwards vous attend au bar."

She inhaled loudly.

"Ça va, Madame? Ça vous convient?"

It was an effort to answer. *"Oui, bien sûr, je serai là dans cinq minutes. Merci."* She replaced the receiver.

Henry Edwards was waiting for her downstairs at the bar. Jesus! What was he doing here? She ran to the bathroom mirror. No, the strappy red sundress did nothing for her. Her arms looked too big. What would she wear? Her white skirt and black T-shirt? No, it was too hot for a waisted skirt. Her loose mauve trousers maybe? Or the

237

blue dress? It had short sleeves. Her clothes, on the open wardrobe rail, seemed hopelessly wrong.

Five minutes, she'd said. She had to hurry – he was waiting for her. Henry Edwards was no doubt a busy man and here she was behaving like a giddy schoolgirl. It was very decent of him to have called this soon to meet her and she couldn't keep him hanging on while she decided what ensemble to choose. What did Henry Edwards care if her upper arms were too fat? She grabbed her handbag and her room key and hurriedly left the room.

He was sitting on a high stool by the small circular bar. Dark curly hair, broad shoulders, pale grey suit. Immaculate. Amy nervously approached. "Doctor Edwards?"

He stood up to greet her. "Henry, please, let's forego the formalities. Amy, I presume. *Enchanté*!"

Beautiful voice, deep and smooth. Cultured accent. He was very tall and lean. Big brown eyes guaranteed to melt any woman's heart. His handsome face was sallow, clean-shaven. His expression was open and friendly. Nervously she fiddled with her handbag strap.

To her surprise, he kissed her on both cheeks and then on the right one again. "This is the Rochelais way!"

She blushed.

"Will you join me for coffee?"

He was so polite, so engaging and personable that she doubted if anyone had ever refused him *any*thing. "Thank you."

He signalled to the barman and was served immediately. Something in his demeanour commanded respect.

"It's very good of you to have taken the trouble to contact me so promptly," Amy said, as she sat up on a high stool.

"I don't start at the clinic until eleven today, so I thought I'd take the opportunity to call to meet you. I was pleased when Wendy phoned me. She knows I love to see people from home."

Ireland wasn't home for him, Amy reflected, but it was gratifying to think that he made no differentiation.

"Do you know Wendy well?"

"No, I'm a friend of a friend. Catherine Cole introduced us recently when I visited her home. I'm from Dublin."

"Yes, yes, of course," he answered hurriedly. "Wendy said. I was wondering about your accent – couldn't place it for a moment."

"The Dublin accent is fairly recognisable, I'm told," Amy replied gauchely.

"You sound a bit like Mary Robinson – same intonation."

The former Irish president?

"Catherine Cole," he went on, unaware that he'd amused her, "I don't know her at all. Wendy told me she worked with my father but that was before my time. Of course the old man was very famous in medical circles."

He offered her a cigarette which she accepted.

"My father died ten years ago. You knew that?" He leaned towards her and lit her cigarette. "Of course, Wendy would have filled you in. After my divorce I moved here to La Rochelle and then, shortly after my father's death, my mother invested in a property nearby."

"It must be nice for you to have her here." Inane.

"She doesn't live here all year round. We kept the family home in Surrey and a skeleton staff. Mother moves home for the winter. She leads a double life, as she jokes."

Death, divorce, emigration – he'd covered them all in less than a minute.

"You live with her?"

"No, but we see one another almost every day. I have an apartment over the clinic. It's convenient and it suits my needs. My mother lives alone – apart from a housekeeper. Old Grace Thornton has been with the family now for over forty years."

He was describing a lifestyle far removed from Amy's experience: a privileged, wealthy world of big houses, villas, apartments, live-in staff. But there was nothing of the braggart about him, nothing boastful in his tone. People like Henry Edwards took it all as a matter of course.

"At this stage old Grace is more of a companion than a servant. Of course my mother always treated her staff very well."

All except *one*.

"My mother's very easy to look after and she's generally quite well in spite of her advanced years."

Amy nodded politely. She wasn't at all sure what to say next. The incongruity of it. She'd come to France with the explicit purpose of meeting this man and finding out all she could. Now, here he was, sitting next to her, ready to tell all, to give her unsolicited information, to talk about his family and his work and his life, no holds barred – and *she* sat there dumbly.

"Are your parents still alive, Amy?"

The suddenness of the question startled her. "My father is – he's an invalid now and lives in a Nursing Home."

"Very sad," he clucked sympathetically. "And your mother?"

Her mother? In his innocence he asked about her mother – a woman who was destroyed by his family – used, abused and discarded. "My mother died a year ago," she said quietly.

"It's hard losing a parent. I think when the second one dies it must be worse – makes one more aware of one's own mortality. Puts us in the front line, so to speak."

Bizarre conversation to be having after a few moments' acquaintance, although it didn't seem to faze Henry Edwards. She pushed herself to be more communicative. "Did you go on for medicine because of your father?"

"I suppose I did, actually. He left me a large legacy and I don't just mean money. Mother thinks I inherited his talent."

Now what? Before she'd time to formulate another question or come up with a relevant comment, he spoke again.

"Being the son of an eminent physician has its drawbacks. I'm content to be a general practitioner – my father was disappointed. He was sure I'd have specialised but ambition was never one of my virtues."

"It's not always a virtue," Amy said.

"Indeed not – my sentiments entirely."

His impish smile made Amy warm to him.

"How long will you stay in La Rochelle?"

"A week."

"That gives us ample time to get to know one another."

She felt like Judas Iscariot.

His mobile phone rang and, excusing himself, he answered. Once he spoke in French, he became spirited, excitable. She only caught half of what he gabbled into the mouthpiece.

"An emergency," he explained as he rang off. "One of my elderly patients has been taken to hospital – suspected heart attack. She's very highly-strung and is asking for me. I'll have to go, Amy. I'm most awfully sorry. I thought we'd have a longer chat."

"That's perfectly all right. I understand."

"So, how about tonight? Would you care to join me for dinner?"

"That would be lovely."

"Do you like shellfish? Seafood is the thing here."

"I can take it or leave it, to be honest."

"Well, there are plenty of alternatives. Suppose I drop by at, shall we say, eight o'clock?

Amy readily agreed. He stood up, shook hands, smiled and walked away. She sat at the bar for fifteen minutes more, staring into space, her coffee gone cold. She decided to go to her room and phone Sarah. She was dying to talk to someone.

"You've met him, Amy. That was quick." Sarah was excited. "What's he like?"

"Friendly and courteous. Easy. Mild-mannered."

"High praise. Come on, tell me more. What does he look like?"

"Very attractive. Dark hair. Tanned."

"French-looking? Yummy!"

"Yes, but he's decidedly English in his manner."

"Stuffy?"

"No, no, far from it. He couldn't have been nicer or more talkative. At the same time he's very genteel. I'm having dinner with him tonight."

"It's all arranged? That didn't take long. I'll say one thing for you, Amy – once you make up your mind, you don't mess about."

"He's picking me up at eight o'clock."

"So everything went OK? You got on well together?"

"Hard to say in such a short space of time but . . . yes, I think so. He went out of his way to be friendly."

"There, I told you – no hassle at all. You'll soon have him eating out of your hand."

"No hassle? Sarah, I could barely reply to the man. I sat here *umming* and *aahing*. He must take me for a moron. I was trying so hard not to say the wrong thing, not to give the game away, that all I could do was make dumb comments."

"I'm sure that's an exaggeration."

"It isn't. I don't think I can keep this up."

"Of course you can. Tonight will be easier."

"Easier?"

"If he's as chatty as you say he is, there'll be no problem getting all the low-down – candy from a baby."

"I wish I hadn't started this at all," Amy said despondently.

"But you just said that he was very nice."

"That's not the point. What if he knew why I'd really sought him out? What would he think if he knew I was spying? Do you think he'd be so sociable with me if he knew the truth? Can you imagine how he'd react if he found out that I was here to pry into his mother's affairs, Sarah?"

"Did he mention her?"

"In glowing terms. Then he spoke about his father."

"The mighty Valentine."

"He gave me the impression that his father was demanding, even overbearing. Told me he had a lot to live up to. Reading between the lines, I'd say their relationship hadn't been idyllic."

"God, more bloody family woes. How are you going to wangle a meeting with Jane Edwards?"

"Good question."

"Never mind, you'll cross that bridge when you come to it. Phone me tomorrow and let me know how things are going. You're really brave, Amy, the way you're handling all this."

"I don't feel brave. Anything but. What's new with you? Is Jack back home yet?"

"No way. He has to suffer a bit more yet – a few more days in the

B&B should do the trick. Oh, wait till you hear the latest! He sold the mobile home. The creep actually made a profit. Anyhow he's going to buy me a new car. Conscience money."

"Sarah, you're a caution! I'd better go. I'll check in with you again tomorrow. Is the morning the best time to get you?"

"It is, yeah. Hold on, Amy, I almost forgot to tell you. I had a card from Amsterdam yesterday."

"Clodagh? How is she getting on?"

"Terrific. In fact so well that she's decided to stay."

"What! Stay in Amsterdam? Are you serious?"

"She adores the place and she's made a load of friends – one special one, from what I can deduce. She'll phone me when she's found an apartment and a job. She's going to let her own house. Crazy, isn't it?"

"Crazy but wonderful," Amy replied.

* * *

She spent the morning in the old port. After visiting the Tour de la Chaine, she strolled along the Cours des Dames, pottering around the tourist shops. She bought a map and a guidebook on the area and lunched in a crêperie on the quayside. The *gouffres* stuffed with ham and mushrooms were delicious washed down with a sweet cider.

Amy called the waitress and ordered an espresso. She didn't feel too uncomfortable sitting on her own and nobody around seemed to pay any attention to her. She planned to spend the afternoon by the hotel pool, reading the novel she'd bought that morning.

Amy glanced at a middle-aged woman sitting at the table by the door. She had her hair pinned up, casually falling around her neck and the sunglasses perched on top of her head. She looked stunning and the whole effect seemed effortless. Amy envied the French their sense of style.

Most of the people eating here were French. That's what Amy liked about this place: *Les Français en vacances*. It gave much more of a taste of the country listening to the language being spoken everywhere. She loved the smell of garlic too and all the aromas of cooking. She leaned back in her chair and looked out at the boats. The colours seemed more vibrant in the sunshine. It was so picturesque. She'd have to pluck up her courage and book a trip to one of the islands. She could check the sailing times at the departure dock on her way back to the hotel.

Amy lit a cigarette. That was another thing she loved about France – everyone smoked. She didn't feel like a social pariah.

She wondered where Henry Edwards would bring her for dinner. There was no shortage of good restaurants. She'd overheard two people chatting at reception this morning. They'd gone into ecstasies about some place they'd been to last night. And on the evenings she had to dine alone she could stay in if she wanted – the Novotel was recommended in the brochures. But, somehow, she knew she'd venture out to try some of the other restaurants. She'd come this far on her own – and it wasn't as difficult as she'd feared.

She was beginning to feel at home which she usually never did when she was away – at least not for a few days. But there was something very relaxing and congenial about La Rochelle which helped to calm her a little. Although it didn't take from the fact that she was here on a mission – a mission that would inevitably plunge her into the very heart of her problems.

Thirty-three

Amy couldn't take her eyes off Henry Edwards as he scanned the wine list in *Le Cardinal*. He looked so sexy: grey streaks at his temples, beautiful full lips.

The elegant blonde owner knew Henry of old and had welcomed them most cordially, chuffed that one of her patrons had chosen *her* restaurant to entertain his foreign guest. She placed them at a centre table where they had ample opportunity to see and be seen. Amy liked the understated decor; pale peach colour on the walls and matching tablecloths. It wasn't a large establishment but mirrors gave the impression of greater space.

"Vous préféreriez le menu en anglais?" The owner suggested helpfully as she went to get it.

"Menus here are particularly difficult – lots of local dishes and you won't find those words in a dictionary," he explained to Amy. "Wendy mentioned that you speak French quite fluently."

"I wouldn't say that," Amy contradicted, "but I am very interested in the language. Still, you need to live in the country to be able to fully communicate – to understand nuances and innuendo!"

"Indeed." He smiled. "But a working knowledge certainly helps. They say you're truly fluent when you dream in French."

"And do *you?*"

"It depends on what I'm dreaming about!"

"I don't usually remember my dreams – except the ones I'm woken from abruptly." Amy buttered a chunk of bread. "It bugs me

245

when that happens – you know, you're in the middle of a glorious dream and something wakes you – just as you're getting to the good part!" She blushed. "I hate that, don't you?"

"It depends on *who* is waking me," he said with a wink.

Amy took a long sip of water and thought about lighting a cigarette. She hadn't bargained on such light-hearted banter coming from Henry Edwards but she welcomed it. Her tummy had been acting up all evening – a mixture of panic and guilt, she supposed. At least there was nothing threatening about this repartee. The arrival of the menus put a temporary halt to all conversation.

Amy followed Henry's recommendation and chose *foie gras* for a starter, while he tucked into a large plate of mussels.

"How's the Chablis?" he asked her.

"Divine. The food is gorgeous," she enthused. "Do you dine here frequently?"

"I come in once or twice a month, usually. Sometimes I go next door to *La Côte Boeuf*. It's very good, too. My mother likes to dine out in the evenings."

"Is that so?" Amy put down her glass. This was her chance. "You should have brought her along. I'd have liked to have met her."

There, she'd said it and her boldness surprised her.

"She had a prior engagement, unfortunately. Perhaps some other evening? What are your plans for tomorrow?"

"I was thinking of taking the boat to L'Île de Ré."

"You'll enjoy that." He wiped his mouth carefully with his napkin. "There are some lovely beaches and you'll like the villages – white houses with green shutters, flowers everywhere and the light is amazing. You'd get a much better idea of the island if you hired a car – or better still a bicycle."

"I haven't been on a bike for years – except in the gym! I can take a bus around the island and stop off wherever takes my fancy."

The main course arrived: grilled breast of duck for Amy and suckling pig for Henry.

"So, your mother lives in the town?" she asked, as she cut herself another piece of Brie from the cheese selection. France was not for diets!

"Yes, about five minutes from the centre."

"A town house?"

"No, it's a villa. Mother likes her comforts. She has two reception rooms downstairs, a large kitchen and adjoining dining-room. Five bedrooms, three bathrooms – plenty of space. She's used to that. The garden is on the small side but it's very secluded. Privacy is a must for my mother."

"It sounds wonderful," Amy said. The old bird must be rolling, she thought. "Doesn't she find a big place like that lonely?"

"Not at all. Grace is her constant companion and she has many visitors from England. She enjoys entertaining. Her brother has just gone back to Surrey. He owns a stud farm."

A *stud* farm – wait till Sarah heard that!

"And my wife is coming over next month. She usually spends a few weeks here. Sonya stayed on with mother in the family home in Esher."

He'd only mentioned his wife in passing this morning, Amy noted.

"I suppose you think it strange – my mother and my ex-wife living together?"

"Slightly," Amy confessed.

"It's a convenient set-up, actually. They have common interests; theatre, ballet, the opera. They're both part of the hunting set, a scene I must admit I was never partial to, but *chacun à son goût*. In any case, she and Sonya are the best of friends."

"Très civilisé."

Henry smiled. "Yes, I suppose it is. Sonya and I parted on good terms – our divorce was by mutual consent. When Sonya told me of her decision to stay on, I felt the whole arrangement was ideal."

Amy didn't think she could stomach such a chummy *arrangement*. This lot sounded like characters from a Jilly Cooper novel. "So, you'll be looking forward to your wife's visit?"

"I always do." Henry motioned to the waiter to bring coffees. "I'll take a few days off work to spend time with her. Sonya loves sailing."

247

"I love the sea," Amy said. "Do you own a boat?"

"I have a yacht. It's moored over in Minimes. You must visit there; it's the largest marina on the Atlantic coast – moorings for over 4,000 boats."

Henry offered Amy a Gauloise but she declined politely and lit a Marlborough. Duty-free cigarettes were no longer available on flights and she had to content herself with this brand. "Would you like to come sailing with me?"

Amy smiled with pleasure. "That would be heaven."

"We'll organise something."

"Great." She wiped her lips daintily with her napkin. "I meant to ask you; how was your patient this morning when you called into the hospital?"

"Madame Cossard? Oh, she was distressed and confused but it wasn't her heart – a panic attack. Not a pleasant experience. She needs a lot of support. Psychological problems are often worse than physical."

Amy agreed.

"Careful handling and counselling; that's how I'm going about it. Her husband died a few months ago. She hasn't come to terms with his death at all. He did everything for her. They were inseparable. Now she's lost – afraid to go out on her own. She was on her way to the pharmacy to collect her tablets when it happened."

"What did happen?"

"Palpitations, shaking all over, loss of balance. This time, she fell. A passer-by stopped his car and drove her to the hospital. She refused to see the doctor there until they contacted me."

"She obviously trusts you," Amy said.

* * *

A trip on a yacht! Amy was sitting in her room back in the hotel. She took off her shoes; her feet had swollen in the heat. What would one wear for a yacht trip? She'd never had this problem before. She'd phone Sarah early tomorrow. Amy laughed to herself as she imagined Sarah's reaction to all this. Maybe she wouldn't like Henry? She'd probably consider him snobbish – but he wasn't.

He was wealthy but he didn't flaunt it. The restaurant had been lovely but certainly not ostentatious.

My wife belongs to the hunting set.

Run-of-the-mill to him. He wasn't boasting.

My mother has a villa.

That was his life and he didn't know anything else. It wouldn't have occurred to him that anyone might be critical of his possessions. He wasn't crass.

Why was she trying so hard to like him? It was his mother who had ruined hers. Amy mustn't forget why she'd come here but at the same time she had to keep an open mind. Whatever his parents did, it wasn't Henry's fault. He was a baby at the time

She remembered Sarah's words. *These people think they can ride roughshod over everyone. His mother sacked yours, spread all kinds of rumours about her and wrecked her life and do you know what? I'll lay you ten to one she doesn't even remember your mother's name.*

Amy had the sickening feeling that her friend might be right.

Thirty-four

Maurice's meeting with the accountant yesterday had yielded some good news; his finances were in a very healthy state, so it was all systems go for next week's interviews: having a third vet would ease the workload and bring in new clients, ensuring even better returns.

He'd heard of a young vet who'd trained in England in acupuncture. Acupuncture for animals – why not? It worked for humans. This guy had recently returned to Dublin and was seeking employment. Maurice would interview him; see what he had to say for himself.

He lit a cigar, sat down on the new brass bed in the flat and pondered his future. Due to a cancellation, Goodmans had been able to install the new windows. The white PVC made the rooms much brighter and would be easier to maintain than the old timber frames. He'd spent the last three nights, since Amy went away, sanding the floors and painting the flat, and was delighted with the results. Once the smell of paint had disappeared it would be habitable.

His next move depended on Amy.

Surely she'd be happy about his decision? She'd always wanted to get rid of the house – saw it as a millstone around their necks. Now he'd come around to her point of view.

Why pour thousands into a property they no longer wanted?

He'd berated Amy for clinging to the past but hadn't he indulged himself in the very same way? He'd walked around the house yesterday, seeing ghosts and shadows in every corner: his Aunt Maureen and her snotty-nosed kids on ceremonial visits; his grandmother, in her fox-fur coat, hobbling into the sitting-room for afternoon tea from his mother's best china; his friends running amok at his eleventh birthday party. Sights and smells and sounds. The family home. It didn't warrant that title any longer.

Dust. Memories . . .

His mother poked her head out of the scullery window and called him in from the garden. "Maurice, your dinner's getting cold."

He kicked the football into the shed. "Coming, Mam."

"Come on, love. Wipe your shoes on the mat like a good boy. Are you hungry? I cooked your favourite: corned beef and cabbage and nice floury spuds. Rice pudding for afters."

Her navy-and-white apron, her everyday attire, covered her plain tweed skirt and worn jumper. He glanced in disgust at her red rough hands and the broken fingernails. She pushed a lock of her grey hair out of her eyes – an habitual gesture. His mother had never been young.

"Where's Dad?"

"In the attic tidying away some stuff."

Stuff.

She deposited a heaped plate in front of him and went back to the range to serve up his father's dinner.

Maggie's stuff.

The smell of cabbage filled the kitchen. His mother turned on the wireless. She sang along to the tune about baby's knuckles and baby's knees but her heart wasn't in it. Eight-year-old Maurice wasn't stupid. His mother sang because she didn't want to cry.

Maggie had died months before. His little sister. Six years of age. Pneumonia. Complications. What were complications? An angel gone back to God – that's what everyone said. Maurice couldn't fathom it. Why would God want a six-year-old girl? They weren't much fun. But he was fond of her in his own way. She was all right for a sister.

A part of him missed her: walking her to school in the mornings; teaching her to play snap; helping her to read; running to the rescue when she was scared of spiders in her bedroom, bandaging her knee when she fell. His mother promised that when summer came around again, he'd be allowed to take her to the Blackrock Baths and teach her to swim.

That would have been massive. Maggie would never see summer now. She'd never swim.

Maurice sprinkled pepper over his mashed cabbage and listened to his mother's soft crooning. She was fading from him, retreating into some faraway place that Maurice couldn't reach. She'd cried and cried for weeks.

His father, never a great talker, just sat and moped in front of the fire night after night. Then he'd started to go to the pub again and they didn't see him much. When he was at home, he occupied himself with odd jobs or else he sat and moped.

They had a lot of fights. His mother and father. Maurice, shivering in his bed upstairs on the cold wintry nights, heard them arguing below. His mother tried to speak in hushed tones but his father, especially when he'd been drinking, roared as loud as the ass in Brennan's yard.

"Moving? I've no intention of moving, woman! This is our home!"

"It's too big for us, Dan. What do we want now with all this room? There'll be no more children." A choking sob. "It's too hard to clean. I'm heart-scalded with all the housework – and all for what?"

"Amn't I tired telling you, Pearl? We're not moving and that's final. I know what you're thinking but you're wrong. Going to a new place won't make it any easier. Maggie's gone, gone from us forever and nothing will bring her back."

"I can't stay here without her. I haven't been into her room since the funeral. I can't. My heart will break."

"She'll be closer to us here. We can remember her better."

He heard his mother drag her chair away from the fire. The sound of water filling the kettle.

"I hate this house. I hate it."

Silence.

When Maurice thought it was over and he'd curled into a ball under the heavy army coat that draped his bed, he heard his father shouting again.

"Is it *me* you hate? Is that it? I'm responsible in some way for my daughter's death? Well? It's me you blame, isn't it, Pearl? I should have got the doctor earlier – isn't that what you think?"

"No, Dan, no. Don't keep going over and over it."

"It's you, Pearl. You're the one who won't let it go."

"You see what I'm saying? We'd all be better off if we left this place. It would be good for the boy."

"Maurice loves it here."

"A child will get used to anywhere."

"But I won't. No, Pearl, you'll have to accept that we're not going anywhere. I'll be carted out of here feet first."

And he was. Eventually.

Maurice stubbed out his cigar. He lay back on the new bed and closed his eyes. Why were these memories haunting him? Plaguing him. Why now after such a long time?

His mother was dying. Slowly. Painfully. He and Amy were married and living with her. His wife was gentle, kind, loving to her mother-in-law – patience personified.

"Maurice, I can never make this up to Amy. The girl's a treasure. She does everything for me, no compliment at all." Her eyes moistened. "This isn't what I intended for you, Maurice."

"Ssh, Mam. Get some rest."

"No young couple should be starting married life like this – trapped by an old crabby sick woman."

"You're not crabby." He fixed the bed-jacket around his mother's shoulders. "Don't fret, Mam. We both love you. Why wouldn't we look after you?"

"It's not right, son. It's not fair to Amy. Why don't you sell up? You'd get a good price for this place and I could go –"

"No, Mam. Everything's fine the way it is."

His mother shook her head, hopelessly. "Will you make me a promise, son?"

"If I can."

"Will you agree to sell after I'm gone?"

"Mam, don't —"

"Maurice, say you'll do that one thing for me. Amy needs a new house, somewhere bright and airy, somewhere that'll be a fresh start for the two of you. And when the babbies arrive —"

"Mam, that's what I've been waiting to tell you. Amy's two months pregnant."

The old lady chortled. "I'm so glad for you. I've been praying for this. Maurice, you'll have to get a new place for the baby. You and Amy and the baby. I'll go to my grave easier now that I know." She clutched at his arm. "Always do your best by her, Maurice. She's a good girl."

"I will."

"Amy's your wife — she has to come first. Your poor father was the best in the world but he never listened. Knew it all. Don't be like him, Maurice. Be good to her. Promise."

Had he kept his word? He'd seen his wife wash and feed and tend to his mother for two years and yet when it had come to her own father . . . Joe Shiels was shoved into a home. Amy hadn't fought him over that decision. Maybe the fight had gone out of her?

"How goes the enemy?" his granny used to ask. The enemy: time. The thief who creeps up furtively, unnoticed, unobserved. But certain dates, years, occasions stand out: the wet windy October night he'd joined the drama club and met Amy; their first clumsy kiss in his old Cortina; their wedding reception in the Gresham Hotel; Dawn's red bike with the stabilisers; her first day at school; her Communion. Years and years and years and always Amy's question:

"When are we going to move, Maurice?"

"Soon, we'll move soon but not now. Let's get the surgery sorted first. All our money is tied up in it."

Eight years passed.

"Can we think about it now, Maurice, before Dawn starts Secondary School? Sarah and I went looking at the new estate yesterday. The houses are lovely. Smaller than this one but spacious enough – better planned. It's not as if I'm asking you to move from Blackrock."

"I'm up to my eyes, Amy. I can't deal with it now." He glanced up from his paperwork. "Can't you see how busy I am?"

Ten years further on.

"I'm worn out, Maurice. I've been over with my mother all day. She's very low. I don't think she'll last much longer. I can't keep two houses going."

"Claire should be doing more to help."

"She does her bit but I'm the one who's there on a daily basis. I'm not complaining; it's just that our house is really getting to me. It needs money spent on it."

"Money, money, money. I'm not made of it, Amy. My overheads are huge."

"Right, but if we sold here you'd make a profit, Maurice. A smaller house would cost less to maintain. When can we sit down and discuss it seriously?"

"Soon."

A grey showery morning in the cemetery. Her mother's funeral. Soon.

Her father selling his house. Moving into the Home. Soon.

Amy's growing depression and lack of interest. Soon.

Maurice opened his eyes. Tomorrow morning he'd ring the auctioneers – get a surveyor out to assess the value of the house. The property market was booming. What better time to sell?

Amy would be ecstatic when he told her. No doubt about it. He looked at his watch. Ten p.m. What time was it in the States? He had to talk to Dawn.

256

Thirty-five

Atlantic City was a furnace. Torrid waves of heat hit hard; steaming, sizzling and scorching, broiling the land, the animals and the populace. Most unusual in an area known for its moderate climate. The average July temperature was in the mid to late twenties but today it had soared to 35°.

Dawn sprawled on the narrow bed after her shower. The gushing water had barely cooled her tingling body when she was sticky and sweating again. She'd spent the morning slaving away in a local far-from-salubrious motel and the afternoon selling supposedly real orange juice in her tacky T-shirt with its moronic GET A FRESH SQUEEZE HERE emblazoned across her chest.

Crowds, heat, honky-tonk. Bars. Casinos. Fun. She was luxuriating in the insanity of it all. It was a far cry from Dublin and her parents and college and Paul. The house they'd rented near the beach was tiny but at least her bedroom was adequate – Angela's was so cramped that when she opened the door she banged into the bed.

The latter burst in, out of breath and puffy-looking.

"What's up with *you?*" Dawn asked.

"Nothing."

"You're like a bleeding beetroot."

"I've been scrubbing my face."

"With a Brillo pad?"

"No. Smart-ass."

"What the hell happened?"

"If you must know – a bloody big seagull did a plonker on my face."

Dawn howled with laughter.

"Shut up! It wasn't one bit funny. I was hurrying home by the boardwalk after six hours selling Taffy to loud-mouthed fat tourists, who should all be on diets and avoiding sweets like the plague, when this yoke flew over my head and decided to drop a load."

Dawn spluttered.

"My face was covered in white shite – I think I swallowed some. I'll probably die of a weird disease and all you can do is sit there and laugh."

A knock on the door saved Dawn from having to mutter something suitably sympathetic. Jason, from upstairs, put his head around the door. "Phone call for Dawn."

"Sailing on a yacht today? Fabulous, Mum. Who's the tycoon?"

"He's hardly that, Dawn. He's an English doctor who's settled here. Catherine Cole was the contact."

Dawn wondered about this. Ever since her mother's visit to England she'd been behaving strangely. Everything had altered – mostly for the better but there was a lot that Dawn didn't understand. "I was amazed that you took another holiday on your own. Of course Dad is so hard to shift. More power to you, Mum. You're very brave. I don't know if I'd have the nerve to travel alone."

"It's actually a liberating experience. I'm tired of relying on others. And I'm not totally alone. Henry's been very good, showing me around, bringing me for meals."

Who *was* this Henry? Her mother seemed very taken with him. Was there something going on? No, no, it wasn't possible. And yet? Her mother's voice sounded very strained. *Had* something happened? Was she having an affair? Was she feeling guilty now talking to her daughter?

"When you're away," Amy continued, "it's nice to meet someone from the area. Gives you a better sense of the place."

Dawn wanted to get off the subject of Henry Edwards. "What's it like? I'd have expected you to head for Nice or Cannes. You love the south of France."

The Edwards didn't live in Nice. "I wanted to see the West Coast for a change. La Rochelle is different – less tourists."

"Middle-aged and boring?"

"It's definitely not boring. The *Francofolies* started this week. A music festival: jazz, reggae, concerts in the street. The bikers have arrived *en masse* – a bit like an Irish *fleadh*."

"Doesn't sound like your scene, Mum."

"It wouldn't be normally but I'm enjoying the atmosphere." Again Amy felt like a fraud.

Was that *all* she was enjoying, Dawn wondered. "Have you been on to Dad?"

Amy instinctively reached for her cigarettes. "No, not since I came away."

She obviously hadn't wanted to phone home. Was this another sign? Dawn decided it could be. "He phoned me last night. You've heard the latest? It's good, isn't it"

"What is?"

"Dad – deciding to sell the house."

Silence.

"The house, Mum. He's having it valued this week."

Amy's breathing quickened.

"Mum?"

"Yes, yes, I'm here. Sorry, Dawn, you've given me a bit of a shock. He *told* you he's selling?"

"Yeah, at first I couldn't believe it. How long have you been nagging him about moving?"

"I gave up a long time ago."

"He's all excited – full of plans. Talked about getting somewhere smaller. Said he was sorry he hadn't done it years ago. I think it's superb – just what the two of you need."

Amy twiddled with the telephone wire.

"Mum?"

"Yes?"

"You've got your way finally."

"Not *my* way, Dawn."

"Come on, you've been at him for years about selling. It's finally paid off. Since you went to France he told me he'd thought about it seriously and reconsidered. He did his sums and decided that selling up was for the best, particularly now with house prices so high."

"How often have I told him that?"

"Well, now he agrees with you."

"Your father is acting independently of any resolve of mine. I don't know what he's up to. I haven't been included in his decisions for years."

Dawn had put her foot in it. "You'd better ring him, Mum. Have a chat."

"Maybe." She'd no intention. "How's work, Dawn?"

"A laugh a minute – it literally is. Total lunacy. Everybody is nuts, great *craic*, though. Americans are far more outspoken than we are, more outgoing but in lots of ways they're more conservative – it's a bizarre mix. The woman I work for in the hotel has been very good to me. Still, I'm thinking of leaving that job. I've been offered a better one in the Taj Mahal."

"The what?"

"It's a huge casino – gambling salons, restaurants, bars. Full of rich New York women who descend in droves. I'll make a fortune in tips."

Hardened gamblers, drug pushers, gun-slinging gangsters, touts, criminals – Amy imagined it all. "I hope it's safe, Dawn."

"It's tightly run and well supervised. Don't worry."

"And how are you getting on with the others?"

"Great. Angela's a riot. There are two lads from the Science faculty living upstairs. This is their second year here so they know the ropes and they look out for us. We go out in a gang and we've met some American students who are really friendly."

"Sounds good."

"It is, Mum. I'm thrilled I came. You were right about it being a learning experience. The work's hard but the social life is great."

"Are you minding yourself, Dawn?"

"Here it comes – the sermon! Don't worry, I'm eating properly and getting enough sleep and I'm not involved in any illegal activities."

"And Paul? Have you been talking to him recently?"

"God Almighty, I almost forgot to tell you. The bastard's out of action."

"Ben Cosgrove?"

"Yes, Paul got a letter from Izzy. She's still in Jersey. There was a small piece about Ben in one of the British tabloids. You know he was working for a builder in Birmingham? Apparently he fell forty feet from a scaffolding."

"Fell?" Amy gasped. "Drunk?"

"An *accident*. Probably pushed. Word had it that he'd been fighting with half of the brickies. I have my suspicions that one of Izzy's brothers had something to do with it."

"Are Izzy's brothers in Birmingham?"

"No, but they have *contacts* everywhere."

"Forty feet, my God! Was he killed?"

"Paralysed. He won't walk again."

"I can't put my hand on my heart and say I'm sorry, Dawn. But it's pretty gruesome all the same."

"He got what was coming to him, Mum. Nemesis, you might say."

"How is Izzy?"

"Paul said her letter was very short. She's working and seems to have settled. Listen, this call must be costing you a fortune. Give me a buzz next week and we'll talk again. How long more will you be staying in France?"

"Five days. The time's flying."

"Same here."

"When are you coming home, Dawn?"

"End of September, I guess."

"You won't work till then?"

"No, Angela's aunt has invited us to Boston for a holiday. We can get a bus to Newark and then a direct flight."

"You might as well see as much of the country as you can while you're there."

"Definitely. Oh, I won a hundred dollars last night in one of the casinos."

Amy didn't hear her. Her mind was elsewhere.

"Mum, are you OK?"

"I'm miffed, Dawn. Deciding to sell the house – not a word to me. What came over him?"

"An impulse, presumably."

"Your father doesn't have impulses."

"Aren't you pleased?"

"I suppose I am at the back of it but I'm really annoyed the way he went about it. It would have been nice to have been asked my opinion."

"Don't let this spoil your holiday, will you? I shouldn't have opened my big trap. I'm sorry I let it slip, Mum. I took it for granted that Dad would have told you by now."

"Of course you did. You've nothing to concern yourself about, Dawn. This is between your father and me. Don't give it another thought."

"I'd better go, Mum. Talk to you soon."

"Where are we off to tonight?" Angela, dressed in a slinky black mini dress was transformed. Her make-up was perfect and her hair glossy.

"Let's avoid the casinos. You lost a fortune last night."

"You didn't. Dawn, I want to give it one more try – I think my luck has changed."

"Have you forgotten the seagull?"

"Maybe it was a good-luck omen."

"I doubt it." Dawn pulled on her new white top. "We'll settle for a few jars in The Irish Pub."

"All right. How's your Mum?"

"Hard to know. She said she was enjoying her holiday, telling me where she'd been, what she was doing – dinners out, sailing on a yacht – all seemingly very jolly but I thought she was really tense. Her voice was high-pitched and shaky. She was telling me how great the place was but it was as if she was deliberately exaggerating or something – I can't put my finger on it but I feel as if there's more going on than she's pretending." No need to tell Angela that she suspected her mother might be having an affair. If she spoke the words it would make them true. "I made matters worse – jumped the gun and told her about Dad selling the house."

"She didn't *know?*"

"No." Dawn sat at the bedroom mirror, took a make-up brush and dabbed some blusher on her cheeks.

Angela whistled slowly. "That news must have gone down like a lead balloon. You'd think he'd have told her, Dawn. That would freak me out – if someone made those kinds of decisions for my life without even *telling* me. Your mother has quite a lot to put up with, doesn't she?"

"There's a pair of them in it. My parents are a law unto themselves. Nice people separately but together a disaster."

Angela frowned.

"They'd be better apart," said Dawn. "They can't see that or they don't want to admit it. I refused to consider the idea for ages but when you look at it logically, the answer is there. I think they should seriously consider separation."

"Do you, Dawn? That's a bit drastic."

"It isn't. They rub each other up the wrong way. It's more than trivial rows and arguments. They don't have the same outlook on life. Dad's very driven and that causes awful tension. I wasn't aware of it myself until I moved out. And Mum needs . . . she's very sensitive. He has a way of putting her down without even meaning to – he's super-efficient, very organised but when he makes up his mind, he's a bulldozer – mows down obstacles in his way. He doesn't confide in her any more; does his own thing. That's not a partnership."

"You blame him?"

"No, I don't. I don't blame her either. They bring out the worst in one another, that's the sad fact of the matter. You're lucky, Angela – you've only one parent to cope with. Your mother is sound."

263

"Single parents get a lot of bad press – typical dysfunctional family, according to popular psychology."

"Bull."

"You think so?"

"Your family is less dysfunctional than mine."

"Thanks – I think."

Dawn grinned.

"May I borrow this?" Without waiting for a reply, Angela popped one of Dawn's lipsticks into her bag. "How come we're so normal?"

"We don't know that we are. All the neuroses will probably come out when we've got kids of our own."

"I'm not going to have kids," Angela said emphatically.

"Me neither." Dawn took one last critical look at herself in the mirror. "Are the lads coming with us tonight?"

"No, Roy's working and Jason's meeting that girl from San Francisco."

"I knew he had his eye on her."

"Did Roy tell you what happened last night? They went for a meal in that Indian place off the boardwalk – what do you call it? Anyhow, this dark-skinned bloke in a turban came up to them, gave a little bow and announced: "My name is Robert. I'll be your waiter tonight."

"So?"

"Dawn, he had a strong Dublin accent!"

It was past midnight when they got back. Dawn dreaded getting up at six a.m. for her chambermaid duties. She'd decided to hand in her notice the next morning, although she'd have no guarantee she wouldn't be on the early shift in the casino – they opened twenty-four hours a day. Atlantic City – a less glitzy version of Las Vegas. The rich visitors, pursuers of the great American dream, spending disgusting amounts of dollars in the casinos and then the other side of the coin – the grinding poverty of the inner city with its mostly black unemployed population.

The phone conversation with her mother was still on her mind, even after having consumed three pints of Budweiser and two Screwdrivers.

"Selling the house might be the best move my Dad has made."

"First move to a split?"

Dawn chewed her lip. "That's not what he intends. He's ready to look for somewhere smaller for the two of them. But, like I said earlier, I don't think it's going to happen."

"Give them time, Dawn. I bet everything will work out."

Dawn doubted that her mother would agree. How would a new house change anything?

Thirty-six

Jane Edwards sat under a large yellow sun umbrella on the patio in her back garden, sipping an iced tea. She'd given Grace the morning off because Henry was calling and she wanted to speak to him in private.

She shifted her seat out of the sun's pervasive glare. Her son had seen this Irish woman four or five times now and she didn't quite like it but couldn't say why. A vague uneasiness, an uncomfortable heaviness had descended on her since Henry had first mentioned that the woman was from Dublin. Doubts and regrets surfaced – maybe guilt, too. She hadn't mixed with any Irish people since . . .

Jane saw her as vividly as if she stood before her now: a young girl holding a baby, softly singing a lullaby. A tall, graceful girl with a fresh complexion and bright green eyes. More sinister images followed: uncontrollable crying, shouting, shaking. A face full of rage; a shrewish voice.

Jane Edwards shivered in the sunlight.

Henry, dressed in jeans and a blue T-shirt, breezed into the garden and kissed her on the cheek.

"Morning, *Maman*. May I help myself to some tea? It's hot today."

"By all means, Henry. Aren't you working this morning?"

"No, this afternoon." He stretched out on a sun lounger and pulled his shirt over his head.

"You'll need some cream," his mother warned.

267

"I'm not staying long."

"Even so, Henry. You, above all people, should know the dangers of sun on unprotected skin."

"The garden looks well. Has André been in? The roses are exceptional this year."

"He does a good job and he's reliable – most important in a gardener. Henry, I've been thinking."

"Yes?" He closed his eyes and felt the warm rays on his face.

"Would you like to bring your Irish friend to tea here with me?"

"If you like. She did say she'd love to meet you." He brushed a wasp away. "But don't feel pressurised."

"She wants to meet me? Why?" Jane asked curtly.

Henry opened his eyes and looked at his mother. "Because she's heard all about you. From some friend who used to work with Father."

"Oh?" Jane's chest tightened. "That's interesting. Will you invite her for Friday?" She hesitated, her breath caught. "Nothing fancy – just a light meal. I don't want Grace to have too much bother."

"Of course not. Yes, Amy will be delighted. She's expressed great interest in the family."

"Has she?"

Henry settled himself more comfortably.

"What class of a person is she?"

"Very reputable, Mother. Husband's a vet and the daughter has completed First Year Veterinary in University."

"And what does *she* do?"

"She's a housewife like your good self."

"I am *not* a housewife, Henry."

"No, you're a lady of leisure. Amy used to work with her husband but she gave up the job to look after her mother who died a year ago. She's been offered the job of managing a bookshop when she goes home. She's very interested in books."

"Very admirable."

"I knew you'd think so."

"What's her surname?"

"Kennedy."

The old lady stroked her chin. "How did you say you got to know her, dear?"

"I told you. Wendy Barrett phoned me."

"Wendy, ah yes. I never remember her mentioning Irish friends."

"Mother, you've lost touch with Wendy and she wasn't ever an intimate of yours."

"That's true – your father knew her better." Jane took off her sunglasses and squinted at her son. "Bring her along, Henry. I'd like to meet her too. What age would she be?"

"Forties, I suspect. I was hardly going to ask her that, Mother. Younger than me, at any rate."

"Where exactly is she from?"

"Dublin." Was his mother getting forgetful?

"Dublin is a big place. What area, Henry?"

"A fashionable seaside suburb on the southside of the city – what damned difference does it make?"

"No need to get excitable, Henry. These things are important."

"Not to me, they aren't."

"And this Amy's husband – a vet?"

"Yes, he has his own practice. I sincerely hope that if she does come for tea you won't grill her, Mother."

"I like to know everything about visitors to my home, Henry. You take everyone at face value. What do you *really* know about this woman? Precious little."

"I like her – she's good company. That's all I need to know."

Jane needed to know a lot more.

* * *

He found her sitting in the shade on a park bench. Amy didn't see him approach; she was intent on her book.

"Bonjour!" Henry sat beside her. "What's this? Something deep and meaningful?"

"It's a novel I picked up yesterday in one of the bookshops: *Une Maîtresse Femme*. It's about France under the Occupation. Have you read it?"

"No, I don't read as much as I should and rarely novels." He glanced at the cover. "It looks dark."

"I'm enjoying it." She marked her page and closed the book. "How are you?"

"Well, thank you. What are planning for the rest of the week?"

"What day is it today? I've lost all track of time."

"That's what you're supposed to do on holidays. It's Wednesday."

"Right, well, I'm going to sun myself by the pool for the morning. After lunch I'll go to see the Aquarium in Minimes, spend the afternoon there and then dine in the hotel tonight. Tomorrow I'll take the bus to Châtelaillon to spend the day on the beach. All very organised but lazy and self-indulgent."

"As it should be," he said, smiling. "My mother wants to know if you'd come to tea at her place on Friday."

Amy's stomach went into spasm.

"Would you like to?"

She clenched her hands. "Love to. What time?"

"I'll collect you at the hotel at around four-thirty." He offered her a mint, which she accepted. "Nothing fancy, Mother says, just a light repast. She's anxious to meet you."

Not half as anxious as Amy was.

"She'll probably ask you a million questions but don't let that put you off – she's naturally curious. Are you all right, Amy? You seem . . . preoccupied."

She sat up straight and uncrossed her legs. "I've had some news from home."

"Bad news?"

"My husband has decided to sell our home."

He took her by the arm, excitedly. "But that's marvellous. You told me that's what you've always wanted."

"Sarah said the same when I phoned her."

"Why the long face, then?"

"I heard the news from my daughter."

"Aah."

"He hasn't got around to telling me yet – too caught up with his plans."

"Have you phoned him?"

"No."

"There you go."

"He should have phoned me."

"You sound exactly like Sonya when she's ticked off." Henry pulled a funny face.

"Don't dismiss this as female perversity, Henry. I have a right to know about my own situation."

"I agree. I do. Perhaps he wanted to surprise you? I mean, after all this time, he's finally taken your feelings into account."

"*You* can give him the benefit of the doubt."

"But you won't?"

"There's method in his madness. Maurice always suits himself. Oh, he'll convince himself that this decision is for my benefit, but I know him too well."

"Dare I say that you sound cynical?"

"Yes, I am. Once again, Maurice has all the control. Henry, all my life I've been manipulated."

He put his arm around her. "Amy, if that's how you genuinely feel, it's time you did something about it."

"I will."

"You need to discuss the matter openly with him." Henry scratched his head. "Sometimes we men don't understand what you women want. You have to spell it out, Amy. I could never figure out what Sonya wanted. She expected me to read her mind. Your husband needs to be told."

"He has been – time and time again. At this stage I'd be flogging a dead horse. He's done his own thing once again – it's time I did the same."

"You've made up your mind, Amy?"

She inclined her head. "I have."

"Don't be too hasty."

"Hasty? Me?" She raised an eyebrow. "Not my form, Henry. Not my form at all. In fact I've always thought for far too long about everything I do."

"You have to consider all your options." He checked his watch.

"I have to go, I'm sorry. I'm not trying to cut you off – we'll talk again if you'd like."

"Why? To give me the male perspective?"

"It seems like you've had a bellyful of that."

"Yes, I have. By God, I have. Henry, did you and Sonya ever learn to communicate?"

"After much effort, yes."

"And did you succeed in understanding one another?"

"Eventually."

"And?"

"We got a divorce."

"Touché!"

"You have a point." Henry laughed at his little pun. "I'd better be off. Surgery in ten minutes. See you on Friday, then?" He stood up. "Oh, Amy, I have another idea. There's a concert in the cathedral on Friday evening at eight. Soul and Gospel. It's the alternative festival – two American singers – would you be interested?"

"A concert in the cathedral; what a nice idea."

"The acoustics should be excellent. I'll get the tickets."

"Will your mother join us for the evening?"

"I wouldn't even ask her. She's only interested in classical music. No, we'll have tea with her and that should be enough."

"Enough?"

"To satisfy her curiosity about you. She's perplexed."

Amy hoped he couldn't hear her heart thumping.

"I think it's because you're Irish." He stooped and kissed her on the cheek. "My mother has extremely eccentric ideas!"

Thirty-seven

The villa was impressive but not in a flamboyant way: handcrafted furniture, polished floors, understated decor. Jane Edwards had good taste. She received them in her comfortable *salon*. Amy, very nervous but doing her best not to show it, shook the hand Jane Edwards proffered and took a seat by the marble fireplace.

The older woman was cordial but cool. While Henry chatted to his mother about the arrangements for his wife's impending visit, Amy stole sly glances at her hostess. Jane Edwards negated all Amy's preconceived notions: she was quite small and petite. Why had Amy imagined she would be tall? Because of Henry? Her steel-grey hair – no sign of a tint or dye – was cut fashionably. Her eyes were a vivid blue, the eyelids dusted with the faintest trace of eyeshadow. She wore a dark mauve dress, elegant in its simplicity. She could have been considered beautiful, were it not for her large aquiline nose which gave her an aristocratic air. But her mouth was small and pretty.

"Henry, perhaps our guest would like a glass of sherry." Jane pointed to a sideboard where a silver tray contained dainty glasses and a crystal decanter. "Or wine, if you prefer?"

"Yes, a glass of wine would be lovely," Amy replied. Her voice sounded different, as if it belonged to someone else.

Jane took the chair opposite to her. Amy felt she was attending an interview. "Henry says a glass or two a day of red wine is good for the heart, don't you, dear?"

He served Amy her drink, then his mother. "Yes, I do, and it's one bit of advice you actually heed – I'm happy to say."

Jane laughed but it was forced. "Don't pay any attention to my son. He's a dreadful tease. I always go by your advice, Henry. Why wouldn't I? I trust your medical judgement implicitly."

He threw his eyes to heaven. "And what about my other advice?"

"Well, dear, that's somewhat different. You've no head for financial matters, have you?" She leaned forward in her seat and mock-whispered to Amy: "He's hopeless when it comes to money. Utterly hopeless."

Despite the pretended criticism, Amy caught the affection in her voice. She beamed proudly every time she looked at her son.

"I always do what you tell me, Henry," she asserted. "I'm a model patient."

He stooped down and kissed the top of her head. "And a model mother, too. You're perfectly right when you upbraid me for my fiscal shortcomings."

Jane pushed him away playfully. "You see? Every word out of his mouth is in jest. When do I ever reproach you for anything?"

"Never," he admitted. "Your generosity and praise know no bounds. Like every mother, you feel your offspring can do no wrong – and while this may be somewhat short-sighted, it's very reassuring. Wouldn't you agree, Amy?"

Why was Henry being so stiff and formal? What was all this about? Amy felt exactly as she had done when she was cast as an ingénue in one of those stilted drawing-room comedies they used to stage in the early days of the drama group. Lousy scripts. "I agree that parental approval is reassuring when it happens," she said, forced to emulate the mood of the moment, "but, unfortunately, not all parents are so uncritical."

"Indeed," Jane Edwards eagerly agreed. "Of course parenting is one of the most underrated jobs. We parents get no training, do we? Where to draw the line between criticism and praise, punishment or reward – that's a problem. It's very difficult to get it right."

"Yes," Henry interrupted excitedly, "it is and most people get it

274

sadly wrong. Honestly, they haven't a clue how to treat children – I see it in my practice all the time."

"But you've no personal experience, dear," his mother said coolly.

"A bone of contention," Henry explained with a smile. "I decided long ago not to have children of my own – I'm much too selfish – do you find that strange, Amy?"

"Not really," she replied honestly.

"Far too much to get wrong," Henry continued. "Even the psychologists can't agree, can they? And then there are social and philosophical trends, which constantly change. The whole subject is mind-boggling. What was considered good for children years ago is a completely different story today. When I was young it was a case of *children should be seen and not heard.*"

"You were always heard, Henry," his mother declared, with a laugh.

"I was an exception, Mother. Come on, you have to admit that children years ago were kept firmly in their place. We were made to conform – especially at school. We were rarely allowed to have an opinion on anything and, if we did actually come up with any innovative idea, we certainly didn't get the chance to express it. Corporal punishment was rife. The system was quite barbaric – certainly in the public schools. Amy, what was your experience?"

"School was strict, yes."

"And what about home?" his mother asked.

Amy considered for a moment. "My father was very mild-mannered but my mother was harsh," she murmured.

"Of course being strict is another way of showing care," Jane said diplomatically, "although I was never a believer in punishment. There are other ways of teaching a child. Encouragement for one thing. You have a daughter, Amy? Grown up now, I believe."

"Dawn is nineteen."

"Well past the difficult stage."

"Dawn has never given any trouble."

"That's to your credit – you and your husband. I believe children grow up happier and more self-confident in a home where both parents agree on childrearing and share the responsibilities."

"My husband was and is an excellent father," Amy replied, piqued by Jane's temerity.

"Like your father, Henry. Valentine was devoted to you from the moment you were born. You were a gorgeous baby. Everyone doted on you, even the servants."

Amy bristled.

"You were an exceptional child – very bright but very well-behaved." Jane crossed her legs and sat back in her chair. "He was a delightful little boy," she crowed to her guest.

"This is highly embarrassing." Henry opened the top button of his shirt. "It's hot in here. You're making me hot, Mother, with all this hyperbolic nonsense."

"Sit over there by the open window and cool down, dear."

Henry pulled a funny face behind his mother's back, then filled Amy's glass again.

"Thank you," she said, glad of the relief the wine provided. It helped her to relax a little. "You have a beautiful home, Mrs Edwards." Hypocrite, she scolded herself for this shameless ingratiation.

"Would you like to see the rest of the villa?" Jane turned to her son. "Bring Mrs Kennedy around, Henry. Upstairs, from the landing, you get a lovely view of the harbour and the towers. It was the view that persuaded me to buy this house. After that," she said imperiously, "come back here and chat with me. We can get to know one another better."

Henry noted Amy's worried expression. He felt for her – his mother could be quite overbearing when she chose to be. Today, she was polite but stiff, a bit frosty, playing the grand lady of the manor and he had humoured her. Amy didn't deserve the haughty treatment.

"Off you go, Henry. Take your time – Grace won't be serving tea for half an hour yet. And don't forget to show Mrs Kennedy the garden. Why not bring your drinks outside? It's a balmy evening."

"You're not very comfortable here, are you?" asked Henry as they walked down the lawn. "I couldn't help noticing and I apologise for my own ridiculous behaviour. Mother likes formality – you can see that. It gives her some reassurance. She doesn't like the way society has changed. She says we're all too familiar, too slipshod, never observing the social niceties and she tries to keep things the way they were. I suppose I'm silly to aid and abet her but usually it's quite harmless. You mustn't let my mother intimidate you, Amy. Anyhow, we can leave as soon as afternoon tea is over." He smiled, took her arm and led her to a garden seat underneath the cherry blossom trees.

Amy was embarrassed by his concern. "No, no, it's not your mother. I'm feeling a bit down today, that's all. Brooding on home problems – it's difficult to switch off."

"You're going through a bad time, Amy. You've difficult decisions to make."

"I think I've finally made them. It's easier to get things into perspective when you're away. I know what I want now. At least I know what I don't want. I have to leave Maurice and start again – for both our sakes. The routine was killing me."

He lit a cigarette and exhaled loudly.

"Same bloody things happening day after day, week after week, month in month out, year in year out. I began to think I was going mad." Amy glanced shyly at Henry. "You'll wear your doctor's hat now and tell me it's all part of this stage of my life, won't you?"

"Yes," he agreed, "but that doesn't make your feelings any less real. It's obviously high time you changed your life."

"I have choices." She smiled. "We all do."

"Choices are the hard part. But if you're sure of what you want, you have to see it through – although that can be very hard."

"Doing nothing is worse. I was very depressed for such a long time – I still get gloomy, as you can see today. I was getting quite paranoid too – I realise that now. I was totally self-obsessed – not much fun to live with."

"You're very hard on yourself." He stroked her shoulder.

"I don't know how my daughter put up with me – or Maurice either. I was out of it for most of the time – it's hard to explain it. It was like being someone else, watching what was going on but

277

not caring or trying to participate. Weird. They tried everything to help me but nothing they did was any good. I was beyond contact, I suppose. Getting out of bed was a major ordeal. That was only a few short months ago – hard to believe."

"Yes, looking at you now, it is hard to believe." Henry swished a fly away.

"You begin to think that everything is in your own head. You blame everything on the depression but sometimes the problems are genuine. Mine were. Ours were, I should say. Maurice did play his part, although he mightn't see it like I do. Anyhow, therapy has helped me to accept that what I felt was real. That the loneliness and isolation weren't all my fault and that I'm not going mad!"

"Mad?" He scoffed. "No such thing. You strike me as being very balanced, Amy."

"A chip on each shoulder?" she joked.

He hugged her close to him. "You will make the right decision in the end. Just follow your gut."

"That's what my therapist advised. For how long should counselling go on, Henry? I don't want to become too reliant on Sylvia. I want to stand on my own two feet."

"You'll know when you're ready to leave her. Stick with it for the moment. You're still tense – I didn't realise how tense until this afternoon."

If he only knew the reason why!

"You must learn to relax. Tension is a real killer."

"Yes, Doctor." She smiled. "And how do I learn to relax? Play soothing tapes? Yoga? I've already joined a gym. Still I feel as if I need something more – and not pills. I'm not taking any more pills. HRT is quite enough!"

"HRT can cause depression in some people, Amy. You might need to look into that. Try alternative medicine. I'm a strong believer in herbs."

"Unusual for a doctor. My GP loves writing prescriptions."

"I don't. I never have. Acupuncture is good. Ah, there's something else that could work for you: bio energy. Have you heard of it?"

"Yes, vaguely. Does it help?"

"I believe so. It can restore lost energy. Sometimes it alleviates aches and pains – it helps the body to heal itself. And it can give a tremendous feeling of wellbeing."

"I could definitely do with some of that!"

"Henry, there was a call from the clinic while you were out in the garden. I told the girl you were busy. She asked you to phone back – something about interviews, she said."

Henry slapped his palm to his forehead. "Of course. How stupid of me. I meant to do it earlier. I've a lot on my mind today. Stéphanie has given in her notice. She's our receptionist," Henry explained to Amy. "She's been with us now for five years. Wonderful worker. She'll be hard to replace. Will you excuse me, Amy? Mother will entertain you while I make that call." He winked at her and went out to the hall.

Jane Edwards smiled stiffly. "I believe you used to work for your husband in his veterinary clinic. I expect that work would be quite similar. Bodies are bodies whether they're human or animal!" She noted that Amy wasn't amused by her observation. "Henry tells me you're not working now."

"As a matter of fact I will be taking up a job soon," Amy replied. "I've been asked to manage a bookshop near my home."

"And what will that involve?" Jane peered over her glass.

"I'm not sure. A lot of work by the look of it. The shop needs total reorganisation. I expect I'll have to deal with the book suppliers, sometimes the publishers, the accounts, and of course the customers. The lady who owns it has asked me to have the list of all stock computerised so that will take up most of my time for the first few weeks. I'll have to interview for some part-time staff as well."

"You're going to be very busy with that and your family commitments," Jane observed dryly.

"Keeping busy is good for you, so they say. I've been quite restless recently, bored with staying at home, so I'm looking forward to going back to work and this job will be a change."

"I don't like change much," Jane remarked. "Not at my time of life. Routine suits me fine. I don't like surprises."

279

Was that some sort of warning, Amy wondered? "I'll be making big changes in my life, Mrs Edwards. That's one thing I do know. However, as you pointed out, I do have family commitments. My father isn't well. That's why I only came away for a week."

Jane asked herself why this woman's father should have precedence over her husband.

"Are you enjoying yourself here? Do you like La Rochelle?"

"Yes, I like the easy-going atmosphere. It's not too hot either. I love the South of France as well, particularly Nice, but it's very hot there. I find I can't take much heat any more – another sign of ageing, I suppose." She laughed nervously. "I'd love to have a holiday home here," Amy added quickly. The third drink had loosened her tongue. She knew she was talking too much but she couldn't stop herself. "It's becoming fashionable to buy houses abroad now – lately *The Irish Times* has featured villas in Spain and Italy and France in the Property Section. Very attractive prices."

"Is that so?" Jane responded indifferently.

Henry came back with an ash-tray and a big smile. "It's all right if we smoke, isn't it Mother?"

"By all means. I may join you for one."

"You don't smoke," he said. "Or is that one of your little secrets, eh?"

"I've no secrets from you, Henry."

"All women have secrets – that's how they keep us on our toes."

"You do say the most absurd things." Jane Edwards stood up slowly. "Why don't we go out to the patio for afternoon tea first, Mrs Kennedy? Afterwards we can all have a little smoke." She took her son's arm. "Then I'd like to speak to Mrs Kennedy alone, Henry. You may help Grace with the dishes. Also, I want you to replace a bulb in the kitchen light. It's too much for Grace to be standing on a ladder at her age and I can't get hold of that maintenance man who did some work for me last year. It's impossible to get good help these days."

"You only met Wendy Barrett once?" Jane raised an eyebrow. "My son led me to believe you were a friend of hers."

Amy was glad that Henry had left them temporarily. His presence made her more self-conscious. The conversation over afternoon tea had been as strained as earlier and Jane Edwards showed no signs of thawing out although she had deliberately got rid of her son. It was clear that she wanted to get Amy on her own. That was OK – Amy had carefully rehearsed what she wanted to say. "I was introduced to Wendy by an old family friend – Catherine Cole."

Jane's hand trembled slightly but enough for Amy to notice. "Catherine Cole?"

"She and Wendy have known each other for a long time. They first met at St. Gabriel's." Amy pretended not to hear her hostess's sharp intake of breath. "They've kept in touch although Catherine moved south with her husband after her retirement. She and her husband have a beautiful home and they're enjoying country life. Of course she still makes trips to London and meets up with Wendy."

Jane sniffed. Amy waited. A few moments of silence ensued, each woman eyeing the other until Jane cleared her throat and asked: "They're both retired from nursing? Goodness, how time flies. It's a hard life and nurses never get enough credit or money for the job they do – I always said that to Valentine."

"I think Catherine misses it."

"I'm sure."

Jane sipped her coffee. Her suspicions about the woman before her had been well-founded. Amy Kennedy had finally mentioned Catherine Cole. A challenge? She couldn't let her visitor see that she was in any way put out. "When did you last see Catherine?"

"Very recently. I had a holiday with herself and Sam, her husband. Your name came up in conversation a few times. Catherine knew your husband well."

Definitely a challenge. Jane placed her glass on the patio table. "I vaguely remember my husband mentioning her. They didn't work together for long, I think. Catherine Cole left paediatrics to go into the general ward if my memory serves me correctly."

"That wasn't her choice at the time – Catherine told me that there was a misunderstanding between them." Amy's courage was mounting with every word.

281

"Perhaps you're right. Valentine never discussed the details of his work with me. He was the soul of integrity."

The charade went on.

"I suppose you don't meet many of your husband's colleagues nowadays?" Amy asked.

"One or two, that's all." Jane put on her sunglasses.

It would be harder now to gauge her reactions, Amy thought. "Valentine's associates did keep in contact for a while but, you know how it is, the years pass and people move on."

"But you did meet Catherine Cole recently," Amy persisted, "at the opening of the new wing. She told me she spoke to you." Damn the sunglasses. What would Jane's eyes betray? Her small smile was impossible to fathom.

"I don't remember. She told you that?"

"Yes. She was most definite."

"Oh, maybe you're right." Jane shrugged. "There were so many people there that day, I scarcely knew to whom I was speaking."

Dismissed. She'd dismissed it with great aplomb. Now what?

"May I have a cigarette, Mrs Kennedy?"

Amy obliged. "Please call me Amy."

"Thank you." Jane leaned forward and Amy lit her cigarette, noticing again the slight tremor in the old lady's hand.

Time for a breather. "Mrs Edwards, may I visit the bathroom?"

"Of course. It's the first door to your left at the top of the stairs."

Jane Edwards was worried. More than worried – afraid. Who *was* this Amy Kennedy? Jane didn't trust her. Oh, she was polite and well-spoken and very respectable but there was something almost menacing about her. The discussion appeared normal; her tone was warm and companionable, her gestures easy and natural – too natural – as if Amy had practised the lines; not missing a cue and at all times in control. Jane had deliberately sent for her to find out as much as she could but now the shoe was on the other foot. The conversation was pointed.

Jane had gleaned one very important fact: Amy knew Catherine Cole. What had she called her? *An old family friend.* How great a friend? Someone she would confide in? They had spoken together about Valentine. How much had Catherine Cole known at the time? How much did Amy Kennedy know now?

And why was she here?

How should she behave when this impostor came back to the table? How long could Jane keep up this act? How much, in safety, could she say? And how would she know if she'd said too much? She'd put the ball firmly back in Amy's court.

If only Valentine was here now. He'd know what to do.

Henry, having helped the housekeeper with the dishes and fitted the light bulb, came back to the garden and took his seat. "You two have been getting acquainted, Mother?"

"Amy knows a lot about us, dear," Jane informed him.

"I wouldn't say that," Amy broke in, "just bits and pieces. I'm glad to have met you both. It's good to be able to put faces to names one has heard about."

"You have us at a disadvantage." Jane was quite defensive now. "I'm not sure exactly what you've heard."

"Nothing bad, I hope?" Henry said. "Have we family skeletons you were keeping from me, Mother?"

Jane's face hardened. "Why don't you ask Amy?"

"I know very little," Amy replied. "I did hear your husband highly spoken of."

"Valentine was well-liked. Let's go back indoors. I'm feeling quite chilly." Jane stood up, led them back to the sitting-room and went to the mantelpiece. She took a silver-framed photograph and passed it to Amy. "That's my husband. Handsome, you will agree?"

Very handsome. Tall, grey-haired, same brown eyes as his son but there was an arrogance in his expression that Henry didn't share. Amy decided to take the bull by the horns. "Catherine was particularly friendly with a girl who used to work for you."

Jane's eyes narrowed, fuelling Amy's resolve to keep on. "She was Irish, as a matter of fact."

"An *Irish* girl used to work for you? You never told me that,

Mother." Puzzled, Henry turned to Amy. "How did you know that, Amy? Did you know her, this girl?"

"She was a distant relative." Amy reached for her cigarette packet. *Distant* covered it all right.

"How extraordinary," Henry exclaimed. "Tell us more."

Amy, to avoid Jane's unnerving stare, focused on her lighter as she lit up. "It wasn't that extraordinary at the time – a lot of Irish people emigrated to find work – mostly to America but thousands of others went to England. Many were forced to do very menial work." Amy tried not to sound bitter.

"I'd say she was glad to have found such a good position," Henry said tactfully. "My parents were great employers. I told you that, didn't I, Amy? We had the same housekeeper for twenty-five years and Grace has been with you now for how long, Mother?"

"Over forty years."

Amy couldn't let them sit there congratulating themselves on their wonderful record as kindly patrons. "The Irish girl didn't stay long, did she? She left your employment suddenly."

Jane Edwards ran her tongue over her lips. "It was a long time ago, Amy. I'm surprised you heard about it at all – it was before you were born."

"Yes, it was." Amy held her gaze.

"She was very unhappy with us, as I recall. She missed Ireland."

"What was her name?" Henry was intrigued.

"Elaine," Amy murmured.

"Yes," Jane said slowly. "Elaine Doherty. But she got married soon after she left our employ, I was given to understand. We lost touch."

"Shiels was her married name," Amy replied calmly.

"And she's a relative of yours?" Henry asked. "You never said a word, you sly old thing. What did she work as, Mother? An upstairs maid?"

The casual way he said it made Amy want to slap him. It wasn't his fault. He had no idea what effect his words would have on her.

"She looked after me." Jane was barely audible. She sat primly, her hands folded in her lap. "And you, for a short while, Henry."

"A nanny? You never let *any*one look after me, Mother. I was too precious, that's what you always said." He gazed at her affectionately. "She wouldn't let me out of her sight when I was child, Amy." He walked over to his mother's chair and stroked her cheek tenderly. "You mollycoddled me."

Jane gripped his hand.

* * *

The cathedral in the Place de Verdun was packed. A woman beside them, a patient, Amy gathered, chattered in whispers to Henry while Amy studied the programme: Eric Bibb, a big name in the States for blues and soul music and Cyndee Peters, a celebrated Gospel singer. Should prove an entertaining evening – if her headache would stop pounding. Wine or tension or a combination?

Amy admired the stained-glass windows which reflected the orange glow from the makeshift stage lights, erected under the silver pipes of the organ at the end of the church. The stone walls shimmered in the candlelight. Romanesque arches. Hushed voices all around. The audience was mixed – young and old. The atmosphere was serene but a large macabre painting of the Crucifixion on a nearby wall unnerved Amy.

The concert began to polite applause. Eric Bibb started with "Going Down Slow" followed by "The Needing Time", a moody air. While she listened, Amy's thoughts ran wild. If asked, she'd have been hard-pushed to describe the visit with Jane Edwards.

Starched. Laboured. Yes, she'd been up to high doh. And Jane, for all her put-on composure, had been deeply troubled too. Had Henry noticed? Amy closed her eyes and listened to a hillbilly version of a Gospel song called "Lonesome Valley."

"Are you enjoying it?" he whispered.

"Very much so."

"Looks like they're dividing the night between them. It will be Cyndee Peters after the interval."

A man behind coughed; they got the message.

The rich smooth voice of Cyndee Peters rang out; deep and

mellow, lamenting the trouble she'd seen. How apt. The music should have had a soothing effect but Amy was too keyed-up. Her thoughts went back to every word Jane had uttered, every gesture, every nuance. Amy replayed them over and over in her mind. Words she'd spoken and those she had not.

She had three days left here. She'd come with a specific purpose and she wouldn't go home until she'd accomplished what she'd set out to do. She had to catch Jane Edwards off guard. Tomorrow she'd pay an unannounced visit to the villa.

Thirty-eight

Jane Edwards pushed her breakfast tray away. She wasn't hungry. She felt tired and fractious and was tempted to stay in bed, but that would only make her more despondent. Should she talk to Henry? And say what?

We did it for you. All for you. We loved you. We acted in your best interests.

How could he accept it? How could anyone? What he didn't know wouldn't hurt him – and that was Jane's *raison d'être* – to keep Henry from getting hurt. Wasn't that the aim and motivation for all her past actions? For all of Valentine's? Everything had been done to protect Henry.

And now this woman had appeared after all these years? She'd followed a trail that had led her here. What did she want?

Grace entered the room with a large bath towel and a silk dressinggown draped over her arm. "I've run your bath, madam."

She was becoming very stooped, but it would be cruel to suggest retirement after forty years' loyal service. Grace needed to be needed.

The housekeeper folded the items over a chair and went to collect the tray. "Oh dear, you've hardly touched it. You need a good breakfast to start the day, madam. You must keep up your strength."

"Yes, thank you, Grace."

"Will you be lunching at home today?"

287

"I will, but there's no need for you to stay in. A light salad will do."

"Very good. I had it in mind to visit Madame Bertrand, the butcher's wife. She's ill."

"Certainly go, Grace, and give her my regards."

"I'll bring her some of my strawberry jam."

"That's a kind thought. Be sure to leave a jar or two for me – you know how I adore your preserves."

Grace beamed. "And the doctor does too."

The peal of the front doorbell sent Grace scurrying – she was still incredibly quick on her feet.

"Mrs Edwards is indisposed. I'm sorry." Grace was about to close the door but Amy held her ground.

"I'll wait."

"That would be inadvisable. Mrs Edwards is not free at the moment to entertain visitors."

"I must see her." Amy was adamant.

Grace curved her lip condescendingly. "Who shall I say is calling?"

Amy refused to be deterred by this woman's obvious slight: the housekeeper gave no indication of recognition although they had been introduced only the evening before.

"Amy Kennedy is my name. I was here yesterday. I'm a friend of Doctor Edwards and I need to speak most urgently with his mother."

Reluctantly the housekeeper let her into the hall. "Please wait here."

Grace didn't like this woman. She was too pushy. She climbed the stairs very slowly and disdainfully. She wasn't going to be dictated to by any self-proclaimed *friend* of the doctor's.

Amy, standing by the hall table, noticed the framed photographs on the wall. She moved closer to study them. One was of a superb ivy-covered mansion in large grounds. Must be their Surrey home. It was magnificent. So, this was where Henry had grown up and this was where her mother had worked – as a servant. There was a photograph of a small boy dressed in tennis gear. Henry presumably. He looked buoyant and bright-eyed.

Amy had never been more determined. No matter how hard this

morning's meeting was going to be, how unpleasant or hurtful, she wouldn't be satisfied until she had answers.

All the answers.

The housekeeper came back. Her dark expression matched her black dress. "Mrs Edwards will be down in twenty minutes, if that is convenient." Prim.

"It is."

"She asks that you wait for her on the patio. This way, please."

Amy followed the housekeeper out to the garden and took a seat under the umbrella.

"May I offer you something to drink?" Polite but stiff.

"No, thank you. I'm fine."

Amy was not fine. Nerves, misgivings, dread and disgust battled for supremacy in her overtaxed brain. She lit a cigarette. She repeated the salient points and arguments over and over in her mind. She wouldn't be fobbed off today. She was very clear about what she had to ask and to say. She was ready to reveal her own identity.

"Good morning." Jane Edwards sat down on the seat directly opposite Amy. Like the previous evening, she adopted a false composure.

Amy muttered hello.

"It looks like rain, doesn't it? The sky is quite overcast. Perhaps you would prefer to talk indoors?"

"Whatever you choose."

"We'll stay here, then. Let's have some tea. I'll call Grace."

"Mrs Edwards, if you don't mind, I'd like to get on with this. I've come a long way to meet you and my time here is running out."

Jane laid her cheek on her hand in a way calculated to irritate. "Pardon?"

"I haven't much time left in La Rochelle. There are things I have to clear up and you're the only one who can help me to do that."

Jane Edwards pursed her lips. "So, you admit to having come here with the express aim of seeking me out."

"Yes, I do." Amy outstared her.

"I knew it. From the moment I laid eyes on you I was suspicious," the older woman declared openly.

"Ditto," Amy boldly replied.

"You're a phoney, Mrs Kennedy."

Amy gritted her teeth and counted to ten.

"And poor Henry was totally taken in by you. He showed you nothing but kindness and this is how you repay him. I hope you're pleased with yourself. Is that the way you usually carry on?

"*I*'m not the phoney, Mrs Edwards."

"Certainly, you are. You're here in my home under false pretences. You wormed your way surreptitiously into my son's favour – you used him to get to me." Jane pulled her chair closer to the table. "Would you mind telling me why?" Her eyes glinted, her cheeks reddened but her voice remained steely.

"I think you know why."

Jane Edwards drummed her fingertips on the table. "Did Elaine send you?"

Amy shook her head. She said nothing. Let the old girl sweat.

"This *is* about Elaine, isn't it?"

Amy nodded slowly, thoughtfully. Gestures, she decided, were sometimes more efficacious than words. Her silence was having the desired disturbing effect on her hostess.

Jane rubbed her forehead. "What does she want? Money?"

"Elaine doesn't want anything," Amy replied, infuriated by the slur. "I do."

"Mrs Kennedy, could you stop playing games, please?"

"I'm not the game-player, Mrs Edwards, you are – you and your late husband."

Jane's temper rose. "How dare you speak to me like this! Who do you think you are? More to the point: who exactly *are* you and what business have you to pry into my personal life?"

"Your personal life has had an inordinate influence on mine," Amy retorted, choking with the rage she was trying so desperately to keep down.

"Poppycock! Either tell me who you are and what you want or I'll be forced to ask you to leave."

Forbidding tone but Amy held her ground. "I'm a relative of Elaine's. I'm here to find out your version of her story. I want to know everything," Amy asserted. "I want the truth."

"Did she send you?" Jane asked again.

"No. I came on my own behalf."

Jane averted her eyes from her unwelcome guest. "Why are you snooping around now, Mrs Kennedy? Why now?"

"I only heard the story recently."

"What story?"

"About you and your husband firing Elaine Doherty and sending her home to Ireland."

"We had every right to do that – we were her employers and she didn't fulfil her role. To put it kindly, she was far from satisfactory. We did what we had to do." Jane fidgeted with her lace handkerchief. "I don't see that it's any of your concern, Mrs Kennedy. I find your meddling extremely impertinent."

Amy ignored the insult. "Firing her was one thing. However, you went much further than that. You accused Elaine of something abominable, Mrs Edwards. You blackened her character with a vicious lie which was detrimental to her health and happiness."

"How dare you! Such impudence!" Jane went purple in the face. "You have no business –"

"*You* had no business toying with the life of another human being," Amy flashed, then she took hold of herself again. She had to calm down. It was vital that she kept control if she wanted this woman to answer her questions. She couldn't botch it up now – there was too much to lose. "I accept the fact that Elaine was unsuitable and you had the right, the duty even, to get rid of her. But the way you did it was inhuman. You and your husband accused her of being responsible for the *death* of your child."

Jane, poker-faced, sat and glared at the grass. She was hot and flustered. The garden began to swim before her eyes. Finally, she looked up. "There's a lot you don't know."

"Which is why I'm here."

"What did Elaine tell you?"

"Nothing."

"Nothing?"

"Not a word."

"Elaine told you nothing?"

"No."

"And who . . . ah, Catherine Cole, of course."

"Yes, Catherine Cole. Were it not for her I wouldn't have known the first thing about this. I'm very grateful to her."

"I wouldn't be if I were you."

"Is that some kind of threat?"

"No, Mrs Kennedy, merely a statement of fact. Elaine Doherty was not as innocent as you seem to think."

"She was innocent of what you denounced her for – Henry is living proof."

"Living proof – thanks to me and my husband. Elaine Doherty was a very sick girl. Disturbed." She brushed aside Amy's effort to interrupt. "She was dangerous – guilty of neglect, gross neglect. She was employed to look after our child and, for a short while, she managed well. Then, a few months after the baby's birth, Elaine became agitated and nervy – at times hysterical. At other times she was sweet and good-natured but, all in all, neither my husband nor myself thought her capable of looking after a baby. She became wilful and disrespectful to me, which was inexcusable, but, more importantly, she was cranky and harsh with the child. She had an uncontrollable temper."

"But you blamed her for *killing* the child," Amy hissed.

Jane Edwards slumped in her seat. "Our accusations were based on what we knew, Mrs Kennedy. The baby was maltreated. We found cuts. Bruises from pinch-marks."

Amy felt sick.

Tears stung Jane's eyes. "It was a shocking discovery for Valentine and myself. If you saw his little body – scarred and marked. I blamed myself for not having kept a closer eye on Elaine. But when we did eventually understand what was going on, we had to get rid of her."

"But the lie – how can you justify the cruelty of that?"

"Mrs Kennedy, I would have done anything to save that baby."

Jane Edwards moaned softly. "I did what I had to do. I didn't see any other way out."

"Please, you must tell me why," Amy whispered, her hands clenched on her lap. "It's really important. I have to know."

The old woman rocked back and forwards in the chair, sobbing now, her shoulders shaking.

"Mrs Edwards, please. I'm begging you."

Jane Edwards sat up rigidly. "You're her daughter, aren't you? That's why you're here. You're Elaine's daughter."

Thirty-nine

Amy gave her time to digest this news. After Jane had gathered her thoughts, she spoke in hushed tones. "I often wondered about her after she left us. Tell me about her, Amy. I'm glad she married and got her life back together again. I'm glad she had you."

Unconsciously, she'd reverted to the Christian name and her expression had mellowed. Amy saw her now for what she was – an old spent woman.

"She often spoke about her boyfriend, Joe," Jane continued.

"My father," Amy said.

"She'd told me that they couldn't afford to get married at the time which was why she came to England. She intended to save every penny we paid her. People went through hard times back then."

The Edwardses hadn't.

"I knew it wasn't over," Jane sighed. "I hoped and prayed it was but I knew, deep down I knew that Elaine would come back to haunt me. Valentine was able to put her out of his mind but I never could." She thumped her chest. "Your mother has been here tearing at my heart since the day she left. I can still see the hurt in her eyes, hear the deep resentment of her words. She cursed me and she cursed Valentine." Her voice cracked. "I was afraid of her then. I still am – afraid of the damage she might do."

"There's no need to fear her any more." Amy swallowed hard. "She died from cancer a year ago. It was a painful end."

Jane stared at her. "She's dead? Your mother's dead? Oh, dear. I'm sorry. I don't know what . . . I'm sorry to have spoken the way I did. I didn't know she was . . . I'm sorry."

She didn't look sorry. She looked relieved.

"Mrs Edwards, I don't know how you can offer me condolences. All her life, since she left your employ, my mother suffered. I did and so did my sister Claire. God knows what my father went through. What you did to her ruined her life and ours too." Although Amy's words were acrimonious, her tone was surprisingly mild.

Jane wrung her hands. "There's so much to tell. Elaine didn't have an easy life. We did try to help her."

"That's not what I was told," Amy said.

"You have to understand my position. Elaine had to be dealt with – she disrupted our family life. She created too many problems. But that's not relevant for you, is it? She was your mother and naturally you loved her."

"I tried to. I tried all my life. She wasn't happy. Nothing I did pleased her. She caused a lot of suffering for us and for herself. As a child I didn't understand. I wished and prayed that I could help her. I felt it was my fault."

"Children do experience guilt when parents are unhappy. I'm so sorry for you. It must have been terrible. Quite terrible."

Amy was galled. "I didn't come here for your pity, Mrs Edwards. I'm waiting for you to tell me what really happened."

"I did what I had to and what you've told me has confirmed my belief that what I did was for the best."

"How can you look me in the face and say that?"

"You've just admitted that you suffered at the hands of your mother." Jane clutched at her cardigan. "Don't you see? That was our belief all along – Elaine wasn't fit to look after a child. She was too unhappy, too stressed out to be a good –"

"Maybe that was down to you, Mrs Edwards? Isn't it possible that you were responsible for my mother's misery – that you *caused* it?"

"No. Elaine created her own torment. She was responsible for what happened to her."

"Responsible? You said she was disturbed. How could she be responsible if she . . . how could you have shirked *your* duty? You and your husband used my mother and when it suited you, you threw her on the scrapheap."

"No, no, no. We did *every*thing we could to help her." Jane, conscious that she'd shouted, looked towards the open window of the kitchen, no doubt fearing that her housekeeper might have heard.

"I can't fathom you, Mrs Edwards. You can sit there and justify anything to yourself. She was young, inexperienced, away from home, friendless except for Catherine Cole. She was a member of your household."

Jane's expression clouded. "You're so far off the mark. Elaine was very difficult – she tried to take over. She went from being obedient and submissive at the beginning to being demanding and . . . she was unstable. Valentine suspected slight schizophrenia."

Amy's dismay turned to anger. "But what caused her to be the way she was? The way you treated her possibly worsened her illness."

"I hope not." Jane rubbed her temples. "I sincerely hope not. I was very fond of her at first. But she changed dramatically after . . . after the baby was born."

Amy knew she was about to hear it all now and she braced herself.

"When your mother came to us, she was young and full of life. You could hear her laughing and singing all over the house. She was pleasant and docile and kind to everyone. Valentine gave her the job of looking after me because I wasn't well with my pregnancy. She was employed to take care of me but also to cheer me up and she did. We became good friends."

Amy very much doubted that but she didn't interrupt.
"Elaine was very bright but she lacked a formal education. I helped her with her reading. Afterwards, she became an avid reader: Dickens, Hardy, Tolstoy. She borrowed books from our library. Valentine was impressed. When she wasn't working, she buried herself in books."

Yes, Amy remembered. The only time her mother seemed to find peace was while she was reading quietly in her armchair.

"When the baby came along, Elaine seemed all right but, after a while, we began to notice little things. Odd things. She became snappish, irritable, irrational."

Amy tried to banish from her mind the temper tantrums, the spitefulness, the cruelty she'd endured from her mother.

"Things went from bad to worse. We paid her well but she started to borrow from the other servants. She went through her savings. Our kitchen maid at the time complained of having money stolen from her room. Then Valentine suspected that she was drinking."

"Drinking?"

"On the sly. She was a secret drinker. It got out of control."

"But she never drank," Amy protested. "I never saw her touch a drop."

"Would you have known?"

Her mood swings, her inconsistency, her paranoia. Locking herself in her bedroom and then the prolonged hospital stay. It all began to ring true.

Jane continued. "Her health deteriorated. She was pale and sickly and desperately tired. She wouldn't eat. She became more and more morose. I was growing stronger and she was becoming weaker and weaker, physically and mentally."

"I still don't understand. If you weren't pleased with her, why didn't you let her go? You could have found her a position elsewhere?"

"I could never have recommended her as a nanny. I told you about the crazed way she treated the baby. She was dangerous."

"Your husband was a well-known doctor. What about his contacts? He should have known how to handle the situation. Why didn't he get psychiatric help for her? Why didn't *you* get her help?"

"I wanted to but Valentine wouldn't hear of it. He had to avoid scandal."

"Scandal?" Amy cried out. "My God Almighty, what kind of a man was he? And you? Had you no compassion?"

"I went by my husband. My first duty was to him."

"Your husband could have done something – he had colleagues who would have helped. Why didn't he seek that help?"

"He had his reasons."

"If you had no pity for my mother, why didn't you do something for the baby?"

"We did."

"What? What did you do? You were ignorant of the situation until it was out of control. Do you call that responsible? If my mother was as unhinged as you make out, it was your duty to get her help. Maybe drugs would have cured her. She was in your employ and you deliberately ignored her condition. Your treatment of her was . . . appalling."

"Do you think we should have had her committed?" Jane retorted. "Is that what you'd have wanted?"

Amy paused and tried to calm down. Fear was eating away at her. She was terrified of what she might hear next and yet she was morbidly fascinated by the story and she had to hear it to the end. She took a few deep breaths.

"Mrs Edwards, please. None of your explanations makes sense."

The old lady mopped her brow. "Amy, I think I've said far too much already. Your mother's dead. Why open up old wounds?"

"I *have* to know."

"I'm thirsty. I must take my blood-pressure tablets."

Was this a plea for mercy? If so, it wasn't working.

"You look as if you could do with something to refresh you. I'm going to call Grace."

Amy's feelings were torn – she wanted to be angry, to be furious with this woman; instead she felt only a deep sadness and regret. She smoked a cigarette and waited for the conversation to resume again. This would be the third version of her mother's story – would she finally hear the truth?

"I think it's best I start at the beginning," Jane said, wiping her lips with her napkin. "Valentine met Elaine at the hospital. He had observed how hard she worked as a nurse's aide there and knew she was miserable in the job. So, having consulted me, he offered her a position with us."

"Yes, Catherine told me," Amy said impatiently. "I don't want to go over old ground."

"There's something you don't know, something significant. When she came to us, she was pregnant. She was, what used to be called, a fallen woman."

Amy's face burned. A sudden uncontrollable flush spread over her cheeks and down her neck. She felt faint.

"It was a very frightening time for Elaine," Jane said slowly, almost to herself. "Unmarried girls who had babies were completely ostracised in those days, but you must know all that."

Her mother had been pregnant. Unmarried and pregnant. Amy's throat constricted.

"We took her into our home as an act of mercy. We felt it our duty to help her. The alternatives were unthinkable."

Homes. Laundries. Charity. Amy wiped the sweat from her brow. She was burning up and she found it difficult to breathe. She sipped the cold lemonade and a pain shot through her forehead between her eyes. Her mother had been pregnant. Hadn't she suspected something like that all along? Somewhere deep inside of her, Amy had suspected. She'd never said it to Sarah or Catherine Cole – never voiced her suspicions. Not even to herself. But when Jane Edwards said the words, Amy had instinctively known.

"Valentine saved her face by moving her from London. Your friend Catherine didn't know *that,* did she?"

Amy was too crushed to reply.

"We *were* good to her. When her condition became obvious I moved her out of the big house and settled her in the cottage at the end of the garden. She had complete privacy there – her own quarters. We had it redecorated for her: whitewashed walls, new furniture, everything. She was very comfortable."

Her mother had a baby before she was married. How utterly ironic. The woman who'd instructed her all through her adolescence on morals, self-respect, self-control. The woman who was obsessed with *respectability.* She'd lived a lie her whole life long.

Tell the truth and shame the devil.

She must have gone through hell.

And Amy's father – had he known? Had she told him? Had she admitted her disgrace when she came back to him? Yes, yes, he must have known. That's what he'd meant when he told Amy she might find out something that would hurt her.

Oh, God, it was a nightmare. And there was worse to unfold. Finally, Amy found her voice. "You kept her on after she had the baby?"

"Of course. We weren't going to abandon her when her son was born. She had nobody else to turn to – not even her great friend, Catherine Cole. She was too ashamed. I tried to get her over her guilt. I tried to get her to love the child."

"She didn't love him?" Amy whispered.

"She saw him as a punishment for her sins. Her Catholic upbringing had left an indelible mark."

"Oh God."

"The child was beautiful. A little angel. She called him Cormac."

"What happened to him?"

Jane ignored the question. She talked on and on, but it was no longer for Amy's benefit. She was reliving the past aloud.

"Her mood and her health had deteriorated so badly that Valentine was extremely concerned. We gave her a holiday. She went to visit Catherine Cole in London and that very week the baby died."

Everything began to fall into place: there *had* been a death; a funeral. A *real* funeral. A baby died – the Edwards hadn't lied about that. Was her mother the cause of his death? Had she killed her own son?

Jane had closed her eyes. A sad smile played around her lips. She was back in another time.

"Did my mother cause the baby's death?" Amy croaked.

Jane sat up abruptly and pulled her cardigan over her shoulders. "The child had colic. He was very fragile. Nobody can be sure. It was a cot death. One night when he was particularly fractious, I was wakened by his screams and I got frightened, I hurried to his

301

room and . . . I found him . . ." Her voice strangled. Jane Edwards took a deep jerky breath and Amy poured her another glass of lemonade. She gulped at it, spilling it down her grey blouse. Her breathing quickened and her lips quivered. She fought for the breath to continue. "I thought he was asleep." Another long drink from the glass. "He was dead. His little body was cold and his lips were blue. I'll never forget it – the sight of that little mite . . . dead. Cold."

"Was my mother to blame? How can you be so sure?"

"She was too rough with him. Some babies are very hard to manage – constant crying, screaming; waking up at all hours of the night demanding attention. It can be daunting and some women can't handle it." Jane shuddered. "Elaine couldn't. She simply couldn't cope. She didn't love him as I did . . . she didn't cherish him." She laughed, much to Amy's horror. "He was so pretty, so chubby. Such a smiling face."

"Chubby?" Amy's chest heaved. "But he was poorly, you just said. He had colic."

"Did I?" Jane stared wildly at her.

"If he was fragile," Amy said, clutching at straws, "he must have died from natural causes. A cot death. It happens all the time." Amy spoke faster. "It was natural causes, wasn't it?"

"Perhaps."

"So, why lie to her? Wasn't it enough that she lost her son? Why did you have to wreak vengeance on her?"

Jane buried her head in her hands. "It wasn't vengeance. It wasn't that at all."

"Tell me why you got rid of her in such an dreadful way? Why didn't you let her attend her son's funeral? Catherine told me she wasn't allowed back to Surrey. You kept her at bay in London while you buried her child. How could you have been that cruel? You should have let her bury her son. That would have been the kind thing to do. She might have got better." Amy grabbed the older woman by the arm. "She might have learned to accept it."

"Accept it?" Jane echoed hysterically. The tears ran down her face. "Don't you understand? *My* son was the sickly child, Amy, my son. Elaine's child was healthy. Robust. Full of smiles and chuckles."

"Oh, Jesus."

"For Elaine he was a nuisance, an inconvenience, a mistake."

"No."

"She didn't want him or deserve him."

"Stop it," Amy screamed. "Stop it."

"This way she got out of her predicament. She had the chance to start her life again. What chance had I? I could never have more children. It wasn't fair."

Consternation swamped Amy's mind as the truth finally seeped in. She jumped up from the table. "You switched babies? You . . . you kept Elaine's son after you buried your own?"

Jane bowed her head.

"You did, didn't you? My God, you switched babies."

"We did what we knew was right," Jane pleaded. "She couldn't love him the way we did. She couldn't have given him such a good life. You know Henry. You've seen how he has turned out. He's a brilliant doctor. He's led a charmed life. He's balanced and happy and contented. How would he have ended up with *her*? Elaine wasn't fit to be a mother."

The truth of her words stung.

"But you had no right," Amy jumped up from the table, beside her with anguish. "You had no right at all. Elaine's child belonged with her – no matter what. How could you sit and pass judgement on her? There's no excuse, moral or legal or human, for what you did. You had no right to take away a child from its own mother."

Jane bowed her head. "We'd tried so long to have a child of our own."

"That's no excuse," Amy cried, her fists held tightly in front of her as if she was about to strike.

"We adored him."

"He wasn't yours to adore." Amy slumped back into her seat.

Her mother's baby. He was her brother, she realised suddenly. Henry Edwards was her half-brother. Her brother. Amy sat and shook. Her whole body shook.

"We swore we'd give him everything he needed – a happy

childhood, good memories, a brilliant education, a fine upbringing. We lived up to those promises and you can't deny that."

"That's not the point," Amy groaned. "You changed his name; you changed his identity. You played God. Henry – Cormac – didn't belong to you or to your husband –"

Amy froze. How could she have been so stupid? Why hadn't she realised it? Or deep down had she known that too? "Tell me," she said bitterly, "tell me the whole horrible truth. Am I right?"

"Yes." Jane muttered. The ringing in her ears was back again and it got louder. "Yes, now you know it all. Valentine was the baby's father."

Forty

The sky blackened and the clouds burst. Hot heavy rain beat down. Amy shakily helped the distraught woman into the house. It was hard to know which of them was the more upset. As she gripped Jane's arm, Amy felt the weakness, the fragility of the bones.

Grace came running out to help. "You'll get your death, Mrs Edwards," she fretted. "Come inside. This is madness." The last words were directed at Amy.

Madness.

They sat in the sitting-room. Grace had lent Amy some clothes – a skirt and top which didn't fit but would do until Grace had dried her dress.

Borrowed robes.

"Madam, come up to bed," the housekeeper pleaded as she towel-dried her employer's hair. "You're worn out."

"It's all right, Grace. Just a few more minutes."

With a scowl and a menacing glare at the intruder, the housekeeper plugged in an electric fire. A last warning shot to Amy: "Just a few minutes."

Jane took up the story again. Amy sat in stony silence and listened to the account of how young Elaine Doherty had fallen for Valentine Edwards. The doctor was handsome, authoritative, charismatic; Elaine was head-over-heels in love. Flattered. Seduced. He'd had many mistresses, Jane explained. Acceptable for a hot-blooded male who exuded charm, power and sensuality. But Elaine was smitten, bewitched, duped – expected a long-term commitment.

Marriage.

"She actually believed Valentine would divorce me," Jane said. "It was woeful. She became besotted by him, deadly jealous of me. Once she was established in the cottage, she thought herself secure, that it was only a matter of time before he'd come around to her way of thinking."

Cold shivers ran up and down Amy's spine. She listened intently to the tale Jane told but it sounded fantastical – a bodice-ripping saga from the romantic fiction Amy had read as a teenager. Poor girl meets rich boy. The girl in the story was a complete fabrication who bore no resemblance to the hard woman Amy had known – or thought she'd known.

"She had a great capacity to fool herself," Jane continued. "Elaine believed that because she had his son, their relationship would be cemented. No doubt Valentine promised her the sun, moon and stars. That was the way he operated with his women."

"What about *you?*" Amy was incredulous. "How did you bear it? How did you sanction his conduct? Having his young lover in your presence . . . and their child? How could you stand it?"

"I had to," she replied simply. "We all had to. Mistresses were – and indeed still are – common in our circle. It's a fact of life we learn to accept early on."

Amy wanted to smack her.

"Elaine wasn't the first but she was the last. When we lost our baby, Valentine did change. He devoted his life to Elaine's child and, from then on, to me. He had what he wanted, you see – he had his son."

And Amy's mother was not part of the package. She couldn't be. The lump in Amy's throat grew bigger. "He was callous beyond belief."

"He was a good husband to me. He had his needs and I, being ill much of the time, couldn't satisfy them, but I was in love with Valentine all my life."

Amy couldn't take any more. "I have to go." She stood up.

Jane, startled, gaped at her. "Will you tell Henry?"

"That's not *my* job."

"You think it's mine?"

"He's entitled to know."

"He knows he's loved. Isn't that enough? Amy, I implore you. Don't do anything that will ruin my relationship with my son."

"*Your* son." Amy eyes smarted.

* * *

She left the villa in the teeming downpour. Her dress was sodden again but she didn't notice. She walked the narrow streets back towards the hotel, her tears mingling with the falling raindrops. When she got to the Parc Charruyer, she sat on her favourite bench and thought. And thought and thought.

Her mind was a maelstrom.

* * *

Jane Edwards took to her bed with a hot port. She was weary. Bone weary. Her eyes were sore from weeping. But, miraculously, she felt better about everything. A tremendous sorrow had given way to mitigation. A huge weight had been lifted from her shoulders. The lie, which had hounded her, ruined her peace of mind, had been wiped away. One other person on the planet knew the truth – or at least the edited version of it.

She felt free.

And Henry? Would he be told? Amy Kennedy – what kind of a woman was she? Vindictive like her mother? She was angry, very angry now and with due cause. She'd want to lash out, to take revenge. But why hurt Henry? Why destroy his life?

* * *

Her brother. Henry Edwards was her half-brother. His roots were half-Irish. This strong, warm man was related to her in the most

307

intimate way. He must be told. He had been most vilely abused by lies, deceit, corruption. His birth, his life, his whole existence had been a falsification.

Amy had been sitting on the park bench for more than an hour and was soaked to the skin. She hadn't noticed that the rain had stopped. She'd sat and cried. She was boiling mad at first but now she felt nothing but sadness. And frustration: Henry Edwards was not who he thought he was. Every atom of Amy's being cried out for justice, fairness, truth. How could she ignore now what she knew? She was his sister. How could she play dumb and say nothing?

Why should *she* propagate the myth?

Forty-one

"Deux messages pour vous." The receptionist, discreetly ignoring Amy's soggy clothes and wet tousled hair, handed her two notes.

"Merci. Je peux commander un café?"

"Bien sûr. Un grand crème?"

"Oui, je serai là, assise par la fenêtre."

"D'accord." The girl telephoned the order to the kitchen staff. "Tout de suite."

Amy, conscious of her unkempt appearance, ignored the stares from a woman at a nearby table in the foyer. She took a seat by the window and glanced at the two telephone messages. The first was from Sarah asking her to phone.

What would she tell Sarah? How much, in honour, could she tell? Had she the right to lay bare her mother's darkest secret? To what purpose? To unburden herself? No, that would be wrong. Amy had trespassed; invaded her mother's past and, as she had been warned, opened the hornet's nest. Now she must suffer the consequence – the loneliness of knowing.

The waitress served her coffee. The second note was a message from Maurice. He'd made contact at last. Was this to tell her about selling the house? Presumably. It didn't seem to matter any more. Her anger against her husband had abated because she knew now how pointless it was – it sapped her energy and that was all. It had absolutely no effect on him. He was blithely unaware of it and if he *did* know he couldn't begin to understand how his actions affected her.

Amy put the notes in her handbag. After her coffee, she'd go up to her room, get out of these wet clothes, have a shower and decide what she'd tell Sarah. Then she'd ring Maurice at the surgery. But what if there was bad news? About her father? He might have suffered a relapse. Amy left the coffee and hurried to the lift.

* * *

"No, no, your dad's out of the woods. He's up out of bed now and walking around on one of those frames."

He'd hate that – an assault on his dignity.

"I went to see him yesterday. He's in fine spirits, Amy."

Her father had always put on a good face.

"Did Dawn phone you?" Maurice wavered. "I'm sure you're annoyed. I wanted it to be a surprise but I certainly didn't mean for you to hear the news like that. Amy, are you angry with me?"

His disquietude appeased her. She'd gone past animosity.

"How do you feel about selling?"

"You know how I feel, Maurice. It's what I want."

"We have a lot to discuss, Amy, and this time I'm ready to listen. I've made a few blunders but they weren't intentional. I'll make it up to you if it's the last thing I do."

She suddenly felt sorry for him.

He coughed nervously. "How are things going there?"

"OK."

"When are you coming home?"

She couldn't make out his tone. Wary? "Monday. I'll be home around six in the evening."

A pause. It felt like he was about to say something else but then changed his mind. She heard him sigh, then he went on: "I bumped into Nancy Mulhearn in the shopping centre. She's all excited about you taking over as manager. I told her you'd done a marvellous job for me in the surgery and that she was lucky to have you."

That was praise indeed coming from Maurice.

"Amy?"

"Mmh."

"Did you hear what I said? About Nancy?"

"Yes, sorry Maurice. I'm not with it."

"You sound tired."

"I am a bit."

"Did you . . . did you find out what you wanted to know?"

"No." She certainly hadn't got the information she *wanted*. She'd got a horror story.

"Are you disappointed?" he asked gently, misinterpreting her words as she'd intended.

"A bit." Lies, she was telling lies and it was easier that way.

"It's probably all for the best, Amy."

"Probably."

"Will I pick you up at the airport in Monday?"

She deliberated.

"Amy?"

"If you want to, Maurice. That would be nice." She stared out of the window at the gardens below. Now that the rain had stopped, the sun was making a weak comeback. "Is everything all right with you? How's work?"

"Good, apart from a few casualties. A stray cat died from feline AIDS and do you remember Bruno, the bulldog? We had to put him down. It was a sad business but he had to be taken out of his misery. The cancer had spread. That's the part of the job I deplore." He was relieved to be able to talk about work – a safer subject. "Oh, I'm employing a new vet. I've no choice at this stage – the workload is mounting. I've some other plans too that we need to talk over."

His excitement and exuberance reminded Amy of how he was when they'd first met. But it was too late.

"I'd better go; I'm up to my tonsils. See you Monday. I'm looking forward to it," he added shyly.

She wasn't.

"Bye, Amy. Take care."

"You too."

The first hurdle was over. Next was Sarah. And Catherine Cole?

She'd be on tenterhooks, waiting for the great revelation. Better to get it over with. Amy took her address book from her suitcase and dialled the English number.

"Amy? I've been thinking about you. How *are* you? Where are you phoning from?"

"The Novotel. I've just come back from a visit to Jane Edwards."

"And?" Catherine's voice went up.

"It was difficult," Amy replied.

"What was she like?"

"Very defensive."

"Blooming sure. Amy, tell me."

"She wasn't what I expected, Catherine. She's physically quite frail but a formidable kind of woman. Indomitable."

"Did you confront her?"

"Eventually."

"This is like getting blood from a turnip! What did she say? Did she remember Elaine?"

"Oh, yes, she remembered her all right. She had a different version of events."

"She would, naturally she would. Was she covering up?"

"No, she came clean." Amy chose her words carefully. "It's not as we thought, Catherine. We were wrong."

"Wrong?"

This was it. Whatever she said now would quell the story forever. Her mother, crippled by fear, had kept the real truth from Catherine. That had been her choice and Amy felt obliged to abide by it.

"The baby did die."

"What?"

"Yes, he was very sick."

"He actually died. They were telling the truth. But your mother – it wasn't her fault? It couldn't have been – she was with me in London when it happened."

Amy gripped the receiver tightly. "There are degrees of guilt, I suppose. She wasn't directly responsible for the baby's death but apparently she had been very rough with the child and who can prove now that she hadn't precipitated his death? Jane Edwards has convinced herself that my mother was to blame."

Catherine groaned.

"From what Jane Edwards said, I believe my mother was very sick at the time."

"That's what I told you, Amy. She was in a dreadful state when she came to London."

"Jane was genuinely concerned about her health, she said, and that's why they sent her to you for a rest."

"Rubbish! That was their first step in trying to get rid of her. I always felt there was more to the whole business than met the eye."

Catherine would never know how right she was.

" So, this Henry *is* the second child."

"Yes, he is."

"The good doctor managed to produce a fine healthy son and heir in the end." There was acidity in Catherine's voice. "The family line sustained."

A healthy son. Good stock. Continuance. And her mother had been the brood mare – but the family line was polluted. Irish blood ran in Henry's British veins and, what Valentine had never bargained on – his progeny, his longed-for heir, unless he produced a son – which was now unlikely from what Henry had said – was the *end* of the line.

"What's Henry Edwards like?

This was the easy bit. "He's a lovely man; kind, down-to-earth."

"We did hear that Jane was a good mother. Remember what Wendy said?" Catherine reminded her. "Is he like her?"

"He's his own person, Catherine, but Wendy was correct. They're very fond of each other. There's a close bond. His mother worships him." With very word Amy uttered, she stabbed her own heart.

"How do you feel now, love?"

"Empty, Catherine. I feel empty."

"But your trip wasn't in vain? Maybe you understand your mother better?"

"A lot better."

"That's good. I'm still a bit flummoxed by it all, Amy, but at least it's over for you. You've learnt the truth and you'll have peace now."

Amy had to hang on for a few more minutes. She wanted to bawl, to scream, to have a bloody good cry.

"Sam and I were talking about you only the other day. We'd love to have you to stay again. Sam enjoyed your visit no end. Or if you'd like to leave it until the autumn, maybe Hallowe'en? Maurice is invited too, of course. And Dawn, if she'd like to come."

"Thanks, Catherine. Things are a bit up in the air at the moment on the home front. I'll call you soon, though."

"Do, Amy. Keep in touch."

* * *

Amy told Sarah the same story. She was practically reciting it by rote. The more she recounted it, the more she believed it herself.

Sarah was flabbergasted. "Gee, who'd have thought it, eh? The second son – and they called him by the same name – weird."

"Not unheard of, though."

"No, I suppose they got some comfort from it – this Henry replaced the first. It's nice in a way. You know, the whole idea of perpetuity. One child dies but maybe lives on in the other."

Henry Edwards: the desired offspring; the baby who would carry on the family name and tradition – but he was sick, weak and destined to die. Cormac Doherty: the replacement; a strapping baby boy – the answer to the Edwardses' hopes and dreams.

And Elaine? An Irish Catholic, away from family and friends, cut off, abandoned and alone. Too embarrassed to confide her trauma to her best friend, humiliated by her condition – her son a constant reminder of her sin. Elaine, her mother, who had been so fastidious, so respectable, so morally upright.

Tell the truth, Amy, and shame the devil.

Truth. Shame.

"Sarah, there are things I found out I can't tell you. I can't tell anyone. They're too private."

"I understand. Please don't try to explain. I can hear how distraught you are. Whatever you found out is your business, Amy. You're not compelled to say anything else."

The tears, that Amy had stemmed all day, trickled slowly down her cheeks. "I feel like an eejit," she whimpered.

"You're grand."

"I'll never forget all you've done, Sarah. You've been –"

"Amy, don't start. You've been a good friend to me all my life. There's no need for thanks."

But Amy was thankful.

"You've only two days left there. The time has flown."

"Yes, it certainly has."

"Jack phoned me this morning. He's begging to come home."

"Are you going to let him?"

"Yeah, he's done his time. It'll be a while before he takes me for granted again. I'm not so thick as to think he's had a road-to-Damascus conversion – but maybe he'll stop and think the next time, Amy. Because if he's unfaithful again I *will* leave him – I've made that crystal clear. You think I'm crazy, don't you, to take him back?"

"No, I don't. You're right to fight for what you want. Maurice is coming to the airport to pick me up."

"You're kidding!"

"No, he wanted to and I hadn't the heart to say no."

"Have you sorted things out, Amy?"

"In my head I have."

"The end of the road?"

"It has to be, Sarah. For his sake as much as mine. I hope I have the guts to carry it through."

"You have. You'll survive this, Amy. So will he, but it's not going to be easy for either of you."

"We can't continue persecuting each other. Staying together would be worse. There's Dawn to consider. She'll be hurt. All I can do is to try and make it as easy as I can for her. Do you think she'll understand?"

"She's not a fool. But it could be a rough ride – accepting that

315

your parents are splitting up is difficult at any age. You'll know how to handle it when the time comes."

"I hope so."

"What'll you do tomorrow, kiddo? It's your last full day there."

"I have to see Henry. I want to thank him for his kindness. I'll bring him to lunch."

"It's funny isn't it? How you hit it off so well with him considering you were complete strangers a week ago."

Strangers. Siblings.

Tomorrow, she'd meet Henry. Her half-brother. Her lost brother. This would be her final act in La Rochelle and the most difficult one.

Saying goodbye.

And when she got home there was her father to face. How many lies would she have to tell him? He knew about Elaine's baby – she was certain. But he believed the child to be dead.

Tell the truth and shame the devil.

What about the charity of silence?

Forty-two

Henry brought her for lunch. Still very emotional and troubled by everything she'd discovered, Amy was afraid she might break down and reveal all. She dreaded this final meeting – being forced, once again, to play the fraud.

The *brasserie* was busy. Amidst the chatter, laughter, to-ing and fro-ing of waiters and waitresses, Amy relaxed. She filled him in on the latest developments at home and her plans for the bookshop. He talked about his practice, his wife's imminent arrival and his sailing plans for the weekend. Then he mentioned his mother:

"She was a bit nervy this morning. She's in bed – blood pressure sky-high. I have to monitor it carefully. Her heart is not strong. She said you called to see her yesterday. That was nice of you."

Amy winced.

"I have to accept that she's not getting any younger. Still, she has a few good years left if she minds herself. Amy, I can't tell you how much I'll miss her when her time comes. She's always been my protector – my champion. I've been lucky. They say it's the only perfect love – that between a mother and a child."

"It can be." She pretended to study the menu.

"In my case, it's true," he continued blithely. "My mother gave me the most perfect gift of all – the gift of being wanted. Not every child feels that and it's such a tragedy."

"My mother was different." Amy poured still water from a large glass bowl. "Not affectionate. She found it hard to show her feelings."

317

"That was tough on you," he sympathised.

"Dad was very kind-hearted, very loving, but I never felt I was truly wanted by her. I think I was an inconvenience." She gave a faint laugh.

He didn't think it was funny at all. "What about the name she chose for you? *Aimée*. She who is loved."

Poor Henry. If he honestly believed her mother – their mother – had thought of that when she was choosing her daughter's name, he was woefully mistaken. She had been named by her father after an aunt.

"Your name lets you know how your mother felt when you were born."

She didn't argue. She accepted a glass of the white wine Henry had ordered. She took a sip and found it was light and fruity.

"My name simply states that I'm from a long line; Henry was my great and my great-great-uncle's name. Tradition and all that jazz. It's not the name I'd have chosen for myself." He grinned.

"It suits you." The name Cormac didn't fit him at all. He *was* a Henry.

Henry, who had a hearty appetite, chose the cheese plate instead of dessert. Amy hadn't been hungry but she'd made herself eat the salmon salad. He was paying for the meal and she didn't want to sit there fiddling with her food, causing him concern.

"I'm so glad we met, Amy. I've enjoyed my time with you. I'll miss you."

"Same here."

"You're always welcome for a holiday, you know that." He checked his watch. "I have to be back at the surgery in thirty minutes. Would you like a coffee?"

"Not for me."

"I hate having to rush away – I should have taken time off work – spent the day with you."

"I wouldn't expect that, Henry. You've given up a lot of your time already."

"We won't say goodbye – we will meet again."

318

"Henry, thank you for everything. You've made my time here very special."

"It was a pleasure – genuinely. You will come back to La Rochelle, won't you?"

She'd never be back.

He called the waiter. *"Je veux régler, s'il vous plaît."* He took something from his pocket. "My mother asked me to give you this."

Amy opened the envelope. It was a photograph of a young girl, with red hair and fresh face, sitting on a garden seat, a daisy chain around her neck.

Elaine.

"Mother told me she found it hidden away at the back of her wardrobe. Apparently it's that relation of yours who used to work for her. It's an old photo – a bit grainy."

"It's lovely," Amy whispered.

Henry handed the waiter his credit card. "My mother told me to thank you. Apparently there was some misunderstanding, some unpleasantness, but Mother said your visit cleared the air, whatever she meant by that. Who *was* that girl, Amy? Did you know her well?"

"Not as well as I'd have liked to." Amy placed the photograph back in the envelope.

Jane Edwards had taken a risk – a calculated risk. This was her way of saying she knew Amy would do the right thing by her and by Henry. "Say goodbye to your mother for me, won't you?"

"Will do."

They walked arm-in-arm from the restaurant and when they arrived out on the street, Henry embraced her. Amy closed her eyes and clung to him.

"Au revoir, Amy Kennedy. *Bonne chance.* Be happy."

When she opened her eyes, he was gone.

Forty-three

The drive home from Dublin Airport had been chaotic: the traffic crawled along, bumper-to-bumper, through Drumcondra and it hadn't eased much as they drove through the city centre and out towards the southside. Conversation had been kept to a minimum.

Maurice carried her bags into the hall. To Amy's amazement, the whole house had been painted.

"I got the decorators in – thought it might help to up the price," he explained. "I was bloody lucky to get them at short notice. One of my clients – Reggie Shortt, the guy with the Alsatian, – his brother-in-law owns the firm of decorators, so they fitted me in between other jobs. Do you like the colours? What do you think? The hall is much brighter, isn't it?"

She'd begged and begged for this. Now, when he was ready to sell, he'd got around to it. Maurice would never change.

There was a huge bouquet of flowers on the hall table with a card from Claire:

Welcome home, Amy.

They sat in the kitchen, the evening light fading. They'd talked for hours and Amy was exhausted.

"I guessed how you'd be feeling," he said hesitantly. "That's why I've moved into the flat. You need time here on your own. The auctioneer has been out to view the place but there's no rush. I told him you would decide the right time."

"Now is the right time, Maurice. You can go ahead."

He brightened a little. "That's handy because there's a builder who's very interested in a house in this area. He's actually made a private offer."

No rush!

"A good offer?" She tried to share his enthusiasm.

"Unbelievable! Five hundred thousand! Amy, I was totally gobsmacked. You see we're lucky to have so much garden space, the auctioneer said – this bloke is more interested in the site than the house itself – hence the huge offer."

£500,000!

"If we do decide to . . . if we can't work things out . . . of course we don't have to make any definite arrangements yet . . ."

Her eyes smiled sadly at him. He was still fooling himself. Funny, that. Maurice was always the one with the answers, the solutions. His past arrogance and self-assurance had always infuriated her – now she began to see it might have been a camouflage all along.

"You're entitled to half the money," he muttered quickly. "I've spoken to my solicitor. We have to have things legal and above board."

She was taken aback. She hadn't thought that far ahead – hadn't considered the financial implications at all. She'd been so caught up in her mother's story, so totally absorbed by recent revelations that her own situation had seemed remote. When she thought about her marriage at all it was only in human costs. Of course, Maurice would have looked into the finances. That would probably have been one of his first considerations.

"Don't look so shocked, Amy. If the worst comes to the worst at least I want to get everything settled properly and fairly. I want to be fair."

Signed. Sealed. Delivered. Everything in order – typical of him. Amy sat there, numb. All the animosity towards her husband had gone. He was in many ways like a small child who was trying his best to be better. She wanted to put her arms around him.

"You'd prefer we went our separate ways?" His eyes were pleading for her to refute although his voice was a bit stronger.

"I think it would be for the best, Maurice."

"I felt that would be your answer but, I suppose I was still half-hoping we could . . . I don't know."

"Salvage our marriage?"

"Yeah."

"Maurice, we've tried. We can't go on and on, dragging things out, postponing the inevitable."

"Where did it all go wrong, Amy? Was it when Dawn left?"

That had brought matters to a head. When Dawn lived with them they were a family. Bickering, squabbling – yes, but a family. It was when she and Maurice were left to their own devices that reality hit home. Her depression, awful as it had been for them all, had been the catalyst.

"Neither of us is to blame, Maurice."

"Did we try hard enough? Maybe I didn't?"

This was the first time he had ever admitted to doubting himself. Remorse and recrimination. Guilt – she'd gone beyond it.

"I do love you, Amy. I admire and respect you greatly. I didn't tell you that often enough and that *is* my fault."

"Maurice –"

"We were happy when we got married. We had it all." He groped for the right words. "I didn't pay attention. I missed the signals. My mother warned me – she told me I had to put you first."

His shoulders sagged – the little child inside the man. Amy finally went to comfort him. "Maurice, please don't." She stood behind him and put her arms around his neck. "We had more than twenty years together; good times and bad, ups and downs. That counts for a lot. Those years will never be wiped out."

"Our marriage wasn't a waste, was it?"

"How can you even think that? Look at what we have, Maurice – a wonderful daughter. Dawn was born of our love – how can that be a waste? And we were right together for a long time."

He held her to him. "We were, Amy. We were a team. Why did it have to change?"

We cannot live the afternoon of life according to the programme of life's morning – Amy had recently learned the wisdom of those words but she wasn't going to demean the moment by quoting Carl

Jung. Yet she did believe those words to be true for her. She had begun to see her life in stages and this one was definitely over. She couldn't wear the mask any longer.

"This needn't be the end of everything, Maurice. We've shared too much to throw it all away. We won't be living together but it doesn't mean we have to sever all contact."

"Maybe living apart will . . . oh, Amy, what am I saying? Who am I kidding? I don't want us to separate. I don't. It's going to be hell living alone. Lonely."

She hugged him tight. "For me as well."

But Amy knew the greater unhappiness was the loneliness of being with someone when you no longer shared, truly shared, a life.

"We'll still have each other, Maurice, and Dawn."

He stood up, turned to face her and kissed her cheek. It was so unlike him that she almost started to cry. A huge ball of pain buckled in her belly.

"I'll leave you to your unpacking." He sighed. "Back to my bachelor flat."

His hangdog expression tore at her. "I'll call over tomorrow to see you."

"Would you, Amy?"

"Of course. Ring the auctioneer, Maurice. Set the wheels in motion."

He picked up his jacket and went to the kitchen door. "Should I phone Dawn?"

"Yes, I will as well."

"I don't know what to say to her."

"When you hear her voice, the right words will come. Maurice, it won't be a shock for her."

"Do you not think so?"

"No, Dawn is very perceptive."

"But this is heavy stuff, Amy. How can we admit to our daughter that we've given up – that we've failed?"

"We haven't failed. We've faced up to our situation. It's the honest thing to do. We're ending something but we're moving on to something better for both of us."

"I'm not as sure as you are. I keep thinking that if we gave it one more try –"

"Maurice, don't torment yourself. We have to accept who we are and where we are now. *If onlys* will drive you distracted."

He looked at her sitting there, more composed than he'd seen her in a long time. Yes, she was upset but in her eyes, he read relief. No matter what she said now, what words of comfort she offered, what she couldn't disguise was the relief in her eyes. "I'll see you tomorrow." He had to get out of there.

* * *

Claire waited two days before she came to see her sister. "What can I say, Amy? Although I suspected it might come to this, it's still a blow. You and Maurice splitting up – how will he cope?"
Interesting, it was Maurice she was worried about.

"You'll be OK, I know that. You're the stronger. Women usually are."

"I didn't know you felt that way, Claire." Amy poured her another whiskey.

Claire glanced around the sitting-room. "This place is totally transformed. Much brighter. Pale yellow walls – is it primrose?" She frowned. "No, it's paler than primrose."

"You'd have to ask Maurice. He chose the colours. Yes, I quite like the room now – ironic, isn't it? I'll probably miss the place."

"Amy, are you thinking clearly? Maybe marriage guidance might –"

"No, Claire."

"I feel awful about a lot of things. You were right about me – everything you said. I was a bitch, a selfish bitch. I'm trying to do better."

"That's all any of us can do."

"It's not easy, this soul-searching business." She pouted. "I saw Jack last night in the supermarket. He was with Sarah and the girls. Anna and – I don't even know the younger one's name. Isn't that horrible? He must have mentioned her name but I don't remember it."

325

"Helen," Amy supplied.

"He'd bought those gas-filled balloons for them. They were laughing and kid-acting at the check-out. Sarah was holding his hand. They looked happy. I heard him laughing at something Sarah said. I was in the next queue – he didn't notice me."

"You'll forget him, Claire."

"I'll have to."

* * *

Her father was looking better, his complexion was healthy and his eyes were bright. They sat in the day room and he listened to his daughter's story – the parts she chose to tell him.

Joe munched on the French chocolates she'd brought back for him. "Hearing about the child, Amy, how did that affect you?"

"I felt numbed by it – to think of all the suffering Mam went through."

"By God, did she suffer." He shook his head sadly. "I tried to make it up to her."

"I know you did."

"She was inconsolable, Amy. At times I felt she was losing her mind. I thought that when we married, that when you came along . . ."

"Dad, it's all right."

"No, it isn't. Your mother's loss was our loss too, but the Lord works in mysterious ways. Frightful as it is to think, maybe it was better that her baby died? Your mother would never have managed."

She let him go on without interruption. The floodgates of his memory had opened and weren't to be blocked now.

"Elaine was guilt-ridden. Her spirit was broken, Amy, and I couldn't do a damn thing about it. It's no excuse but that's why I never interfered with your mother's treatment of you and Claire. Any harsh words from me, any intervention on your behalf, would have driven her over the edge. I know she was too cross with you and Claire, too driven – but she loved you both. She'd never have purposely hurt you."

326

Amy didn't know that at all. "You know the Edwardses accused her of killing the child?"

"They were wrong, Amy. Your mother was not capable of that at all." He gripped the sides of the chair. "We know that woman had it in for Elaine. She resented her deeply. No, no, Elaine would never have deliberately harmed her child."

Maybe not deliberately, Amy wanted to say but she kept silent. She thought it very moving that her father defended his wife so stoutly.

"Poor Elaine! Having been through that experience, she couldn't handle criticism from me. One time she smacked you and I objected . . . she went to pieces: locked herself in her room for days. I had to take time off work to mind you and Claire. The doctor had her hospitalised. After that I tried not to interfere. I didn't want to aggravate the situation. All I could do was to see that she kept up her medication."

Amy didn't mention the drink.

"It's terrible to think of the child's death but what sort of a life would he have had? What future? It chills me to think about it."

"Could you have accepted him, Dad?"

"Me? Of course I could, Amy. He was Elaine's son – I'd have loved him as my own. But he'd never have been that, would he? No matter how much I wanted it. Your mother was used and exploited but she never acknowledged that, especially not to herself. She revered Valentine Edwards. I swear she loved him to the end of her days. I was a poor substitute."

"No, Dad, you're so wrong about that. She never felt about him the way she did about you. Her feelings for him were based on fantasy – nothing more. She knew you all her life. She married you."

"When you were born, Amy, there was such excitement. My parents, Elaine's parents, all the family and neighbours and friends gathered around you in the Nursing Home. Your birth was a cause of celebration. How must she have been feeling? Everyone kissing and hugging and congratulating us. What a nightmare for her, knowing her first-born – a child who'd have been reviled and rejected by all those same well-wishers – was buried in the cold clay of an English graveyard. What must *that* have done to her?"

Amy. She who is well-loved. The first child of a married couple. Legitimate. Respectable. Welcome.

"And yet she knew that her little boy would never have been accepted in the Ireland of the fifties. Elaine could never have come home. Her life and the child's life would have been destroyed. I'd have lost her." His eyes filled up. "Maybe God took the baby out of kindness? Maybe it all turned out for the best?"

"Yes." Amy edged closer to her father on the couch.

"You won't say anything to Claire?" he asked nervously.

"No, Claire will never know – it wouldn't do her any good. And Mam wouldn't like it."

"You're an honourable woman, Amy. I'm very proud of you."

"And I of you, Dad."

Forty-four

Six weeks passed. Hectic weeks. Amy loved the shop: working with Nancy Mulhearn, organising the bookshelves, setting up the computerised lists, chatting to the customers, dealing with the wholesalers, showing the ropes to the new sales assistant and the two part-timers. She got a buzz out of it all. It was good to be employed again; to be out and about, meeting people. Being useful.

The sale of the house had gone through without too much trouble and Amy had another week to quit the house and settle in her new home – a modern town house in Avondale Lawns. She fell in love with it at first sight when Claire had driven her to see it. It was close to Blackrock village and the DART station. She was, in effect, only moving streets away. Her new house was a stone's throw from her husband's premises – an arrangement they were both happy about.

Maurice had supervised the removal men. He was going to keep his father's mahogany bureau and china cabinet but he agreed that the old suite – his mother's pride and joy – would have to be dumped. The only item she wanted from the house was a silver tray. Amy remembered her mother-in-law sitting up in her sickbed, polishing the tray with gusto, crooning away to herself. That was Amy's abiding memory of Pearl Kennedy – her singing.

Amy had left the house and visited Sarah during the clear-out. It was the end of her old life, and although she welcomed the change, it was hard to watch the bits and pieces, the emblems of her life with Maurice, being cast away. He must have felt it too.

The phone rang shrilly in the empty hall, breaking into her quiet reverie.

"Mum? Hi!" Dawn's chirpy voice.

"Hello, darling."

"I'm phoning to let you know that we're on our way to Boston. Angela's aunt will meet us at the station. She's taken time off from work to show us around."

"That's very nice of her."

"Speaking of work, how's it going?"

"Dawn, I'm thrilled with myself. I thought it would be more difficult to get into the swing of things but I've taken to the job like a duck to water."

"Good for you, Mum. When are you moving to the new house?"

"In a few days."

"You won't be sorry."

"In a way. I hadn't expected to be as unsettled about it as I am. You can't live for twenty years in a place and not put down roots. But the new house is bright and airy. The kitchen gets the morning sun."

"Have you any room for a lodger?" Dawn asked. "I'll need somewhere to stay for a while when I get back."

This was a white lie. Paul had already arranged the lease on a small house in Irishtown and Angela was going to share with them. This time there'd be no dicey flatmates. But Dawn wanted to stay a couple of weeks with her mother to help her to settle in.

"No problem, Dawn. There are three bedrooms. You can have your pick."

"Thanks, Mum. It's strange, isn't it? This is the last time I'll be dialling this number."

Amy paused. "Dawn, how are you feeling about everything?"

"It'll take a bit of time to get used to the idea. You and Dad are the best in the world and I love you both. The writing was on the wall, Mum. I've known for a long time that it might come to this.

I'm a big girl now. Don't worry about me. If it's any consolation, I think you're doing the right thing."

Trust Dawn to *say* the right thing.

"I only want you to be happy. You and Dad."

"We're getting there. Your father's bringing me out for a meal tonight and he'll help me move next weekend. Claire's been kind too. And Sarah, of course. I'm surrounded by help."

"Rightly so. I have to admit something, Mum. In an ideal world you and Dad would have stayed together but I know that's not possible. At least you're still on good terms. And," she added, "now I have two homes to visit." What she didn't say was that her parents' separation would actually be easier for her in lots of ways. She'd been like a go-between in the last year, trying to please both of them.

"Dawn, I've seen more of your father lately than I did when we were living together."

"He said the same thing when I spoke to him last night. He seems to love the flat."

"He has it like a show-house – everything neat and tidy and in its proper place – no one to disturb him."

"Peace, perfect peace." Dawn chuckled. "I'll call you from Boston with the details of my flight home."

"Dawn, wait! What about my new phone number?"

"You gave it to me. I have it off by heart. The first four digits are the same – I just had to learn the 582."

"The apple doesn't fall far from the tree!"

"Pardon?"

"Nothing, love." Dawn was just like her father – organised, factual. "Bye, love. Enjoy the rest of your holiday."

"Thanks, Mum."

"Love you."

"Me too."

Amy replaced the receiver. She went into the kitchen and poured herself a stiff brandy.

Forty-five

The wind howled, the rain pelted and Amy drew up the collar of her coat. She placed the potted plant on her mother's grave. Elaine had always loved red geraniums.

He's alive, Mam. Your son survived.

A gust of wind answered her.

A new name. A new identity.

The cold air stung her cheekbones and made her eyes water.

He's tall and strong and handsome. Successful. And he's happy.

She took a bunch of tissues from her handbag, leaned over and wiped the wet mud from the marble tombstone.

Elaine Shiels,

Beloved wife and mother.

You'd have liked him, Mam. You'd have approved.

An elderly man, a gardener, was digging by the wall near her mother's grave. He nodded at her and continued on with his work. Amy approached him.

"Afternoon, Missus." He doffed his peaked cap. "Visiting a loved one?"

"Yes, my mother."

"God rest her." He made a sign of the cross. "Long dead, is she?"

"Not that long, no."

"You never get over it – losing your mother. The worst loss of them all. But sure the poor soul's at rest now."

Amy willed it to be so.

"She's looking down at you, watching over you. Mothers never give up on their children – that's what my ma used to say, God be good to her." He took up his shovel again. "You picked a wild afternoon for your visit, didn't you?"

"It's stormy, yes. Will they survive this wind?" She pointed to the saplings he was tending. "They look delicate."

"Delicate?" he scoffed. "Not a bit of it. It'd take a damned sight more than a few auld squally showers to do them fellas any harm. You see, it's the roots. That's what it all comes down to in the end. Good roots. That lot now will weather anything – rain, cold, frost, wind. No trouble to them. They've been well planted and with a bit of care and attention they'll thrive, never you fear, Missus."

As she walked away she heard him muttering to himself. "Roots, it's all down to having good roots."

The sun filtered through the dark clouds. As she passed along the footpath, Amy glanced at the names and dates on the gravestones and wondered about these dead people. How had they died? How had they lived? What did they accomplish? Who and what did they leave behind? Were they still missed? How were they remembered?

A visit to the cemetery put everything into perspective: she was at a crossroads in her life and had much to look forward to – a new job she loved, a new home, a new existence. Tomorrow she was going to see about a new car – her final bid for independence. She was excited and optimistic.

She was also afraid – by its nature, change aroused misgivings, fears and some regrets. But that was OK, Sylvia had assured her. She'd made mistakes and no doubt she'd make more. All part of the pageant. Whatever the future had in store, she knew she could deal with it.

Amy reached the cemetery gates and looked back. She could see her mother's tombstone standing proud and erect against the driving rain. She thought she heard a voice calling to her. She stood, frozen, and listened.

It was only the whoosh of the wind through the trees. Stillness filled her heart. She smiled and moved on. There would be no more voices.

Between Amy and her mother, there was no unfinished business.

334

Forty-six

Surrey 1951

The baby's scream shattered the night. Tears of frustration flooded down the burning cheeks.

"Stop it, stop it!" the woman hissed.

The little body convulsed in a paroxysm of temper and the cry became a piercing shriek. The crinkled eyes squeezed to slits as the mouth opened wider in a long bloodcurdling wail.

"Stop it!" She rocked the cradle roughly and glowered down at the tear-stained face. "Go to sleep!"

The terrified eyes bored through her soul.

Silence reigned again in the darkness as the night light flickered, spreading ethereal shadows on the mahogany panelled walls. Rigidly the woman walked to the window, drew back the heavy brocade curtains and looked out over the moonlit fields. A cluster of stars sparkled, momentarily softening her spirits.

The baby gurgled, spat, then half-choking cried again. It started as a low keening but infuriatingly turned into the same loud howl as before.

A boiling cauldron of anger bubbled. She had to keep the brat quiet – this was her third night pacing the floor; if she didn't get some sleep she'd go mad.

Jane Edwards dashed across the room and grabbed the hysterical

Mary McCarthy

infant from the warm blankets. Scalding hot tears splashed from the swollen eyes. She shook and shook the tiny bundle until her arms ached. The eyes rolled backwards in the baby's head, the body became limp.

And the crying stopped.

THE END